NOTHINGNESS

The light was failing rapidly now, and I stepped onto the terrace on my way back to my room. The view from the edge of the terrace would be marvelous. Just a quick look before I left!

The wind caught me, blowing cold from the sea, moaning and sighing over the weathered stone like the cry of a lost soul. I shivered, started to turn back, then continued forward until I was standing next to the shattered balustrade. The slate-grey sea spread out below me; the sky stretched grey and empty to the horizon.

I laid my palms on the balustrade, leaned my weight upon them, gazed down into the boiling, pounding waves. Then, as I started to draw back, the rail beneath my hands gave way. For what seemed an eternity, I teetered there, arms flailing. Then a gust of wind whipped around me, overbalancing me — *or was it hands upon my back?*

And slowly I toppled into the yawning void . . .

THE ROMANCES OF LORDS AND LADIES
IN JANIS LADEN'S REGENCIES

BEWITCHING MINX (2532, $3.95)

From her first encounter with the Marquis of Penderleigh when he had mistaken her for a common trollop, Penelope had been incensed with the darkly handsome lord. Miss Penelope Larchmont was undoubtedly the most outspoken young lady Penderleigh had ever known, and the most tempting.

A NOBLE MISTRESS (2169, $3.95)

Moriah Landon had always been a singularly practical young lady. So when her father lost the family estate over a game of picquet, she paid the winner, the notorious Viscount Roane, a visit. And when he suggested the means of payment—that she become Roane's mistress—she agreed without a blink of her eyes.

SAPPHIRE TEMPTATION (3054, $3.95)

Lady Serena was commonly held to be an unusual young girl—outspoken when she should have been reticent, lively when she should have been demure. But there was one tradition she had not been allowed to break: a Wexley must marry a Gower. Richard Gower intended to teach his wife her duties—in every way.

SCOTTISH ROSE (2750, $3.95)

The Duke of Milburne returned to Milburne Hall trusting that the new governess, Miss Rose Beacham, had instilled the fear of God into his harum-scarum brood of siblings. But she romped with the children, refused to be cowed by his stern admonitions, and was so pretty that he had the devil of a time keeping his hands off her.

Available wherever paperbacks are sold, or order direct from the Publisher. Send cover price plus 50¢ per copy for mailing and handling to Zebra Books, Dept. 4040, 475 Park Avenue South, New York, N.Y. 10016. Residents of New York and Tennessee must include sales tax. DO NOT SEND CASH. For a free Zebra/Pinnacle catalog please write to the above address.

F. JACQUELYN HALLQUIST

THE DARK SECRETS OF GREYSTONE MANOR

ZEBRA BOOKS
KENSINGTON PUBLISHING CORP.

ZEBRA BOOKS

are published by

Kensington Publishing Corp.
475 Park Avenue South
New York, NY 10016

Copyright © 1993 by F. Jacquelyn Hallquist

All rights reserved. No part of this book may be reproduced in any form or by any means without the prior written consent of the Publisher, excepting brief quotes used in reviews.

Zebra and the Z logo are trademarks of Kensington Publishing Corp.

If you purchased this book without a cover you should be aware that this book is stolen property. It was reported as "unsold and destroyed" to the Publisher and neither the Author nor the Publisher has received any payment for this "stripped book."

First Printing: January 1993

Printed in the United States of America

Chapter One

Greystone Manor, 1844

How often I have longed to be a child again, to stand once more upon the old stone bridge in the early morning light, my small hand held warm and safe in that of my father, Lord Samuel Garth. What Papa thought as we stood together, gazing at our ancestral home towering stark and weathered above the cliff's top, I do not know. I only know that I thought it most beautiful. Never did I see the broken stone arches, the chipped and crumbling balustrades; never did I see the ruts, and stones, and limbs of fallen trees choking the road that leads from the bridge to the manor door. Rather did I behold it all through the eyes of love: my home, strong and safe, filled with affection and joy.

In summer, the canticle of birds calling sweetly in the long-neglected park, and the purling of the beck that flows beneath the old stone bridge mingled with my piping voice while I chattered on as small children are wont to do. And if an inexplicable sigh escaped Papa's lips from time to time, I was much too young to notice or to understand.

I neither knew nor cared that my beloved manor house had stood upon that spot since the year 1583, when the first Samuel Garth raised a stone peel there with his own hands. Thereafter, each succeeding generation added a wing or a wall until the house eventually encompassed even the moat that at one time encircled the dwelling. Today the waters that once filled the moat flow within the walls, following a channel that leads through the very foundations of Greystone Manor.

It is water from the stream flowing under the old bridge that fills that moat, even today. Sometimes in early spring, fed by melting snow, the quiet little stream becomes a wild and turbulent river. It overbrims its banks and turns the moat into a raging torrent that swirls and froths and plunges its way through the stone foundations of the manor house until, with one final thunderous roar, it flings itself over the cliff onto the rocks below, and thence, into the sea.

But during the long hot days of summer, it becomes a gentle stream that gurgles and coos its way between grassy, flower-strewn banks. It was a spot much favored by my brother, Adam — stepbrother, actually, though to our young minds it seemed a difference of little consequence — and me. And as we grew older, my stepbrother Adam and I, we often waded there, dabbling first our toes and then our heels, playing a delicious game of I Dare You.

One golden afternoon when I was nine, as we played there on the bank, I slipped and fell into a shallow pool, an event that, in itself, was not unusual. I scrambled to my feet, laughing and giggling, and with Adam close behind, I hurried home, soggy skirts held high to flap about my thin bare legs.

However, on that particular day, my stepmother, Elizabeth, met us at the door, and I could tell by the expression on her face that she was not pleased. She took me by the arm and said, her voice stern, "I have told you before, Victoria, you are getting too old to run about in such a fashion. Both your father and I are sorely displeased by such unseemly behavior. Now go upstairs at once and change your clothes, then come down to the kitchen and sit by the fire until your hair is dry."

I made a saucy face at Adam behind Elizabeth's back causing him to burst into a fit of giggles, and thereby earning for him a sharp reprimand. I did not wait to hear the end of it, but hurried upstairs to do as I was bid. Elizabeth was a kind and loving stepmother whom I adored, but I knew she would brook no impudence, neither from me nor from Adam.

When I was dressed and dry once more, I took myself off to the kitchen, where I found my stepbrother sitting silent in the chimney corner, gazing into the fire. As I approached he glanced up, smiled, and made room for me beside him in the inglenook.

Elizabeth and Lueddy, who sat at the table mending, also looked up at my approach. They smiled at me, a little sadly I thought, though I could not tell why. I was certainly none the worse for my drenching.

As I settled into the seat next to Adam, I heard Elizabeth say, "She much resembles her mother, doesn't she, Lueddy?"

"The Lady Amanda? Aye . . . indeed she does," Lueddy agreed.

Elizabeth sighed. "I'll never forget the night Dr. Johnshaven came home and told me the Lady Amanda had died. . . . I wondered how Samuel would manage with a newborn babe and no family to help him."

Lueddy nodded her head, her face sober. "Never dreamin' ye'd be alone yerself so soon after . . ."

A far-off look came into Elizabeth's eyes. "Those were sad days. So many people ill, so many lost . . . gone so suddenly. . . ." She put down her work and rested her hands upon the tabletop.

"Aye, 'tis true." And Lueddy, too, sat for a moment, her hands idle upon the top of the table.

I had heard the story from their lips many times: how some months after my mother's death in childbirth, an outbreak of dysentery carried off a large portion of the local population, including Adam's father, the village doctor. It was a story I never tired of hearing.

7

After a short silence, Lueddy commented, "She do look like her mother, m'Lady, but when I looks at her, it be me little bird I sees."

"Samuel's mother, the Lady Christina?"

"Aye, Christina . . . me little bird."

Whether my dawning maturity had made me more sensitive to the feelings of others, or the weight of passing years had left Lueddy less resilient, I do not know. But for the first time I detected an unmistakable note of sadness in her voice when she spoke of my grandmother.

"From the day she were born, t'was me as cared for her. Not nurse nor governess could take the place of old Lueddy." The memory brought a smile to light the old woman's nearsighted eyes. Lueddy's situation, her place in our household, was unique. She was neither family nor servant—friend, I suppose, though in truth we always thought of her as one of us. I loved her dearly.

Elizabeth reached over and patted one of Lueddy's careworn hands. I scrunched myself into a more comfortable position on the ledge in the inglenook. This was the part of the story I liked best, the part that always filled me with pride.

"This house were always full of people a-comin' and a-goin', an' so many beautiful things . . ." Lueddy gave her head a sorrowful shake. "They's all gone now . . . ye'll never know, such beautiful things as was in this house."

With a little sigh, Elizabeth picked up her mending and the two women bent over their work once more. An oppressive silence settled over the kitchen—a waiting silence. I looked about, not sure what I expected, but there was nothing to see save the shadows cast by the firelight, dancing in the corners.

At last Elizabeth spoke. "The Lady Christina was ill for such a long time."

"Aye, m'Lady, her were never strong . . . an' after her married *him* . . ." Lueddy emphasized the *him* with a curl of her lip, as if she had something distasteful in her mouth.

Elizabeth's gaze, which she now fixed upon Lueddy's face, was questioning.

Lueddy shook her head, brushed back a wisp of grey hair that had escaped her cap. "Handsome, he were . . . with a smile to break an angel's heart." Lueddy's voice trailed away.

Again the silence closed in, thick, palpable. Elizabeth stirred uneasily in her chair. Lueddy glanced about with a nervous twitch of her head. Only the fitful shadows, adrift in the far corners, moved.

The sudden rattle of coal settling in the grate echoed loud in the quiet room. I started and moved closer to Adam. He put a comforting arm about my shoulders.

Abruptly, Lueddy dropped the petticoat she was mending and clasped her hands tightly together. "I should never have left her, no matter *what* that man as was her husband said!"

Never before had I heard such anger in Lueddy's voice, or a story that began with those words. Suddenly uneasy, I huddled still closer to Adam.

"Then you were not here when Christina's husband disappeared?"

"No, m'Lady, I were gone, all the summer long. Then, one day, I didn't know why, I just decided to come back an' see me little bird." This, indeed, was something I had never heard before. Lueddy had stopped speaking, but the expression on her face was quite terrible to see. I waited, scarcely breathing, for her next words.

When finally she spoke, it was in a voice strangled by emotion. "Oh, m'Lady . . . if only I had knowed. . . ." She hesitated, and the silence grew unbearable, but no one seemed able to speak.

At last Lueddy resumed the tale. "The day I come home, I found her sittin' in great hall, just sittin' an' starin'. An' when she saw me, first she began to weep, an' then her laughed an' said, 'There you are Lueddy! For shame to be so slow! Go tell Papa our guests are arriving.' "

Lueddy took a deep breath, swallowed, but she could not control the trembling of her voice. "An' then me little bird, her stood up an' began to dance. Round and round . . . smilin' an' talkin'—but not to me . . ."

Lueddy's voice broke and she began to sob. It was the only time in all my life I ever saw her cry, and it was more than I could bear. I sprang to my feet and ran to throw my arms about her. It was Elizabeth who finally calmed us all, and sent Adam and me off to the nursery to play.

I don't remember when it occurred to me that the *him* of whom Lueddy spoke with such distaste was my grandfather; but after hearing the story I always wondered why he had run away, why Lueddy looked so sour when she mentioned him. As a matter of fact, Adam and I once asked her.

"Never ye young 'uns mind!" and she scowled at us so fiercely, we never dared mention the subject again.

However, the motives of my grandfather did not interest us nearly as much as did the manor house itself. In those days, while Adam and I were yet children, all the rooms in the east and west wings, as well as the rooms above the second floor, remained closed and forgotten. And all those chambers, halls, and galleries that had stood cold and abandoned for so many years held great fascination for the two of us.

Many a day we hid ourselves away in the more accessible areas, or wandered through those empty halls and chambers, staring at the shrouded furniture. Dust and cobwebs were everywhere and we discovered, to our chagrin, that many of the rooms in the east wing, as well as upper-story rooms in the south wing, were locked. Longing to explore those rooms, we devoted countless hours over the years to a diligent search, but we never found any keys.

Nonetheless, as we grew older, we grew bolder, and we pushed the game of exploration into almost every nook and cranny of the old house. But even Adam could not draw me into the north wing.

My fear of the north wing was born when I was perhaps five years old, on a day when Adam and I went to play in the stable. There was an old carriage there that had stood in a corner, unused and gathering dust, for more years than anyone now living could remember. On that particular day we climbed up onto its front seat, and Adam immediately gathered up a handful of imaginary reins, clucked to a make-believe horse, and shouted, "Ho, horse, giddy up!"

Following my stepbrother's lead, I reached up to settle a make-believe bonnet more firmly over my mop of thick black curls. "Beautiful day for a ride in the park," I affirmed in my most grown-up tones, and I turned this way and that pretending to admire the scenery.

As I did so, from the corner of my eye I caught a glimpse of a fat black and white cat just disappearing through a small door down behind the carriage. In an instant, without a second's thought, I scrambled down from my perch and followed after, calling, "Here, puss, here, puss!"

The cat neither paused nor slackened her pace. Tail held tall and straight above her back, she continued down the long narrow corridor we had entered and disappeared through a doorway at the far end. I hurried after her, calling plaintively, "Wait for me, puss!"

She did not wait, but kept on at a steady pace, just beyond my reach. I followed doggedly behind through room after room, until at last she led me out onto a terrace, where I found myself standing in the gathering dusk, looking down from a vast height. Far below, heaped and tumbled rocks, grey and jagged, spilled out into the sea.

Fascinated, I forgot the cat and stood watching the pounding waves that surged over the fallen stone—breaking, leaping, foaming, reaching upward, only to fall back upon themselves with a mighty roar.

And all the while, the damp sea wind whistled and shrilled about me, tearing at my hair, stinging my eyes, biting through the thin summer garments I wore into my already chilled body. I watched the pounding surf and I listened to the wind screaming through the ragged wall, and I realized, with a clutch of fear, that it was not only the wind I heard. Blended with it and through it, and rising above it, was the voice of a man, howling in hate and anger, shrieking in pain and anguish.

And with the realization came fear, stark terror that stopped the breath in my throat, froze my heart with horror. I turned from the crumbling wall and started to run, blindly, through the darkness, tripping, falling, scrambling up and running again, seeking to escape that nightmare wail.

A maze of halls and chambers lay between that small broken door in the stable where I had gained entrance to the north wing and the place where Papa found me, hours later, huddled in a corner, blue with cold, too filled with dread to make a sound. However, when Papa picked me up, I burst into a fit of hysterical weeping, and though he held me tight in his strong arms, my cold little face buried against his warm neck, it was long before he could quieten me, before the trembling left my body.

"There, there, child." His voice was deep and gentle. "Papa has you now." He held me close and continued to whisper words of comfort as he carried me back to Elizabeth, who was pacing nervously before the fire in the great hall.

"Found her in the north wing," Papa said.

Elizabeth ran to us, took me in her arms. "She's not hurt?" She tossed the question to my father, and in the same breath said to me, "Are you hurt, little love? Tell Elizabeth, where does it hurt?"

The hysterical sobbing, which had subsided as Papa carried me back, burst forth anew at the sight of Elizabeth, and I clung to her, only weeping more loudly in answer to her questions. Not until the following day was I able to tell them anything of what had so terrified me, and even then, being such a young child, I could tell them very little. "It was a man," I said uncertainly.

"What did he look like? What did he do?" they wanted to know.

I could only shake my head. "I could hear him," I said at last.

"What did he say?"

"I don't know," I said, ". . . but I could hear him," and I started to cry once more. I could see the disbelief in Papa's eyes and it made me feel ashamed.

"There, there, darling, don't cry. It was only the wind," Elizabeth assured me.

Papa added, "The wind and your imagination. Don't let your imagination play you tricks, Victoria," and he ruffled my hair with a gentle hand. Yet there was an edge in his voice that told me he wanted to hear no more of my imaginings.

Nevertheless, despite Elizabeth's assurances and Papa's warnings, I knew it was more than the wind I had heard, and for months thereafter the sound of it, moaning in a chimney or wailing about the walls, would recall for me that dreadful tortured voice, sending me into a paroxysm of fear. And though I dearly loved to go exploring about the house, would happily follow Adam wherever else he might lead, from that day onward I balked at entering the north wing. Many a long year was to pass before I would venture there again.

On the day Elizabeth married Papa, the family fortunes had been at a low ebb. This I knew from bits and pieces of gossip heard here and there as I grew up. Indeed, it had been clear enough for even me to see, though I must say it never really concerned me. As I have said, I was a happy child, and never having known great wealth, I could scarcely miss it.

However, from the day of their wedding onward, conditions on the estate steadily improved. Tenant farmers, who had deserted the land to seek their fortune in the ironworks of Birmingham and Manchester, returned. Brutalized, disillusioned, demoralized by conditions in the city slums, they were happy to be working the land once more. With the new iron plows and iron-toothed disk implements for harrowing, the crops they tended produced a plentiful harvest, providing richly for farmer and landowner alike. And the stud—Papa's pride and joy—began to prosper.

By the time I was reaching the age of ten, Elizabeth was no longer engaged in cooking and mending and cleaning. Rather, she devoted her time to planning and organizing, and overseeing the running of the house. Lueddy continued to do the cooking, but a housemaid, a scullerymaid, and a charwoman had been hired. In addition, a number of gardeners, whose job it was to restore the park, had been taken on, as well as a boy whose sole duty it was to muck out the stable.

However, the kitchen, a small dining room, and the great hall continued to be the only rooms in use on the ground floor. A magnificent stairway with a railing of hand-carved English yew led from the great hall to a second-story gallery. Seven bedrooms opened onto this gallery, but only two of those rooms were in use. Papa and Elizabeth shared one. I shared the other with Adam while we were young, and that room was always referred to as the nursery.

Elizabeth bore Papa a son, John, in 1847, and then there were three of us to share the room. However, with the approach of my tenth birthday, Elizabeth called me to her side one day and said, "Victoria, love, you will be a young lady soon."

I smiled at the thought. "I know," I said proudly.

Now it was Elizabeth's turn to smile. "And as a proper young lady, you will require a bedroom of your own."

A bedroom of my own! I did not like the sound of this. But surely Elizabeth could not be serious. It would be a great extravagance to prepare a room for me alone. Of late, there had been more money to spend—I even had a new dress. But a room of my own? I looked at Elizabeth, the smile fading from my lips. I found the idea not at all pleasing. In fact, the thought of facing the night and the darkness alone was terrifying, and I said, "No! If you please, Elizabeth, I'd rather not."

"Young ladies do not share a bedroom with two young gentlemen," Elizabeth observed. Her tone was firm, and though I could see the sympathy in her eyes, I knew it would be quite useless to argue.

And so I moved into a room of my own. My grandmother, the Lady Christina, had been its previous occupant, and, Papa explained, many of the beautiful things that remained in the room had been hers.

The floor was covered by a carpet, thick and soft, patterned with roses the color of Burgundy wine. The walls were hung with heavy tapestries on which exotic shrubs, trees, flowers, and birds, all stitched in silken thread, glowed and shimmered when touched by the least glimmer of light.

One small bird in particular gave me great delight. He perched upon a frond of fern near the head of my bed. If the slightest breath of air rippled the tapestry, the fern would appear to sway as in a gentle breeze, and the little bird with it. The play of light over the silken thread gave the illusion of movement to his round black eye; indeed, his entire head appeared to change position at times, and when I was lonely or blue, or out of sorts, I would sometimes sit cross-legged upon the floor and talk to the wee fellow.

In the eastern wall of my room, there was an elegant fireplace with a hearth of burnished brass, and a wide mantel of rose marble on which stood an elaborate French ormolu clock, telling the passing of the hours with delicate, tinkling chimes. In front of the fireplace there was a chaise longue upholstered in ivory satin damask. On the opposite side of the room stood a canopied bed with delicately carved posts of burnished rosewood. The room also contained a stately walnut vanity and armoire, as well as a table and several chairs.

But that which I prized above all else was a diminutive escritoire. It, too, was fashioned of rosewood that glowed with a mellow patina born of age and loving care. Its slender legs were covered with a delicate tracery of carved leaves and vines, which extended around the sides and over the back of the little desk. But most endearing of all, to my childish heart, were two exquisite silver ink pots, each with a pillow-shaped top upon which reclined a chubby porcelain cherub, and each cherub held aloft a beautiful pink-plumed quill.

"The writing table belonged to my mother," Papa said as he showed me the room. Then he added, in a strangely distant voice, "She loved that little desk. . . ."

All the bedrooms facing the gallery also opened through heavy French doors, onto a wide balcony that ran the length of the southern side of the house. When these doors were thrown wide on a balmy summer day, the view was breathtaking. The weed-choked park looked like a great green forest. Beyond it the farms, each with its own small cottage, became a magic land of elves, while far across the valley the shining white church steeple, like a slender finger, pointed the way to heaven.

The balustrade enclosing the balcony, though chipped and broken, did support an ancient vine that bore neither leaf nor blossom. It clung tenaciously to the shattered stone with thick dry fingers, and on the first night I slept in my room, I dreamed this dream about it:

I stood on the balcony, leaning against the balustrade which, in my dream, was unbroken. There was an ancient vine of flowering wisteria entwined upon it, and the cloying scent of its blossoms gave the texture of satin to a warm and gentle breeze that caressed the bare flesh of my throat, my shoulders. I leaned over the balustrade and flung my arms wide, as if to gather in all the beautiful world I could see spread out below me, and I laughed aloud, because the happiness within me would not be silent.

Then, without warning, the breeze stiffened and grew

chill. I drew back from the balustrade, and from the corner of my eye I perceived a dark shadow, over against the tower wall. Terrified, I tried to run, but I could not force my feet to move, and the shadow began to grow, becoming a formless, writhing darkness that seeped across the balcony toward me. I opened my mouth to scream, but no sound issued from my lips, and struggle as I would, I could not run.

Then, just as the blackness seemed about to overshadow me, the doors to my room swung open. A dark-haired child with laughing black eyes stepped forth, smiled, and held out her hands to me.

In the morning, when I wakened, I looked all about my room, somehow expecting to see her there. I was quite disappointed to find her gone. At breakfast, I could not wait to tell everyone about my visitor. "She was so beautiful, and she is going to be my friend," I announced, fairly dancing up and down with enthusiasm.

Papa's face darkened. He put down his fork and looked at me, his eyes fierce. "That," he said, and his voice was harsh, "is utter nonsense. There was no one in your room last night. No one—do you understand? And I never want to hear such foolishness from you again!"

In all my life, Papa had never spoken to me in such a stern and accusing voice. Being by no means a shy child, I promptly opened my mouth to speak in my own defense. "But Papa, I *saw* her. I—"

Papa, actually shouting now, interrupted me. "Enough! I will hear no more. It was a dream, only a dream. I will not have you pretending your dreams are real!"

Filled with consternation, I shrank down into my chair, tears brimming in my eyes.

Elizabeth laid a soothing hand upon Papa's arm and murmured, "Don't frighten the child, Samuel. She meant no harm."

Papa took a deep breath, turned to look at Elizabeth. "I have seen what harm there is in this kind of nonsense . . . and she is the image of my mother."

As Papa spoke, they both turned to look at me. I bit my lip to stop its trembling. I had heard the stories about my grandmother, and I understood what Papa meant. It was also clear to see in his face that he did not believe a word I had spoken and that he was sorely disappointed in me. Suddenly, I felt sick at heart.

Thereafter, I dreamed of the dark-haired maid quite often. I would seem to waken and she would be sitting at my escritoire, her blue-black hair falling in a profusion of curls over her slender shoulders. Sometimes she would rise and beckon me to come and stand with her before the open French doors, to walk with her upon the balcony. Then, bathed in the soft fragrance of wisteria, we would stroll together, gazing across the moon-washed landscape while the night breeze fluttered the dark curls upon her forehead. In the deep, velvet-cushioned stillness that filled the night, I could feel her joy, and as I grew older, I became aware of an inner excitement, an undefinable longing and wonder that were hers, and yet my own.

When I awoke in the morning, I would remind myself that it had only been a dream, but it did not feel like a dream, and in all those years of growing up she was the only childhood fancy I shared with no one — not even Adam.

Chapter Two

Greystone Manor, 1847-1851

As we grew older, Adam and I—for my half-brother John was still too young to be our companion—we delighted in roaming the countryside. We rode our ponies where we would, fair weather or foul, along the cliffs, down to the village, or amongst the fields and cottages of the farmers. Our favorite path led upward and westward along the brow of the cliff overlooking the sea. Twisting, turning, drifting, the path often comes so close to the edge that even today, when riding there, I close my eyes to shut out the dizzying drop to the jumbled rock so far below.

Times beyond number, Adam and I stood at the top of the cliff gazing out across those changing waters. Sometimes they were dancing and frothing with whitecaps, sometimes undulating with a slow, ponderous rhythm, sometimes heaving and crashing mightily against the foot of the cliff. Though that restless stretch of sea water may be black as ink on a storm-tossed morning, it warms to a glowing translucent green when the weather is fine and still.

But the air is seldom still upon the cliff's top, and on a bright and windy day, we always found it exhilarating to ride our ponies at top speed up the steeply rising path with its many twists and turns. Such is the foolhardy bravery of youth!

At the very top of the cliff, the path turns back and down to dip into a low-lying glen laced with moss and feathery fern. In spring and summer, the vale is gay with bluebells and anemone, the air sweet with wild thyme, rosemary, and clove-scented pink and lavender gilliflowers. In the center of the dell, a spring bubbles up to fill a small rock basin, and as children, we often stopped to water our ponies there.

It was there that Adam first kissed me. We sat on the lip of the stone basin while the horses snuffled noisily in the sparkling water. The summer sky was bright blue overhead. The morning air was athrob with the secret life of woodland creatures that moved unseen through bushes and sedge. And there were bees humming their busy song in the blossoms all about us.

I watched them with a wary eye until Adam assured me, "You need not be afraid, they won't sting unless you bother them."

He had not yet finished speaking when a large and furry bee, the color of warm honey with stripes of midnight black encircling its body, settled itself upon my cheek and plunged its sting deep into my tender flesh. I cried out, as much in fright as in pain, though the pain was not inconsiderable.

Adam gasped in surprise, then brushed the offending creature from my face. For an instant, shock held me immobile. It was long enough for Adam to lean forward and extract the sting still buried in my cheek.

For a moment longer I sat, my gaze darting back and forth between Adam and the dying honeybee before I fell to sobbing and wringing my hands, shaking my head about until my thick, dark curls escaped the confines of their ribbons and fell in wild disarray over my forehead and down my back.

The wound did burn and throb, but I must confess, I quite enjoyed being the center of attention, even when I had an audience of only one. Adam's response to my performance was particularly gratifying.

Filled with concern, he put his arms about me and held me close, whispering, "Please, Victoria, please don't cry. It will be all right. Truly. It was only a bee . . . don't cry."

When at last I allowed myself to be calmed, he took his handkerchief, dipped it in the cool, clear water of the pool, and ever so gently bathed my face. "There. Now it will be fine," he said.

But it did not seem fine to me, for already my cheek was puffy, my eye swollen shut. I gazed at him reproachfully.

After carefully studying my wounded countenance, he shook his head and murmured, "Poor little sister. You do look very strange." His mouth began to twitch and he started to laugh, but the laughter died upon his lips.

His eyes held mine and my heart began to pound. And that is when he kissed me, his lips soft and sweet and warm against my own.

We were neither of us prepared for the tide of emotion unleashed by that innocent kiss. We were, after all, but youngsters, I not yet thirteen, Adam scarcely two years older. Bewildered, we stood for a moment, staring at each other.

Abruptly, Adam said, his voice loud and curt, "We'd best go home and let Lueddy see to you." He helped me mount my pony, and we rode back to the manor in silence.

There was a subtle change in our relationship following that first kiss. Adam became more protective of me, I more inclined to decorum and modesty. And if we did take to exchanging kisses from time to time, it was always with much giggling from me and blushing from Adam. Truth to tell, I am certain we knew even then that we were sampling forbidden fruit, yet it seemed but a pleasant pastime.

It was at about that time, when the rowdy games of childhood lost their appeal, that my stepbrother took to carrying paper and pencils about with him wherever we went. He had always had a talent for drawing, and now he took great pleasure in sketching, especially pictures of me or of Greystone Manor.

He never seemed to tire of dreaming up some new pose for me: standing in the garden holding a single rose, or on the bank of the stream with an armful of wildflowers; on the back of my pony with my hair flying free, or sitting decorously on a stone bench in the park. Whatever the pose, he always drew me exactly as he saw me, even if it were with a smudge on my nose or my hair in disarray.

But Greystone Manor he portrayed as he imagined it had looked when it was new, or as he would have it look when he restored it. For that was Adam's dream: to master the art of architecture and one day restore Greystone Manor to its former glory. I thought it an excellent plan — indeed, whatever Adam wanted seemed excellent in my eyes.

Thus, the happy, carefree years of childhood and youth flowed one into another. We rode the countryside or picnicked in the park. On warm summer days, we waded and splashed in the stream flowing under the old bridge; and when the winds of winter swept in across the North Sea, burying our world in ice and snow, we played hide-and-seek in the stable, or chess before the fire in the great hall. And always together.

Only in the early morning, when I was up and about before him, was I without Adam, and whenever a kitchen cat was delivered of a litter of kittens, I would arise at an even earlier hour. I loved to sit in the chimney corner stroking the mother cat's head, scratching behind her ears, listening to the contented song she sang deep in her throat whilst her babies nursed. I could never wait until the wee ones had their eyes open and began to stagger about on their unsteady little legs.

On one such morning, in a cold October, as I sat with a dear old mother cat, my reverie was disrupted by the rude sounds of scuffling and sniggering just beyond my range of vision, around the corner of the inglenook.

"Ye best never let Master hear ye," a high-pitched

young voice exclaimed. "He'd have yer hide, he would!" This last was accompanied by another burst of giggles.

"But 'tis true, all the same. Daft, her were. Loony as any Tom-o'-Bedlam. Always a-talkin' to folks as weren't there. I know, 'cause me ol' granny heared her, an' she tol' me all about it." Now the voice took on an affected tone. " 'I'd be charmed, I'm sure. Oh, I'd love to dance another turn with a handsome gen'leman like you . . .' " This sally prompted yet another peal of laughter.

I could feel hot, angry color burning in my cheeks, and tears of shame started in my eyes. I knew of whom they spoke, who it was that they were mimicking: my grandmother, the Lady Christina.

Around the chimney corner, the conversation continued. "Me old granny do say she ought to a been put away. 'Tis a wonder ol' Lueddy weren't afraid to stay with her . . ."

Tightening my lips and clenching my fists, I was about to step right out and confront them then and there, but Lueddy, at that very moment, came into view from behind the brine vat on the other side of the kitchen. A sudden scurry of departing footsteps told me the two offenders had beaten a hasty retreat.

Dashing the tears from my eyes with the back of my hand, I settled myself against the wall once more and sat staring moodily into the fire. For the very first time, I seriously contemplated the relationship between my grandmother and me. All my life, I had heard people say of me, ". . . the very image of Lady Christina."

Papa himself said it, though he always looked somewhat less than pleased when other people mentioned the resemblance. And I knew why. Everyone said Grandmother was very beautiful, but that I looked like her was not what worried Papa—it was the fear that I was like her in other ways, too.

At that moment, Lueddy caught sight of me and said, "Fie, young miss, to sit there daydreaming. Git along with ye now. 'Tis almost time for breakfast."

Dear Lueddy. I jumped up, threw my arms about her and gave her a great bear hug, before I ran off to my room to brush my hair and wash my hands and face. With all thought of the Lady Christina forgotten, my heart was glad once more.

The most exciting event of our young lives was the Great Exhibition that was to open in London in May of 1851. For months, the newspapers were full of it. Indeed, the whole of England was abuzz with excitement, eagerly anticipating this marvelous affair.

It was Prince Albert who had first conceived of this great undertaking, and its theme, Progress, was his inspiration. It was expected that practically every country in the world would be represented, and the exhibits were meant to display the Works of Industry of All Nations.

How Adam and I longed to go! We read everything we could find on the topic, then we took to dropping hints designed to pique our parents' interest, hoping thus to promote a visit to this most extraordinary of events. "It's going to be *so* educational," or "Every *true* Englishman will be certain to attend," or "It is the *only* patriotic thing to do," and so on. Elizabeth and my father listened, and smiled, and said nary a word.

March winds were still blowing when I descended to breakfast one morning to find Papa and my stepmother, deep in conversation, a letter spread out on the table between them. When I entered, they both looked up and beamed at me. Then, without preamble, Elizabeth announced, "Victoria, love, we have been invited to spend the summer in London with my dear friend, Drusilla, and her husband, Phillip Hornaby."

I could feel my eyes growing big and round with surprise, but before I could think what to say, Elizabeth continued, "Your father and I have decided that we will accept their kind invitation."

Abruptly my excitement spilled over. Hands clasped together, I stood on tiptoe, and bobbed up and down. "Really, truly? We are going to London? All of us? And we can visit the Exhibition?"

Papa nodded, his eyes aglow, but his voice remained solemn. "That is the plan. Do I perceive that you are pleased?"

I ran to him, threw my arms about him. "Oh, Papa, I love you!"

Then I turned to Elizabeth, who continued, "You and I shall go to London early, in April. That will give us time to have some new costumes made."

I'm certain my eyes assumed the size and shape of saucers. New costumes! That must mean something beautiful and stylish! Having never worn anything except homespun in summer and worsted in winter, I must admit I was even more excited by the prospect of a new dress—or maybe two or three, for Elizabeth had said *costumes*—than by the thought of viewing the Great Exhibition.

"Taffeta, Elizabeth, sky-blue, with a bonnet and mantle to match!" I fairly danced with excitement.

Elizabeth laughed. "We'll see when the time comes, love, but, I promise something pretty."

"With lots of lace and ribbons?" I added hopefully.

Papa's smile was indulgent, but Elizabeth repeated firmly, "We'll see."

Papa and Elizabeth had worked very hard over the years, and under their careful husbandry, Greystone estate had flourished. However, what money there was had never been spent on fripperies. On that morning, however, Papa placed a hearty kiss on Elizabeth's cheek and said, "It is time, madam, to enjoy the fruits of our labor. Spoil the child a little!"

"You, sir," Elizabeth retorted, "have already spoilt the child more than a little." But there was a merry twinkle in her eye, for truth to tell, neither Adam, nor little John, nor I suffered from lack of cosseting.

The Exhibition was not to open until the first of May, but as planned, Elizabeth and I went down to London early in April. Papa and the boys were to join us there nearer the end of the month.

As had been arranged, we were to stay with Elizabeth's dearest friend, Drusilla, who was married to a very rich and very famous doctor who counted among his patients members of the royal household. The two women, who had been friends since they were girls, had always maintained a lively correspondence, but this was their first opportunity for a visit since Elizabeth had married Papa.

Now, with the approach of the Great Exhibition, the two women deemed it the perfect opportunity to renew their friendship and to present Elizabeth's new husband, sons, and daughter to Drusilla and her family.

Thus it was that Elizabeth and I boarded the train early one bright morning the first week in April. I remember the strange, musty odor in the compartment where we sat, and the soft plush seats that clung to the skirt of my wool dress.

I sat myself close to the window and pressed my cheek against the glass, waving and blowing kisses to Papa and John and Adam. They stood upon the platform, unwilling to leave until they could be certain we were safely on our way. And for a moment I was almost overcome by a rush of homesickness. I wished that I could jump off the train and stay with Papa, Adam, and little John.

Of course I did not truly want to stay behind, and I was just telling myself what a silly goose I was when the train gave a great lurch and began to clank and sway. My head went thump! against the back of the seat. I grabbed Elizabeth's arm with both hands and, fairly overcome with fright, I shrilled, "What's the matter, Elizabeth? What's happening?"

Elizabeth patted my hands and clucked reassuringly. "There, there, Victoria. You have nothing to fear."

"But why is the train shaking so?" I demanded, my heart pounding.

"It is just the way trains are, dear. Sit up, and behave like a young lady."

We were now lurching and swaying along at an amazing clip, and the rattling and clanking were most unnerving. Nevertheless, I took a deep breath and slowly sat up. Outside the window, the landscape seemed to flow by, like a constantly unrolling tapestry. Lost in the wonder of it, I soon forgot the noise and began to enjoy myself.

When the conductor came to take our tickets he said, "And how do you like riding the train, Lady Victoria?"

"It is truly most exciting," I declared.

"Can you tell me when we shall arrive in London?" Elizabeth asked him.

"We'll be there by nightfall, m'Lady. This train will do thirty-five miles an hour on the straightaway." The conductor looked so proud, I wondered if perhaps he owned the train, but I did not ask.

When Papa had remarked at dinner the night before, "People who live near the train tracks are complaining bitterly of the noise and soot," I had not clearly understood what he meant. Now, when I pressed my cheek against the window and peered upward through the glass, I could see billows of steam, and coal smoke laced with ashes and fiery sparks, all spewed from the engine and trailing out behind us, spreading over the countryside like a highwayman's cloak.

Suddenly I felt a surge of sympathy for those who dwelt beneath that cloud. It must, indeed, make everything grimy and dirty. However, youth is not given to dwelling on such matters, and I would not have foregone the train ride for all of that.

It was enchanting to watch the fields and villages rush by. The day, too, rushed by, and we reached London all too soon. The train slowed to a crawl, then bumped to a stop beside a narrow platform. A porter came bustling into our carriage and began lifting down our cases and bags, while Elizabeth and I descended from the train.

The platform was by then swarming with people, but before I had time to take it all in, an extremely solemn and painfully thin man in a tall beaver hat strode up to us.

With a small bow he addressed himself to Elizabeth. "Lady Garth, Countess of Greystone?" Then, unaccountably, they both burst out laughing and gave each other a hug!

I was staring at them, open-mouthed, when Elizabeth turned to me and said, "Dr. Hornaby, may I present my stepdaughter, Lady Victoria Garth."

I wasn't certain what I should do, curtsy or offer him my hand. Before I could make up my mind he took me gently by the shoulders, smiled warmly down at me, and said, "Please call me Uncle Phillip, and if I may, I'll call you Victoria. In the Hornaby household we save all the folderol for court."

With a grateful smile, I replied, "Thank you, Uncle Phillip. I would be most pleased if you would call me Victoria."

He stepped back then and gestured toward an elegantly attired young man who stood close by. "Countess, Lady Victoria, may I present my son, Thomas."

Elizabeth's eyes grew very wide and she clasped her hands beneath her chin as she looked back and forth between father and son. "Is it possible?" she murmured at last. "Can the three-year-old roly-poly I remember have grown into this handsome young man?"

Now Thomas stepped forward. "Indeed it is I, m'Lady," and he started to make a formal bow.

But Elizabeth cried, "Thomas, Thomas, though more than a dozen years have passed, am I not still your Aunt Elizabeth?" And moisture filled her eyes. Then they, too, gave each other a warm hug.

However, when Thomas turned to me, I quickly offered him my hand and tried not to look as shy as I felt. He really was a most handsome young man, with thick, sandy hair and a dusting of freckles across his nose.

He bowed over my hand with a flourish and said, "A great pleasure, Lady Victoria."

Soon we were in the phaeton, riding through the streets of London. Elizabeth and Phillip sat in the forward-facing seat, chatting as if they had seen each other only yesterday. Thomas and I sat opposite them, listening politely.

From time to time Uncle Phillip would address a remark to me, and I would answer carefully, for I felt much in awe of him at first. No matter what I said, I had the feeling he was searching for some deeper meaning in my words. I feared that somehow he could discover something about me that even I did not know.

I had overheard Elizabeth tell Papa while we were planning our trip that Uncle Phillip's special field of interest was the care and treatment of the mentally disturbed. That, too, I found intimidating. I couldn't help but wonder if he knew about my grandmother.

Aunt Drusilla, for so she insisted I call her, was waiting to meet us at the door when we arrived. A chubby, effervescent redhead, she greeted us with hugs and kisses and tears of happiness. She seemed, on that first meeting, as different from Uncle Phillip as night from day. However, as time passed, I perceived that Aunt Drusilla was much more than she seemed, and it was obvious that she and Elizabeth, though only friends, held one another in warm sisterly affection and took great pleasure in one another's company.

As for Thomas, he appeared to be a happy, lighthearted young man, intelligent and knowledgeable, though clearly more interested in the latest London gossip than in affairs of business, medicine, or state. At supper that first evening he regaled us with stories about the royals, the comings and goings at court, and progress on the Crystal Palace.

"Do you know why they call it the Crystal Palace?" he asked, shifting his gaze between Elizabeth and me.

I knew, of course. Adam, with his avid interest in art and architecture, had explained it to me often enough. Nevertheless, I followed Elizabeth's lead and shook my head. I was glad that I had done so when I observed how much Thomas enjoyed explaining it. It must, I decided, be something men like to do: explain things.

"Because it is made entirely of glass . . . about three hundred thousand panes, as a matter of fact."

When Adam had tried to tell me about all that glass, I had found it unbelievable. Now I declared in amazement, "Impossible!"

"Well, the frame is of iron, of course, but the walls are all of glass. It is absolutely magnificent."

I closed my eyes and tried to picture such a fabulous edifice. I could not.

"It has cost a total of 75,000 pounds sterling," Thomas was now informing us. "The Queen donated a thousand pounds of her own, and Prince Albert gave five hundred. The rest has come from Englishmen in all walks of life." This I could easily believe. Had not my own Papa made a sizeable donation? Though I said nothing, I couldn't help smiling proudly.

Adam and I had read in the newspaper that there were those who claimed the palace looked more like a greenhouse than an exhibition hall. Actually, from the sketches provided with the article, I thought it did rather resemble a greenhouse. Nevertheless, I felt sure no true Englishman could view that magnificent structure with anything but pride.

After supper, while our elders sipped their wine before the fire, Thomas and I sat in a corner playing whist. He was a jolly companion, and already I felt quite at ease in his company.

However, when the day was over and I climbed at last into bed, I lay awake for awhile, remembering all that had happened, savoring all the new experiences. And the very last person I thought about before I slept was Adam, and I wondered if he missed me as much as I missed him.

Chapter Three

London, 1851

After breakfast on the morning following our arrival in London, Drusilla, Elizabeth, and I repaired to Drusilla's sitting room. The two women were soon deeply involved in reminiscences.

Drusilla asked, "And has your father never forgiven you for running away with the young Dr. Johnshaven?"

My ears pricked up. I had never heard anything about Elizabeth running away.

My stepmother was shaking her head. "He has not, and I know he never will. I do not waste time mourning the past." She smiled at Drusilla. "My life is much too full of happiness to dwell on sorrows best forgotten."

Drusilla nodded. "You always were a most sensible girl."

A warm, pleased chuckle accompanied Elizabeth's response. "You did not always think me so."

Drusilla laughed, too. "Well, time has proven me wrong . . . for which I am grateful. You were indeed right when you followed the dictates of your heart and married your idealistic, if improvident, doctor."

Elizabeth's sigh was gentle. "He was a good man. And if life with him brought me little in the way of worldly goods, it was rich in love and the satisfaction of bringing some comfort into the lives of those less fortunate."

"A fulfilling and worthy life, indeed," Drusilla agreed.

"We were always very happy," Elizabeth continued. "My only regret is that he did not live to see his son grow to manhood. But enough of the past, dear Drusilla. You have already met my beautiful daughter." As she spoke, both women turned their heads and smiled at me.

Suddenly shy, I lowered my eyes, but I felt inordinately pleased.

"Now," Elizabeth continued, "I am eager to have you meet my son . . . or *sons*."

"And I am most anxious to meet them. But I am even more anxious to meet this second husband of yours, Lord Samuel Garth, Earl of Greystone. What is he like?"

A tender smile preceded Elizabeth's reply. "He is a fine man, Drusilla. A strong man . . . a man who has suffered much, achieved much."

When Elizabeth paused, Drusilla urged her on. "Pray, tell me more. How has he suffered?"

"Well, it is a long story; however, I will make it as short as possible. You know, I'm sure, that Earl of Greystone is a very old title. It dates from the twelfth century."

"A very old title, indeed," Drusilla agreed.

"It was bestowed upon the first Samuel Garth for bravery in battle, defending the life of the king. Over the generations, the Garth family became both wealthy and powerful, but the estate began to decline under the ninth earl. He was Samuel's grandfather. From all accounts he was a good man, well loved by all his people, but apparently he had no head for business."

Drusilla nodded. "It happens in the best of families."

"Still, things might have been all right had not his daughter, Christina, married a real scoundrel."

I stiffened. *Surely Elizabeth was not going to tell Drusilla about him!*

But Drusilla was instantly intrigued, of course. "This *scoundrel* she married—what was his name?"

Elizabeth looked perplexed and her response came slowly. "In truth, Drusilla, I have never heard his name spoken."

For a moment, Drusilla only stared at my stepmother. When she did speak, there was disbelief in her tone. "You have never heard his name?"

"Never," Elizabeth declared emphatically, then added, "The Lady Christina was the last of the Garth family, it was written into her marriage contract that she and her children should retain the family name."

"The Lady Christina was Lord Samuel's mother?"

Elizabeth nodded.

"And the . . . scoundrel . . . he was? . . ."

"Samuel's father."

I winced, and even though no one was looking at me, my cheeks burned. To have not only a grandmother who was daft, but a grandfather who was a scoundrel — whatever possessed Elizabeth to reveal such shameful family secrets?

Elizabeth, oblivious to my humiliation, continued, "The wretch stripped the estate of all its treasures, then left before Samuel was born."

Drusilla, her eyes wide with shock, said, "Surely you are not telling me that the Lady Christina's husband simply walked away and left her?"

Elizabeth nodded. "Not only alone, but destitute and with child."

Drusilla looked askance at my stepmother. "But how could that be? Where were her parents?"

"Unbelievable as it may seem, within a year after Christina's marriage, both her father and mother died, leaving the young bride entirely at the mercy of her husband."

"But surely," Drusilla insisted, "there must have been someone — an uncle? a brother? a close friend?"

"I thought that, too," Elizabeth agreed, "but it is apparent that no one came forward. And to make matters worse, Christina's husband sent Lueddy away —"

Interrupting, Drusilla asked, "Who was Lueddy?"

"She was Christina's nursemaid, who doted upon her charge. Nevertheless, the blackguard turned her out. The Lord only knows what would have become of her if our pastor had not arranged a place for her in the next shire."

"But there must have been other servants," Drusilla insisted.

"No. Lueddy says that all the other servants fled soon after Christina's mother died. She claims they were afraid . . . although of what, exactly, she will not say."

Drusilla, obviously dumbfounded by this story, had raised her fingers to her open mouth, and sat shaking her head, her gaze never leaving Elizabeth's face.

"So you see, the Lady Christina was, in truth, entirely alone and destitute. Exactly what happened, no one knows, but it is certain that when Samuel was born, there was scarcely anything left of the estate save the manor house and the land."

Please, Elizabeth, say no more! I sought by the sheer power of thought to silence my stepmother.

But she pursued her narrative relentlessly. "In any event, whatever happened, it was too much for the Lady Christina. She was little more than a child, and her mind . . . well, it was never the same."

By that time, I was so mortified I wanted to jump up and run from the room. But I knew such action would only call attention to me, and that I could not bear.

As for Drusilla, she was, at least for the moment, speechless. It was a condition of which I highly approved.

However, Elizabeth, with single-minded concentration, continued, "But the strangest thing of all is that Christina, to her dying day, waited for her husband's return, and spoke of him in loving terms. She seemed totally unaware of the desperate situation in which the blackguard had left her. All this I know from Samuel himself."

Clucking in dismay, Drusilla commented dolefully, "It indeed goes to prove that love is blind."

"Perhaps so," Elizabeth murmured.

A silence descended on the room. Outside the window, a gentle breeze stirred the branches of an early-blossoming apple tree, filling the air with sweet perfume. In the distance, the call of a street hawker blended with the rhythmic clop, clop of his horse's hooves. I began to relax. Surely my stepmother would say no more.

But Drusilla was not to be put off. Brows knit in perplexity, she asked, "But if Christina was all alone, who delivered the baby? How did they survive?"

And Elizabeth was more than willing to supply the answer. "Christina might easily have died there, alone, had not Lueddy taken care of her, and of Samuel, too, after he was born."

"But I thought you said—"

"Yes, yes, but she returned. She couldn't bear the separation, so she came back. Fortunately, the husband had already disappeared."

"But how in the world did the woman manage?"

"Lueddy always had a garden patch, raised a few chickens. And the few tenant farmers who were left paid their rent in foodstuff and wool. Somehow, they survived."

"Remarkable!" Drusilla exclaimed, shaking her head again. "Quite remarkable!"

"Indeed," Elizabeth agreed. "Sam was sixteen when his mother died. She left him with nothing save the rundown estate, unpaid taxes, and a magnificent rope of matched pink pearls."

Abruptly my chagrin turned to curiosity. A rope of matched pink pearls? Why had I never seen them?

But even as the thought formed in my mind, Drusilla was posing the question for me. "What did Samuel do with the pearls?"

"Well, with the rope of pearls for collateral, he borrowed a quite considerable sum, and went to work!" Elizabeth spoke the words with such an air of triumph, it broke the tension. They both laughed.

"And now I think we should have a cup of tea." So saying, Drusilla rose to her feet and gave the bellpull a tug. Within minutes a white-capped and aproned servant arrived, carrying a heavily laden silver tray. Everyone was silent for a few minutes while cups were passed and buttered scones and strawberry jam offered round.

But as soon as we were all contentedly sipping and munching, Drusilla said, "Please, continue, Elizabeth. What happened next?"

My stepmother, who was very proud of her husband and all he had accomplished, needed no urging. "People in the village say that during the years following Christina's death, Samuel did the work of two men. He helped the few farmers who still remained on the land to repair their cottages, clear their fields, and to plant and tend crops. He also purchased a fine herd of dairy cattle and added a line of blooded horses, which he has bred into a prosperous stud.

Elizabeth paused and Drusilla remarked, "I have heard of the Greystone horses. They are highly prized by their owners."

The words brought a glow of pride to my stepmother's countenance, and served to soothe my own wounded pride as well.

"So the estate is prospering again, is it?"

"Indeed," Elizabeth confirmed. "The changes Samuel has wrought are little short of miraculous."

With these words, my stepmother reinstated herself in my good graces, though the shame of having a stranger know all about my daft grandmother and despicable grandfather would not be easily cast off.

Drusilla stared at Elizabeth, her eyes thoughtful. At last she spoke, hesitantly. "I seem to remember reading somewhere . . . something about a magnificent collection of jewels. Now that I think about it, I'm sure it was the Greystone jewels."

Greystone jewels?

"You are quite right. The Greystone jewels were famous. Unfortunately, they disappeared along with Christina's husband. Goodness only knows how she managed to save the pearls." Elizabeth sighed and fell silent.

Why, I wondered, had *I* never heard of the Greystone jewels? And why did Elizabeth choose this moment to stop talking? I would have liked to ask her to tell me more, but decided to leave it until we were alone.

For a while, the two women sat quiet, each lost in her own thoughts. The morning sun, shining through the lace curtains, brought warmth and cheer to the little room where we sat. Despite the pain and humiliation Elizabeth's words had inflicted, I began to relax. After all, I reasoned, Drusilla wasn't really a stranger. No doubt she and Elizabeth had shared many a secret during all the years they had been friends. I yawned. The room seemed to grow warmer, and my eyes began to droop, my head to nod . . .

". . . your husband's first wife?" Drusilla's question brought me wide awake once more.

"A lovely young woman," Elizabeth replied without hesitation. "Her name was Amanda. She was the youngest of Sir Alfred Mangrove's eleven daughters."

"Eleven girls! What in the world had their poor father done to deserve such a fate?" The laughter following Drusilla's remark was warm and sympathetic.

"Well," Elizabeth smiled, "whatever his short comings, having sired eleven daughters and not one son, Sir Alfred did his best by his children. They say he was inordinately proud of them, too. However, village gossips also say that when Samuel asked for Amanda's hand in marriage, Sir Alfred agreed very readily, despite the estate's straightened circumstances. In fact, it is rumored that he seemed quite relieved to have one more of his brood provided for." Elizabeth's smile faded and she sighed as with a heavy heart.

"What happened to her?" Drusilla prompted.

"Well, all who speak of her say that the Lady Amanda was a sweet and good child, but a child nonetheless. And poor Samuel . . . he had never had a childhood himself. After he married Amanda, he quit working so hard and spent long hours laughing and playing with his beautiful bride. For what little time they had, they were happy together, Drusilla. It was a happiness they both deserved, and for Samuel, it was happiness long overdue."

A questioning look pursed Drusilla's lips, sharpened

her glance. "Do you not mind speaking of your husband's happiness with another woman?"

My stepmother's answering laughter bespoke both self-assurance and contentment. "Ah, Drusilla, my dear, you must know there are many kinds of happiness. Samuel and I have found a joy in each other that is ours alone, and it has nothing to do with anyone else. I have borne him a son, my little John."

"But there is more to a happy marriage than bearing children," Drusilla exclaimed softly.

Again, Elizabeth laughed. "Oh, indeed! But what Samuel shared with Amanda, I shared with Adam's father. Samuel and I have something more . . . something deeper. I suppose it is what our first marriages would have become, had death not intervened." A gentle, faraway look softened Elizabeth's face. "Samuel is a kind, a gentle, a warm and loving man." She stopped speaking and a wave of rosy color suffused her cheeks.

"We are the most fortunate of women, dear Elizabeth," Drusilla conceded, and they sat in silence for a while, smiling at each other in, I thought, a most smug and self-satisfied way.

I had listened to their conversation in quiet fascination. I had always known, of course, that Elizabeth, though I loved her dearly, was not my mother. Amanda was my mother. Yet when I heard her name, I felt nothing.

It came to me then that no one ever spoke of Amanda, or scarcely ever. She had lived and loved, had worked and played and dreamed her own dreams; she had borne a child and died, and no one ever spoke her name. There was nothing to mark her brief sojourn upon this earth save me—and even in me she was denied, because I reminded everyone of my grandmother.

Without warning a lump formed in my throat, and a kind of loneliness and grief I could not express filled my heart. I rose from my chair and slipped unnoticed from the room.

Chapter Four

The following week was busy, filled with getting acquainted, then with shopping and choosing patterns. Next came long hours of standing while Miss Twitchle, Drusilla's seamstress, fitted, pinned, and turned hems. During the second week, however, there were fewer demands upon my time, and very little to interest me in Uncle Phillip's elegant house: no puppies, no kittens, no horses. And with time heavy on my hands, I was sorely missing Adam.

Thus, when Thomas proposed a sightseeing expedition, I was filled with excitement. Elizabeth and Drusilla also viewed the suggestion with favor, and when Uncle Phillip had given his consent, it was decided that we would leave directly after breakfast the next day.

The first of my new gowns had been finished, a simple two-piece walking out costume of moiré silk in a beautiful shade of blue. The jacket, cut in the military Zouave style—it was all the rage that season—was trimmed with bright red silk braid. My bonnet, too, was of blue, the same shade as the dress, and the ribbons that tied under my chin, and the plume that curved around the bonnet's crown, were of the same red as the silk braid. When I looked at myself in the mirror, I could not help but feel pleased at the effect, at the way the blue accentuated my eyes, the red complemented my dark hair and fair skin.

Drusilla's maid coiffed my hair for me, arranging it in the latest fashion. First she parted it in the middle and drew it tight and smooth over the crown—not an easy task with hair as thick and curly as mine. Then she brushed the sides into fat ringlets, called spaniel curls because they were pulled forward and allowed to hang down in front of the ears so that they could be seen under the brim of one's bonnet.

When Thomas saw me thus attired, his eyes filled with admiration. "Lady Victoria," he exclaimed. "You look quite . . . quite . . . devastatingly beautiful."

I felt a blush mount in my cheeks—I was not used to such flattery. But I managed to say lightly, "Surely, sir, it would take more than a simple country girl to devastate a handsome young man like you."

Laughing, he offered me his arm and we were ready to depart. At the last minute Elizabeth tucked a pound note into my reticule and whispered that it was mine to spend as I pleased.

London, on that beautiful bright spring morning, seemed a wonderful place to be. The Hornaby residence was located in a quarter of the city known as Belgravia. Lilacs bloomed in the square in front of Uncle Phillip's house, filling the air with their fragrance. The sky was clear overhead, and the birdsong I had heard all my life in the park at Greystone Manor seemed fresh and new when sung here in the streets of London.

How lovely it was to be alive, to have a whole long glorious day before us, a day to fill with who-knew-what adventures. I leaned on Thomas's arm and gazed up into his face.

He smiled down at me and said, "What a beauty you are, Lady Victoria. Why, even the flowers in Mama's garden pale beside you."

Oh, what a delicious feeling, to be admired by a handsome young man! But I answered modestly, "Fie, sir, to tease a poor simple lass so!"

"But it is true," Thomas insisted. "I swear, you quite outshine the leading beauty at court."

A hansom cab had been called, and now Thomas

handed me in with gallantry befitting royalty. Indeed, brimming with excitement, I was feeling very much the young lady of station. If only, I thought, Adam were here . . .

But Thomas, a lighthearted companion, gave me no time for moping. The morning hours, filled with sightseeing and shopping, passed quickly. We drove through Picadilly Circus and Trafalgar Square, and paid a very short visit to the Tower of London—I found it a most depressing place. To raise my spirits, I insisted Thomas take me to a shop where I might spend the money Elizabeth had given me.

We went to Harrod's, an establishment that had opened its doors only two years before. There were so many beautiful things to buy, I was tempted to spend every penny of my pound on myself. But, of course, I did not. In the end I bought handkerchiefs for everyone: lovely lace-trimmed ones for Elizabeth and Aunt Drusilla, large white monogrammed ones for Papa, little John, Adam, and Uncle Phillip. For myself, I purchased several yards of ribbon and a pair of gloves.

Then we went to Madam Tussaud's. This last stop was great fun. The wax figures were so lifelike, I actually asked directions of one, thinking it a guard. How Thomas laughed!

He took me to Claridges for lunch. I was quite overawed, never having dreamed there could be a place, other than Buckingham Palace, so sumptuously furnished. The carpets were thick and soft, heavy velvet and silk brocade hangings framed the windows, chandeliers of gold and crystal glittered with red and blue fire in the candlelight. Here and there, potted palms in huge porcelain urns provided seclusion for couples seated on love seats, chatting quietly while they waited for a table.

The dining room was paneled in rich dark oak, the tables spread with white linen and laid with the finest china, crystal, and silver. Each table also held a bud vase with a single rose. The menu was all in French, and

Thomas, at my request, chose for me. First, we had a lovely clear soup, followed by plover's eggs, then salmon in aspic. For the main course, there was partridge prepared with a savory glaze and accompanied by a lovely red wine. I could quite easily have finished several glasses, but prudently, I restricted myself to one. Last of all we were served a selection of small cakes, each delightfully iced and decorated, some with bits of candied fruit, others with currants or raisins.

When we had quite stuffed ourselves, we went for a stroll in Hyde Park. The day had turned unseasonably warm, but it was cool under the trees and we dallied for a while, listening to the speakers. One fellow, loudly exhorting his brethren to seek salvation, denounced the falling away of the faithful and the attendant rise of drunkenness; another emphatically decried the lot of the working man and the failure of the government to do anything about the widespread unemployment; yet another railed against the rise of crime in the city, loudly voicing his fear of the ruffian gangs that prowled the streets.

I'm shamed to admit that neither Thomas nor I were in the mood for such depressing fare. Indeed, I was embarrassed by the shouting and gesticulating of the more emotional speakers. And so we walked on, intending to cross through the park to the site of the Crystal Palace, which was nearing completion.

"It has really been great fun," Thomas was saying. "There was such a to-do over the elm trees, you know. Just wait 'til you see!" He was enjoying his story as much as I. Surprisingly, it was one that Adam and I had missed.

So I listened with great pleasure, and Thomas became increasingly animated. "The faction that wanted the Crystal Palace in the park insisted the land be cleared, but the nature lovers were just as insistent that not one tree should be touched."

Heatedly, I interrupted, "How dreadful that the people who loved the trees did not win the day. I, too, would have done my best to save them, had I been here at the time."

"What makes you think they did not?" There was a gleam in Thomas's eye that set me on my guard.

"Why, sir, you did say the Crystal Palace is in the park, did you not?"

"I did, and it is. But the champions of the trees didn't lose. It was finally decided that there was nothing for it but to build the Palace large enough to accommodate the elms!"

"Tsk, Thomas . . . surely you jest. Trees cannot grow inside a building!"

But Thomas gave a solemn nod, and explained, "The architect used a vaulted transept, like in the nave of a cathedral, to raise the roof high enough to clear the tallest tree, and now the elms are growing right inside the building."

"La! You're teasing me!" And I tossed my head, unbelieving.

"No, no. It's true, I assure you."

"Then it must be marvelous to see," I said cautiously, still not certain that he was serious.

"Smashing!" And Thomas smiled pridefully, as if he were personally responsible for the entire project.

I gazed up at him, thinking what a fine handsome young man he was, and he squeezed my hand, which he held tucked into the crook of his arm as we walked along.

On that bright and beautiful afternoon, strolling in the park with Thomas, the Crystal Palace sounded incredible to me, and I could scarcely wait to see it. If only Adam were there to see it with us, I thought. Then I smiled, thinking what fun it would be when he did arrive and I could show it to him.

We hurried on, and as we approached the center of the park, I noticed a most peculiar group of people standing near the head of the path we were following. Actually, only one figure was standing. The other two were kneeling, one on either side, clinging, in what seemed abject desperation, to the central figure. They were clothed in the filthiest, most ragged collection of tatters I had ever seen, and fastened around the upper arm of each was a metallic band about four inches wide.

The two who were kneeling had their faces hidden against the thighs of their fellow, who stood, eyes blank, gazing straight ahead; and though the lips moved, no sound issued from the mouth. A battered cup was grasped tight in the outstretched hands, and as we drew near I could not help but stare at this strange trio.

Were they male or female? Of the crouching figures, there was naught to see save their ragged covering. And even with the poor creature who was standing, neither the body, which was completely shrouded by a loose-hanging cloak, nor the stringy, matted hair and vacant eyes gave any clue as to gender. Not, I suppose, that it really mattered. Misery is misery, no matter who the sufferer may be.

I was more sickened than frightened by my first glimpse of these people. I stopped, clutching frantically at Thomas who was chattering on, oblivious to my consternation. "Thomas, look! What's the matter with those people?"

Thomas, following the direction of my gaze, stopped short, and tried to turn me back the way we had come. "Victoria, I'm so sorry, I shouldn't have let you see them. Come, let us take another path."

But I would not be distracted. "No, no, Thomas. They are ill. We must try to help them." I could feel tears rising in my throat. Though we had seen any number of dirty and ragged people in the streets that morning—the sight had somewhat dimmed my first feelings of admiration for the great city of London—none we had encountered earlier had had this look of utter helplessness about them.

"But they aren't ill, Victoria, at least not as you mean." The strain in Thomas's voice revealed his distress. "They are—or were—quite mad. It's these poor devils about whom Father gets so infuriated. He insists they are sick and should be treated with the same care as any other invalid. Support for his views is growing, but not nearly fast enough, I'm afraid."

As he spoke, Thomas sought again to turn me back, away from the dreadful sight, but I would not go. I was still intent upon giving aid to the poor creatures, and I tried to pull Thomas toward them, saying "Come. If nothing else, we must see that they are taken to hospital."

"Ha!" Thomas snorted derisively. "Those poor devils have already had treatment in hospital: St. Mary's of Bethlehem, better known as Bedlam."

I glanced at him with surprise. The tone of his voice, the expression on his face belied the impression I had had of a carefree, self-centered, albeit charming, young man-about-town.

"*Despite* the treatment," he continued cynically, "they have recovered enough to be sent out to beg. Those armbands are their badges of office, and those cups the tools of their trade."

Thomas's voice had become unsteady, and I suddenly felt very close to him. It was the same feeling I always had at home when Adam and I would find some sick or wounded woodland creature. Except, I thought, Adam and I were always able to provide them with shelter and care . . .

Thomas was still speaking and I forced my attention back to him. "Father says it's a crime to treat the poor fools so, but it's the law!"

This was indeed a side of Thomas I had not seen before. No longer was he the charming, gay, lighthearted lad. In his place there was a sober, sensitive, and much troubled young man.

"Father is right, I think, Victoria. Look at them. They are sick. No human being looks like that from sheer perversity!" Thomas was becoming increasingly agitated. "You would not believe how they are treated at Bedlam. You can visit for a ha'penny any day of the year, and there are those who consider it a jolly way to while away an hour or two."

Since I would not be turned back, Thomas now tried to hurry me along. However, as we passed the poor Bedlamites, he dropped a guinea piece into the cup held by the vacant-eyed figure.

At the clink of the coin, the smaller of the crouching figures twitched spasmodically, the head jerking around so that the face became visible. I shall never forget how thin that small countenance was—thin to the point of emaciation. The eyes were screwed tight shut, but the mouth hung open, revealing the even, pearly-white teeth of a child. An ugly, suppurating sore festered on the lower lip, oozed down the small, pointed chin.

Feeling both queasy and frightened, I clung to Thomas's arm, shrank close against his side, but I could not tear my eyes from that fearsome tableau. And still the central figure stood immobile, staring into space. The lips continued to move, delivering no sound, a thin trail of spittle hanging out the corner of the mouth.

Bitterly, Thomas continued, "The crowds gather about the gates of St. Mary's on a Sunday afternoon and jeer at the poor creatures, who are chained in the yard for the public's amusement like beasts in a circus. They laugh and toss stones, and they yell, 'Hi, Tom-o'-Bedlam!' "

But I listened no more. Those last words rang in my head, awakening the memory of that long-ago morning when I sat in the chimney corner tending a mother cat with her litter of kittens. *"Daft, her were. Loony as any Tom-o'-Bedlam...."* That's what they said, and they had laughed. My heart began to pound, and watching that wretched Bedlamite gazing into space, mouthing soundless words addressed to some unseen being, I thought, *Surely my grandmother was not like one of these poor creatures!*

And as if to mock me, my mind summoned up the memory of the words, *"Always a-talkin' to folks as weren't there...."*

A chill coursed through me. For a moment I feared I might faint right there in the park, and, struggling to gain control of myself, I whispered, "Thomas, I should like a cup of tea now, if you please."

We left the park at a rapid pace, and though we made no further mention of the three we had encountered there, they continued to haunt me. Several days later, I chanced upon one of Uncle Phillip's medical journals. I picked it up and began idly paging through it. But what I saw there shocked me into rapt attention. It was an issue devoted to the problem of madness, and though I was both revolted and nauseated by what I read, read it I did, from beginning to end.

The articles were complete with pictures of the accommodations afforded patients of St. Mary's of Bethlehem. Also included were detailed drawings of various pieces of special paraphernalia used to administer so-called "harmless tortures," which were guaranteed to return the hapless patient to a state of normality. In the margins, Uncle Phillip had noted some additional treatments applied to those patients who managed to survive the filthy conditions, the abominable food, the isolation and darkness, and the brutality of the keepers.

By the time I had finished my perusal of the journal I was, quite literally, sick. I lost my breakfast and went to bed for the remainder of the day to nurse a pounding headache. And I couldn't help thinking, *God in Heaven, 'twould be better to be dead than to be mad!*

I never spoke to anyone about the matter, though often in the days that lay ahead I would remember those poor miserable Bedlamites I had seen in the park, and I would recall with fear and horror the fate that awaited all hapless victims of madness who should find themselves guests of St. Mary's of Bethlehem.

Chapter Five

Papa and the boys arrived the last week in April. I did not realize, until I saw him, how much I had missed Adam. At dinner that night, seated next to Thomas and across the table from my stepbrother, I could feel my heart beating quick and light in my breast. I felt like laughing and clapping and whirling about for joy, but some entirely new and totally foreign sense of modesty held me in check. All unawares, I had crossed into that limbo twixt childhood and maturity where every step is filled with mystery and joyful pain.

That was the first time I ever thought of Adam as other than my big brother. Suddenly, he was a young man whose very smile made my breath catch in my throat. I looked at him, sitting across the table from me, and when his blue-violet eyes caught mine, just for a moment I was lost in another world. Then shyness overcame me and I bowed my head toward my plate.

When I looked at him again, not raising my head but glancing shyly up through my lashes, he was smiling a most masterful and grown-up smile. I giggled with delight. Fortunately, someone was relating a story of an amusing nature and my giggles were masked by the general laughter.

No word acknowledged what had passed between us that evening, but thereafter Adam granted me a deference that somehow altered our relationship. In my new dresses, with my hair elegantly brushed and coiffed in the latest fashion, I was no longer his little sister. I was a young woman, and I felt a warmth, a glow when he was near that belied the sisterly affection in which I professed to hold him.

On the first day of May, the Great Exhibition opened in the Crystal Palace. We were all up early and I dressed with great care. My gown was of striped French silk in shades of grey accented with sprigs of rosy peach-colored blossoms. The bodice, secured with tiny pearl buttons, fit tight about my waist and over my bosom, accentuating the fullness that had developed there, seemingly overnight. The sleeves, done in the full pagoda cut, flared wide below the elbow to display the puffed organdy sleeves of my chemisette, which was the same shade of rosy peach as the sprigs of flowers on the dress.

The skirt, made up of three wide ruffles and supported by one of the new-style hoops, swung gracefully with my every step. I had spent hours practicing with those hoops. Elizabeth and Drusilla had impressed upon me the necessity for keeping control of my skirts at all times. Even a chance mishap that revealed (God forbid!) an ankle, would mean disgrace and the end of any hope for social acceptance.

We had not been much concerned about such things at Greystone Manor. Living so far removed from the mainstream of society, with money so scarce for so many years, Adam and I had been allowed to simply grow, to observe nature about us without any thought of shame or embarrassment. Elizabeth and Miss Jones, our governess, had, of course, taught us proper deportment and the social graces; but the prudery — if I may make so bold a judgement — that marked our Victorian society had not been practiced at Greystone Manor.

But I digress. For the great day, Papa had purchased for me the most beautiful bonnet I have ever seen. It was constructed of heavy grey silk and trimmed with peach-colored silk roses, tucked with feathers, and finished with long velvet ribbons to tie under the chin.

Elizabeth said I was too young for such a hat, but Papa would hear none of it. "Let the child enjoy the day. There will never be another like it in all our lives," he insisted, and Elizabeth finally relented.

When at last I was ready, I hurried out of my room and started down the stairs. All the men waited below, talking and laughing. But when they heard the rustle of my skirts, they raised their heads to look at me. Their conversation ceased abruptly. I hesitated, uneasy in the sudden silence. Then I saw on each upturned face an expression of such admiration, it brought the color to my cheeks, set my heart fluttering. Lifting my chin a bit higher, I descended the stairway slowly, giving each of them, in turn, a glance, a smile.

I had almost reached the foot of the stairs when Adam and Thomas, both at the same instant, stepped forward, causing them to collide with one another; and while they were setting themselves to rights once more, Papa offered me his arm.

But it was Uncle Phillip who said, "How beautiful you are, Victoria. We shall have to keep a sharp eye on you, or some young gallant will surely carry you away."

Elizabeth and Drusilla joined us then, and we went immediately to the carriage that awaited us at the door. The Crystal Palace, as we approached, blazed like a huge diamond in the morning sun, and we all gazed at it, spellbound, until we reached the entrance.

Because Uncle Phillip knew so many people at court, we were escorted through the crowds and taken directly to a spot, marked off by silken ropes, where we would have a clear view of the festivities. I was gawking, marveling at the trees—for, as Thomas had promised, they were actually growing right inside the building—when there was a great fanfare of trumpets announcing the arrival of the royal family. It was precisely twelve o'clock, noon.

I was so excited, I quite danced up and down. Elizabeth, always prepared, slipped me her vial of smelling salts and whispered, "Here, dear, tuck this into your reticule and take a sniff should you feel faint."

The royals were escorted by the Household Cavalry. Queen Victoria—for whom I was named—was accompanied by Prince Albert, in full regalia, and two of the older children. As they entered the hall there was a flourish of trumpets, followed by the rustle and sigh of silk as all the ladies curtsied low, marking the progress of the royals through the hall to the dais that had been raised to receive them.

The queen was so beautiful, my heart almost stopped with admiration. Her dress was pink and silver and she was wearing a diamond tiara. Diamonds hung from her ears as well, and a diamond necklace encircled her throat. Nor was that all. There were bracelets and rings, and a huge pin in the shape of a cross, all set with diamonds that blazed and flashed and sparkled as she moved slowly forward. So close were we to the dais upon which the royal family sat, I could have reached out and touched the sleeve of the queen's dress as she passed.

Her face was absolutely radiant as she acknowledged the loud cheers of the crowd, and the children waved and smiled most amiably. Prince Albert, too, looked very grand as he read a report on the fair, and though he was not widely admired, for our beloved queen's sake his speech was well received.

There were several speeches then, and the Archbishop of Canterbury offered a prayer, after which a chorus of one thousand voices sang Handel's "Hallelujah Chorus." It was truly glorious, and had I not had Elizabeth's smelling salts, I fear I should have been taken with the vapors.

It was late in the afternoon when the ceremonies ended. We returned to Uncle Phillip's house in silence, too overcome by the excitement of the day for idle speech. It had been a marvelous and exhausting experience, one I will remember forever.

We visited the Crystal Palace many times during the ensuing weeks, and each time we went, we saw something we had not seen before. Exhibits had been sent from all over the world, and represented the newest and best that each country had to offer. Some of the things were utilitarian, some artistic in nature.

I was much taken with a magnificent howdah, complete with a fringed awning, that was sent all the way from India. Constructed of ivory, inlaid wood, and richly embroidered fabric, it sat atop a stuffed elephant draped with silver and gold trappings. The fair officials had had to borrow the elephant from a museum in order to display the howdah properly.

The carved ivory furniture, also from India, delighted most of the ladies who saw it, but I could not help but think about those huge gentle creatures who had died to provide the raw material.

The one exhibit that everyone, men and women alike, found irresistible, was the fabulous Koh-i-noor diamond. It was displayed in a burglarproof cage of gilded steel and was said to be more valuable than all the rest of the fair's exhibits added together.

John, who had inherited our father's love of the land, was particularly fascinated by a huge machine called a reaper. It had been sent by the Americans. "Do you realize," he said to Papa, "that machine could revolutionize farming? Just think of the possibilities."

Some of the American display was, however, a bit disappointing. Nothing but heaps of Indian maize, and pyramids of soap and dental powder. This elicited much good-natured joking at the Americans' expense.

"I have heard," Thomas said, "that the Americans, in their own optimistic manner, requested far more space than they could properly fill. A bit cheeky, don't you agree?"

"For shame, Thomas!" I reproached him. "They are our cousins, after all, and most inventive, too."

"Yes," Adam put in, "and speaking of invention, have you seen that statue, *The Greek Slave?* It's quite beautiful, and most ingeniously displayed."

"Where? I want to see," I exclaimed, instantly all agog.

Adam led the way, and with my first glimpse of the statue, I was captivated. It was its very simplicity that made it so beautiful: an undraped, yet obviously modest young woman, lovely to behold. Then, even as we gazed upon her, she began to move.

Startled, I clutched at Adam's arm, exclaiming, "Oh, my!"

Adam covered my hands with his own and looked down at me with a reassuring smile.

Thomas, after giving the statue a quick examination, remarked, "It is only an example of that American inventiveness you so admire, Victoria. See? There in the base of the statue, someone turns that crank, the gears inside mesh, and round the young lady goes."

During the early days of the Exhibition, Elizabeth worried and fretted over me, fearing to let me out of her sight. "Did you see in the paper last night?" she would say. "The anarchists are plotting to overthrow the government. They are even threatening to blow up the Crystal Palace!"

However, Papa said he was sure the rumors were highly exaggerated, and Uncle Phillip insisted they were entirely without basis. In the end, I was allowed to accompany Adam or Thomas whenever I chose to do so. Actually, I had only to mention that I should like to come or to go, and both those young gentlemen would immediately offer to be my escort and protector. And it always ended with both of them accompanying me.

What fun we had, the three of us. Despite the enormous crowds, the jostling, and the waiting in queues, everyone was in a holiday frame of mind. As for my two gentlemen, their generosity knew no bounds. If Adam bought me a raspberry ice, Thomas would buy me a sweet to go with it; when Thomas gave me a souvenir doll attired like Queen Victoria, nothing would do but that Adam give me a small plush bear. All in all, for me it was a wondrous, never-to-be-forgotten summer.

The evening before we were to return to Greystone

Manor, we all sat together in the small salon of the Hornabys' house, talking about the various exhibits and the events that we had enjoyed most.

Aunt Drusilla remarked upon the Indian cashmere shawls, so fine, so delicate that they could be drawn through a finger ring. Elizabeth said she found the eau de cologne fountain, where ladies could dip their handkerchiefs, a charming idea. And both women gave high praise to the colorful French chintz.

Uncle Phillip suddenly interrupted our reminiscences to ask, "Have any of you seen this article in today's paper?" Without waiting for a reply he read us a commentary that said, in part, ". . . the only miscreants apprehended during the entire twenty-three weeks that the exhibition has been open were twelve pickpockets, and eleven persons caught trying to remove minor exhibits."

Thomas, with a perfectly straight face, replied, "No, father, I did not see that article, but I did read a couple of days ago that among the unclaimed lost articles were three petticoats and two bustles."

Drusilla tapped him smartly on the knuckles with her fan, and said, "That is hardly a subject for mixed company, young sir!" but everyone else laughed heartily.

The next morning, as we were leaving the breakfast room, Thomas whispered, "Will you come up to the solarium with me, Victoria?"

The solarium was a lovely room on the third floor, filled with flowering plants and shrubs and furnished with wrought iron tables and chairs and benches, all painted white and padded with cushions in lovely rainbow colors.

"One last visit to that lovely room would be welcome," I agreed, and I held fast to his arm, laughing up at him as we mounted the stairs.

Thomas was tall, like his father, but his coloring more nearly resembled that of his mother. He had thick, reddish-brown hair, hazel eyes alight with intelligence and humor, a rather prominent nose, and generous mouth. When he smiled, a dimple that I found most enchanting appeared at its corner. All in all, I thought, as I observed the play of expression on his face, he was a very handsome young man.

When we reached the solarium, he half-closed the door behind us and led me to one of the wrought iron benches. Then he took both my hands in his and said, "I am going to miss you, dear Victoria."

Something in the tone of his voice made my heart beat faster, my breath come a little quicker. "I'm glad," I said, "because I shall miss you, too, Thomas."

"Please promise you'll write to me." His eyes, gazing into mine, added their plea to his words.

"And will you promise to write to me?" I asked, smiling, trying to hide the sudden confusion I felt.

He nodded gravely, then raised my hands to his lips and kissed my fingertips, one by one, while his eyes continued to gaze into mine with such tenderness, it brought the warm color mounting in my throat, suffusing my cheeks. The soft touch of his lips on my fingers sent little shivers of pleasure pulsing through me. I felt excited, exhilarated, and without thinking I leaned toward him, raised my lips to his. We stood thus for a long moment, the silence closing us in. Then, even as Thomas bowed his face toward mine, the sound of footsteps pounding up the stairs broke the stillness.

A moment longer Thomas held my hands, then he released me just as the door burst wide. A breathless Adam entered and proceeded to make a great pretense of getting Thomas's opinion on some matter of absolutely no importance. I thought how very flattering it was that all that summer, whenever I chanced to be alone with one of these young men, the other promptly appeared. I also thought how very fortunate I was, for I was truly fond of both of them, though they were as different as two people can be.

Adam was the dreamer, the artist, moody and changeable, even as the everlasting sea that beats against the crags below Greystone Manor. How very dear he was to me.

And Thomas, dear comfortable Thomas, was so kind and such a good friend. Yes, I thought, I shall miss Thomas sorely.

Together, the three of us descended the stairs. Thomas and Uncle Phillip rode with us to Victoria Station, and when it was time to say goodbye, I could not speak for the tears clogging my throat. Uncle Phillip kissed me on the forehead. At the last minute before boarding the train, I stood on tiptoe to kiss Thomas lightly on the cheek.

The trip home was exhausting after the long exciting summer, and I suppose it was because the whole adventure was over, or because I was tired and yet unable to relax, that on that first night home I had a terrifying dream.

I stood upon the balcony, waiting. I paced back and forth, staring over the balustrade, watching the lawn below, searching the dark shadows under the trees at the edge of the park. Then a figure appeared, emerging from the darkness, moving quickly toward the house, and even as my heart began to beat faster, the sudden joy I felt turned to fear.

A terrible blackness arose, eddied and flowed about me, then receded, leaving me chained to a wall in a dark and musty cell. The din of insane laughter echoed all around me. Shivering with cold, covered with filth, I cowered against the damp wall to which I was fastened, whimpering, while the pain in my manacled arm became a searing flame. Then, through the wild laughter that beat inside my head, I heard the creaking and scraping of a door, and a burst of light filled the tiny cell.

I opened my eyes to find myself safe in my own bed, my room awash with moonlight and fragrant with the scent of wisteria. My dream friend, the lovely dark-haired girl, whom I had not seen since we departed for London, stood at the foot of my bed, contemplating me. I sat up and smiled at her, and she beckoned me to follow her out onto the balcony.

I did not realize until I wakened in the morning that it had been a dream within a dream.

Chapter Six

Greystone Manor, 1851-1852

For Adam and for me, our trip to London to visit the Great Exhibition marked the end of childhood. With the dawning of maturity, our relationship lost the easy camaraderie we had once enjoyed, and a strange new kind of tension developed between us that was at once frightening and gratifying.

Even as my bosom had blossomed, Adam's voice had deepened, his shoulders broadened. Now we walked where we used to run, sat and talked where we had once rolled and tumbled. No longer did I follow Adam about like a devoted pup. Rather, I began to feel the power of my womanhood, and I was not above exerting it, though never meanly or with thought to hurt.

For Christmas that year, Drusilla sent me a bonnet trimmed with chinchilla and a muff to match. I put them on immediately to go for a walk in the park. Adam helped me don my boots and we set out at a brisk pace.

There had been a fall of snow during the night. The boughs of the evergreens were laden with white, and the fragrance of pine filled the air. There was no sound save the crunch and squeak of snow under our boots. We stopped at the head of the path that meanders through the woods to the old bridge. The sun, at that moment, broke through the clouds and struck sparks of flame from each ice-sheathed leaf and blade of grass.

"Oh, Adam," I breathed. "How beautiful the world is . . . it makes my heart burst just to look at it!" But when I glanced up at him, I saw that his gaze was fastened on me. My breath caught in my throat, and I could feel the warm color begin to rise in my cheeks. Unaccountably flustered, I turned from him, gathered up my skirts with one quick gesture, and, as I had done so often as a child, started to run, shouting over my shoulder, "Race you to the bridge."

Adam caught me just where the path enters the trees, caught me in his arms, and swung me about. We were both out of breath and laughing. But as we clung together, looking into each other's eyes, something strange and wonderful happened. Slowly, Adam's arms slackened their embrace, his hands moved up to frame my face, and he bowed his head until his lips were touching mine.

A sensation akin to a draft of warm wine flowed through me, leaving me weak. Indeed, I think I should have fallen, had he not suddenly clasped me so close against his chest that even through my heavy fur-lined pelisse I could feel the pounding of his heart, racing even as my own.

Abruptly, Adam's lips left mine and he buried his face in my hair, whispering over and over, "I love you. . . ."

His voice, little more than a breath in my ear, sent shivers of delight all the way down to the tips of my toes. "And I love you," I whispered, nuzzling my cold face into the warm hollow beneath his chin.

Then for a moment we drew apart, though still within each other's arms, and looked deep into each other's eyes. A small gust of wind moved the branches of the trees overhead, causing huge white crystals of snow to come drifting down. They caught in Adam's hair, fell onto my upturned face.

With a sigh, I offered him my lips once more. He bent his head and his eager mouth claimed mine. Then his mouth opened, my lips parted, and the tips of our tongues touched.

We had kissed before—many times before—but never like this. And never before had our kisses unleashed such a maelstrom of sensation. My whole being seemed to come alive, and as his tongue brushed my lips, I was suddenly intensely aware of all the most intimate parts of my body. His tongue moved over mine. Moaning softly, I pressed my body even closer to his, wanting him to touch me all over.

Fortunately, no matter how hotly the flames of desire may burn within, to consumate love in the snow would be a very chilling experience. Still, I do not dare to contemplate how long we would have remained, exchanging kiss for kiss, had not dark clouds moved in from the sea, obscuring the sun. An icy wind began to blow. Cold seeped in through our cloaks, and even the passion of newfound love must cool before the onslaught of inclement weather. At last we knew we must seek shelter in the manor house or freeze. We returned to the great hall, eyes shining, cheeks glowing, mouths tremulous with kissing.

From that day onward Adam and I could not stand side by side without our fingers touching, and our eyes never tired of gazing into those of the other. Each moment alone together became an opportunity to taste again the sweetness of each other's lips, to tentatively touch and explore the wonders of each other's body. Oh, the sudden intake of breath when gentle fingers found a new source of delight, the aching wonder of the longing mounting between us, the pain of unrequited desire. . . .

I knew, of course—as did Adam—that there were certain things reserved for the marriage bed. Exactly what, I could not guess, though I supposed Adam was not as ignorant as I. However, lack of knowledge did not inhibit us—did not inhibit me, at any rate. What might have happened in such circumstances, what undoubtedly would have happened had we been left to ourselves, remains conjecture, for no longer did Adam and I ever find ourselves alone for any length of time.

Our total involvement in one another had not gone unnoticed. Elizabeth or Lueddy always managed to be near if we were in the house, and Papa would appear at odd moments during the day, no matter where we happened to be. If all else failed, John was sent to ride or walk with us, much to his disgust and our distress.

Thus, we lived the rest of that winter and the summer that followed in one long blur of happiness, of stolen kisses and burning promises, of stormy tears and forgiving laughter. And in all those wondrous months, only one cloud darkened my world. It was the knowledge that in the coming autumn, Adam was to go to Europe. It had long been understood that he should spend at least a year on the Continent, completing his education, but I had steadfastly refused to acknowledge that the day of parting would come.

From time to time Adam tried to reason with me. He would say, "It is for only a year, Victoria, and you know how important it is that I complete my education."

"But why can't you complete your education here in England? Surely at Oxford or Cambridge—"

"The finest schools of art, the best examples of classic architecture, are in Italy and France. Please, Victoria, try to understand."

"But if you stayed here, Papa would let us marry right away."

Adam would scowl. "You forget that I have no inheritance, no estate. I must make my own way in this world."

"That is not true! Has not Papa given you his name? He will see to your inheritance as well."

"I cannot accept what is not rightfully mine. Until I have made my own mark, I cannot . . . I *will* not ask for your hand."

In the end all my pleas, all my tears, availed me nothing. Still, I would not be convinced that Adam would truly go away while I must remain at home. Thus, when the day of parting came, I was in no way prepared.

On the eve of Adam's departure, we slipped away after tea and rode up to the cliff top. Miraculously, no one sent

John along to keep us company. It was a balmy, cloudless evening, and the moon was already riding high in the heavens when we reached the summit, though dusk had only just begun to gather.

Alone together for the first time in months, we dismounted and walked over to the rim, where we stood leaning against a great grey outcropping of stone. In silence we gazed across the darkling water, while from the forest behind us came the sleepy chirruping and twittering of woodland creatures settling themselves for the night. We did not talk; only stood quietly in the gathering dusk gazing out to sea. I was filled with a pain and emptiness I could scarce endure, and seeking comfort, I turned to look up into Adam's face.

He was gazing down at me with an expression that frightened yet thrilled me. Those feelings that his very nearness always awakened in me, so bewildering, so exhilarating, yet so akin to pain, raged in me now, blotting out everything except my need. I raised my hand and laid my palm gently along the curve of his jaw.

The wonder of that touch overwhelmed us. With a strangled cry, Adam gathered me close in his arms, held me tight against his lithe, strong body; the warmth of him, the strength of him, the pounding of his heart, became one with the throbbing of my own body. And when his mouth closed over mine, I was filled with an exquisite longing, an all-consuming need.

Desperately I clung to him in the deepening dusk while the gentle sea breezes caressed us, wrapped us in whispering softness. Adam kissed my eyes, my cheeks, the curve of my throat, while I whispered brokenly, "Beloved, my heart . . ."

Then he spread his cloak upon the ground and pulled me gently down beside him. The stars were a shining canopy overhead, seeming almost close enough to touch in the velvety blackness of the autumn night. With shaking fingers, Adam unfastened the small pearl buttons holding the bodice of my riding habit tight and smooth, and slipped aside my chemise. The touch of his fingers on my skin set me aflame, and I was filled with joy seeing the wonder in his moonwashed face when he beheld my bare breasts.

His lips parted with the whisper of a sigh. He cupped a breast in his palm, and as he stroked the dark shadow that was its roseate crown, I closed my eyes and reveled in the sensations his touch sent coursing through me. Then his lips, warm and soft, began to move over their swelling fullness, and when his mouth closed over the nipple, I cried out, cradling his head in my arms close against my eager flesh, while the secret places deep within me throbbed, ached for his touch.

At that very instant, carried on the still night air, came the distant thud of horse's hooves. Abruptly, Adam wrenched himself from my embrace, sat up, turned away. His voice was strained and harsh when he said, "I'm sorry, Victoria. I should not have done that."

"But Adam—" I started to whisper.

"It is not right."

"But I love you," I insisted. I could not believe that he could turn away from me now, not when my body ached for his touch.

"And I love you."

"Then . . ."

"No! Not until we are married."

"We shall marry soon enough!" When he made no reply, I started to cry.

He turned, then, and looked at me once more. I held out my arms to him, but he shook his head, his expression grim. "Please don't make this any harder than it already is, Victoria. I cannot risk bringing you disgrace."

"I don't care," I sobbed. "Please . . ."

He only shook his head.

At last, with hot bitter tears scalding my cheeks, I, too, sat up. With fingers that shook, I rebuttoned my bodice while Adam wiped away my tears. Then he stood, pulled me to my feet, and helped me smooth and rearrange my hair before we returned to the horses. He lifted me into my saddle, but before he could leap onto the back of his own horse, all the emotions churning inside me suddenly coalesced into an ungovernable sense of frustration.

Scarcely thinking what I was doing, I wheeled my horse about and rode off at a wild, reckless pace, which I did not slacken until we reached the wall of the manor, though Adam followed close behind, shouting for me to stop.

It had been a foolhardy thing for me to do, and yet it served to shock me back to reality. By the time we reached the stable, my emotion was spent. I waited mutely for Adam to dismount and give me a hand down. A stable boy led the horses away to be groomed and fed, and Adam and I returned to the great hall and, with forced gaiety, joined the others in a glass of sherry before retiring.

Adam departed the next day at dawn. Elizabeth and Papa gave him an affectionate hug in farewell, and he and John clapped each other fondly on the shoulder. Last of all, he turned to me, took my face in his hands and kissed me on the forehead. He did not say goodbye. Then he was gone, down the road and across the bridge. I watched until he was out of sight, my heart heavy, my thoughts bleak.

As much as I had dreaded this separation from my beloved, I had never dreamed how difficult, how full of hurt it would be. Only in the weeks that followed Adam's departure did I truly come to understand the wretched misery of loneliness. The moment I opened my eyes in the morning, the pain would catch in the pit of my stomach and squeeze my heart, until the ache left me weak and listless.

Neither did I take comfort in the sympathy offered by my family. How could they possibly understand how I felt? How could *they* know how much love hurt? Didn't they realize that Adam and I had been inseparable for fourteen years? Now he was gone. How could anyone console me?

For days I continued to wander about the great old house feeling empty and aimless, and I thought constantly about Adam. I remembered how his fair hair grew thick and full, and the silky feel of it under my fingertips; I recalled the way his blue-violet eyes could darken with passion, like stormy skies above a gale-tossed sea, when he held me in his arms; or yet again, I would think of the joyous sound of his laughter, his dear voice calling. . . .

I remembered the games of our childhood, the rides along the cliff, the hours we had spent in searching out the dustiest nooks and crannies of Greystone Manor; the puppies and the kittens and the baby birds that together we had tended and loved.

But the memory I cherished above all others was of that last night on top of the cliff, when I had lain beside him. I would close my eyes and feel again his lean hard body pressed close to mine, the strength of his arms holding me, the gentle touch of his hands, the warmth of his lips. And I would shiver with desire.

I had discovered at last the bittersweet pain of happy memories. Slowly, I came to terms with my loneliness, telling myself that if for a while I could have only the letters he wrote, at least I was secure in the knowledge that Adam loved me.

However, one cannot survive forever on memories alone, and with the passage of time, I found other pursuits to help me pass the days. True to his word, Thomas wrote to me faithfully, almost every week. I enjoyed his letters. They were filled with gossipy bits of news from court as well as comments upon the political and social issues of the day. And now that I did not have Adam to fill my every waking hour, Thomas's letters took on a new meaning for me. I made an honest effort to understand what he was saying, and to answer as thoughtfully as he had written.

Thomas had decided to follow in his father's footsteps,

to become a doctor; and, like Adam, he went to the Continent to complete his education. He was particularly interested in the work being done by M. Jean Martin Charcot in his neurological clinic in Paris, where they were using mesmerism to treat patients suffering from mental disorders. However, despite the long hours he spent with his studies, Thomas did not fail to write to me regularly, even though I was far from prompt, and often remiss, in answering.

Adam, too, wrote regularly, letters which I had to share with the family, of course. Hence they were filled with comments on his studies, the museums and palaces and cathedrals he had visited, the changes occurring in the art world.

Under the new emperor, Louis Napoleon, Paris was becoming the center of fashion and frivolity. As Adam became better acquainted with the city, his letters were laced with anecdotes about afternoons spent with new friends at various sidewalk cafés, and evenings seeing the sights at some of the well-known night spots.

One place he seemed to enjoy was named The Dead Rat—it still sounds a bit unsavory to me. Another was the Moulin Rouge. This one I remember because it was famous for its entertainment, particularly a dance called the cancan. It entailed the exposure of legs and ruffled undergarments, and was executed with great enthusiasm by rather bawdy women. Though Adam described this spectacle with great delicacy, the newspapers did not. Elizabeth and I could not help but wonder what he was doing in such an establishment; Papa only laughed.

In one letter, Adam included sketches he had made of the gowns ladies wore to such places: crinoline skirts that billowed wide to reveal lacy petticoats, and necklines that were cut perilously low. He also tried to describe for us the new dances favored at the outdoor dance palaces: the mazurka, the polka, and the waltz. I could scarcely wait for him to come home and teach them to me.

But best of all, sometimes my beloved would enclose a

special page, just for me, filled with all those tender things I longed to hear. Then I would cry happy tears and for days thereafter carry the sheet of paper, on which his words of love were written, folded small and tucked into my bodice close to my heart.

But letters alone can fill just so much time, and thus it was that for the first time in my life, I began to find some pleasure in the work set out for me by my tutor, Miss Jones. She was a quiet, nondescript little person, my Miss Jones, with mousy brown hair, and rather close-set grey eyes that were downcast most of the time. Her nose and mouth were small and thin as, indeed, was all of Miss Jones.

Early on in our relationship, before Adam went off to Europe, when Miss Jones and I sat together in the study pursuing my lessons, she would glance at me in her own shy way and say, "There are so many wonderful things to know, Lady Victoria, so many wonderful and exciting books to read . . ."

I would clamp my lips tight shut and stare at her. I did not dare to make a pert reply, for Papa would surely have been sorely displeased. Rebellious I might have been, but I did not care to risk Papa's displeasure.

Miss Jones could not, however, misunderstand my expression. She would sigh and murmur, "I know you would much rather be out and about . . . but if I could make you understand how important . . ."

Her words invariably vexed me to a point beyond the reach of caution. "What could possibly be important about something that happened a hundred years ago?" I would interrupt rudely.

Without fail, these words brought an even deeper sigh from Miss Jones, and I always knew that tears were gathering behind her downcast eyes.

Chagrined, I would mutter, "There, now, I'm sorry . . . truly I am. I promise I will finish the chapter by tomorrow." And before Miss Jones could regain her composure, I would be out the door, off to look for Adam who, long since, had completed his assignments. This scene was repeated regularly throughout my childhood. However, with Adam gone, there seemed to be nothing else to do. Thus it was that I discovered the joy, the comfort, the pleasure reading can bring.

In bygone days, the Greystone library had been quite famous. Overwhelming in size alone, it occupied the better part of the east wing, but had been unused and closed off for years. Within a month after her arrival at Greystone Manor, however, Miss Jones had asked and received permission to reopen the library. She began the task with the occasional help of Gillian, a willing, albeit slow-witted girl who had been hired to help with the general housework.

Now, perceiving the change in my attitude, my growing interest in the books she had already provided me, Miss Jones decided to try to make of me an ally in the project. "These books, many of them, are quite priceless, Lady Victoria," she explained, her eyes shining. "If only we could get a young man with a strong back in here to remove all this furniture. . . ."

For, indeed, the room appeared to have become the repository for every unused or unusable table and chair in the house. The floor space was choked with odd pieces of furniture, and the windows were so dirty, the light that did trickle through served only to emphasize the gloom. Dust shrouded everything, except in that small area Miss Jones and Gillian had managed to clear.

"Just think what books may reside on those shelves beyond our reach, Lady Victoria! Now, if you could prevail upon His Lordship to send us a sturdy young man . . ."

Her voice trailed off, and I sensed that she was overcome by her own temerity. But the idea appealed to me, and I lost no time in presenting the plan to Papa—dear Papa, who could deny his only daughter nothing upon which she had set her heart.

And so it was that within the week, young Jimsy, a brawny, gangling youth, presented himself at the manor and, herded along by Miss Jones and myself, began the task of removing the clutter. It was slow, tedious work, but at long last the accumulation was removed and stored elsewhere, the windows washed, the floors swept and polished, the rugs beaten and relaid. The shelves were cleaned and the books all received a preliminary dusting.

A chimney sweep was called, and when his work was done, a fire was kindled in the great fireplace. A massive structure open on two sides, it was set in a central wall that served to divide the library into two sections, the northern and the southern. This wall extended for some ten feet on either side of the fireplace and ended in graceful trefoil arches admitting free passage from one half of the library to the other. The fireplace was surrounded on each side by an imposing mantel of black marble and flanked by floor to ceiling bookshelves.

Indeed the library walls were almost completely lined with book-filled shelves. Those portions of the walls that were exposed were covered with tooled leather, and the outside wall was pierced by twelve tall, narrow, lancet windows arranged in groups of three and set with leaded panes of colored glass.

The floors throughout the library were of polished stone, covered by elaborate Persian rugs patterned in shades of garnet, royal purple, and gold, accented with rich browns and muted greens to form intricate, geometric designs that seemed to pulse with a life of their own when the firelight played over them. How long those rugs had lain, shoved into untidy heaps and covered by dust, I do not know. Once they were beaten and brushed, however, and were spread once more upon the floor, the colors were as bright as the day the woollen yarn first came from the dyeing vats.

Miss Jones and I spent considerable time selecting the furniture for the library from unused parts of the house. When at last we were done, I wrote Adam a long letter describing the more beautiful pieces. Among the most impressive items were a pair of magnificent, hand-carved gilt console tables with marble tops. And to provide for the ease of the user, each table was flanked by a number of large and richly carved cane chairs.

For the spaces facing each other through the fireplace, we chose two huge leather-covered sofas. When seated upon either of these couches, one could look through the fireplace into the opposite half of the room.

Last of all, we decided upon a large, heavy desk of dark oak that appeared to have been part of the original furnishings. Several of its drawers were locked and no sign of a key was to be found. The drawers that were open contained sheafs of paper, quills, sealing wax, several ledgers, and a multitude of miscellaneous objects.

Once the cleaning and refurbishing of the library was finished, Miss Jones began immediately the arduous task of cataloging the books. I, myself, could find no joy in such a dull and repetitious task, and for a while I left Miss Jones to her own devices.

Then, one particularly cold and blustery day, finding time heavy on my hands, I chanced to remember the old desk and the accumulation of papers it contained. It occurred to me that amongst them there might be something of interest. Indeed, I might even find the keys to the locked drawers! So I joined Miss Jones in the library with the admirable intention of sorting through and cleaning the desk.

I found the ink on many of the papers so faded that the letters were beyond reading. These I put into a neat stack until I should gain permission from Papa to destroy them. Those that I could read were very dull and dreary, having to do with the various phases of upkeep of the manor, or unpaid bills, or requests for this and that. They did not seem of any particular importance after all these years — the latest, dated 1782, was addressed to my great-grandfather. Nonetheless, these, too, I stacked neatly together for Papa's perusal before I should dispose of them.

Then I turned to the ledgers. The first, dated 1759, contained debits and credits of the tenant farmers, and was of little interest to me. The second appeared to be a kind of personal budget that had been kept assiduously by one Jeremiah Garth from 1747 until 1780, and I soon dubbed it *Jeremiah's Journal*. It listed such fascinating items as a new wig, powder for said wig, a box of snuff. I giggled as I skimmed the first few pages. Jeremiah must have been a bit of a fop, and I felt certain I should not have been greatly impressed with him, even though he was one of my ancestors.

The afternoon, by then, was far spent, and the dull reading had made me quite drowsy. I closed *Jeremiah's Journal* and picked it up. I would take it to my room to finish at my leisure. The third ledger could wait for another day. I shoved it back into a drawer, bade Miss Jones a good afternoon, and left the warmth of the library for the eternal cold of the dark, drafty hall. The sudden change in temperature served to drive the sleep from my head, and by the time I arrived in my chamber, I was feeling quite wide awake once more.

I laid the journal on the mantel between the ormolu clock and the gift Adam had sent me for Christmas—a miniature of himself in a handsome silver frame. I smiled at his painted likeness and thought, my Adam: so handsome, so exciting, so very dear. In the autumn, when Adam returned, what fun we would have reading *Jeremiah's Journal* together. The thought was a smile in my heart, and I determined to write to my beloved immediately.

First, however, I removed my dress, loosened my lacings, and put on the satin peignoir Elizabeth and Papa had asked Adam to send me from Paris the Christmas past. The gift had been from my parents, but it had been chosen by my beloved. So thinking, I wrapped my arms about myself, closed my eyes, and allowed my mind to carry me back to that last evening on the cliff top. And so vivid was my memory, I could feel his lips on mine, could taste their sweetness. I could hear his voice, husky with emotion, whispering "I adore you, Victoria."

As I let the memories flow through my mind, I was suddenly overcome by a feeling of shyness, as if someone were reading my thoughts. I felt the warm blood rising in my throat, staining my cheeks crimson. My arms dropped to my sides. I opened my eyes and glanced quickly about my room. There was no one there.

Of *course* there is no one here, you silly goose, I told myself. Then I sat down before the little escritoire, selected one of the pink-plumed quills, and dipped it into the ink pot. As I began to write, the clock upon the mantel began to chime. Never before had I noticed how delicate, how silvery bright was its tinkling voice. The room was filled with the rich fragrance of wisteria.

I put down the quill, reached up, and removed the combs from my hair. As I shook loose the tight coils into which I had had it wound whilst I was working in the library, I closed my eyes and luxuriated in the feel of it spilling down over my almost bare shoulders.

When I opened my eyes, I was standing before the fireplace, though I had no recollection of rising to my feet or of walking away from the desk. My dream friend, the dark-haired girl (though now she seemed more a woman) was seated at the desk holding one of the quills in her left hand. Though she had not visited me for some time, and in the past I had seen her only by the light of the moon, I recognized her immediately, and I was neither surprised nor frightened to see her there.

How lovely she was. And though she seemed older, her blue-black hair still curled in gay abandon over her shoulders and down her back, as it always had done. I also observed that in the light of day, her skin was like ivory, her cheeks and lips the color of ripe peaches. But it was her eyes that held me, beautiful dark eyes filled with sadness and pain.

She contemplated me with a gentle smile, yet the smile held a quality of sorrow that I found almost unbearable. I tried to reach out my arms to her, but I could not. She turned from me then, took a firmer grip upon the quill, and began to write. Although I could no longer see her face, I knew that there were tears upon her cheeks, and I was filled with an anguish I somehow knew was hers.

And even as I watched her, the late afternoon light that had filled my room grew dim, and the wind began to shriek outside, causing the high French doors to rattle and creak. My dear God! I thought, Hurry! Hurry before it is too late!

My head snapped up and back with a violent jerk, and I blinked my eyes. I was sitting at the escritoire, the quill in my left hand. Someone was pounding on my door.

Then, before I could gather my wits, Gillian burst into my room, her words fairly tripping over one another in her haste to utter them. "Come quick, Lady Victoria, come quick! 'Tis Mr. Adam has come home, and he's brought his new wife with him, he has!"

Chapter Seven

Nausea, thick and hot, clawed at my stomach and constricted my throat. The heavy beating of my heart was painful in my chest, and I was frightened. I heard Gillian's words, but my mind rejected them. My head seemed stuffed with cotton, and try as I might to pull my thoughts together, my groping senses found only emptiness.

The young woman — where had she gone? And why was Gillian babbling such nonsense? I was disoriented, and my eyes did not want to focus. I put down the quill and tried to stand up, but my trembling legs refused to hold me.

Gillian rushed forward to assist me, but her chattering did not cease. "Oh, Lor', Lady Victoria," she was saying, "M'Lady Elizabeth sent me to fetch ye, she did. Come quick, her said."

Still trying to gather my thoughts together, I continued to gaze about the room, looking for the young woman who had sat at my desk. "Did you see her, Gillian?"

"Aye, m'Lady. I see'd her."

Gillian had stopped talking, thank goodness. I made a desperate effort to control my own whirling thoughts before asking, "Where is she now?"

Gillian's dull eyes widened, filled with uncertainty. Her mouth opened, but she said nothing.

What was the matter with her? Could she be ill? I put out my hand and touched her flushed cheek. No. Her face was

73

warm, but not unduly so. Exasperated, I repeated my question. "Where is she now?"

"She be in the great hall . . ." The excitement had died out of Gillian's expression and she gazed at me, obviously puzzled. "Be ye all right, m'Lady?"

"Of course. Who is she, Gillian?"

Now Gillian's look became one of utter bewilderment. At last, apparently finding my question completely incomprehensible, she shook her head and repeated, "Come quick. Lady Elizabeth wants ye."

"I don't understand," I muttered, as much to myself as to Gillian. "I must have fallen asleep."

"Please, m'Lady. Lady Elizabeth said to be quick. . . ."

All through this exchange, some part of my mind had been fastened on Gillian's words, "Mr. Adam has a new wife. . . ." How ridiculous! What had made the addleheaded Gillian say that? Adam would not be back until late in the coming summer; he had said so in his last letter. As for a wife—it was impossible! Gillian always got messages all mixed up. I knew she couldn't help it, poor thing, but at the moment my head was throbbing and I couldn't help glaring at her. I felt like shaking her!

Abruptly, Gillian took a step back. "Please, m'Lady, don't look at me so."

I took a deep breath, ordered myself to remain calm, and said, "Then tell me again: Why did Lady Elizabeth send for me?"

"Truly, m'Lady, it be 'cause Mr. Adam come home again. He come home not ten minutes gone, and he brought hisself a wife with him, he did. He got hisself married, he did, an' please, m'Lady, I must fetch ye to the great hall to meet her."

The room seemed to darken. Breathing was becoming more difficult. *Adam is going to marry me!* The thought had a steadying effect. Gillian was talking nonsense, of course. It was obvious that I must dress and go downstairs if I were to learn the right of it.

But even as I sought to soothe myself with these sensible considerations, on another level my mind was filled with dire thoughts. Could it be? *Could* Adam have married someone else?

"Come, m'Lady. Let me help ye with yer laces," Gillian was urging. I stood up, let Gillian slide a dress over my head, button buttons, tie ties. Dazed, I did not take time to arrange my hair, but followed her meekly from my room.

Adam is home! The words suddenly flashed through my mind as if for the first time. My heart leapt. I gathered up my skirts as if I were a child again, and ran past Gillian to the head of the stairs.

He has a wife. . . . I halted in midstride. Slowly I began to descend.

I paused when I reached the landing. From there I could see Elizabeth, seated on a small settee to one side of the fireplace. Her face looked drawn and tired, but she was smiling—or at least, her lips were arranged in a gentle curve. Papa and Adam stood side by side, their backs to the fireplace. It put a catch in my heart to see them together again. Papa so solid and gray and gnarled, like one of the ancient oaks in the park; Adam so slim and fair. Again, elation gripped me. Throwing all caution aside, I fairly flew to the foot of the stairs.

Jimsy, who had stayed on after the opening of the library to be trained as a footman, had lighted the last of the candles on the mantel and was just turning to the wall sconces. As he applied flame to wick, soft light flooded the room.

Now I could see Adam quite clearly. He was gazing at someone I could not see, someone seated in a great wing-backed chair facing the fire. I stopped short, tried to tear my gaze from his face. It was indecent to look on such a surfeit of love and pride and self-giving written on his countenance, when it was meant for another.

I looked instead at Papa and Elizabeth. They were looking at one another, their expressions unreadable. No one spoke. No one moved. My limbs had gone all heavy and stiff, but I advanced until I was even with the wing-backed chair. There I hesitated, not knowing just what was expected of me under such strange circumstances. Apprehension gnawed at my breast with dull teeth. I was afraid to even glance toward the chair, afraid to see the woman at whom Adam was looking with such blind adoration.

Abruptly, Adam turned his gaze on me and smiled. I flew into his arms and clung to him then, too overcome with emotion to speak.

For a long moment he returned my embrace. Then he held me back and looked down into my face. "Dear little sister," was all he said.

He had not called me *little sister* since our trip to the Great Exhibition. Only words, but they put a world between us. He could not have hurt me more had he plunged a dagger into my heart. My arms fell to my sides. I couldn't speak.

It was Papa who broke the silence. "Gillian has told you, Victoria, you now have a sister-in-law. It is our wish, Elizabeth's as well as mine, that you should welcome her to the family."

Then, addressing Adam, "Would you do us the honor of presenting your bride to Victoria?"

There was a rustle of silk behind me. Slowly I turned to face the sound. I knew then why Adam's face had betrayed his adoration of this woman.

He must have spoken, but I did not hear him. I was aware that she, also, spoke to me, but the words I could not distinguish for the blood singing in my ears. I mumbled something inane in reply and stood frozen, a wooden smile twisting my lips, whilst my spirit recoiled from her as my flesh would recoil from a viper! Oh, I knew her—my soul knew her that very moment, though my mind could give her no name.

Tall, she was, almost as tall as Adam. Her hair, pulled straight back from her high, smooth forehead, and looped in heavy burnished coils over her ears, was a deep rich brown from which the candlelight struck sparks of red and gold. Her face was a perfect oval, her lips full and sensual.

But her eyes were her most arresting feature, at once beautiful and, to me, frightening. They glittered. At first glance I thought they were green, but the color changed subtly with each movement of her head. The lashes surrounding them were long and thick and feathery, of the same hue as her hair. Her brows, too, were of that deep rich brown, and they formed perfect arches over those large, wide-set eyes.

Her figure was full but lithe, and she moved with a fluid feline grace. I could not tell how old she was, but I felt certain that she was older than Adam. I also knew, as only one woman can know of another, that her knowledge and experience of life were arrant.

She tilted her head to one side and reached out her hands to me, though a curtsy would have been more proper. A warm, tender smile touched her lips, and all the while, those marvelous green eyes glittered.

I wanted to run, to hide myself away, but with an effort of will I had not known I possessed, I took her hands and mumbled through lips that felt stiff and cold, "May I, too, bid you welcome to Greystone Manor."

"Thank you, dear Lady Victoria. I do so wish that you may truly come to think of me as your sister." Even her voice was beautiful: low-pitched, warm, caressing.

I could think of nothing to say in reply. I nodded my head, feeling gauche and dowdy as well as heartbroken. This was Adam's wife, this beautiful woman — his *wife* — and, I told myself, I must not cry . . .

"Come, dear, sit here by me," Elizabeth urged, her words seeming to come from far away. I turned uncertainly toward the sound.

"Here, dear," she repeated. I started to step around the low table that stood before the settee on which she sat, but my legs did not want to obey me. I stumbled, and bumped into the table, causing a great clatter.

Elizabeth rose to her feet, reached out to steady me, but it was my new sister-in-law, Helaine — for that was her name — who took my arm. "Oh, my dear," she said in that warm intimate voice. "Are you all right?"

My face flamed hot with embarrassment, and I could not

look at anyone. "I'm so sorry," I stammered. "I'm fine . . . how very clumsy . . . do forgive me."

Helaine released my arm and I, burning with humiliation, dropped awkwardly into the seat beside my stepmother. Elizabeth's hand found mine amidst the folds of our skirts, between us on the settee. Her touch on my already cold fingers was like ice. However, as I settled myself next to her, she returned her attention to Helaine, and only the hint of a quaver in her voice belied her calm expression.

She was saying, "Would you like a little refreshment here, Helaine, or are you too tired? Would you prefer to retire to your room?"

Helaine had not returned to the wing-backed chair, but had moved over to stand demurely beside Adam. There was a sly possessiveness about her, a self-assurance, a vague something that chilled me, left me feeling ill. A loving smile warmed her face as she returned Elizabeth's gaze, but she waited for Adam to respond to his mother's question.

With a tender glance at his bride he said, "It was a long trip and we are tired, Mother. We would be grateful if we might retire to our room."

"Of course," Elizabeth agreed. "I think you will find your rooms next to the western turret the most comfortable for the time being. Would you like dinner sent up, or will you join us in the dining room at nine o'clock?"

Helaine chose to answer this time. "A tray in our room would be lovely, if you please, Lady Elizabeth. It has been a most tiring day."

I thought she did not look tired at all, but I said nothing. It didn't matter. I had only one desire: to escape to my own room, to be alone with my sorrow and hurt.

Samuel rang for Gillian, who appeared immediately, still wide eyed and curtsying feverishly. I strangled an hysterical impulse to laugh, and the wooden smile remained frozen on my cold face.

"Take a light for Mr. Adam and Miss Helaine. Show them to their room, by the western turret, Gillian."

Then, with a glance at Adam, Papa added, "Your baggage will be there already." Not once until now had I seen Papa look directly at Helaine.

When I left the hall a few moments later to return to my room, Papa and Elizabeth were standing together before the fire. Although I had asked and received permission to withdraw, they seemed unaware of my departure.

I ran up the stairs and along the dark, cold gallery to my own door, rushed inside, and threw myself down across my bed. *A wife!* The sting of those words was too painful for tears, and at last I sat up again, on the side of my bed, rocking myself back and forth.

Filled with mute misery and despair, I could not stem the flow of memories, memories that flayed my very soul. I recalled the empty promises, the idle dreams; with anger and humiliation I remembered that evening on the cliff top, the way I had offered myself to Adam, begged him. What an utter fool I had been!

Rendered numb at last by the searing pain of my thoughts, I stood up and took a deep breath. A chill was creeping into the air. The fire had burned low, and my room was dark except where the silken threads of the tapestries caught the glow from the dying coals. My little yellow bird, perched upon his lily stalk, seemed to watch me with a bright, inquisitive eye.

I crossed to the mantel and lighted the lamps. The coal I put upon the fire took flame readily enough, and I spread my cold fingers near to catch the warmth. I was relieved when Gillian appeared a few minutes later to announce that no one was going down to dinner.

"I'll fetch ye a tray straight away, m'Lady," she promised.

When my tray arrived, I made a pretense of eating, but the food stuck in my throat. The fire burned low and I went to bed. Oddly enough, I went right to sleep, but my sleep was fitful, plagued by a strange and unaccountable dream.

I watched my dark-haired dream friend moving with awkward steps along a narrow mossy ledge, only inches above a channel filled with swirling, sucking waters. We appeared to be in some subterranean chamber, and even as I watched her, I could feel the dank, stagnant air of that place, thick and clammy in my own lungs, suffocating, adding to the panic that threatened to engulf me.

Hurry! Hurry! Don't look back! . . . The words burned in my brain. Then, reaching the foot of the stairs at last, I felt a surge of relief. But as I took a step upward, my foot caught in the ragged hem of my gown and I lurched forward, fell heavily upon my side.

But it isn't me—it's her! whispered a voice somewhere deep in my mind; yet the nightmare held me in thrall. Somehow it was I who clawed frantically at the moss-covered steps, scrabbled upward on hands and knees, tore my fingernails on the rough edges of the cold stone.

Whimpering, gasping for breath, I reached the top at last, pushed open the tower door, and stumbled out into the clean night air. Then somehow I was at the French doors, and I passed through them as fast as my advanced state of pregnancy would permit.

But I am not pregnant! Again, my sleep-clouded mind sought to separate me from the dream.

Abruptly, the clock upon the mantel began to strike the hour. Its chimes played a delicate tune against the rhythm of it's ticking, and I began to dance, round and round, floating on the music, happy—so very happy. Joyously I raised my head to look into the face of my partner. Then my blood turned to ice. Those cruel snarling lips, those eyes, glittering green. . . .

Soundless screams, tearing at my throat, wakened me. I did not sleep again that night.

Chapter Eight

I lay quite still upon my back, staring up into the rosy folds of the moreen canopy draped above my bed. I felt tired, depressed, yet relieved to have the long sleepless night behind me, and I was glad when Gillian arrived with my morning tea. Nevertheless, I closed my eyes when she entered my room, and pretended to be asleep. I did not want to talk to anyone, least of all Gillian. I heard the clink of cup on saucer when she placed the tray on my bedside table, and the rattle of coal in the scuttle when she set the fire to blazing on my little hearth. Then I heard her moving softly about the room, setting things to rights; I did not hear her leave.

Much later, when I opened my eyes again, I realized that while pretending to sleep, I had actually drifted off at last. And as I slept, the fire had burned low. Now my room was warm, but my tea was cold. There was a cold, hard knot in my stomach as well, and an aching pressure behind my eyes. I rolled over and curled myself into a ball, toying with the temptation to stay in bed all day. I wanted nothing so much as to go back to sleep—to forget . . .

Oh, God, it cannot be true—it must not be true. Surely it was all part of that wretched dream. Yes, that must be it. . . .

For an instant hope warmed my heart, only to die aborning. I knew that the woman with the green eyes, the expression on Adam's face when he looked at her—they had not

81

been a dream. Only my fierce pride kept my eyes dry.

The sound of the great clock chiming its full-throated call from the landing urged me to be up. I arose at last, rang for hot water, and when it arrived I washed and dressed without enthusiasm. However, as I descended the stairs, I held my head high, determined to salvage what I could of my dignity and self-respect.

Papa and Elizabeth were in the breakfast room before me and had long since finished eating. Still they lingered, their half-full cups of cocoa grown cold. When I entered they looked up, bright smiles painted on their faces.

Papa said heartily, "There you are, Victoria. Good morning, my dear."

Elizabeth added brightly, "Is this not pleasant, the three of us together at the breakfast table? The bad weather is good for something."

It was a cold, wet morning, but the weather had never kept Papa indoors in the past. He might plead the inclement conditions as a reason for remaining with Elizabeth and me on this particular day, but I was not fooled.

Neither could I bear to look at them and see the guarded hurt and sympathy in their dear faces. Eyes downcast, I bade them good morning, poured myself some cocoa, and took my accustomed place at table. Feeling awkward and ill at ease, I made a great to-do of breaking my currant bun and dipping it in my steaming cup, all the while wishing I could think of something bright and cheerful to say. But my misery went too deep for that.

After a painful silence, Papa cleared his throat and commented on the possibility that the skies might soon clear. "It would be pleasant to see the sun," I said.

That subject exhausted, Elizabeth asked if I had slept well. I lied.

No one mentioned that which was uppermost in all our minds. The painful silence returned.

When Adam entered the breakfast room soon thereafter, alone, a flutter of joy touched my heart, but I did not jump up and run to throw my arms about him as would have seemed natural the previous morning. He stopped just inside the doorway and looked at each of us in turn: first Papa, then Elizabeth, then me.

I gazed at him, searching his expression for some hint of feeling. We had loved each other so desperately, so completely—at least, I had *thought* he loved me too. But I could not read the expression in his eyes; dark pools, they were, and his thoughts were hidden in their depths.

His solemn scrutiny awoke in me an unaccustomed shyness, brought a flush to my cheeks. I lowered my gaze, plucked at a crumb lying beside my plate.

At last he spoke, his tone low and grave. "It is good to be home."

I raised my eyes once more. He was still staring at me, his face as grave as his voice. For an instant our glance met and clung. My breath caught in my throat, but the moment did not last.

Adam's eyes dropped, although he continued speaking. "Helaine bids you all good morning, and begs to be excused. She has a headache and is very tired after the long journey."

Papa nodded. " 'Tis good to have you home, Adam," he said.

Elizabeth added, "Fill a plate for yourself, then come and sit here beside me."

Adam poured himself some cocoa, selected a cinnamon bun, and moved around the table to take his place next to his mother. No further mention was made of Helaine. Adam and Elizabeth talked about the places he had been, the life he had led at university. From time to time his eyes smiled across the table at me, but there was a wall between us.

When at last breakfast was over, Papa stood and said, "Come, Adam. We must have a little talk."

Both Elizabeth and I knew, as did Adam, that the time had come for the accounting. Without a word, he followed Papa from the room. I would have returned to my own room, had not Elizabeth leaned toward me and said softly, "Wait, Victoria. I think you and I should talk a bit, too, and this is perhaps the best place."

Then she rose and moved around the table to sit beside me. She said nothing for a long moment. There were circles under her eyes, and tired lines about her mouth. I felt resentment welling up inside me; resentment, hurt, and anger. I wondered anew how Adam could have committed such an ill-conceived, thoughtless act: to marry without the consent of his parents, to marry a woman we none of us knew. It was unthinkable.

And he had betrayed me! But that was an anguish I could not face, even in thought.

Elizabeth sighed. "Victoria, dear . . . you must know that this marriage of Adam's has come as a great shock to all of us." She paused. Another sigh. "But what is done is done. Your father and I have concluded that it would be best for all concerned if we simply accept the situation."

I nodded, not meeting her gaze.

After a long pause, she continued, "We all love Adam . . . and we must learn to give the same affection to . . ." her voice faltered. She swallowed. ". . . his wife."

Never! I thought. *Never, never, never . . .*

Impulsively Elizabeth had reached out, taken my hands in hers. Now she continued speaking. "Victoria, little love, would you like to go to London for a while? Buy some new clothes . . . go to the theater?" Her eyes searched my face. "Samuel and I know how . . . how difficult this is for you. It was your father's suggestion. Perhaps a month in the city would be just the thing. It would be a joy to Drusilla and Phillip, and Thomas has been waiting a long time for you to visit."

There was a pleading note in her voice, and I was reminded anew that my love for Adam, my dreams and plans, had never been a secret. I was filled with confusion and shame. A painful flush suffused my cheeks, and try as I would, I could not meet Elizabeth's sad gaze. It seemed to me a pitying look, and I longed to flee to my room, to hide myself from everyone and everything.

But with great effort, I controlled my voice and answered

with all the dignity I could muster, "Truly, Elizabeth, I do thank you and Papa, but I have no desire to go to London alone, to stay with Uncle Phillip and Aunt Drusilla. Neither do I understand why you should think I would wish to do so. I am perfectly happy right here." At last I managed to raise my eyes to meet hers, and the pain inside me translated itself into a defiant stare.

Another long, drawn-out sigh from my stepmother. Then she patted my hand. "It is only that you are very dear to us. We wish your happiness with all our hearts. If you do not want to go, think no more about it. But should you change your mind, you have only to speak." She continued patting my hand absently.

When I made no further comment, she straightened herself in her chair with a quite noticeable effort, then rose to her feet. "And now what will you do?"

It was a perfunctory question, but with her eyes, so full of love and concern, fixed on me, I forced myself to assume an air of insouciance I was far from feeling. "Why, now the rain has ceased, I think I shall change and take Blue Boy for a run. I have not been riding in such a long time." My voice sounded high-pitched and affected, even to me, but Elizabeth seemed not to notice.

She smiled vaguely as we moved toward the door. Before we parted, she said, "Please be back and dressed by three this afternoon. Samuel is presenting the staff to Helaine at that hour in the great hall. You should be present.

"Yes, Elizabeth," I agreed obediently.

And with that she went off to her workroom to organize her day, give what orders or direction she deemed necessary, and insure that the household continued to run smoothly.

I returned to my room, changed into a riding habit, and hurried off to the stables, which, as I have already indicated, lie within the walls and are enclosed by the house, itself.

What in the early days had been an open courtyard was at some later date roofed over, and servants' quarters built above. Connecting this closed area with the outside world is an ancient drawbridge. Lowered into place over the moat for a last time, so long ago that no one living today remembers, it has since rusted solidly into place. The water that fills the moat under this drawbridge is the same as that which flows under the old stone bridge spanning the stream that borders the park.

Although the beck flows shallow and calm, the water in the moat runs deep. In the autumn, when rain falls steadily, or in early spring when the snow begins to melt, it is often a rushing, foaming, swirling body of turbulent water that actually laps at the underside of the bridge as it flows beneath. Where the curve of the moat meets the wall of the tower, the water swirls itself into an angry, sucking whirlpool, above the drain that empties into a channel in the foundations. Ultimately, the water reaches a place atop the cliff, where it flings itself in a mighty cascade over the edge and down to join the heaving, churning sea a hundred feet below.

As I mounted my horse, Blue Boy, I noted that the cold, wet rain of the morning had given way to a rowdy wind blowing in from the west, and although the sun was still hidden now and again behind the scudding clouds, there was a hint of spring in the air. Sap would be rising soon in the trees, and already crocuses were poking their heads through the dark rich soil so recently covered with snow.

After months of inactivity, Blue Boy was ready for a run. His excitement communicated itself to me, and I felt my bruised spirits respond to the sun and wind even as my body responded to the movement of the animal. As we passed through the gate in the outer wall, I gave Blue Boy his head. "Go, Boy, go!" I whispered, and he leaped forward with such a surge of speed and strength that he almost unseated me.

However, I clung to his back and sought neither to check nor to guide him. He carried me full tilt down the path, thundered over the old stone bridge, and continued at breakneck speed along the road that leads to the village. The cool air whipped over my face, stinging my cheeks, my ears, and for the moment easing my bitter thoughts. It was not until we reached the outskirts of the small town that I finally pulled Blue Boy in.

The Greystone horses are not bred for riding, but because Blue Boy was much too large for a lady's carriage, where he could have been used singly, and because his size made it difficult to match him with another for double harness, it had been decided early on that he would be kept as a riding horse for one of the boys. But I had fallen in love with him the day he was foaled, and insisted that he should be mine.

What a rumpus ensued! John, who fancied the handsome creature for himself, declared that the animal was too big for me to handle. "Don't be ridiculous, Victoria," my young brother had said patronizingly. "You are much too small, too lacking in strength to handle a horse this size." Then he'd had the effrontery to add, "You'd best stick to your pony."

Made furious by his masculine posturing, I *demanded* Blue Boy be given to me. "Not only am I the eldest . . . I am by far the better rider!" I fairly flung the words at my little brother. (Though he was already head and shoulders taller than I, I would always think of him as my little brother.)

The truth hurts, as they say, and now John was as angry as I. The argument went on and on, leading nowhere, since it was Papa who would have the final say. It presented him with a very ticklish situation, because no matter what he decided, it was certain to look as if he were playing favorites. However Papa, with great tact and diplomacy, to say nothing of considerable expense, settled the affair to everyone's satisfaction: he purchased a very handsome hunter—one upon which John had set his heart some time before.

Ultimately I was proven right in my claim that I could ride Blue Boy, for with this huge animal, as with all of God's creatures, love prevailed. We had a perfect understanding, my great black horse and I. He answered my lightest touch, my quietest whisper. In fact, at times we seemed to communicate with a clarity seldom achieved through spoken language.

Thus, his headlong dash had been easily slowed to a sedate walk by the time we reached the first cottage on the edge of the village. We passed without incident down the length of the street, picking our way carefully past children, chickens, and stray dogs.

As soon as we had left the village behind us, Blue Boy broke once more into a gallop. The path from there curved around and upward, then back toward the cliff top before it finally straightened out and headed inland. At the spot in the road closest to the summit, we turned aside and made our way cross-country to the cliff path.

We were now at a considerable height above the manor, though truly not far from it. It must have been shortly after the lunch hour by then, and the sunlight, which was very bright, cast small but intensely black shadows from every smallest projection. It highlighted the house, underscoring the balconies, highlighting turrets and terraces.

I suppose that in the past, Adam and I had ridden this very path a hundred times or more. We had stopped at this very spot and looked down on the manor, just as I was doing now. Yet, all of a sudden, as I gazed down at that beloved structure of moss-covered stone, I felt as if I were seeing it for the first time. Perhaps it was an aftereffect of the rain. The air was crystal clear, and what moisture remained suspended in the atmosphere acted as a magnifying glass, focusing, in minutest detail, the old house under my gaze: its towers, its mullioned windows, its crenelated walls.

And as I sat there on Blue Boy's back in the bright afternoon light, with the wind tossing his black mane and pulling at my own dark hair, I was utterly overwhelmed by a crushing tide of love and foreboding. I bent forward over Blue Boy's great arched neck and cried. The tears that had not come the night before now wracked my whole body with convulsive sobs, and my hands trembled so, I had to knot them into fists and press them tight against Blue Boy's strong, warm neck to calm my anguish.

He stood steady as a rock until I had regained control of myself, moved forward only when I urged him down the trail toward home. By then the wind, exhausted by its early morning roistering, had subsided into the gentlest of zephyrs. All about me, the cliff top was delicately etched with the first pale greens of spring. The cloudless sky was a soft cerulean blue above the azure waters of the sea, and early-blooming forget-me-nots were a fragile mist of blue amongst the rocks on either side of the path.

Scarcely seeing the beauty around me, but feeling its soothing touch deep inside, where I was hurt and mute, I urged Blue Boy on down the path. As we passed through the dell, I noticed that the stone bowl of the spring was full to overflowing. Here, furry curls of hart's tongue thrust their heads through the dark, rich soil, and pennyroyal grew thick, though it would be another month before it bloomed.

Blue Boy stopped for a noisy drink, and I was tempted to slide down from his back and splash some clear, cool water over my tired face, to wash away any traces of tears that might remain. *To sit again upon the bowl's stone edge, where we had sat the day Adam gave me my first kiss....*

At the memory, tears began to form once more and I dashed them angrily away. *Only a fool would cry for such a betrayer!*

Forcing my attention outward, I noted that from my present vantage point, sitting astride Blue Boy there in the dell, the west wall of the manor was clearly visible, as was the terrace on the north, the place where I had stood as a child, looking out to sea, when I had heard the man screaming.

And as I looked down, a figure in a long, cowled cloak of dark brown, carrying a large wicker hamper, appeared. A mischievous gust of wind caught the hood and tossed it back, releasing a cloud of red-gold hair. The gusting wind died. The hair fell over the shoulders of the cloak and hung down past the wearer's waist. It could be no one but Helaine.

She set the hamper down, then walked to the balustrade and stood staring out across the wind-whipped water of the sea. How in the world had she found her way out there? And to what purpose? For as long as I could remember, the north wing had been closed, all its entrances sealed.

At last she turned, looked upward toward the cliff top where I sat. It was not possible for me to tell if she could see me. In any event, she made no move to salute me, nor I, her. Neither did she long remain standing there. Rather, she turned and hurried back to the hamper, picked it up, and vanished into the interior of the north wing.

How exceedingly strange! Automatically, I urged Blue Boy forward once more, while my thoughts continued to whirl. What could she have been carrying in that hamper?

Without warning, a covey of quail fluttered up out of the sedge. Blue Boy tensed for flight, then relaxed as I ran a gentle hand along his neck, clucked soothingly, even as my thoughts continued doggedly on: and why was she alone? Where was the bridegroom?

A harsh, cynical laugh escaped my lips. The bridegroom, indeed! My heart twisted as I remembered how impatiently I had waited, longing for Adam to come home — Adam who had kissed and caressed me in the moonlight on the cliff top. But Adam belonged to Helaine now. He would never belong to me!

At the thought, a great yawning emptiness blossomed inside me, a huge black hole filled with pain. I pulled Blue Boy to a stand, waited for the ache to subside. We were close under the wall of the house now, so close, I could reach out my hand and touch the rough gray stone of which it was built. And as I sat there, from the depths of my grief and misery I cried out, "God help me!"

The sound of my own voice startled me, but it was not my anguished cry that unnerved Blue Boy. Rather, it was a rattle and rush of noise above us. For the second time that day, he almost unseated me with a tremendous forward lunge, and there, where we had tarried but a second before, a hail of stones rained down, spread themselves across the soft, damp earth of the path.

The sense of foreboding that had forced itself upon me as I sat at the cliff's top earlier was strong in me once more. I gazed stupidly at the new-fallen stones, then lifted my head to stare upward. We were at the northern end of the western wall. At that point it rose straight and smooth, the only openings those narrow arrow slits once used by archers in defense of the manor.

After that great forward lunge, Blue Boy stood like a statue beneath me. The fear that had seized me at first sight of the stones subsided. No harm had been done. Even had I been struck, there was not one piece large enough to have done much damage. Still, it had been disturbing.

At length I urged my mount forward once more. He moved sedately on down the path to the great gate, which had been left open anticipating my return. A groom waited in the stable to help me dismount and to care for Blue Boy.

The shock, attendant upon the surprise and fear I had felt when those stones came falling down, remained with me as I made my way back to my room. How could such a thing have happened? It was almost as if someone—but that was impossible! Who would want to hurt me?

It was past two o'clock when I gained the cozy warmth and safety of my own room once more. Mechanically I began to change, remembering Elizabeth's admonition to join the family in the great hall at three.

It was very near that hour by the time I had readied myself. Therefore, lest I should encounter Adam and Helaine, I chose to take the long way round, down the back stairs to the ground floor, and make my entrance into the great hall through a small side door.

Elizabeth and Papa stood before the fireplace, expressions calm and unreadable. My stepmother's hand lay upon her husband's arm. There was a gentle smile about her lips, but I noted that it did not reach her eyes. Papa stood at ease, his gaze fastened upon a distant nothing. John, of course, was absent. He had left the previous autumn to take up his studies at Oxford, and was not expected to return until June.

I observed with some alarm that Lueddy, too, was missing; but being so late to enter, I dared not ask questions. The rest of the servants stood in a line just beyond the fireplace.

No one spoke, but they all smiled and ducked their heads as I entered.

Only Miss Jones stood slightly apart, neither fish nor fowl, as the saying goes. My heart went out to her. Her's, I fear, was a lonely life, but perhaps she liked it that way. She had her books, and she seemed to care for little else.

The grandfather clock that stood on the landing now announced the hour with dignified, deep-throated, chimes. It was precisely three o'clock, and on the instant, Adam and Helaine appeared at the top of the stairs. I thought for a moment that Adam looked drawn, but decided it was a trick of the light and shadow upon his thin face. However I did not have time to ponder this idea, for even as it danced through my mind, I found my eyes drawn and held by Helaine's compelling figure.

How exquisite she was. She smiled as she descended the stairway, a tender, intimate smile full of warmth and friendliness, and ingenuous affection. "Please like me," said that smile. "Please be my friend."

A sudden chill passed over me.

Helaine was wearing a modestly cut gown of creamy merino wool trimmed with Irish lace. Her hair was brushed straight back from her high, smooth forehead, and caught into a mass of Psyche curls that cascaded down the back of her head and fell in tight ringlets over one shoulder.

I wondered how she had managed, in so short a time, to get her hair, hair that had been falling long and free down her back not two hours before, into such an arrangement. I learned later that her maid and her trunks had arrived while I was out.

As Adam and his bride descended the stairway, Elizabeth and Papa moved forward to welcome them. They met at the foot of the stairs, where Papa took Helaine's hand and touched his lips briefly to her forehead. Then he offered her his arm and led her back to me. Elizabeth took Adam's proffered arm and they followed after. When Papa presented Helaine to me, we touched cheeks as protocol demanded. Papa then returned her to Adam who proceeded to present the staff.

The entire affair took less than a quarter-hour. Papa then dismissed the servants and begged to be excused himself, saying he was needed at the stud. Elizabeth invited Helaine to accompany her on a tour of the manor, and suddenly Adam and I were alone. I turned at once to the fire, but I could feel his eyes watching me.

Then he was beside me, his arm about my shoulders, and he began to speak in a voice that sounded strained and unhappy. "I should have written to you about Helaine," he said. "I would have had I been able . . . please believe me."

He paused, waiting, I suppose, for me to speak, but I could not. With a sigh he continued, "Please forgive me, Victoria. I hope you will always be my friend, as well as my little sister."

I turned, then, and gave him a scathing look. Did he really expect that just because it suited him, I could forget what we had meant to one another—the promises we had made? He wanted to be my *friend?* He wanted me to be his *little sister?* Tight-lipped, I lifted my hand and slapped him full across the face.

The color drained from his cheeks, leaving an angry, red-mottled mark where my palm had struck. For a long, painful moment we stared into each other's eyes. Then I turned back to the fire lest he see the trembling of my lips. I did not move until I heard the final echo of his footsteps as he mounted the staircase. Then I made my way back to my own room, via the same route I had followed coming down. There was a dull ache behind my eyes, and my brain felt hot and dry inside my skull.

In my room once more, I changed into the peignoir. It was fashioned of peacock-blue velvet and was lined with cerise satin. Cool and smooth, it clung sensuously to my bare arms and shoulders. I pulled the pins from my hair, picked up my brush, and stood, irresolute. It was only then that I remembered the letter I had started to write to Adam. Could it have been only twenty-four hours past?

A grim smile touched my lips as I reflected on the happiness that had been mine when I started that letter. I put my brush down on the mantel, and crossed to the corner, where the escritoire stood. I could not remember what I had written, but there was at least the beginnings of a message on the sheet of paper I had left lying upon the polished surface of the desk. I picked it up and started to read.

As I did so, the hair on the back of my neck began to rise and a knot of fear gathered in my stomach. Is it possible to think more than one thought at a time? It seemed to me my head was filled to bursting, a dozen ideas all clamoring for recognition. Who was she? Where had she gone? Surely she had been part of a dream!

I looked again at the sheet of paper still clutched in my hand, but my fingers shook so violently, I had to put the paper back on the desk before I could read again the message scribbled thereon in a round, childish hand:

Carter, beloved, come quickly! If you leave me now, I shall surely die. Even Lueddy cannot save me from the . . .

The rest of the message was lost in an unintelligible squiggle.

Chapter Nine

The dark-haired woman I had seen sitting at the desk — she *had* been in my room. This proved it, for I knew no one named Carter. But who could she have been? Where did she go? What did this strange message mean? What was I to do? Elizabeth, of course — she would know.

I snatched up the piece of paper, dashed from my room, and rushed along the gallery to Elizabeth's quarters. I was pounding frantically on the door when I heard her voice behind me.

"Enough, Victoria! I am here beside you."

Taken unawares, I gasped and spun to face her.

"Why, Victoria, little love. You're white as a sheet. Come . . ." She paused, opened the door. Then, as she drew me along inside, she asked, "Whatever is the matter?"

I had not given any thought to what I would say, how I would explain, so I simply thrust the paper into her hands.

She glanced down at it, then fixed a questioning look on me. Finally she asked, "And what am I to make of this?"

I found my tongue at last. "It was on my little desk, Elizabeth. The girl . . . the woman with the beautiful curly hair . . . she was in my room again. She must have written it and—"

Abruptly my stepmother held up her hand, gesturing for silence. "What woman?"

Suddenly, I remembered that no one knew about my

dream friend. Because that was all she was: a dream. In my shock and excitement at finding the note, I had not stopped to consider these facts. I stared at Elizabeth in consternation. What was I to say now?

When I remained silent, Elizabeth repeated, "What woman, Victoria?"

My mouth had gone dry, and I could not think what to say to make Elizabeth believe me. Believe what? That I had dreamed about a woman with dark curly hair, and she had written a note? When I took time to consider, even *I* did not believe that. Yet I had seen her! Was she a dream? But Elizabeth was holding the note in her hand. Suddenly I realized I didn't know what to believe myself. But I had to tell someone, and Elizabeth loved me—she knew I always spoke only what was true.

Finally, I blurted, "She's my friend, but I don't know who she is. I always thought she was a dream, but she wrote this note, and she . . ."

My stepmother was shaking her head, staring at me, disbelief mirrored in her eyes.

"But it's true, Elizabeth She—" In my distress, my voice had risen, grown overly loud. I stopped speaking, tried to swallow.

Slowly Elizabeth lowered her gaze to the piece of paper once more, appeared to read it carefully, then looked again at me. "And who is Carter?" The question was put softly.

"I don't know," I said.

"You did not write this?"

Spurred by the expression in her eyes, I replied hotly, "Of course I did not write it! I told you—she did."

Elizabeth continued to stare at me, obviously nonplussed. Slowly, the look of impatience her face had assumed was replaced by one of concern. Finally she said, "You are upset, little love. Let me take you back to your room. You should rest awhile, have a cup of tea. We shall talk about this," she held up the piece of paper, "when you have had a chance to collect your thoughts."

I went cold inside. Elizabeth didn't believe me. But she

had to believe me! "Please, Elizabeth, please! Listen to me. I know how strange this sounds, but she was there—in my room. And she wrote that note. . . ."

My stepmother was shaking her head, slowly, back and forth. There was a strange look in her eyes. Sadness, yes, and something else. Pity!

I wanted no one's pity! Abruptly, I drew myself up to my full height, held out my hand. "Never mind, Elizabeth," I said coldly. "It was thoughtless of me to trouble you. Please, just give the paper back to me and I will go."

She hesitated, seemed about to speak, then changed her mind. Slowly, she handed the paper to me. I snatched it from her, turned, and fled. Back in my own room once more, I wadded up that miserable scrap of writing and flung it across the room. Then I sat down upon my chaise, pulled my knees up under me, and turned so that I could rest my cheek against the smooth, cool back. I felt trembly inside, and my thoughts were in chaos.

I should have known better than to go to Elizabeth—to anybody—with such a silly story. The dark-haired woman was, after all, only part of a dream. She could not have written anything. I knew that—and yet, if not she, then who? One of the servants? But not one of them could read or write, except Miss Jones. Could she—? *Would* she—? Of course she would not! I finally admitted to myself that it was a puzzle for which I could find no answer. The best I could hope to do was put the whole incident out of my mind.

And how was I to do that? Work on my embroidery? Choose a new book to read? Perhaps a walk in the park would clear my mind. But I remained seated, curled against the back of the chaise. I was still sitting, doing nothing, when a gentle rap upon the door roused me from my lethargy. "Come," I called.

Immediately the door swung open, and Adam stepped into my room.

Just the sight of him set my heart to pounding. I gazed at him in amazement, utterly nonplussed. The ugly red marks left on his cheek by the stinging slap I had delivered less than an hour before were no longer in evidence. Indeed, his face was pale, his lips set in a grim line. He moved forward until he stood at the foot of the chaise staring down at me, and still he did not speak.

Slowly, I lowered my feet to the floor, sat up straight. "Why are you here?" The words, the tone of my voice, could have been addressing a total stranger.

"I must talk with you, Victoria."

"You should not be here in my room. It would be best if you were to leave immediately." My words were correct but the tone was uncertain.

"Please, Victoria, don't send me away. I must talk with you!"

Before I could dissent further, he stepped around the end of the chaise and dropped down beside me, all in one swift move. He clasped his hands tightly together between his knees and leaned toward me. A lock of pale gold hair fell across his forehead and his eyes, gazing into mine, were stormy.

I tried to think, but he had caught me unawares and vulnerable. Now, with him so near, I could only remember how much I loved him, the feel of his arms about me, the tender warmth of his lips. . . .

He was speaking, the words tumbling out. "I beg of you, Victoria, forgive me. Please, tell me you forgive me. I must know that you don't hate me."

"Oh, Adam, I could never hate you!" My response, like the wave of longing that washed over me, came unbidden.

"I never meant it to happen. All those months I was away, I never thought of anyone but you . . . then I met Helaine. . . ." His eyes begged me to understand.

But his words brought only pain. For a moment I had forgotten the woman, and the mention of her name was like cold water dashed in my face. I started to turn away.

"Victoria, *please!*" His voice was ragged. He reached out, took my hands in his, raised them to his lips, then pressed them to his cheek.

I know I should have snatched my hands away, but I could not. His touch burned, weakening my resolve, melting my strength.

At that moment, a flicker of movement outside my French doors caught my eye, and turning my head, I beheld a strange woman. She stood just outside, staring balefully at the two of us, her eyes unblinking, her expression one of pure hate. A chill shuddered through me and I recoiled in fear.

Adam, too, turned and looked over his shoulder. His whole body stiffened. Then he released my hands and started to his feet, stood scowling at the woman peering in at us.

Her lip curled. She tossed her head, then turned and stalked away.

Adam, his face livid, hands clenched at his sides, muttered, "Damn that woman!"

Shocked as much by Adam's reaction as by the appearance of the stranger, I demanded, "Who is she? Do you know her?"

"Do I know her? Ha!" It was an ugly sound. "That old witch is Helaine's maid."

"Old witch?"

"Her name is Stella."

So Helaine's maid had seen Adam in my room, kissing my hands. Innocent though the gesture had been, the look on the woman's face did not bode well for either of us. My ire began to rise. Did I not have enough to cope with? Had Adam not given me pain enough?

Abruptly I leaped to my feet and began pushing Adam toward the door. "You have to go." I shouted. "Get out of my room at once!"

But he would not move. His eyes, gazing at me now, held a hunted, haunted look. "First, promise me you will talk with me tomorrow. We can ride up to the cliff top together."

I knew I should say no, emphatically, but at that look in his eyes, I hesitated . . .

"I beg of you, Victoria."

And still I vacillated, standing there, looking up into his eyes: longing for the warmth of his embrace—thinking how he had betrayed me; aching for the sweet caress of his lips—remembering he belonged to someone else now; hoping he would say something that would ease the hurt. I closed my eyes and the words just seemed to slip past my lips, "I don't know . . . maybe. . . ."

He remained, indecisive for a moment, at last accepting the inevitable. He bowed his head. "All right," he sighed. "Until tomorrow." Only then did he leave.

Alone once more, I paced the floor, distraught. What should I do? My heart told me one thing, my common sense another. If only there were someone with whom I could discuss it, to whom I could unburden myself. But there was no one.

It was growing late, time to dress for dinner. I rang for hot water. Gillian appeared shortly, and when I had washed my hands and face, she helped me into one of the dresses I had brought back from London—was it almost three years ago? It took only a moment to braid my hair and wrap the long coil about my head, and I was ready.

I descended the stairs and crossed the great hall slowly, my thoughts somber. It was the sound of someone speaking my name that brought me out of my reverie. I was standing just outside the dining room door. Papa and Elizabeth were already inside, and, I realized, they were discussing me.

Elizabeth was saying, ". . . something to do with a dream, a girl who is her friend."

Papa snorted. "I will not have it, Elizabeth! We have been too lenient with that girl."

"Samuel! Please! She has had a bitter disappointment. It is no wonder . . ."

Shock held me speechless. I knew I should not be eavesdropping, but I was so stunned, I could not move.

Papa's voice had risen. "That is no excuse! Life is full of disappointment, and she must learn to deal with reality. I'll not abide such nonsense from anybody, least of all, my daughter!"

Elizabeth had told Papa. How *could* she! Was it not enough that her son had betrayed me? Trembling with rage, I burst through the door. Startled, they turned to face me.

I glared straight at Elizabeth and shouted, "How dare you! How . . . how dare you talk about me behind my back!"

Papas angry roar interrupted me. "How dare *you* trouble your stepmother with such nonsense?"

"But, Papa—"

"Go to your room! I shall tend to you later."

Elizabeth had gone deathly pale. She stood silent, her fingers splayed upon her cheeks.

"You have no right—" I started.

Papa had gone white around the lips. Now he raised his hand and pointed. "Go to your room. Immediately!"

Without warning, my throat, my eyes, filled with burning tears of anger, of shame, of misery. I whirled about and ran from the room, up the stairs, to my own chamber. Furiously, I dashed the tears from my eyes and began to pace, up and down, back and forth, while inside my skull, my thoughts ran in circles.

And suddenly I remembered the note. I stopped pacing, turned, and walked slowly to the corner, where it had fallen when I flung it from me. I picked it up, smoothed it out, and slipped it into my desk drawer.

Although Adam had abandoned his studies some months early, during the time he was on the Continent he had acquired that special knowledge of art and architecture that had been his goal. Therefore, Papa entrusted to him responsibility for completing the renovation and refurbishment of Greystone Manor. To Adam also fell the task of monitoring expenditures and overseeing upkeep. In short, he became Papa's bailiff.

It was John, Papa's first-born son, who would inherit the title. It would pass to him upon Papa's death. For the present, however, John remained at college, and would do so for at least another year.

As for Papa, the stud was his pride and joy. He would have been content to put all his time, energy, and effort into the management thereof. Nevertheless, he did retain final authority in all matters pertaining to the family and the estate. It was an equitable arrangement, and all three men seemed well satisfied.

It was also decided, during the first few weeks following their arrival, that Adam and Helaine should have a suite of rooms on the third floor. Preparations were made straight away, and the bridal couple took possession of these new quarters soon afterward.

However, at Helaine's insistence, Stella, who had appeared at Greystone Manor along with a dozen trunks on the day following the arrival of the newlyweds, was installed in Adam's old room on the second floor. It did seem odd that Helaine should want her personal maid there, rather than in a room adjoining her own, but neither Papa nor Elizabeth found cause to object, and so it was agreed.

Stella, Adam informed us, had served Helaine for many years—from childhood, in fact. It soon became obvious to all of us that the woman attended Helaine with complete devotion, indeed as if Helaine were still a small child. Helaine, for her part, appeared to trust Stella implicitly.

I, on the other hand, found Stella's presence completely unnerving, and could understand why Adam had referred to her as a witch. Grim, unsmiling, she did not look like anyone I had ever seen before. That is, she did not look English, Welsh, Scottish, or Irish.

Her skin, drawn tight across high cheekbones, was light brown, with a peculiar greyish cast. Probably, I surmised, age had added that tinge of grey, though how old she might be, I could not guess. Her iron gray hair was pulled back and fastened in a sparse, tight coil at the nape of her neck, and her cold black eyes, deep-sunken and set well apart, were distinctly almond-shaped. Her hands were extremely long-fingered and boney, and there was a disturbing fierceness in her sharply hooked nose with its wide-flaring nostrils.

Just the sight of her was enough to give me a chill, and it seemed to me that every time I turned around, she was somewhere visible. Out on the balcony, in the gallery, climbing the stairs—the back of my neck would begin to prickle, and if I glanced over my shoulder, there she would be, watching me with those cold, unblinking black eyes.

I often wondered, worried over, what she had made of that little tableau she had observed through my French doors. Had she reported to Helaine? She would have, of course. Would the two of them guess at the relationship Adam and I had shared? Or had he already told Helaine? The latter idea was so distasteful, I did my best to thrust it from me.

During the weeks immediately following their arrival at Greystone Manor, Helaine and Adam remained aloof, joining the family only for dinner, and that rarely. For newlyweds, it was not considered remarkable.

And following the fiasco with Elizabeth, I, too, took to spending much time alone: sitting in my room, walking the shadowed paths through the park, riding the windswept trail to the cliff's top, with nothing but my memories for company. Despite the ugly scene in the dining room, nothing more was said concerning the episode.

The incident with the falling stones continued to trouble me, but I couldn't decide just what to do about it. The sensible thing would have been to report it to our new bailiff, Adam. But I could not bring myself to do so, lest he think I was pursuing his request that I meet with him alone.

And slowly, the idea began to form in my mind that I myself should go into the north wing. Not only did the origin of the falling stones bother me, but I wondered what Helaine had been doing there. Not since that long-ago day when, as a child, I had followed the cat, had I even contemplated another foray into that closed and abandoned area. Even now, the thought gave me pause; but if Helaine could go there, then certainly I could.

But how was I to get in? The entire north wing had been abandoned long before I was born. Considered to be unsafe, it had been closed off from the rest of the manor. Even the small door in the stable, which had given me entrée so many years ago, had been sealed to prevent further mishaps. For the very first time, it occurred to me to wonder why. Perhaps I should not . . .

But Helaine had been there! *She* had returned safely enough! If she could go there, so could I. Certainly I had more right to be there than she. And so one afternoon, some ten days after Adam had come to my room, I dressed myself in a plain frock of grey worsted, and started out.

I wasn't certain just how one gained entry into the north wing, but after giving the problem careful consideration, I decided to try the old servants' entrance off the kitchen stairs. My deductions proved correct. Turn right at the top of the stairs, down a long hall, and there was the door. However, it was obvious that Helaine had not come this way. Indeed, it was doubtful that anyone had passed through the hallway in a score of years—the accumulation of dust everywhere gave indisputable proof of that.

For a moment, my courage threatened to desert me. I would be alone in there, in that awful place where I had heard the banshee wail. Gooseflesh began to prickle along my arms, and an unexpected shiver ran down my spine.

But, I reminded myself, Helaine had been in there. No harm had come to her. I straightened my shoulders, took a deep breath, and grasped the door handle. It turned easily enough, but the hinges were rusty. Only when I put my shoulder to the task did they finally give way with a moan and a shriek. It was further proof that this was not the way Helaine had come. Nevertheless, I felt a moment of elation as I stepped through into the north wing.

My elation turned to dread as I gazed about me. The room in which I found myself was cold and damp. It was also devoid of furniture. Festoons of spider webbing hung from the ceiling and filled the shadowy corners. Small, dark shapes scuttled across the floor to disappear into the cracks and crevices that marred the moldering walls.

I gasped, jerked my skirt above my ankles lest some creature should seek refuge in its folds. *Go back,* urged a small voice in my head. But I would not. If Helaine could walk through the north wing, so could I. And I was determined, now, to discover what she had been doing here — or die trying. A shiver coursed over me. Quickly, I banished the thought from my mind. I had no intention of dying!

I concentrated on Helaine, once more. As dusty and dirty as this place was, it should not be difficult to determine where she had walked. I knew for certain she had been on the balcony overlooking the sea. It should be easy to pick up her trail there.

However, I decided to try to find my way to the arrow slits overlooking the western cliff, first. If there had been someone there, if someone had *helped* that shower of stones to fall, that too, should be easy to verify.

Still holding my skirts high, I turned left and crossed to the nearest door. It stood slightly ajar, and I was able to pass through without difficulty.

The chamber in which I now stood was twin to the one I had just left. Again I crossed to the nearest door, and just as I reached for the handle to open it, I heard a squealing sound, but soft, somewhere behind me. Could someone be following me? I stopped, listened intently. Nothing.

Still, my heart was beating faster as I continued on my way. Perhaps, I thought, I should have told someone where I was going. I almost laughed out loud. And who, I asked myself cynically, would you have told?

The next door I opened gave into a hallway. Beyond that, I passed through several more empty rooms in quick succession. Then I found myself in a chamber that was somehow different. I hesitated, glanced about, squinting through the gloom. It wasn't the size or shape — and it was just as cold and dirty — but it was not empty!

There, in the corner, was a pile of litter. I moved nearer. It looked like a broken chair with a heap of old rags thrown over it. And what was that under the chair? I moved closer still. It was some sort of a cage or trap. A mousetrap, the kind Cinderella had used to catch the mice for her fairy godmother to turn into footmen.

I shivered. When everything was removed from these rooms, why had that been left behind? I started to turn away, but a flicker of movement inside the cage caught my eye. I turned back, moved closer. There was a mouse in the cage! But how could that be? Any mouse left in that trap should have been long dead, unless someone had only recently set and baited the trap. But this part of the manor was abandoned, so who would come in here and set a mousetrap?

Helaine—could she have set it the day I saw her on the terrace? No, a mouse caught then would be starved to death by now. Could she have come back again, in the last few days? But why would she want to trap mice?

As my mind worried over the problem, I opened the trap and watched as the frightened mouse scurried into the pile of moldering cloth draped over the chair. Then I continued on my way.

Though I moved slowly, stopping from time to time to look over my shoulder, and listen, I made good progress. However, when I reached the rampart walk, I found it most disappointing. Open to the weather, lacking in proper upkeep, the wall with its arrow slits was crumbling. The walkway was littered with detritus and bird droppings. The fall of stones could easily have been caused by a seagull perching there, taking its ease after the storm.

Well, I decided, perhaps there might be something of interest farther along. I continued north along the rampart walk until, at its end, I emerged onto the terrace. As I moved out into the open, I was caught and buffeted by a gusting breeze. I turned slightly, tilting my head to take the full force of the wind on my shoulder, then halted in midstride, staring back at the house. I had never seen anything quite as imposing as the magnificent Venetian doorway that gave access from the back of the manor onto the terrace. I must have seen it when I was here as a child—or was I completely blinded by fear then?

I had absolutely no recollection. So what lay beyond that door? I wondered. Obviously a very large room of some sort. I hurried to the nearer sidelight, suddenly bursting with curiosity.

As I approached, I noted that several of the panes of glass had been broken out, which was helpful, since the others were so encrusted with spider webs and dust as to be totally opaque. The chamber beyond was immense and full of shadow, but I could make out what appeared to be a few pieces of furniture scattered here and there about the room.

I left the sidelight and went to the door. To my surprise, I found that it stood slightly ajar. And, with mounting excitement, I noted that it had recently provided egress, or perhaps ingress, to someone. Helaine? Who else? I asked myself.

Pushing the door open, I stepped over the threshold. Not until I was actually inside did I realize how bright the light had been on the terrace. Slowly, as my eyes adjusted to the gloom, I moved to the center of the room, then turned about, full circle. And having done that, I felt utterly confused.

This huge room, facing the terrace, must have been designed as a drawing room, a place to entertain on a lavish scale. But all the furniture that remained belonged in a bedroom. At the far end of the room, sitting on a dais where one would have expected to find a pianoforte, there was a massive four-poster bed. The bedcurtains were drawn back, and the comforters and sheets were all of a tumble, as if it had been slept in, then never made up.

At the same end of the room, over against the back wall, stood a huge wardrobe. One door hung open, revealing an interior filled with garments: some on hangers, some lying in untidy heaps. A pair of riding boots lay on the floor, one near the bed, the other in front of the wardrobe. There were also a number of chairs, several of them lying topsy-turvy about a large side table.

But most remarkable of all, at the opposite end of the room there were three wicker hampers, very much like the one Helaine had been carrying. As I moved closer, I saw that there were several mousetraps sitting nearby. I was near enough now to note that the wicker hampers had been badly damaged, probably by mice. That would account for the traps. By why the hampers? And why here, in this place that had apparently been used as a bedchamber? I peeked into one of the hampers. It was empty. How very curious, I thought.

I turned around, then, and went back to the wardrobe. It contained coats and trousers, and other garments of a style worn by gentlemen before Papa was born. Could these things have belonged to my grandfather? Without warning, a feeling of revulsion washed over me. Slowly I backed away, then turned and looked quickly about. Gooseflesh rose on my arms.

The light was failing rapidly now, and I was beginning to wish I had never undertaken such a foolhardy expedition. It was time I returned to my room, the sooner the better.

With that idea firmly in mind, I hurried back to the door and stepped out onto the terrace. Out there, it was not so dark as it had seemed inside. And the view from the edge of the terrace would be marvelous. Just a quick look before I left!

No sooner had I left the protection of the doorway than the wind caught me once more. Blowing cold from the sea, it moaned and sighed over the weathered stone like the cry of a lost soul.

I shivered, started to turn back. But Helaine had stood at the terrace edge—if she could stand there unafraid, so could I. There was nothing to fear, after all. Lost souls and banshees were for children.

Leaning into the freshening gale, I continued forward until I was standing next to the shattered balustrade. The loneliness and sorrow that had been kept at bay while I was busy with my explorations began to insinuate itself upon me once more. The slate-grey sea spread out below me. How dreary, how bleak it was. The water far below surged in and out, flinging itself against the base of the cliff; the sky stretched grey and empty to the horizon. Like my life, grey and empty. . . .

I laid my palms on the balustrade, leaned my weight upon them, gazed down into the boiling, pounding waves. The wind wailed through the broken stone; it whispered in my ear, the words not quite clear. And yet I knew, I understood. The water waited below, and there would be no more loneliness, no more pain. . . .

Horrified at the turn my thoughts had taken, I started to draw back, just as the rail beneath my hands gave way. For what seemed an eternity I teetered there, arms flailing. And it seemed to me I heard the sound of feet behind me, running across the terrace. Then a gust of wind whipped around me, overbalancing me — or was it hands upon my back? And slowly I toppled forward into the yawning void.

Chapter Ten

The scream that tore from my throat ended in a strangled cry of pain as I landed heavily on my side. My left arm was, miraculously, crooked around what remained of the baluster; my right hand was pressed hard against the outer surface of the wall below me.

Numbed by shock and pain, I lay there for a few minutes, breathing heavily. What had happened to me? My thoughts were so muddled. Ever so slowly, I wriggled back from the edge before pushing myself to a sitting position. My right hand was lacerated and raw from its encounter with the rough stone wall, and my body felt bruised; but I was able to bend and move my arms and legs. There were no broken bones.

I fished my handkerchief from my pocket and wound it around my hand, which was oozing blood. Then, slowly, painfully, I got to my feet. Belatedly, I glanced over my shoulder. I was alone. Of course I was alone. . . .

But there was a dreadful throbbing in my skull, and I felt sick. Swallowing hard against the nausea, I paused, and as I waited for the giddiness to subside, I raised my hand, ran my fingers through my hair, winced as they encountered a large swelling just above my left ear. The area was warm and sticky, and when I looked at my hand, I saw that it bore a smear of blood.

I stared at the ugly red stains. My head must have grazed the baluster as I fell forward. But my brain was clearing now, working more smoothly. I remembered the wind, whispering. Had I really been about to jump? No. I had started to step back. Otherwise, I would surely have gone over the edge when the balustrade gave way.

Like a slow-rising tide, a thrill of horror crept over me as I recalled that peculiar sound of running feet, the touch of hands. It had not been the crumbling of the rail that had propelled me half over the edge!

I had not been alone here in the north wing, after all. What a fool I was not to have exercised more caution. Someone had shoved me! But who? Why?

Again I swung about, surveying the length and breadth of the terrace. Nothing, only shadows. Had I only imagined the sounds, the pressure on my back, after all?

Suddenly I had only one wish: to leave this awful place and return to my own cozy room. Chilled to the very marrow, I was shivering violently by now, and the light was all but gone. My hand hurt, my leg hurt, my head hurt; in fact, I hurt all over. I knew I must get back to my room. But, I promised myself, I shall be back!

Groggy, hobbling on my twisted knee, I retraced my steps along the rampart walk, intent on making my way back to the kitchen stairs as fast as possible. From time to time I reached up and probed the injured spot on my head, but gently. It was very tender indeed.

Surprisingly, without really thinking about it, I found my way back to the kitchen stairs with no difficulty. In my room once more, I rang for hot water.

Then I started to brush myself off. Immediately a cloud of dust rose about me, setting me to coughing and sneezing, which, in turn, renewed the pounding in my head, the uneasy state of my stomach. I gave it up, and lay down on my chaise to wait for Gillian and the hot water.

And while I waited, my mind continued to explore the mystery. Clearly, the mouse could not have been in that trap for very long. It was also obvious that the poor little creature would not have entered the trap had there not been some sort of bait therein. Hence, someone had recently been in the north wing and had baited that trap. But who? And why?

What about that strange bedroom, with more mousetraps? But that bedroom had clearly not been occupied for years.

And then someone had tried to push me off the terrace! Again, who? Why?

Well, I thought, the only logical answer is: the person who had set the mousetrap! At that point, thinking how cleverly I had reasoned it all out, I felt a positive flush of triumph.

But that faded as I asked myself, why? What would anyone want with a live mouse? And my stomach knotted with fear at the question that followed: why would anyone wish me dead?

The *who,* of course, was probably Helaine. Had I not seen her on the north terrace? But what in God's name would Helaine want with a live mouse? And why try to push me off the terrace? Did she think I would care that she was trapping mice in the north wing? Had I not felt so wretched, I would have laughed.

Gillian, when she arrived, took one look at my duststreaked face, the blood in my hair, and began to wring her hands. "Law, Lady Victoria, what happened to ye? I'd best fetch old Lueddy. She'll know what to do for ye," and she started for the door.

I stopped her. "No! You will not fetch Lueddy. You will stay right here and help me yourself."

Though obviously frightened and skeptical, Gillian at last allowed me to swear her to secrecy, then helped me to wash my hair and clean the wound above my ear.

The blow had left me with not only a nasty headache, but a decided lack of appetite as well. I directed Gillian to tell Elizabeth that I would not be down for dinner. "Tell her nothing else," I said severely, then added, "and bring me back a tea tray."

I had forgiven Elizabeth for telling Papa about the dream girl and the note. After all, I had not asked her to refrain

112

from mentioning the episode, and she had had only my best interests at heart.

For his part in the matter, Papa had said some pretty harsh things, including that he thought I was making the whole thing up in a bid for attention and sympathy. They were accusations that stung me to the quick. However, thereafter the whole affair appeared to be forgotten.

It was Elizabeth, of course, who prevailed upon Papa to let the matter drop. And I was not ungrateful. Nonetheless, it was clear to me that in future it would be foolish indeed to confide in Elizabeth or to seek counsel from my father—at least where my dream friend and all the rest of it were concerned.

Bitterly, I wondered what they would make of this latest circumstance Elizabeth would probably think I was trying to discredit Helaine in the hope of regaining Adam's love, and Papa would probably accuse me of inflicting the wounds upon myself! No. Never again would I seek their aid.

But there was surely an explanation for these strange events somewhere. And, I promised myself dramatically, I would find it, though I died in the attempt. Then they would be sorry!

By the following morning I was feeling quite well again, though the spot above my ear would be tender for a while. Life resumed its daily pattern. At mealtimes, or in the evenings sitting together with my family before the fire, I made a determined effort to put on a brave face. If I could not have their trust, I certainly did not want Elizabeth's or Papa's pity. So I smiled and chattered on about whatever came to mind. And if I caught a knowing glance between them, I would toss my head and talk even faster.

I was also determined to return to the north wing and revisit that strange bedchamber. Had my grandfather—the blackguard—really slept there? Were those his things in that wardrobe? I had to go back, make a thorough search. But somehow the time was never right.

As time wore on, I did make a halfhearted attempt to become better acquainted with my new sister-in-law. On several occasions I sent along a note asking if she would take tea with me in my room, or suggesting we walk together in the garden. I promised myself I would ask her about the mousetrap if she accepted; but on each occasion, when she declined my invitation, I breathed a heartfelt sigh of relief.

Then, just when I was beginning to feel assured that I was to be spared the trial of a sisterly *tête-à-tête,* I received a message from her requesting my presence in her quarters. It read more like a summons than an invitation, and for a moment anger burned hot in my breast. However, I decided finally that it would be childish to let her bad manners spur me to like behavior. Besides, an opportunity might present itself to question her concerning her business in the north wing. And feeling most virtuous, I hurriedly made my toilette and presented myself at her door at the appointed time.

Adam had departed that very morning for London, on matters pertaining to the estate. Thus, I knew that I would be alone with Helaine and her maid, unless, of course, Elizabeth, too, had been sent an invitation. But such was not the case. As I had feared, the door was opened by Stella, and when I moved past her into the room, I found myself alone with my sister-in-law and her grim-faced maid.

The air was heavy with incense, and though the afternoon outside was bright, the drapes were tightly drawn and a multitude of candles provided a gentle light that seemed to accent the opulence with which Helaine had surrounded herself. When Papa had given the newlyweds a free hand in decorating their quarters, I'm sure this was not what he had had in mind.

Fleetingly, I wondered if Samuel was aware of the amounts of money that must have been spent in decorating just that one room. But Helaine gave me only a moment to contemplate my surroundings. Immediately I entered, she took me by the arm and led me to a large sofa upholstered in sumptuous Beauvais tapestry. Seating herself, she drew me down beside her. Then she leaned back against the cushions and turned sideways on the seat so that she was facing me.

"Ah, dear sister. At last we have the opportunity to become better acquainted." As always, her voice was low and velvety.

"Indeed," I answered, trying not to stare. But I could not help myself. I had never seen anyone as strikingly beautiful, or as exotic, as was my sister-in-law.

Her hair had been brushed back, then braided, and the braid wound round and round atop her head. The knot thus formed was held in place by a large two-toothed comb with a long curved handle, from which dangled several tiny golden bells that tinkled with each movement of her head. She also wore large, gold-filigree earrings, and on three fingers of each hand there were heavy gold rings all set with semiprecious stones. As for the costume she wore, I had never seen anything to equal it except in pictures: a kimono-like garment of shimmering emerald green silk, lined with pale lime green satin.

As my gaze traveled over her, a faint smile twitched the corners of her mouth, but she said nothing more. Not even the tick of a clock disturbed the silence. I licked my lips, swallowed, transferred my gaze to my own fingers, which were twisting themselves together in my lap. When Stella suddenly reappeared pushing a black lacquered tea cart, I could not suppress a sigh of relief.

I glanced up just in time to see the look that passed between my sister-in-law and her maid—*exchanging a silent message?*

Helaine nodded her dismissal. Stella immediately withdrew. Had they really exchanged some message, or was my imagination playing tricks? Were they secretly laughing at me for some reason I could not fathom? At least, I told myself, I do not have to tolerate that witch's presence. I knew, of course, that Stella was not a witch, but I thought spitefully, she looks like one!

While my mind was busy with these musings, Helaine had poured the tea. Now she asked, "Milk? Sugar?"

"Both, if you please."

Helaine's hands moved gracefully over the tea tray, and

when my cup was ready, she handed it to me. "I hope you will find this to your liking," she murmured. "It is a special blend I learned to enjoy while I was in the French West Indies."

The brew was very dark and strong, and when I raised the cup to my lips, I found the aroma less than pleasing. I lowered the cup once more, took a deep breath, then forced myself to take a sip. I almost gagged. Helaine had added far too much sugar, and not only were the contents of my cup sickeningly sweet, but the tea had a strange aftertaste. I fought to keep a grimace from twisting my face.

If Helaine noticed, she gave no sign. "And how do you like my tea?" she asked pleasantly.

"It is . . . unusual," I replied, trying to be polite.

With a throaty laugh my sister-in-law assured me, "It is an acquired taste. Drink a little more . . . you will see how good it can be."

Dutifully I raised the cup to my lips once more, but I almost retched, just smelling it, and could swallow only the tiniest sip. I was trying all the while to think of a clever way to bring up the question of the mousetrap, but my mind remained blank. In truth, I had only one thought, which was how to flee my sister-in-law's presence.

"Tell me about yourself, dear sister. What do you like to do? How do you spend your days?" Helaine's tone was sincere, and the eyes searching my face were intent with interest.

I took a deep breath, set my cup and saucer back on the tea cart, and folded my hands in my lap. "Why, I . . . I read. I do lots of things . . . different things."

"What about friends . . . a special young man, perhaps?"

I thought her question entirely too presumptutous. Yet she *was* my sister-in-law. Perhaps in Paris such personal questions were considered thoughtful. Or was she aware that I had been in love with Adam?

Suddenly I remembered the day Stella had looked through my French doors and observed Adam, with me in my room, holding my hands. Again I licked my lips. My mouth was dry as dust, and I had difficulty twisting my tongue around the words when I answered. "My dearest friends are in London. We live so far from anyone here. . . ." I shrugged, unable to think of anything to add.

"Perhaps Lady Elizabeth could take you to London for the season . . . would you like that?"

And what business is that of yours? I longed to say. Instead I replied, "Perhaps next year. I'm really quite content. . . ."

But Helaine ignored my response. "Let me see . . . ah, yes. Your Uncle Phillip and Aunt Drusilla." She paused, and studied me with a speculative look.

Then abruptly, she leaned forward, glanced into my cup. "You have not drunk your tea, my dear. Come, finish it, and I'll pour you a fresh cup."

My heart began to pound. A wave of giddiness swept over me and I rose unsteadily to my feet. "No, thank you, Helaine. I must go. I . . . I have something to do." I backed toward the door as I spoke.

Helaine did not bother to stand. She leaned back and surveyed me, from the tip of my toes to the top of my head, and her eyes glittered. "Do come again soon, Lady Victoria," she murmured, and the sound of her soft laughter followed me as I opened the door and fled.

In my own room once more, I berated myself for having failed to mention the mousetrap, for having let Helaine make me feel so inadequate. Suddenly, I was very tired, and for the remainder of that day, I felt quite ill.

Yet when I went to bed, I tossed and turned, unable to fall asleep. Sleep, nevertheless, I must have done, for suddenly I seemed to waken, and there at the foot of my bed, walking to and fro, wringing her hands and sobbing softly, was my raven-haired friend. At last she seated herself at the escritoire, but only slid her fingers aimlessly over the polished surface.

In the morning I was strangely disoriented when I awoke and found, once again, that it had just been the same old dream. And yet, lying there in my bed, thinking about it, I realized that this dream had been different. The girl had seemed unhappy, and she had grown older—was, in fact, no longer a child. It occurred to me then that, always, she seemed to be my own age, this child-woman who haunted my sleeping hours.

Suddenly another thought made me gasp, sent a shiver of dread down my spine. I got out of bed and, slowly, unwillingly, approached the escritoire. With an audible sigh of relief I found that there was nothing there save the ink pots.

Though I tried to put her from my mind, in the days that followed, the memory of that unhappy visitor began to obsess me. I caught myself thinking of her as if she were real, yet I knew she could not be. And just seeing her again had reminded me of that unfinished letter I had found upon my desk. Could *I* have written it? But I knew no one named Carter. So, if not I, then who? And why?

And such a peculiar message. Day after day I pondered the meaning of those words I had found scribbled upon my writing paper, and I became nervous and tense. Who was Carter? From whom did the young woman seek protection? Why was she going to die? Who *was* she?

I shivered, pressed my fingers to my throbbing temples, reminded myself once again that the dark-haired woman could not have written the note, because she was only part of a dream. And again I asked myself: If she is only a dream, then who *did* write the note? Surely not I! If I had written it, I would remember. And so, like a squirrel in a cage, like a dog chasing its tail, round and round my thoughts ran while my head ached.

An unaccustomed ennui, both of body and of spirit, took possession of me. I lost my appetite, and what I did manage to eat did not sit easy in my stomach. My once boundless energy began to flag, and though my sleep was troubled, all I wanted to do was sleep.

One morning, several days after I had taken tea with Helaine, when Elizabeth said, "Come sit with me for a while, Victoria. I have a plan I should like to discuss with you," I followed her into her sitting room with something less than avid interest.

However, Elizabeth took no notice of my apathy, and once we were seated, she stated in her forthright way, "I think we should give a dinner party to celebrate Adam's return and to introduce Helaine to some of our friends. And John will be back from Oxford by then. What do you think?"

"That would be nice," I agreed without enthusiasm.

"I thought we could invite Pastor and Mrs. Grewe, Dr. Maerrie and his wife, and the squire and Lady Mangrove. Perhaps you can think of someone else?"

I arranged my features in what I hoped was a bright and interested expression. Then, after a pause intended to give the impression of deep thought, I shook my head. "No, Elizabeth. I can think of no one else."

"Perhaps it would be a good time to have Phillip and Drusilla?" I could feel Elizabeth's eyes studying me, waiting for my reaction.

"That would be nice."

Elizabeth's smile was bright, too bright, when she added, "Of course, we would include Thomas. . . ."

I could feel the blood, hot and angry, flooding my cheeks. So that was it. Out of pity for her poor, foolish stepdaughter, she was going to play at matchmaker. Did she really believe that Thomas could replace Adam in my heart? Well, I thought, she is wrong about that, and I neither want nor need her pity.

Defiantly I lifted my chin and fixed her with a cold stare. "If that is your wish, Elizabeth, I shall be pleased to see whomever you may choose to invite to *your* dinner party." With those words, I rose to my feet and rushed from the room.

However, Elizabeth was not one to be easily deterred once she had made up her mind. She presented her plan to Adam at breakfast the following morning. He received the news about the proposed dinner party with hardly more enthusiasm than I. But he thanked Elizabeth for her thoughtfulness, and promised to tell Helaine.

I had seen neither Stella nor Helaine since the day I had had tea in her quarters, and I couldn't help but wonder how she would take the news. But whatever her feelings may have been, she thanked Elizabeth most prettily at dinner that evening, so plans continued apace.

Invitations were issued forthwith, and during the days that followed, Greystone Manor became a veritable beehive of activity. Not only did the guest rooms require airing, but there were menus to prepare, decorations to be planned, Elizabeth and I had to have new costumes, and extra help had to be secured.

Phillip, Aunt Drusilla, and Thomas were to arrive two days in advance of the dinner party, to give us all time to visit. Despite my initial lack of enthusiasm, as the time for their arrival drew near, I found myself awaiting them with great anticipation. Indeed, on the appointed day, I stood with Papa and Elizabeth in the entry, eagerly waiting to greet them.

When the Hornabys had alighted from the coach, Thomas took both my hands in his and smiled down into my upturned face. I must admit that the very sight of him, his frank, admiring gaze, brought me a sense of pride and happiness I had thought never to experience again.

Thomas, like Adam and I, had matured. His cheekbones were more finely chiseled, the line of his jaw more strongly set; but that same enchanting dimple still lurked at the corner of his mouth, and I was beset by a most unseemly urge to throw my arms about him.

Finally, Thomas said, "It has been far too long since last we met."

"It is good to see you again," I replied, and we smiled at one another with warm affection. Then he raised my hands to his lips, brushed a kiss across my fingers while his eyes held mine fast. I blushed and glanced away. He laughed softly, then, and gave my fingers an extra squeeze before he released my hands.

The rest of the day was spent in happy reminiscences, and when twilight fell, Thomas and I went out to the park for a stroll. The moon, shining through the trees, traced lacy patterns on the path. The air was sweet with the fragrance of summer. Frogs chirruped and the bright, clear notes of a nightbird's song added its magic to the evening. We strolled in silence for a while.

Then Thomas stopped, laid his hand upon my arm, and, when he spoke, his voice was soft. "Victoria?"

I, too, halted, turned, looked up into his face.

Again he said, his voice warm and husky, "Victoria . . ." Then his arms were around me, holding me, while his lips brushed gentle kisses over my eyes, my cheeks, found at last my lips.

The feel of his arms about me, the touch of his lips on mine, unleashed something that had been imprisoned, chained, smothered inside me from the first moment I knew that Adam was lost to me. Overcome by my need, I clung to Thomas in the darkness, shamelessly letting his kisses ease the ache that had been knotted inside me for so long. I clung to him selfishly, accepting the comfort of his arms, his lips without thought.

When he would have released me, I only clung the tighter, burying my face against his shoulder, kissing his neck, his chin, nibbling at the corner of his mouth until his lips claimed mine once more with fierce passionate kisses. Only then did I relax in his embrace.

Then he whispered against my lips, "Victoria, heart of my heart. . . ."

Aghast, I suddenly realized what I had done. I think I always knew that Thomas loved me, though I had never given it conscious thought. Now I had given him cause to believe I returned his love. Quickly I moved to draw away from him, to tell him the truth, but he misunderstood my contrition, thinking me overcome by modesty.

Though he relaxed his embrace, he continued to hold me in his arms. In the moonlight, his face was aglow with happiness. Seeing his joy, I hadn't the courage to tell him the truth, and I was filled with shame and remorse when I heard him whisper, "I never dared to hope. I always thought . . .

that is . . ." He laughed softly. "It doesn't matter now," he concluded, and he kissed me again before he released me.

Then his face became serious. "Dearest Victoria." He swallowed, cleared his throat. "Is it too soon . . . dare I hope?" In the moonlight, his eyes searched my face for reassurance.

How I hated myself in that moment. I knew what he was going to ask, and before he could say more, I interrupted. "Perhaps it is too soon. We need time to think." I did not want to hurt him by refusing him point blank, yet I did not wish to lead him on. "It is growing late . . . we really must go back." I murmured unhappily.

Some of the joy died out of Thomas's eyes, but he acquiesced. When we rejoined the others, I saw a pleased glance pass between Elizabeth and Drusilla. I could not read the expression on Adam's face, but Helaine's glance was openly speculative. When her eyes met mine, I tossed my head and looked coolly down my nose. Let them all imagine what they will, I thought, and I turned to gaze up at Thomas.

On the following day, Papa and Adam took Uncle Phillip and Thomas on a tour of the estate while Elizabeth and I spent the day gossiping with Drusilla. Helaine, pleading a headache, did not join us until dinner.

When dinner was over and everyone had gathered in the small salon, Papa said to Helaine, "I overheard you singing the other evening, when I was out on the balcony smoking a cigar."

"And how did you know it was I, my Lord?" Helaine tilted her head archly to one side.

"No one else in this household plays the mandolin."

"Then I must confess, it was I," Helaine laughed.

"Would you favor us with a song now?"

She did not wait to be coaxed, but there was just the right touch of modesty in her demeanor when she replied, "If you found my poor effort entertaining, then I shall be pleased to sing for all of you."

A servant was sent to fetch her mandolin and Helaine, with obvious pleasure, began to play and sing in a soft contralto voice. Sometimes in French, sometimes in German, sometimes in a strange lilting patois I could not place. Sad songs, happy songs, mischievous songs. The candlelight glinted in her hair, turned her bare shoulders to glowing ivory, emphasized the subtle changes of expression in her lovely eyes. She was captivating.

Was there no end to the woman's charms, I thought bitterly. As I listened, I allowed my gaze to move over the faces of the others. I could not see Adam's expression, for he sat with his head bowed, listening intently; but when I saw the admiration in Papa's eyes, in Uncle Phillip's smile, in Thomas's air of enjoyment, I must admit that I felt sick with envy. I was grateful when Elizabeth pointed out that the morrow would be a long day, and everyone said good night.

The following morning, Thomas and I rode to the top of the cliff and then down into the dell. The sky overhead was deep blue, and a gentle breeze herded a flock of fleecy white clouds along the horizon. The meadow grasses, lush and green, were laced with cinquefoil, and the delicate rose-like aroma of wild strawberries vied with the lemony scent of wild thyme.

Impulsively I slipped down from Blue Boy's back and called to Thomas, "Come. Let us gather strawberries and thyme for Lueddy."

Thomas dismounted and came to join me in my search. "And what will Lueddy do with wild strawberries and thyme?"

"Sometimes she dries them to make medicinal teas, sometimes she uses them in her cooking. But if we are very good, she may let us each have a bowl of berries and cream in the kitchen before supper."

No sooner had the words left my mouth than a picture of Adam and me as children, our lips stained bright red with the fruit we had eaten, rose before my mind's eye. My heart twisted and I ducked my head so that Thomas should not see the pain in my eyes.

If Thomas noticed, he gave no sign. "I like the sound of that," he said, "the berries and cream, I mean. But how shall we carry them home?"

I forced myself to smile as I replied, "Why, in this, of course." So saying, I pulled my hat with its fashionable plume off my head, turned it upside down, and began filling it with the small red berries. When it was full, we piled a sheaf of thyme on top and Thomas made the whole thing fast with his handkerchief.

That done, we walked back to the spring, rinsed our fingers, and had a drink. Then we sat down, side by side on the lip of the stone basin. Thomas put his arm about my waist. I made no effort to move away.

Knowing what Thomas intended to ask me, I had lain awake, far into the night, wondering what my answer should be. I asked myself if perhaps it would be unwise to refuse Thomas too soon. After all, I thought, I am very fond of him. I might even grow to love him someday. But I knew in my heart that I was only fooling myself. Reluctantly, I determined to tell him the truth.

So now that the time had come, I took a deep breath and said, "Thomas, there is something I must say to you."

Quickly, he shook his head. "No, Victoria. Please. I understand what you want to say . . . it can wait."

"But I have no wish to deceive you, Thomas. I—"

Again he stopped me. "I am not deceived, dear Victoria." And then he added something I thought very strange. He said, "Do not deceive yourself."

I looked up at him then. Both love and understanding were in his eyes, and I said, "Oh, Thomas, you are so good, so kind. You really are very dear to me."

He leaned forward and kissed me, a tender kiss, before he said, "Someday, my beloved, you may learn to love me as much as I already love you."

The afternoon was, by then, far spent. We mounted our horses once more and returned to the manor. I went straight to my room to rest until it was time to dress.

The guests arrived at the appointed time, were presented to Helaine, and dinner was served on the stroke of nine. The new cook—Lueddy no longer did much in the kitchen—had quite outdone herself. There was breast of quail, salmon poached in milk, a roast of venison, Yorkshire pudding, various side dishes, and a different wine with each course. For dessert, there was a sherry trifle. Elizabeth was a gracious hostess, Papa always a jovial host.

For my part, I sat through the entire meal speaking only when spoken to, picking at my food, feeling very gauche and dull. The self-assurance that I had felt when alone with Thomas melted away in Helaine's presence. I thought again, watching her graceful movements, listening to the exciting timbre of her voice, that it was not surprising Adam had chosen to wed her instead of me.

Her hair, shining red and gold, had been dressed by Stella into a graceful fan on the back of her head, and wispy little curls fringed her forehead, nestled at the nape of her neck, peeked from behind her ears. She was so much more feminine than the rest of us with our fashionable smooth center parts and spaniel curls.

She wore a gown of sea green brocade, cut low in the style of the Empress Eugenie, a fashion that would not reach British shores for three more years. Her only jewels were a pair of gold filigree earrings set with jade the color of green sea water, and a simple pendant of the same material nestled modestly in the cleft between her ample bosom.

Watching her, listening to her, I soon realized that not only was she charming and delightful to behold, she was intelligent. Her knowledge of Garth family history, her grasp of the details of estate management, were nothing less than astonishing. And her questions about the stud, which was Papa's pride and joy, were thoughtful as well as knowledgeable. Papa was delighted and Adam, his eyes downcast, listened with pride.

Neither did Helaine neglect the guests. With artful questions and a look of absorbed attention, she drew Uncle Phillip into a discussion of his interests and accomplishments. She charmed and flattered the aging Lord Mangrove with just the right touch of coquetry. And she did not overlook Dr. Maerrie or Pastor Grewe and their wives. Each speaker, in turn, was rewarded by her complete attention, by a flashing smile, a heartfelt frown, a gasp of surprise as the story reached its climax.

And the lilting voice: "How very droll, Lord Mangrove," or again, "I should have been terrified, Dr. Hornaby." For Pastor Grewe, it was, "What would they have done without your aid and succor?" and for Dr. Maerrie, "To think you were able to save the child after all that!" Even Thomas appeared to be beguiled by her charm and wit. In fact, between the two of them, they kept everyone amused.

I tried to follow the conversation, but my mind was like an unbridled horse, dragging me willy-nilly where it would, and the food was tasteless in my mouth. I forced myself to eat, nonetheless, and I smiled and smiled until the muscles of my cheeks ached with the strain. Once I caught Elizabeth's eyes upon me, and I knew that she was worried. I tried to sit a little straighter, to think of something to add to the general merriment, but I could not. I could only wish, with all my heart, that the interminable evening would end.

And at long last, the final course was finished. The ladies rose to leave the gentlemen to their brandy, but I could stand no more. "Pray, excuse me," I said, "I do have a most annoying headache." My head really did ache, pounding away behind my eyes, but I knew Helaine for one, did not believe me, and I felt stupid and childish.

"Victoria! Dear little sister," she said, her voice full of concern. "You do look pale. I shall send Stella to you . . . she is quite wonderful at soothing an aching head."

Although her words were warm and full of sympathy, her eyes glittered spitefully. I wondered that no one else seemed to notice.

"Thank you, no!" I exclaimed, then realizing how churlish my refusal sounded, I added, "I'm just tired. No need to trouble Stella."

Dr. Maerrie gave me a piercing glance and Elizabeth, her eyes full of worry, wanted to see me to my room, but I refused her offer and hurried out lest she insist. I wanted only to be alone, to bury my tired head in my pillow. Even the disappointment on Thomas's face did not stay my flight. I longed only for the oblivion of dreamless sleep.

Elizabeth must have rung for Gillian, however, because that young woman arrived at my door almost as soon as I. She carried a pot of tea, a pitcher of hot water, and warm towels. She poured the water into my basin, and then, while I disrobed and bathed, she turned down the bed and laid out a nightdress for me. When I was ready, she brushed my hair. I tried to drink the tea, but she had put in too much sugar. I hadn't the heart to tell her, though, for she was trying so very hard to please me.

So I thanked her, made some excuse for leaving the tea, and crawled into bed. She waited until I was comfortably settled, then blew out the lamps, and left. The pounding in my head became more intense and I could not find a comfortable position upon my pillow; neither could I fall asleep. Or at least, I dreamed I was still awake, and I continued to fret and toss upon my pillow until something, I know not what, actually wakened me.

The night was warm and very still. Not the slightest breath of breeze fluttered the vine upon the balustrade, although the lush perfume of its blossoms cloyed the air. No call of sleepy bird, no chirrup of insect, no sound at all; yet something had wakened me.

Only the stars, shining like lanterns in the midnight sky, their light flooding in through the open French doors, gave any point of reference to my groping senses. I lay unmoving, searching my mind for some clue. My head no longer ached, neither did I feel frightened, exactly, only possessed of a disquieting agitation, an urgency of spirit: *hurry, hurry, hurry. . . .*

I sat up and looked about my room. My eyes had accustomed themselves to the starlight, and though I saw only in shades of black and grey, I could see quite clearly. There, standing next to the escritoire, was the child-woman. She seemed to feel my gaze, for she turned about and regarded me with those great dark eyes of hers, eyes filled with the calm of utter hopelessness. An overwhelming sensation of loss flowed through me, filling me with a dreadful, aching emptiness. Still I watched.

My visitor turned once more to the little desk and seated herself. Picking up a quill in her left hand, she removed the top from one of the little ink pots, dipped the quill, and began to write. The plume swayed and bobbed above her shoulder like one of the dancing marionettes I had seen at the Great Exhibition. I longed to speak, to ask her who she was, what she was doing there, but I did not. In truth, I could not. I could only sit there in my bed, watching.

How long she wrote, how long I watched, I do not know. But I had the distinct impression that the room was growing light with the first glimmering of day when, without warning, I was shaken by that same nameless horror that had sent me, as a child, screaming and stumbling through the halls and chambers of the north wing.

Wave upon wave of icy terror washed over me, and my heart pounded against my ribs like a panicked horse rearing and kicking at the walls of his stall. But I could neither move nor call out, although soundless cries tore at my throat. And still I watched the young woman.

In one smooth motion, she dropped the quill and swept up all the papers from the desk top. At the same time, she leapt to her feet, whirled about, knocking over the ink pot, and began backing, groping behind herself with the sheaf of notes, toward the fireplace.

The air became cold—unbearably cold. And even as I watched, a darkness grew within my room, swirling, eddying, flowing after the young woman, rising above her, enveloping her. Her step faltered and she began to sway, then to sink, to crumple, to melt down toward the floor. And even as she fell, the room grew dark as a bottomless pit and I felt myself falling, falling, falling. . . .

Chapter Eleven

Far off, I heard someone calling, and I struggled to open my eyes, to rise up, up out of the stygian darkness that enfolded me. But my limbs were cramped, I felt chilled to the very bone, and when I tried to move, it dawned on me that I was not in my bed. When at last I forced my eyelids open, I saw that I was huddled upon the floor before the fireplace.

Gillian leaned over me, shaking her head in bewilderment. When she saw my eyelids flutter, she cried, "Oh, law, Lady Victoria, what happent to ye? Why be ye sleepin' on floor?"

When I made no response she continued, "Look at yer room, m'Lady. Just look! There be ink spilled all over carpet. Lor' m'Lady, what happened?"

Painfully, I pushed myself to a sitting position and looked about. It was immediately evident that what Gillian said was true. One ink pot, knocked from its silver stand, had come to rest leaning against a quill that lay, forlorn and inksoaked, across a corner of the desk. The pink plume had absorbed most of the spillage, but some had trickled down onto the carpet.

Instinctively I looked at my hands. My fingers, too, were ink stained. *But it was not I who had knocked over the ink pot!*

It was shock, I suppose, but sitting there on the floor, I was gripped by an icy calm. I looked up at Gillian and said, "Don't carry on so girl! Give me your hand."

Gillian, her countenance a mask of uncertainty, helped me off the floor, onto the chaise.

Only then did I see Stella. She stood just inside the doorway, observing me with cold, unblinking eyes. Her steady stare so unnerved me that I snarled at poor Gillian, "For goodness' sake, girl, fetch me a robe . . . can't you see I'm cold?"

I was immediately sorry, of course. Gillian's broad face assumed an aggrieved expression as she scurried off to the wardrobe to return moments later with a large, fleecy shawl. Having tucked it about me, she asked, "Will ye have yer tea, now, m'Lady?"

Still in the throes of that icy calm, I said, "If you please, Gillian."

She turned to the table and filled a cup, then placed it on the stand beside me.

And all the while, though I did my best to ignore her, I was acutely aware of Stella; each time I stole a glance in her direction there she was, like a vengeful stone gargoyle, watching every move.

I thanked Gillian for her kindness, then sent her off to fetch something to clean up the ink. When I looked again, Stella had gone.

Thank goodness, I thought, and picked up my cup of tea — or tried to. My hand shook so that I could not hold the cup to my lips. Quickly I put it back on its saucer, and without warning, two salt tears rolled down my cheeks.

What was happening to me? I wondered. It was only a dream. But then, how did the ink get spilled? Why had I been lying on the floor with ink on my fingers?

At that moment there was a light rap on my door and Helaine, not waiting for my answer, glided into the room — I say *glided,* for that is how she always moved, silently, smoothly. Stella moved the same way. She could walk right up behind you, and you never knew she was there until the hair on the back of your neck began to rise. . . . I shivered.

Helaine had stopped just inside the threshold and stood smiling at me. She was wearing a morning coat of eggshell satin that hung in flowing ripples from an embroidered yoke. It fastened at her throat and wrists with tiny ivory buttons. Her hair was knotted high upon her head, and the ends fell down her back in a stream of shining red-gold.

So shocked was I to see her there, I could only stare, speechless, while a knot formed in my stomach.

"Victoria, dear little sister," she murmured, "Pray, what is the trouble? Have you hurt yourself?"

I tried, with the back of my hand, to brush away the tears that clung to my lashes. "No, no. It was only a small accident. I . . . I tripped."

"You are certain you are all right? Stella was so concerned."

Indeed, I thought waspishly. The old witch was probably *concerned* that I had not broken my neck! Aloud I said, in as cool a tone as I could muster, "As you can see, Helaine, I am fine. Stella should not have troubled you."

Suddenly my sister-in-law crossed the room with that smooth, light step and, smiling warmly, sank down beside me on the chaise. "Sweet little sister," she purred, her voice as warm, as intimate as her smile. "Forgive me for letting so much time pass since our last visit. How shameful to think it has taken an accident to bring me to your side."

For some reason I cannot name, her words made me feel guilty, as if it were I who had been remiss. "No . . . no," I stammered. "There was no need—" and having said the words, I immediately recognized how rude they sounded. My cheeks flamed scarlet. "I mean I'm very glad to see you, but . . ."

Her soft laughter interrupted my disjointed speech. "Never mind, my dear. I understand. We have both been busy, but in future nothing shall interfere . . . we are going to be good friends, are we not?"

I nodded, but I did not feel any degree of certainty. Indeed, I felt angry and rebellious as well as awkward and uncomfortable. I was tempted to order her out of my room, but somehow I could not. I had every right, I told myself. She had certainly given me provocation. And yet she couched her jibes in such seemingly innocent terms. Was it jealousy, rather than true dislike that I felt for Helaine? Was it envy that filled me with resentment, no matter what she said?

Now Helaine tipped her head to one side and observed me with a frank, open stare. "You look tired, Victoria . . . perhaps you have not been sleeping well?"

"Please, do not trouble yourself about the state of my health," I replied, trying to sound haughty. But even in my own ears there was a defensive ring to my words.

Ignoring my request, Helaine continued, "You are quite recovered from your headache?"

"There is nothing—"

But Helaine did not let me finish. She reached out her hand and brushed at the tears drying on my cheeks. "There, dear, no need to pretend with me. Please don't think me presumptuous . . . it is only that I *do* want to be your friend. You have not looked well of late—so pale and drawn. Now the headaches, and last night's . . . accident."

She paused, looked embarrassed, then took a deep breath and plunged on. "There, I've said it. Please do not think me rude. After all, I am a member of the family. It was Stella who told me you had fallen—not to gossip, you understand. No, no. Stella knows how much I want to be your friend."

When I remained silent, my sister-in-law reached out and took both my hands in hers, smiled tenderly into my eyes. "Please, dear Victoria, if there is anything I can do, anything you'd like to tell me?"

Her beautiful face was so filled with kindness and concern, and I was so lonely, so miserable. I gazed into her eyes, and the words seemed to flow unbidden from my lips.

"Oh, Helaine. I don't know what is happening to me. I'm so frightened, and last night . . . I must have been walking in my sleep, and—"

If Gillian had not returned just then, I think I should have blurted out the whole story—told Helaine about my secret friend, and the dreams that had become nightmares. However, Gillian did return, bringing my revelations to a halt.

A flicker of irritation darkened my sister-in-law's brow, but she said nothing except, "Come, dear little sister . . . let me help you."

She put her arm about me, steadied me as I rose to my feet. I did not resist as she guided me back to my bed, and I was soon huddled under the blankets, my eyes closed.

Helaine left immediately, but I could hear Gillian moving about the room cleaning up the ink, setting the desk straight, picking up the tea tray. Then she came over and stood beside my bed. I could hear her breathing, deep and regular. Poor Gillian. I sensed her indecision, her concern.

At last she spoke in a guarded whisper, "Be ye all right, m'Lady?"

I hesitated, then decided it best to answer her. "Yes, Gillian, just very tired. I did not sleep well last night. Please tell Lady Elizabeth I wish to remain in bed today."

Gillian continued to stand beside my bed, fidgeting. However, when I did not open my eyes, she finally departed.

I felt wretched, physically and emotionally. I was so tired, and my thoughts were all muddled, and I didn't know what to do. Silently, my face twisted with the effort to hold back the tears, I began to cry again. I must, indeed, have cried myself to sleep, because when Elizabeth rapped at my door, I wakened with a start.

The morning's sleep, short as it was, had revived me somewhat, and I had recovered my composure sufficiently to sit up and smile.

Elizabeth moved quickly to my bedside. Close behind her came Gillian, pushing a tea cart laden with cups and pot, and all sorts of goodies: a basket of freshly baked rolls, a crock of butter, and a jar of jam, as well as a platter of sliced cheese and cold sliced meats. Another plate held small fruited cakes, and there was a bowl of fresh bilberries and clotted cream.

Now Gillian took a large tray with short legs from under the tea cart and set it on the bed, over my knees, while Elizabeth plumped the pillows behind me. With a nervous smile, Gillian withdrew.

These preparations completed, Elizabeth drew up a chair and sat down close beside me. "There," she said, "I've come to take lunch with you. It has been far too long since we have sat together and talked. I miss you, little love."

Despite the fact that I had long since forgiven her for the incident with the note — for telling Papa — a coolness had remained between us. Now the very sound of her voice was comforting, and the last of my reserve melted. "Oh, Elizabeth," I replied, "I do love you," and though my voice shook and a tear splashed down my cheek, I did manage a watery smile.

Elizabeth now directed my attention to a third person, who had just entered my room: Betsy, the newest member of the household staff. She was carrying a large kettle of water and a spirit lamp. A bright, comely young woman of fifteen or sixteen, her movements were quick and assured. She put the lamp on the tea tray, set the kettle upon it, then lit the wick under it.

When she had completed this task, she stood back and looked at me, her brown eyes bright and admiring. Then, with a wide and guileless smile, she remarked, "Aye, Miss, ye do look right pretty sittin' there."

It was not a fitting thing for a serving girl to say, but the frank admiration that had prompted her words was totally disarming. "Thank you," I said, and smiled back.

Betsy had been added to the household staff shortly after Adam and Helaine arrived. It had been intended that she should help in the kitchen and learn to serve at table. However, rumor had it that she spent more time playing with the kittens and pinching tidbits for the dogs than she ever did in peeling potatoes or washing pots and pans. Nevertheless, it was considered that she did a creditable job of serving, and she was well liked by staff and family alike.

Elizabeth said sternly, "That will do, Betsy! You may go now."

Betsy curtsied and left, almost dancing. I glanced at Elizabeth, then, and saw that she was nodding in quiet approval, despite her mild rebuke. She remained silent for a while. Although her eyes were fixed on me, her mind was not.

She seemed to consider her next words with great care. At length she said, "I am worried about you, little love. You have grown thin and pale this summer. You are too much in your room alone. You are too quiet."

Once more she paused, and appeared to consider her words with great care before she continued. "I have prayed most earnestly concerning the situation, and I do believe Betsy is God's answer. For all she is so young, I believe she would make a happy companion for you. You need a new direction for your days, and Betsy, too, needs help and love. You might even undertake to teach her to read and write. Do you think you would like that?"

Elizabeth's words took me so completely by surprise, I just stared at her.

"I have found her," Elizabeth continued, "on several occasions, seated on the floor in the library holding a book ever so carefully upon her knees, staring at the page, tracing the words with her fingertip, as if she hoped that in some way she might absorb their meaning. I asked her if she could read and she said, 'No, m'Lady, but belike someday I may.' "

Dear Elizabeth. Mimicry of the local accent was natural to her, as easy as breathing, with no hint of malice in it. She had spent much time with the women and children of the village, as well as amongst the tenant farmers. As wife of the village doctor, she had accompanied him on his rounds, and assisted him in nursing the sick. Now, as wife of Lord Garth, she had continued to give comfort and aid to the people in their times of sorrow, always ready to do all that she could to ease their many burdens. She loved them, and they returned her affection.

Now she wanted, yet again, to provide for one less fortunate, and although the idea was a novel one, moving Betsy from the kitchen to a status only a step below that of family, it pleased me. Perhaps, I thought, Elizabeth is right. I do need something new to occupy my time, somebody to think of other than myself, and I asked, "Do you think Betsy would agree, Elizabeth? Do you think she might really like to be my companion, and learn to read and write?"

Elizabeth nodded, and it was obvious from her expression that she was pleased by my response.

"How would we arrange such a thing?"

Elizabeth explained, "I have been concerned about the child from the day she first arrived. She is bright and quick, with a gentle quality about her that belies her humble birth."

Elizabeth paused, as if giving the idea one last consideration, then declared, "Yes, it is the right thing to do. I will have her bring a kitten. It will make a nice opening. She is as tender with our animal life as ever were you and Adam. You see, I have been thinking about this for some time."

Whilst Elizabeth was talking, she handed me a serving of bilberries and a bowl of clotted cream, and while I spooned cream over my berries, Elizabeth selected a roll, which she broke and buttered before handing it to me. I put it on my tray.

"Do you remember when I fell off the spotted pony and broke my arm, Elizabeth? You sat beside my bed then and buttered my rolls for me."

"And poured you tea as well, if I'm not mistaken."

We smiled at each other, memories warm between us. Then Elizabeth spoke again. "Thomas was most worried when you did not come down for breakfast."

I had quite forgotten that the Hornabys were with us, and I felt a sharp twinge of guilt remembering Thomas's never-failing affection. "Oh, I am so sorry. Please tell him I will be quite well again by tomorrow."

"You know they must all return to London on the morrow?"

"So soon?" I was surprised by the feeling of regret that swept over me.

"You are fond of Thomas, are you not, little love?" Elizabeth searched my face with hope-filled eyes. In that moment, I realized how great must be Elizabeth's sorrow: to have her first-born son marry a stranger, without the family's consent; to know the pain his actions had caused me.

"Yes, Elizabeth," I assured her, "I am very fond of Thomas." I hoped my words afforded her some modicum of comfort.

We finished the meal in silence, a comfortable, reassuring silence, and when the tea was finished and Elizabeth had rung for Gillian to come and clear away, I felt more at peace than I had in many a day. Elizabeth patted my shoulder and leaned near to kiss my cheek before she left. "You needn't come down to dinner unless you truly feel able, little love. Now rest. Betsy will be here soon, and I am sure you will find her a joy."

Within the hour, Betsy's forthright knock sounded upon my door, followed immediately by the presentation of her freshly washed self. Her thick chestnut hair had been brushed until it gleamed. Her eyes, too, were brown, and a bright light glowed deep within them, bespeaking a merry, loving spirit.

She stopped just inside the door and beamed at me. "I couldn't choose the fattest, happiest kitten, as me Lady Elizabeth bid me, m'Lady," she announced without preamble. "So I brought me favorite." And out of the folds of her apron, she drew the homeliest kitten I have ever seen.

Pure white, he was, with a thick and glossy coat. But that glossy coat, unfortunately, was the sum total of his attributes. He was of the long, lean, large-boned, well-muscled variety of cat that never gets fat and round and cuddly. His tail was unreasonably long and ended in a point. His ears were large, but his face was small, as were his close-set eyes, and his nose was like nothing I had ever before seen on the face of a cat. Long, it was, and pendulous in appearance, and the pink of his flesh showed rosily through its thin fur covering, giving him the look of a wizened sot or an old beggar.

"Be he all right, m'Lady?" Betsy's eyes were round and questioning.

I laughed and held out my arms. "You could not have

chosen better, Betsy. Bring him here, and we will admire him together."

"He do be a different sort, don't he, m'Lady?"

"Indeed he is," I agreed.

She put the kitten down upon the bed, close beside me and he began to purr and knead the down coverlet intently.

"What do you call him?"

Betsy indicated that she had been unable to settle upon just the right name for this most unusual animal.

"He is very special . . . he should have a very special name." I wrinkled my brow in deep thought.

We sat in silence for a few moments, racking our brains. Then I had an inspiration. "How do you like the name Cyrano?"

"Indeed, it be a fine-sounding name," Betsy offered hesitantly, "but if ye please, m'Lady, what do be special about that name?"

"Well, it was made famous by a Frenchman, a very brave and gallant soldier with the soul of a poet . . . but he had a most unfortunate nose!"

Betsy's eyes danced. "Just like me poor kitty, here!" she exclaimed, and we both laughed.

I liked Betsy immediately, and the feeling seemed to be mutual. Despite the seven or so years' difference in our ages, we seemed to share an understanding, an ability to communicate with just a smile, a nod, a roll of the eye. I felt relaxed, at ease, happier that afternoon, laughing and talking with Betsy, watching the antics of Cyrano, and planning things we would like to do someday, than I had felt for what seemed like a lifetime. Betsy was not in the least awed by the new situation, but took it entirely in stride.

Thus the afternoon passed. The light falling through the French windows began to fade. The kitten curled himself into a ball and fell asleep, and Betsy and I subsided into a gentle stillness.

And as we sat there in silence, Elizabeth's words came back to me. "Betsy," I asked, "do you like it here at Greystone Manor? Do you like working in the kitchen?"

Her response was quick and forthright. " 'Tis warm in winter and cool in summer in the great kitchen, m'Lady. An' Lueddy, her knew me old granny when her were still alive, so I be not lonely. Aye, I do be grateful."

"But are you *happy,* Betsy?" I persisted.

Her look never faltered. "M'Lady, family here at Greystone Manor be gentle folk, an' kind, an' I do thank ye for takin' me in."

And then there it was again—that communication without words. I knew that Betsy thought I was to scold her for being remiss in her chores, for playing with the kittens when there were birds to pluck and herbs to chop.

"Betsy," I hurried to reassure her, "do not think that I would ever scold you. That is not my place, even were it necessary. Rather, I must tell you that Lady Elizabeth has observed that you are a good young woman."

A smile was slowly taking over Betsy's face, a smile that came from within and shone in her eyes. Nodding her head, she stated, "I do try hard, m'Lady."

She is indeed a delight, I thought. Aloud I continued, "Lady Elizabeth knows that I am too much alone, having no friends of my own age with whom to visit and talk. We have discussed the matter and we . . . I . . . should be pleased if you would be a companion for me. You would move into the room next to mine, and I would undertake to teach you to read and to write, to embroider, and to ride. Would you like that, Betsy?"

"Oh, m'Lady," she said. "Ohhhh, m'Lady!"

Thus it was settled, and when Betsy had left my room that evening, I lay back against my pillows thinking that perhaps my life did have some point, some meaning, after all.

I arose early the following morning hoping to have a few minutes alone with Thomas before they all returned to London. Even so, everyone was already gathered at the breakfast table when I entered, and I was greeted by a chorus of *Good morning* and *How are you?*

I took a currant bun from the sideboard and poured myself a cup of cocoa, then went to sit beside Thomas. He had risen when I entered and stood holding a chair for me. His eyes followed my every movement anxiously, and a feeling of guilt swept over me.

After acknowledging the general greeting and assuring everyone that I was quite recovered, I turned to Thomas and said softly, "I'm so sorry I was indisposed yesterday. Do forgive me."

As he seated me, he murmured, "Of course . . . I understand completely. All that matters is that you are well again today . . . that we can have at least a few more moments together."

When he had reseated himself beside me, I enquired, "What time is your train?"

"We shall have to leave for the station within the hour." Regret was clear in his voice.

"Then let us go for one last walk in the park," I said, rising quickly.

"But you have not eaten—"

"I am not hungry . . . I seldom eat breakfast."

Thomas did not argue. We excused ourselves and walked out into the garden. The sky was a glorious gentian blue overhead, and only the gentlest of breezes moved across the grass, whispered in the rose beds, riffled the leaves upon the branches of the trees. We paused at the garden's edge, breathing deeply of the crisp, flower-scented air.

Thomas remarked, "What a beautiful morning."

We continued on across the formal garden, and then passed into the park, where we were soon lost to view from the house. We strolled in silence for a while until we came to a stone bench.

Thomas laid his hand upon my arm. "Shall we rest here for a moment?"

I smiled my acquiescence, and we sat down.

Thomas took a deep breath, then spoke all in a rush, "I know that now is not the best of times to speak, but I do love you, Victoria, with all my heart."

I could only sit with my head bowed, wishing that I could truthfully tell him I returned his love. But I could not.

However, he was not waiting for me to speak. "I have only one more year of internship before I can join Papa in his practice. May I continue to hope? Will you write?"

I looked at him then, and my heart was full of gratitude. "Dear Thomas." My voice shook. "If ever I can fall in love, surely it must be with you."

"Then I am content. I know it would be impossible for you to live your life without love . . . there is too much passion in you. When you are ready, I will be waiting."

I made no effort to resist when he took me in his arms and kissed me, a hungry yet gentle kiss. Rather, I returned his kiss, before burying my face against his shoulder, and I held him close as I replied, "I promise, I will write to you, and you must promise to come visit me again."

He did not answer but kissed me again, then rose to his feet, drawing me with him. "We must get back. It is almost time for us to leave."

A half-hour later, Elizabeth, Papa, John, and I stood at the manor door and waved them all a fond farewell. I don't know why Adam and Helaine were not there.

As soon as the carriage bearing Thomas and his family to the station had disappeared down the drive, I hurried off to the kitchen to visit old Lueddy. Betsy's mention of her the day before had touched my conscience, for I had neglected the old soul for many a week past. When we were children, Adam and I, Lueddy had watched over us, told us stories, tended our cuts and bruises, and kissed our tears away. But as we grew older, matured, we spent less and less of our time in her company. Now, as I hurried along the corridor leading to the kitchen, I realized with dismay that I had not even spoken with her since the day Helaine and Adam arrived from Paris.

When I entered the kitchen, Betsy ran across the room to greet me and lead me to the fireplace, where Lueddy sat rocking in a sturdy wooden chair. I felt a sense of shock when I saw how frail she had grown. She was thinner than I remembered her to be, and her once round and rosy cheeks were pale, and etched with fine creases. However her eyes were still clear, and at sight of me she brightened perceptibly. Stretching forth her hands in greeting, she said, "Lor' love us, m'Lady. Ain't it fine to see ye! Like me little bird come back to me."

Her words brought a lump to my throat and I had to swallow, twice, before I could speak. "Dear Lueddy . . . how are you?"

Smiling, nodding, she replied, "I be fine, fine."

Dropping to my knees beside her, I kissed her sunken cheek. "I'm so sorry I have not been to see you. Let us have a cup of tea and talk a bit."

"Aye, aye . . . a cup o' tea. 'Twould be fine." She grasped my hands in hers with a grip that was surprisingly strong and gazed directly into my face.

At that moment one of the kitchen maids brought me a chair, and Betsy, who had gone to make the tea, returned. Lueddy released her grip upon my hands to accept the cup offered her by Betsy. Quickly, I rose from my knees and sat in the chair.

"Has Betsy told you that she is going to move upstairs to be my companion?"

Lueddy smiled. "Aye. 'Tis a fine thing. Betsy will be safe with ye."

"Safe?"

"Aye, and happy . . . happy."

"It will be a fine thing for both of us. Both of us will be happy . . . and safe." What had prompted her to say *safe?* I wondered. It had an unsettling effect on me.

A shadow moved over Lueddy's face, clouding her eyes. She glanced at Betsy, then back at me.

"It was Lady Elizabeth's idea . . . to ask Betsy to be my companion. I wish I had thought of it myself. I think it a wonderful plan." I tried to keep my tone bright and cheerful, but something in Lueddy's demeanor was making me increasingly uneasy.

"Aye. . . ." The word was uttered on a long outward breath. Then she closed her eyes and seemed to drift off to sleep. Betsy took the cup from the old woman's hands and set it on the floor beside her chair. And for a time we sat in silence. Even the clatter from the kitchen staff seemed hushed. Cyrano appeared from behind the brine vat and jumped upon my knees. I sat stiffly in my chair and tried to drink my tea.

I was just preparing to rise when Lueddy again opened her eyes. She reached out and grabbed my arm, frightening Cyrano, who leaped to the floor and skittered away. Then, with a vehemence that made the hair on the back of my neck rise, Lueddy whispered, "I'll not leave ye again. Never will I leave ye, little bird."

Her words sent an icy chill down my spine, but I could not move for the fierceness of her grip upon my arm. For a long moment, her face remained tense, her eyes bright with fear. Then her lids closed, her body relaxed, her fingers slipped from my arm. Once more she slipped into a troubled sleep.

I stood up and I'm certain all the color had drained from my face and Betsy, seeing my distress, rose quickly to her feet. Coming quickly to my side, she slipped an arm about my waist to steady me. "It's all right, m'Lady. Lueddy be very old, and she gets confused, but she be all right. When she wakes, she'll be fine."

I took a deep breath, pressed my suddenly cold hands together. "Thank you, Betsy." I stood for a moment more gazing down into the face of the sleeping woman. It upset me that Lueddy should mistake me for my grandmother. It frightened me, too. Lueddy had always been so bright, so merry . . . so strong. How could she have aged so in such a short time?

And suddenly I was filled with anger. It's all so unfair! I thought. I have lost Adam, and now Lueddy, too, is slipping away from me. I felt like throwing something, smashing something into little pieces. Instead, I leaned down and kissed Lueddy's soft, wrinkled cheek.

I took my leave of Betsy with as much grace as I could muster, saying, "Come to see me tomorrow and we will begin making plans for the future." Then I returned to my own room.

I don't know what I intended to do. I glanced about, started to sit down, then noticed something odd about the fireplace. I stepped nearer, and observed that the grate contained the charred remains of several sheets of paper. Mystified, I leaned nearer, and the movement of my body stirred the air, causing the burned pages to shatter into a pile of gray ash. But in so doing, it also revealed a small piece of scorched but unconsumed paper at the center of the heap.

I stared at it, and something cold and dark breathed inside my head, *Don't touch it! Leave it there!* But the warning voice deep in my mind could not stay my hand. Gingerly, I reach out, fished the scrap of paper from amongst the ashes, spread it upon the hearth. And as I looked at it, the breath caught in my throat.

I had seen that round and childish hand before. But it was not possible! She was only a dream. Nevertheless, someone had penned the words:

. . . now I know that he is dead — murdered — I will have my revenge.

Chapter Twelve

Betsy was given the room next to mine, and I threw myself whole-heartedly into the task of selecting furnishings for her comfort and helping her settle in. A connecting door made for easy access from one chamber to the other, and in no time at all we had established a pleasant daily routine.

Although this new arrangement, moving Betsy from below stairs to a position so close to the family, was without precedent, little notice was taken by the other members of the family or by the household staff. And Betsy was wise beyond her years. Endowed by nature with common sense and native wit, she did not seek to rush into her new life. Rather, she subsided into a period of metamorphosis, wherein she sought to transform herself from kitchen maid to lady.

She seemed to understand far better than I the importance of knowing the correct spoon to use at table, producing the right inflection when saying *good morning*, the ability to turn a graceful phrase, to recognize the proper time, the proper place, and the proper way.

And she needed to be told things only once. Overnight, it seemed, her *ye's* became *you's*, her *na's* and *nary's* became *not's*, her *wif's* became *with's*. And so it was with everything she undertook. She was determined to learn all that I could teach her, and more if possible.

Even before Betsy's education was well underway, there was the matter of wardrobe to consider—not only for Betsy, but for me. I had long since outgrown the things Miss Twitchle had made for me on our trip to London. Even had that not been so, fashions had undergone considerable change since the days of the Great Exhibition. I believe both Papa and Elizabeth were piqued by the comparison between Helaine, in her beautiful and elegant Paris gowns, cut in the latest styles, and me in my old and far-from-fashionable dresses.

So Elizabeth sent to London for a seamstress — Aunt Drusilla's Miss Twitchle, in fact. She arrived the following week, bringing with her a dozen bolts of cloth, yards of lace and of ribbon, multitudes of buttons, pins, and spools of thread, a baize-covered dressmaker's dummy, and a wondrous new invention called a sewing machine. Together with her treasures, Miss Twitchle was soon installed in a large room in the east wing.

For the next several weeks, Betsy and I spent a good part of our time being measured and fitted and pinned. Nevertheless, we continued our lessons, with Betsy reciting her ABC's and multiplication tables while we stood, enduring the seemingly endless agony of having hems turned, bodices darted to fit just so.

Betsy was an apt and eager student — far better than I had ever been. She took to books like a kitten to cream, and had mastered the rudiments of reading within a matter of days. In truth, I soon found myself hard pressed to provide suitable material for her avid young mind.

Fortunately Miss Jones, to whom we now referred as librarian, had stayed on at Greystone Manor after I completed my formal studies, and was now engaged in writing a history of the Garths. When it became evident that Betsy was, indeed, a gifted student, Miss Jones was overjoyed to take charge of her academic education, leaving me free to concentrate upon such things as etiquette and deportment, sewing and riding.

As for me, I had put that bit of charred paper, with its insidious words, into the drawer with the first unexplainable note, and steadfastly refused to let my mind dwell upon it.

Thus, for a while, Betsy and I were very busy and very happy. She shared with me the love for our furred and feathered friends that I had once shared with Adam. She also evidenced great love for the old house that had given Adam and me so many years of fun and adventure.

For almost a month, I did not dream; neither did I have time to worry about the scribbled words, the spilled ink, the ashes on my hearth. My appetite improved, and I even felt almost at ease on those rare occasions when Helaine was present, though I did continue to speculate concerning her presence in the north wing and the events the day I went there to investigate.

Actually, we saw very little of Helaine. She did not ride, and neither did she seem to care to walk in the park or sit in the garden. It was a circumstance that suited me to a T, for Betsy and I much enjoyed carrying our books or our embroidery out into the garden, where we sat in the shade and either read aloud, or chatted happily.

Adam and his wife did join the family for dinner at least once a week, and did, though very rarely, take tea with us. On those occasions, Helaine was always charming and gracious, but if she stood too close to me, the hair on the back of my neck would rise, and something inside me would turn cold and hard and withdraw into the most secret recesses of my soul.

From time to time I would see Helaine walking the balcony alone in the darkness or, more often, accompanied by Stella. There was a fervid aura of protectiveness, of possessiveness about the woman when she was with her mistress that was unmistakable, even from a distance. Her utter devotion seemed, in fact, for some reason I could not put my finger on, unhealthy. She always walked a half step behind Helaine, her bearing and demeanor full of hauteur and pride.

It did strike me as odd that I saw Helaine with Adam only at formal family gatherings. 'Twas never he who walked with her upon the balcony; never, to my knowledge, did they stroll together in the garden. However, Adam had totally immersed himself in his new duties as bailiff, and he, too, for the most part, remained aloof from the family. Only at breakfast did he appear, alone and relaxed without his wife. He had grown thinner. There were lines about his eyes, and laughter no longer came so readily to his lips.

He made no further attempt to approach me when I was alone. No mention was ever made of the blow I had struck him that day in the great hall. If he bore me ill will because of it, I could not tell. For my part, I felt no guilt—even though, in retrospect, I found myself wishing I had taken him in my arms and comforted him when I had the opportunity, or had thrown caution to the winds and ridden off to meet him—somewhere—anywhere. . . .

My emotions were sorely muddled, my heart steadfastly refusing to believe what my mind so clearly saw and understood. Adam had chosen Helaine.

Nevertheless, for a little while each morning, sitting across the table from him at breakfast, I could pretend that we were still those carefree children who had roamed the manor together, who had ridden the cliff paths wild and free. Yet even then, sitting in the cheerful comfort of the breakfast room, surrounded by the same rich aroma of currant buns and cocoa, with Elizabeth urging us to take just one more bite, and Papa beaming in fatherly benevolence, even then there was a constraint upon us. I could feel, rather than see, a tenseness about Adam's smile, a restraint in his laughter, a vague unease in the set of his shoulders, and my heart would ache.

Oh, I tried to hate him, tried always to keep in mind how he had deceived and betrayed me. And even though I was filled with shame when I remembered how eagerly I had once offered myself to him, I still longed to tell him I forgave him. But the words stuck in my throat.

One morning, not long after Betsy had moved upstairs, Adam failed to make his appearance at breakfast. I dawdled over my cocoa as long as I could, and still he did not come. I had to give up at last and, feeling disappointed and depressed, I went back upstairs.

I wandered aimlessly about my room for a while, trying to think how I could fill the hours until noon. Betsy would be with Miss Jones all morning and so I was alone. Alone, I thought. All alone. And as I stood looking aimlessly about, my glance encountered *Jeremiah's Journal,* still lying on the mantel where I had left it — how long ago, it seemed. But seeing the journal triggered a memory. There had been a third ledger.

At least it would be something to do, I thought, and I left my room to hurry off to the library. I went straight to the desk, sat down, and opened the drawer. All was exactly as I had left it. I withdrew the book, laid it on the desktop, and turned back the cover.

A glance at the first page told me that I had found something that could be of great interest: an inventory of all the treasures that had at one time belonged to the Greystone estate, together with date of acquisition, name of individual who acquired each piece, and, in most cases, the price paid. Included were paintings, silver, china, objets d'art.

Excitement took hold of me. I turned to the next page. Listed there were a number of oriental rugs — I could only assume they were the ones that now lay spread on the stone floor of the library — and tapestries, undoubtably the ones that now hung on the walls of my room. I had never dreamed how valuable they were.

Last of all, the journal contained an accounting of the Greystone jewels. I read the list with growing amazement. Could anyone really have possessed such wealth? Rings and brooches and pendants; diamonds and rubies, sapphires and emeralds. And the pearls — according to the ledger, Christina's father had given her the rope of pearls on her sixteenth birthday.

I closed the book, stared at it, stunned. Then I opened it again, skimmed through it once more. I could not imagine such wealth as those jewels had represented. Had my — that blackguard — really squandered it all?

The excitement that had accompanied the discovery of the ledger, and the information it contained, seeped away. I wondered if Papa had any idea of how wealthy the family had been. But it could hardly matter now, though it might be of some help to Miss Jones in compiling her Garth family history.

With a sigh, I put the inventory with the other papers that were still awaiting Papa's examination, promising myself I would tell him of my most recent discovery at dinner and remind him that all these old papers needed his attention.

Back in my room once more, I glanced at the clock. More than an hour remained until lunchtime. I walked over to my French doors, pulled them open. It was a gorgeous day outside, and it occurred to me that it would be pleasant to walk in the garden, perhaps cut some flowers for the dinner table.

I put on a large-brimmed hat to protect me from the sun, which was shining brightly that morning, and made my way out through the potting room, where I donned an apron and picked up a pair of cotton gloves. Then, armed with a flower basket and some pruning shears, I continued on to the garden.

The question was, what to pick? Everything looked so lovely: dahlias were just coming into bloom, there were daisies in abundance and long-stemmed gladioli. But it was the fragrance of the roses that finally drew me. How lovely they would be, I thought, floating in the crystal bowl Papa had given Elizabeth for Christmas.

I was moving along the path, humming to myself as I proceeded from bush to bush, seeking only the most perfect blossoms. There were bees all about me gathering honey for the long winter ahead. Their soft buzzing reminded me of that day so long ago in the dell—of my bee sting and the performance I had staged for Adam, and of the kiss that had followed. It was a poignant memory and, momentarily distracted, I snagged myself on a thorn.

Uttering a small cry of distress, I jerked my hand back out of the bush, causing a tiny spine to break off and embed itself in my finger. It had gone straight through the fabric of my gloves and was lodged securely in my flesh. I dropped the shears into the basket with the flowers, set it on the ground, and was gingerly removing the glove when a shadow fell across me.

I glanced up to find Adam staring down at me. "Can I help?" he asked, but he had already taken my hand in his. While I stood agape with surprise, he turned his attention to my smarting finger. Deftly he withdrew the thorn, squeezed out a drop of blood to cleanse the wound, then wrapped it in his clean handkerchief.

That done, he continued to hold my hand. In fact, he turned, drew it through his arm, and started to stroll along the path, forcing me to accompany him.

His nearness, his touch, were like magic, setting my pulses racing. I knew I was playing with fire, and yet I could not bring myself to draw away from him. What harm can it do, I asked myself, to walk with him here in the garden?

And so we continued on for a while, in silence, until we came to the edge of the park. The trees were in full leaf. It was dark in the shadows beneath their wide-spreading boughs. We would soon be lost to sight from the manor house. We would be alone. . . .

What prompted me, in that instant before we entered the shelter of the trees, to glance back, I do not know. But look back I did. And there, leaning on the balcony balustrade, was Stella. I cannot explain why the sight of her should have frightened me so, but I stopped short. Wrenched my hand from Adam's grasp.

Startled by my action, he turned to face me.

I did not give him time to speak. "This is madness," I snapped, and turned and fled back up the path. I was actually in the potting room before I remembered the basket of flowers. However, I did not return for them until I had assured myself that Adam was no longer in sight.

I returned to my room much shaken: furious with Adam for having attempted to draw me into a clandestine meeting, for I knew that had been his intent; furious with myself for letting Stella so discomfit me that I had denied myself that small pleasure. We would have done nothing improper, I assured myself. It was just that it would have been so wonderful to be alone with him, to talk. But in my heart, I knew I was only fooling myself.

Perhaps if I had had someone with whom I could share these feelings, I could have come to terms with them. But there was no one. Though Betsy and I were fast becoming good friends, I was not yet sure enough of that friendship to bare my innermost feelings to her.

How could I say to her, "I am in love with a married man. I long for a rendezvous with him . . ." No. It would never do.

Lunchtime came, and my thoughts were still in chaos. When Betsy popped her head through the connecting door to see if I was ready to go down, I asked her to make my apologies to the family. "Tell them I have a headache."

Immediately she was full of concern, but I assured her that it was nothing. The truth of the matter was, I could not face the thought of sitting at table, making small talk. Later, when Betsy returned, I begged to be left alone. She offered to read to me, but I assured her I would be better left to rest. "Perhaps I'll take a nap. . . ."

"If you are sure," she said, and I could hear the worry in her tone. "But first let me brush out your hair. It will relax you. Then you must lie down. A nap will do you good." She made me smile, so like a mother hen was she.

No sooner had Betsy completed her ministrations and left via the connecting door than a rap sounded on the other. When I made no reply, the rap sounded again, and then the door swung open. Helaine stood in the doorway, smiling that small intimate smile that never failed to send a chill through my veins.

She was wearing a simple frock of pale green organdy with long full sleeves, finished at throat and wrists with a froth of Irish lace. Her hair had been smoothed back, then knotted at the nape of her neck, and from her ears dangled a pair of tear-drop earrings set with opals and jade.

"Oh!" she murmured. "Were you sleeping? I'm so sorry if I have wakened you. I only meant to pay a small visit."

Though I offered no word of greeting, she moved across

the room and sat down beside me. "I have been hoping that you would come to visit me," she continued, with just the trace of a moue.

How did the woman always manage to make me feel guilty?

"But," she hastened to add, "I know how busy you have been."

"Yes," I replied, finding my tongue at last, "I have been very busy."

As was always the case when Helaine came near me, I longed to shrink away. For all her disarming smile and gentle words, I sensed a coldness in her. My rash outburst during our previous meeting, when I had revealed my unhappiness to her, had in no way lessened my distrust of her. Indeed, I hoped with all my heart that she had forgotten my confidences.

She reached over and patted my hand. "I understand. After all, we are sisters-in-law, and though circumstances do seem to keep us apart, I insist we shall be good friends." She paused and stared at me.

I stared back.

With a little shrug, she continued, "There must be many things we could share . . . we do have so much in common."

Her words only served to draw the knot in my stomach tighter. For the life of me, I could think of nothing I held in common with Helaine.

"For example, we share the same love."

Startled, I could not hide the agitation her words aroused in me. Was she telling me, I wondered, that she knew how much I still loved Adam? And, of course, Stella, who had watched this morning as Adam was leading me into the shadows under the trees—and it suddenly occurred to me that my sudden flight had undoubtedly given the appearance of guilt—yes, Stella would have told Helaine what she had witnessed, would have recalled for Helaine what she had witnessed the day she stood watching Adam and me through the French doors of my room.

There was something sinister about Helaine's soft laughter as she continued, "We both love . . . this house . . . all the people in it. . . ."

"Yes, of course . . . the house . . . the people," I parroted, my face flaming.

When I said no more, Helaine shook her head, and a fine crease formed between her brows. Her lips parted, and she tilted her head to one side, the better to observe me.

Feeling like a trinket on display, I wondered anew how much Adam had told her about me—about us.

The silence stretched taut and I jumped when Helaine spoke. "Really, Victoria . . . are you quite well? You still look tired."

"Perhaps . . . I have been very busy."

She shrugged, sighed, seemed to consider me with great care before she sat back and glanced about. "How lovely your room is," she murmured. Then, almost as an afterthought, she added, "Did not this very room belong to your grandmother, the Lady Christina?"

"Yes, it did. Some of the furniture was hers as well." Glad no longer to be the object of her attention, I was full of information. It did not occur to me until much later to wonder how she had come by that knowledge—Adam, of course, was the obvious answer.

"They say you are very like your dear grandmother." Helaine let her gaze brush over me, sighed again, and added under her breath, "Poor demented woman."

Shocked by my sister-in-law's lack of tact, horrified by the implication of her words, I could only gape at her.

Helaine leaned nearer, and her eyes glittered. "Did you know," she whispered, "that Christina walked in her sleep . . . she saw things that weren't there?"

The breath stopped in my throat, and the room seemed to swim and sway about me. My mouth worked, but I could find no words to refute what she was saying—what she was implying.

And while I still sought to formulate a suitable response, Helaine rose to her feet and crossed to the door. There she hesitated and turned back. "We must visit again soon, dear little sister. Now sleep well." With a trill of laughter, she raised her fingers to her lips and blew me a kiss.

Then she was gone, but the scent of her exotic perfume lingered in the air just as her parting words lingered in my mind, driving sleep from me, leaving me to sit and stare into the fire. *Like my grandmother,* Helaine had said. *Like my grandmother, who walked in her sleep and saw things that were not there.* . . .

I do not clearly recall the rest of that day. I must have gone to dinner, must have eaten and talked, must have returned to my room. I seem to remember Elizabeth's concerned face and Betsy's worried eyes. I only know for certain that it was near dawn before I went to bed, and then my sleep was restless, filled with dreams through which my dark-haired lady walked and wept.

After breakfast the next morning, Adam followed me from the dining room, took a firm grasp on my elbow, and propelled me along with him to the library. I had no wish to accompany him; but neither did I wish to create a scene, and so I went.

Once inside, he stopped with his back firmly planted against the door. "Look at me, Victoria," he commanded.

I turned to face him, but I could not meet his gaze.

"Look at me!" he repeated, and he put his fingers under my chin, lifted my face until our eyes met. "Victoria . . . you can't go on avoiding me, treating me like a leper. I need you." He spoke in a tone that was flat with controlled emotion.

Had I not been so tired, so numb after the long sleepless hours, the worry, the anger, the hurt, I think I should have laughed. He needed me? Did he not know how desperately I needed him? Had he really thought, when he married Helaine, that he could come home and resume a simple friendship with me? Had he really expected me to forget all that had passed between us? Had he truly believed I would be content to become his adoring sister once more?

But I only said, "I do not seek to avoid you."

Though we both knew that was not true, Adam did not

contest the point. Instead he asked, "Then will you go riding with me this afternoon?"

The muted light from the stained glass windows cast dark shadows under his eyes and smudged the hollows of his cheeks with blue. In the silence of the library, I could hear the beating of my heart, could feel the faint trembling of Adam's hand beneath my chin, was dimly aware of the musty odor of paper and leather and ink.

"Will you go with me?" Adam repeated doggedly.

I took a deep breath, tried to think. I wanted so desperately to say yes — and why shouldn't I say yes, I thought. But the wound to my pride was still too fresh, too deep. I shook my head, not trusting my voice.

"Please . . ." Adam began.

The sound of someone pushing against the door, rattling the handle, interrupted his words. His hands dropped to his sides.

I moved swiftly away, walked to the nearest bookcase and selected a book at random.

Behind me, I heard Adam say, "Sorry, sir. The door seems to have become stuck."

"Indeed, indeed." I recognized the second voice as Papa's, and I turned around.

Papa strode into the room carrying a great iron ring laced almost entirely round with keys: large keys, small keys, plain keys, ornate keys.

As with one mind, Adam and I both knew that those keys Papa carried were the ones we had sought so diligently all through our childhood. For a moment, the passage of time, all the events between us, were forgotten. I laughed and clapped my hands. Papa and Adam both glanced at me and smiled. A sudden burst of sunlight streamed through the windows, and for the first time since Adam's return, the wall that had stood cold and hard between us disappeared.

I stamped my foot in mock exasperation and asked, "Papa, how could you have kept those keys from us all these years? You knew how Adam and I longed to explore all those locked rooms! How could you let us think the keys were lost?"

Papa grinned a sheepish grin. "Hard enough, it was, keeping track of the two of you. There seemed no need to give you more room in which to lose yourselves."

Without thinking, I moved over to stand close beside Adam, and he, just as casually, leaned his arm upon my shoulder, as he was wont to do when, as children, we stood and talked with Papa — or, more often than not, stood to listen to a stern reprimand following some harmless, though probably (for our parents) unnerving and thoroughly irritating childish escapade.

Papa's smile was indulgent. " 'Twas always my intention to give these keys to you both when—" Even as the words escaped his lips, we could see he wished them back.

Adam did not move, but I could feel his body stiffen. The three of us stood, tense, gripped for a dreadful moment in awkward, painful awareness of each other's thoughts. The interlude ended, but now the weight of those dead dreams, unacknowledged until that moment, were added to the already strained atmosphere of the house. I mumbled some excuse, and fled.

As the library door closed behind me, I almost collided with Helaine, who stood just outside in the hall. Trying to avoid her, I lost my balance, and would have fallen had not she reached out her hand and grasped my arm to steady me.

"I'm sorry," I gasped. "Oh—I . . . I'm sorry." I could think of nothing else to say, and only wished to be safe within the four walls of my own room. I tried to withdraw, but Helaine did not loosen her grip upon my arm.

"Are you all right?"

"Yes, yes. Let me go!" I snapped ungraciously.

Her grasp upon my arm only tightened.

I looked straight at her then, into her glittering eyes, and the thought came to me: . . . *like a snake watching a bird*.

A small cry of fright escaped me, and I jerked my arm free. A moment longer we stood, measuring each other, but my gaze wavered and fell. I turned and ran.

Back in my room, I poured some cold water into the basin and bathed my face. I was shaking, and the countenance that looked back at me from the mirror was like chalk. I felt ashamed, frustrated, and thoroughly miserable. Why had I fled the library in such a gauche and naive fashion? Why had I let Helaine see how frightened I was? Why *was* I so frightened?

Inwardly I surveyed my world, gone grey and empty, and I realized that, try as I would, I still could not accept Adam's marriage. And now, for the first time, I gave voice to my true feelings. I stood alone in the center of my room, eyes closed, hands closed into fists, and I said through clenched teeth, "I hate her. I *hate* her!"

I sat down, then, to consider the implications of this newly recognized emotion. And for the first time, I toyed with the idea of going to London for a while after all. It would give me time to adjust, to confront and accept the changes that Adam's marriage had wrought in all our lives. And perhaps if I were away somewhere, someplace where I would not have to face Adam every day, maybe then, I thought, I could accept the fact that he really belonged to Helaine—could never belong to me.

Suddenly a vision of the long, lonely years that lay ahead for me flashed through my mind. It was more than I could bear, and I sought to turn my thoughts to something else— anything else.

First I rang for tea, then took off my shoes and began undoing my buttons, thinking to change into my riding costume. I would take Blue Boy for a run. With him, at least, I felt secure and assured.

But if I went down to the stables, Adam might be there waiting. . . . Instantly my emotions were at war within me: longing to see Adam, determined not to do so.

Gillian arrived. A cup of tea first, I decided. I sat down upon the chaise and poured myself a cup, added a spoonful of sugar and a drop of milk. Then I leaned back against the cushions and stretched my legs out before me. The satin upholstery was cool and smooth beneath my bare feet.

I picked up the cup and took a sip. My face twisted in distaste. I had added too much sugar. I considered getting up and throwing the whole lot in my basin, but I didn't. Listlessly, I took another sip of the tea and continued to sit. Too tired, too dispirited. . . .

The clock on the mantel chimed, and the silvery sound came to me as from a great distance. My head felt strange, numb, and my eyes burned. I pulled the combs from my hair and ran my fingers into its thick coils to shake them loose.

I became aware, in a vague sort of way, that my room was unnaturally warm. My mouth was so dry — I took another sip of the disgustingly sweet tea. I felt stifled. The beating of my heart was slow and heavy, painful in my chest.

The walls wavered and swam, then came into focus, and I gazed about me in amazement. My tapestries still hung from ceiling to floor, just as they always had done, only now, each flower, each tree, each bird, had depth and dimension, as if I were viewing them through Papa's stereopticon.

There, sharp and clear in the semi-gloom, sat the fat green macaw, unconcerned and self-satisfied, watching a sloe-eyed Persian cat whose smug air of indifference I usually found amusing. Above the macaw, a pair of sky-blue lovebirds perched, their bright yellow beaks entwined, and lower down a great white cockatoo prepared to take wing. My little yellow bird clung steadfastly to his perch, his black eyes shoe-button bright.

Off to the left, below and behind my yellow friend, the ferns grew thick and green upon a mossy bank that had its crest somewhere behind my bed. And as I gazed at the wee bird, some small flicker of movement amidst the ferns, perceived only on the outermost edges of consciousness, caught my attention. My heart began to thump violently against my ribs. I peered more closely at the stand of fern behind the bird, thinking I must be mistaken — but I was not.

Why I had never noticed it before, I could not understand. How could I have failed to see that long, sinuous, green and mauve and brown body, twined in and out amongst the fronds of fern, its iridescent eyes glittering with an evil light, its black forked tongue just slithering back into its half-open mouth?

Fear, an icy wave, washed over me. I lay there, staring in horror at the creature as it began to glide forward toward the little yellow bird. Now the serpent raised its head, arching its body up to weave slowly from side to side, its skin catching and reflecting the light with an oily sheen.

I jerked my knees up and pressed myself against the back of the chaise longue. At the soft whispering sound my movements made against the satin upholstery, the snake swung its ugly head around and fastened its glittering gaze on me. It hesitated, then began to glide down the lowest curve of the grassy bank. My breath clogged in my lungs, my vision blurred. Far off, I could hear someone keening, long, high-pitched wails. Then darkness, thick and suffocating, swallowed me.

Chapter Thirteen

When I opened my eyes Helaine was standing over me, one hand resting on the back of the chaise. *But where was that dreadful serpent?*

At the thought, every muscle in my body tensed and I looked wildly about the room. My sister-in-law leaned forward, placed her hand on my shoulder as if to reassure me.

Why was she in my room?

"There, there, little sister, you've been dreaming."

Had I been dreaming? The snake—had it just been part of a nightmare? But it had seemed so real. And what was making those peculiar sounds?

I was trying very hard to think, to put it all together, but I felt so awful. Belatedly, I realized that those odd little whimpering sounds were escaping through my own clenched teeth. There was a slow, heavy pounding inside my skull, and I prayed that I would not be sick.

"Hush, hush," Helaine crooned, her voice soothing and strangely hypnotic.

Slowly, the whimpering faded, ceased. But the fear continued to twist in my dazed mind.

"Victoria, dear, whatever is the matter? You were carrying on so, I could hear you out on the balcony."

I swallowed, tried to speak, but my heart was still pounding in my throat and I was shivering as with the ague. If it had been naught but a dream, it had been a monstrous one. The terror was still strong in me, and suddenly I was glad that Helaine was there. At least I was not alone.

She continued to contemplate me through narrowed lids. "Do you have these spells often?"

Spells? What did she mean? I shook my head, tried to answer, but my mouth was so dry.

When I remained silent, Helaine sat down beside me on the chaise. "Are you certain you are quite well, dear sister? You seemed much perturbed when I met you in the hallway, and now this dreadful spell. . . ."

At last I found my voice. "No, no . . . I'm fine. . . ."

"How can you say that, when you are white as a snowdrift and shaking like a leaf?"

"It was just a dream . . . a bad dream. Please, don't trouble yourself about me."

Helaine only leaned nearer and slipped her arm about my shoulders. "Dear Victoria. Dear child. I can see that you are terribly upset. This cannot go on. Someone in this family must speak plainly, for your sake."

Speak plainly? About what? What was she getting at? I wondered. Still I said nothing.

Helaine continued, "Everyone knows this sort of thing runs in families . . . but you must not worry. The kitchen maid is here to watch over you, though why she did not hear you screaming just now I cannot tell."

I had been trying to draw away from the woman, but at her words, I froze.

Helaine, ignoring my distress, continued. "Just remember, your grandmother never suffered . . . neither shall you."

In stunned silence, listening to her words, I wondered if this, too, was part of the nightmare. And if not, could it be true that all the family knew what was happening to me? Did everyone believe me insane? Had Betsy really been sent to watch over me? I opened my mouth to speak, but no words would come.

Now Helaine drew back and stood up. "You really should be resting, dear sister." With that, she rang for a maid and, when Gillian appeared, my sister-in-law directed her to help me into bed.

At the door Helaine paused, turned back. "Remember, Victoria, straight to bed, and you are not to worry." Then she was gone.

Still, I refused to move until Gillian had looked under the bed and poked into every corner and behind every piece of furniture in my room. I knew I was being ridiculous, but it had seemed so real. However, of the green and mauve and brown snake on the tapestry, there was no sign, a fact that did little to reassure me.

Indeed, if anything, it added to my distress. Obviously my room was just as it always had been, and that hellish serpent had, indeed, been naught but a dreadful dream, a figment of my disturbed mind.

Which brought me back to Helaine's insinuations. Could it be true that Betsy had been put in the room next to mine for the sole purpose of keeping an eye on me? What had Elizabeth said the day she suggested the arrangement? ". . . You are too much alone." That could mean anything.

Utterly dejected, I allowed Gillian to help me to my feet. Then, with what little dignity I could muster, I said, "Please, promise me that you will say nothing to anyone about what happened just now. My behavior has been uncalled for, and it would worry Lady Elizabeth. It was only that I had a very bad dream and it frightened me. You do understand, do you not, Gillian?"

Gillian's dull, flat eyes gave no hint of understanding, but she nodded her head solemnly, and I knew she would not long even remember the incident. I wished with all my heart that I could say the same of Helaine!

My head still ached and I was sticky with perspiration, so I sent Gillian off to the kitchen to fetch a pitcher of hot water. When she returned, she helped me with my lacings, and whilst I washed myself, she scurried about, turning back the covers and piling high the down pillows. Then she brushed my hair and helped me into bed.

It was only after she had tucked the covers about me and

stood back, beaming broadly, that I remembered it was no more than late morning. I should be expected, if not for lunch, most certainly for tea.

But I felt too apathetic, too utterly depleted both physically and mentally, to care. "Please, Gillian, tell Lady Elizabeth that I am very tired and beg to be excused. I will take lunch here in my room, and rest until time for tea."

"Aye, m'Lady, straight away." And off Gillian went, smiling affably to herself.

When I was alone again, all the doubt and fear rushed back to torment me. Could it be true? Was I, like my grandmother, losing my mind? Becoming as those poor creatures I had observed on that long-ago day in Hyde Park?

Then another question began to plague me: if I were mad, what would become of me? Would they lock me in the tower, perhaps, where I could do nobody harm? But that was silly; they had not locked the Lady Christina in the tower.

It was more probable that I should be sent off to London. Could that be why Papa and Elizabeth had suggested I visit Aunt Drusilla and Uncle Phillip? But, no—surely they would not do that to me. And yet, who better to take care of me than Uncle Phillip? *Bedlam*. Would he consign me to Bedlam?

I shook my head and the whispered words, "No, no, no," slipped past my lips, denying the morbid thoughts.

Later, both Elizabeth and Betsy came to see me, but the suspicions awakened by Helaine's words weighed upon me, upon my spirit, and I begged to be left alone. Yet so perverse was my state of mind that as soon as they were gone, I wished them back, longing for someone to share my fear and uncertainty. But whenever someone did come near, my courage failed me, my lips would not form the words of confession; and in the days that followed, even Betsy could not pierce the melancholy that fastened itself upon my soul.

Now, in addition to the nightmares and my once insubstantial fears, I brooded over Helaine's intimation that there really was something wrong with me—with my mind—and that everyone knew. Then it occurred to me that perhaps that was why Adam had tried to urge a clandestine meeting upon me. It was not that he rued his rash marriage, that he had discovered he could not live without my love, as I had secretly hoped (for I now admitted to myself it was so). That had not been his purpose at all. He had been intent upon discussing my illness!

Betsy and I did continue her lessons, and she tried to raise me from my apathy. But I was plagued by suspicion and doubt. My trust in Betsy had been so blighted by my sister-in-law's poisonous remarks, that I found myself reading hidden meaning into all Betsy's words of kindness, all her efforts to bring me comfort.

And try as I would to fight against it, day and night I was plagued by that terrible gnawing loneliness that only Adam's arms, Adam's lips, Adam's love could assuage. My appetite failed once more, as did my once boundless energy and enthusiasm. I seldom rode, indeed seldom ventured outside, but spent much time sitting idle in my room or wandering the shadowy chill halls of the manor.

In my loneliness and distress, I found myself wishing for John's return. He had gone to visit friends from Oxford for a month or so, and I missed him. Although John was only seventeen, he was a great deal like our father: serious, thoughtful, and ambitious in a dogged sort of way.

From the time John was able to keep pace with Papa, he had followed him about, miming Papa's every step and stance. He shared with Papa a love of the land, an understanding of the needs and problems of the tenant farmers, a sure eye for a good horse, and a head for business that far surpassed the capabilities of many an older man.

John and I had never been particularly close. I always thought of him as my baby brother, as indeed he was. Adam, too, had taken that attitude with John. As youngsters, we rarely included him in any of our adventures, not that John ever seemed to mind. In fact, he always looked with great disdain upon our childish escapades.

Like the time Adam and I discovered the secret of the

priest's hidey-hole behind the fireplace in the great hall. For weeks we took great pleasure in secreting ourselves away, then popping out to confound our parents. I shall never forget the day John, who had had more than enough of our theatrics, said, "Do you *children* never get tired of that silly game? Everyone knows you have been in the priests' hole."

Thoroughly deflated, neither Adam nor I missed the proud look that passed between Elizabeth and Papa. It was humiliating. But I always smile, now, at the memory.

John's passion in life, like Papa's, was the Greystone horses. He would spend hours in the stables sitting with a newborn colt or caring for a mare in foal, or in the training ring with a skittish two-year-old. But above all, he loved to walk, to talk, to work with Papa.

The love Adam and I gave to the old house, John gave to the land. Whilst Adam and I were fire and air, John was water and earth. He was my junior by almost six years, but his maturity had always exceeded mine — and Adam's too, for that matter — in many ways. Even as a child, John found our explorations of the old house, our games of make-believe, our whispering and giggling, quite beneath him; and he rarely deigned to waste time in our company. But he was a solid, warm-hearted lad, and I always regarded him with affection, albeit detached affection.

Thus, even after Adam left for the Continent, John and I never shared confidences. So it was for the first time in my life that I now found myself wishing for the sight of his stocky brown figure, his serious, gentle grey eyes. But John would go straight from his friend's house back to school in September, and was not expected home again until Christmas.

Adam made no further effort to see me alone, but when we were in the same room, or met by chance in a hall or gallery, his eyes would follow me. What was he thinking? I wondered. Was he watching for some sign of madness? Or was he, after all, wanting only to be my friend?

From time to time I did visit with Lueddy in the kitchen. Gillian would make us a cup of tea, and I would sit on a stool at the old woman's knee, as I had done as a child, and try to talk with her. But Lueddy had aged, almost overnight it seemed, and her mind sometimes wandered.

Nonetheless, the change in my appearance did not escape her, and she would admonish me, saying "Ye must eat more, m'Lady. Ye an' Master Adam . . . allus too busy to eat, ye young 'uns be."

"But we are grown now, Lueddy," I would try to reassure her.

She would only cluck and shake her head, "Just like me little bird. . . ."

And I would grit my teeth at the anger and fear those words evoked.

One day, toward summer's end, when I went to visit, she appeared to be quite distraught. "Ye'll not let 'im send Lueddy away, will ye, m'Lady?"

I took her hands in mine. Cold, they were, and trembling. "Why, Lueddy, what a question! Of course not. We'd never send you away."

She clung to my hands and repeated, her voice rough with desperation, "Please, m'Lady, ye knows old Lueddy loves ye. Don't let 'im send me away!"

I knelt beside her on the floor and put my arms about her. "Oh, Lueddy, dear, I love you, too. We all love you, and no one will ever send you away." I continued to hold her, whispering words of reassurance, until she relaxed and drifted off to sleep.

Later that day, I made a point of seeking Elizabeth out and talking with her about Lueddy. "Couldn't she have a room upstairs, Elizabeth?"

Elizabeth sighed. "Both Samuel and I have tried to bring her upstairs. She refuses to come. When we sought to insist, she became so agitated, we feared she would make herself ill."

So Lueddy remained below stairs. Summer matured into fall. I filled my days with idleness, though I made a pretense of continuing Betsy's studies. At night, I rarely slept without dreaming strange, disquieting dreams, through which the dark-haired young woman moved, weeping and beckoning, seeming somehow to share my fears and sorrows. That, too, was frightening.

Yes, I was frightened. Twice, following the episode with the nightmare snake, I awakened to find myself standing beside my bed, shivering with cold. But once awake, I could not recall what dream had possessed me, or why I had left my bed. There was only a lingering aura of sadness and a feeling of urgency. I would creep again under the covers to lie staring into the darkness, until dawn streaked the sky with pale light.

I began to wonder, as I never had before, exactly what had been wrong with my grandmother; but I was afraid to ask. My only real pleasure during that endless period was watching Cyrano's antics. He would often find his way into my room, and stay to chase a ball of yarn or his own tail, or stretch himself upon my silken counterpane to sleep the hours away.

Thus, several weeks passed following the day Papa gave the keys to Adam, for that was what I learned he had done. For me, the days were long, dull, fruitless. Though for years I had longed to see into those locked areas of the manor, now that the keys were available, I was reluctant to make use of them.

I would sit in my room after breakfast and think, Today I shall ask Adam for the keys. And because I longed to seek Adam out, to talk with him, to have him join me in the exploration of those long-locked rooms, just the thought of asking him for the keys became sweet torture.

For, having let my imagination go that far, it invariably ran wild, filling my head with impossible ideas. How easy it would be, I thought, for the two of us to become lost, somewhere in the heart of the old house. And then Adam would take me in his arms and tell me he loved me. Just thinking about it, I could feel his lips on mine, feel his hands caressing me as they had done so long ago under the stars upon the cliff top. And my cheeks would burn with shame at my weakness.

The day would creep on into dusk, I would sit at the escritoire, running my fingers over the polished writing surface, afraid to go to bed, to dream, perhaps to rise and walk. For what if, as I slept, I should find my way out into the hall and be discovered?

Sometimes I would open the drawer in which I had secreted the note and the piece of scorched paper, take them out, and read them over yet again.

Carter, beloved, come quickly! If you leave me now, I shall surely die. Even Lueddy cannot save me from the . . .

I wasted much time in pondering that final undecipherable squiggle.

Then I would turn to the other message:

. . . now I know that he is dead — murdered — I will have my revenge.

Each time I touched that scrap of paper, read the words, I would grow cold. Little shivers would rise between my shoulders, and in my stomach a knot would grow. My mind would fill with blind panic, and I would cower in my room as a hunted thing cowers in its lair.

I also spent long hours considering the possibility that the dream woman was real. The ink stains, the bits of paper, the written words were real. Why not the woman, too? But then, why did she disappear when I awoke? Try as I would, I could make no sense of it, confirming the fear that my mind was no longer to be trusted.

Then I would recall the stories about my grandmother, the Lady Christina. Oh, no one — except Helaine, of course — had ever sat down with me and said, "Your grandmother was insane, Victoria, and you are just like her." But a word here, a glance there, a sly giggle, and Papa's refusal to talk about his mother. I had come to understand, all too well, why, when I was still a child, it had upset Papa so if he caught me playing at make-believe.

Oh, yes, I knew all right; but the fact that my grandmother had been mad — mad as a hatter — had never before mattered to me. Never before had the knowledge held any threat.

Despite all this internal turmoil, I continued to go about my daily routine. I had breakfast with the family; I gave Betsy instructions in needlepoint and riding; I had lunch, and tea, and dinner; I made my rounds of the library and the herb garden and the stillroom; I tended a bitch with a litter of pups; I went to church on Sunday mornings. I even smiled, and spoke when spoken to. But I had the strange sensation of being two people: one who walked and talked and ate, and another who lurked inside, just watching and waiting—for what, I dared not think.

Chapter Fourteen

The red and gold leaves of autumn turned to brown. Another successful harvest had filled the barns with hay, the cellars with apples, the granaries with corn. Inexorably, the days grew short, and the cold north wind blew in from the sea, bringing with it ice, sleet, and snow. But our tenant farmers were as snug in their cottages as were we who lived in Greystone Manor.

Sitting at the breakfast table one wintery morning, listening to the howl of the wind outside, Elizabeth surveyed the comforts that surrounded us and asked, "Samuel, do you remember the days when first we were wed?"

Papa put down his fork and gazed at Elizabeth, his eyes full of tenderness. "Yes," he said. "Yes, I remember," and though he said no more, the love and respect he felt for his wife were abundantly clear in the look he bestowed upon her.

I smiled at them, glad to see their happiness.

Elizabeth laughed, a small warm sound, and reached across the table to touch Papa's hand. "We have worked very hard, Samuel, very hard . . . and the Lord has prospered us."

Papa nodded. "Aye, my dear, He has prospered and blessed."

"I have been thinking," my stepmother continued, "it is time we shared our prosperity, our blessings, with our friends and our people."

Again Papa nodded. "And how do you propose we do that?"

"I think," and Elizabeth's eyes began to dance, "we should give a Christmas ball."

Thus it was settled, and for the next few weeks all was in turmoil. Extra help was hired: scullery maids, parlor maids, stable boys, and bakers. Even a French pastry chef was brought to the manor. He arrived with two trunks full of fascinating little pans and other strange and wondrous utensils.

For all the people living on the estate and in the village, there was to be dancing in the great hall, with food and drink aplenty. To this purpose, the great hall was cleared of furniture and decorated as a ballroom. Several of the small parlors on either side of the hall were also cleared, and large tables and racks for hogsheads were installed, in order to provide our guests with all the delicacies in keeping with the season.

The local gentry, and our guests from London, would be entertained on the second floor in a small but very elegant ballroom. Its walls were set with pier glass that reached from floor to ceiling, and down the center, suspended from a gorgeous baroque ceiling, were several crystal tear-drop chandeliers. This room, too, was made festive with boughs of evergreen and sprigs of holly and mistletoe.

Amongst those special guests invited to our Christmas gala were, of course, Uncle Phillip, Aunt Drusilla, and Thomas. I had not seen Thomas since their visit to Greystone Manor the summer past, and I looked forward to our meeting with both pleasure and pain. With pleasure, because Thomas would always be very dear to me; with pain, because I had decided, after weeks of soul searching, to tell him to forget me.

What is more, I was determined to do so before the coming of the new year. He was much too fine a young man to be kept dangling, to waste his affection on me when my heart in its perversity refused to belong to anyone but Adam. I sincerely hoped that Thomas, once freed from our commitment, would meet some nice young woman and forget about me altogether.

John was to return from Oxford on the early morning train several days before the ball. He had not yet met Betsy, and hardly knew Helaine, and I couldn't help but wonder how he would feel about these two women. But most of all, I truly looked forward to just seeing my baby brother again.

The prospect of the coming reunion raised my spirits so much that as I dressed that morning, I hummed a happy tune in glad anticipation. Even as I hurried downstairs, the gay little melody sang itself over in my head.

Elizabeth and Papa had gone to the station to meet their son, and the three of them entered the hall just as I did.

"John!" I called as I ran to throw my arms about him. "Oh, John, I'm so glad to see you."

Though not as tall as Adam, John was broader of shoulder, thicker of limb, and his was a calm and steadfast nature. He put his arms about me, gave me a resounding kiss upon the cheek. "Dear Victoria," he declared. "I have missed you!"

We both laughed. It was such an unlikely statement, for ours had been a turbulent relationship at best.

Papa actually threw back his head and guffawed. "The years have certainly mellowed the two of you," he chuckled, as we turned to leave the great hall.

At that moment Betsy came rushing down the staircase, hair flying, skirts billowing. She barely managed to stop her headlong approach in time to avoid a collision with John. Laughing, she glanced up at him. The laughter died on her lips and her eyes grew round with surprise. Then, unaccountably, she bowed her head and dropped into a deep curtsy.

"Betsy, this is my brother, John," I said, wondering at her reaction.

Betsy did not move.

As for John, he was looking from one to the other of us, then down at Betsy's bowed head, at a total loss for words.

It was Papa who took command of the situation. He

173

reached down and touched Betsy's arm, urging her to rise. At the same time he addressed his son. "This is Miss Betsy, your sister's companion. She has been with us since midsummer, and is a most agreeable addition to our household."

At last Betsy raised her head, rose to her feet, and glanced shyly at John.

Then I noticed the expression on John's face. For a moment he seemed nonplussed. Then he murmured, " 'Tis a pleasure, Miss Betsy."

Betsy took a deep breath, swallowed, and seemed to regain her composure. "Lord John," she replied. "How nice to meet you."

Papa offered Elizabeth his arm and said, "Now, shall we go in to breakfast?"

John offered his arms to both Betsy and me. As we entered the breakfast room, the smell of fresh-baked cinnamon buns, of cocoa and strawberry perserves, tempted me for the first time in weeks. We filled our plates and sat down, I with my back to the door, facing John, who sat across the table. Betsy took her accustomed place next to me.

We were sitting over our second cup of cocoa, chatting quietly, when the hair on the back of my neck began to rise. The expression on John's open, honest young face told me why. He sat for a long moment, owl-eyed, then leaped to his feet, almost overturning his chair.

Now I could hear the rustle of her skirts, smell her exotic perfume, and from behind me came that voice, soft, warm, vibrant. "Good morning Lady Elizabeth, Lord Samuel . . . John."

My breakfast turned to bile in my throat as I felt the touch of her hand upon my head. An affectionate gesture, yet it did not take her crooning "Dear little sister" to let me know she meant it to put me in my proper place, to point out that I was of hardly more significance in the family circle than a child. Betsy she ignored altogether.

Anger seethed in my chest though I strove to keep my face

expressionless. Why, I wondered, after all these months, had she decided to come down to breakfast on this particular day? Did the wretched woman have to spoil everything for me? Yet when she had moved far enough around the table to enter my range of vision, even these angry thoughts were stilled and I, too, became owl-eyed.

As often as I saw her, I was always startled anew by her beauty. This morning was no exception. Her rich brown hair, fastened back with a wide bone-colored velvet ribbon, had been brushed, by Stella no doubt, into a mass of ringlets that caught the morning sunlight and spilled down her back in a shower of gleaming red-gold. The effect was startling. Her lovely face had taken on an elfin, childlike quality, and her large green eyes were dewy with innocence. She wore a high-necked gown of fine cashmere trimmed with creamy lace, a deceptively simple gown that somehow served to accentuate her voluptuous sensuality while bestowing upon her an aura of youthful vulnerability.

She chose the seat next to John. Dear John. While Adam went to fill a plate for his wife, John held out her chair. And when he had seated himself next to her, he strove valiantly to maintain a proper attitude of respectful aloofness toward his sister-in-law. But he was, after all, a very young and very unsophisticated man, and I could only presume that in the months since he had seen her, he had forgotten the degree of her beauty. It was all too evident, at least to me, that Helaine, with hardly the flutter of an eyelash, had made another conquest.

I could not eat another bite, and when I rose to leave the table, Betsy did the same. It wasn't until we reached the stairway that I realized John had followed us.

"Must you ladies retire so soon? I thought that perhaps we could go for a walk."

I started to laugh. "It's far too cold . . ."

But Betsy interrupted, "Have you not noticed how brightly the sun is shining, Victoria? A walk would be most invigorating."

And then, without waiting for my response, she turned to

John and said, "Pray, give us a moment to fetch our cloaks."

I glanced at John, dumbfounded, but he was gazing after Betsy, who was already halfway up the stairs.

And slowly the truth dawned upon me. Though John may have been overwhelmed by seeing his sister-in-law again, he was one man who was not taken in by her beauty and charm!

The day following John's homecoming, the Hornabys were scheduled to arrive on the afternoon train. Despite the pain I felt when I thought of the disappointment I had in store for Thomas, I was filled with anticipation at the thought of seeing him again. By the time lunch was over, I could contain my excitement no longer, and I begged permission to take the carriage down to the station to meet them.

I had expected that Betsy would accompany me, but shortly before it was time to leave, she came into my room attired in her riding habit. Blushing prettily, she said, "Lord John has asked me to go riding, and I said I would be pleased to accompany him. Then I thought I should ask your permission. May I?"

John and Betsy? It was a turn of events that had never occurred to me. Nonetheless, it pleased me no end. "Run along," I said. "Have a nice time."

So I made the trip to the station alone. This day, like the one before, boasted a cloudless sky, and it was a delight to be outside. Dazzling white snow, several days old now, lying heavy on the branches of the trees, glittered and flashed when a ray of sunlight glanced over it. The air was crisp and cold, filled with the pungent fragrance of pine.

I drew long deep breaths, filling my lungs with the sweet clean air. The clip-clop of the horses' hooves beat a steady rhythm to the merry jingle of the harnesses, and my spirits rose as we neared our destination. The train was just pulling in as I climbed the steps to the platform. Waving a cheery greeting, I hurried forward to meet Uncle Phillip and Aunt Drusilla as they descended from the coach.

"Halloo," called Uncle Phillip, and he raised his walking

stick, touched it to the brim of his hat. Aunt Drusilla waved her handkerchief.

"How good it is to see you!" I called back. Then I was beside them, giving them each a hug and a kiss, asking, "How was your journey?"

But before they could answer, I noted that Thomas was nowhere to be seen. My heart sank. "Where is Thomas? Is he not coming?"

Drusilla chuckled. "It is wonderful to see you again, too, child. We had a lovely trip, and Thomas will be along tomorrow."

"Then he is well?"

"He is fine . . . had a rough crossing from Hamburg and felt the need for a bit of a rest today. But he will join us tomorrow, Uncle Phillip assured me. He had been observing me with a practiced eye, and now his face became serious. "Have you been ill, young lady?"

"Oh, no!" The denial sprang too quickly to my lips, and I could not meet his eyes as I added, "I have been quite well."

"You do not *look* well," Phillip persisted. "You are thin and pale, and—"

"You look perfectly lovely," Drusilla interrupted, and I had the feeling she was shaking her head at Uncle Phillip behind my back.

"Yes, yes," Uncle Phillip sputtered, then added, "Perhaps it is the light . . . a trick of the light." But he did not sound convinced.

"Come along," I said, choosing to ignore Uncle Phillip's comments. "I have brought the carriage to carry you back to Greystone Manor. The coachman will be along shortly to collect your baggage."

I was more disappointed at not seeing Thomas than I cared to admit, even to myself. However, I put on a cheerful face and we chatted gaily all the way back to the manor.

The following day we were all up early, and Elizabeth and I spent a harried morning seeing to all the final details. Not until after lunch did we retire to our rooms, to rest until the time came to dress for the ball.

I wanted to go to the station to greet Thomas, but Elizabeth had ruled against it, saying I needed my rest if I was to be at my best for the festivities. Grudgingly, I bowed to her wishes.

Having returned to my room, I actually slept for almost an hour. When I arose, I felt, for the first time in weeks, some small spark of my old enthusiasm glowing within me. How good it would be to see Thomas! However, when I looked at myself in my mirror, noted how thin my face had grown, saw the dark circles that underscored my eyes, the fatigue lines about my mouth, I could scarcely believe that it was really I.

I pinched my cheeks, bit my lips, trying to bring up some color, but it was wasted effort. Only my eyes had color, and they looked enormous in my thin, pale face. It is no wonder, I thought, that Uncle Phillip feared I had been ill. And what would Thomas think?

One consolation, thin as I had grown, was that it took no effort to do up my lacings, and the narrow belt of my hoop skirt fit easily about my waist. With a heavy sigh, I turned to look at my dress. It, at least, was beautiful: silk and wool barege in cornflower blue, trimmed with yards of pale blue silk tulle, pink silk roses, and dark blue velvet ribbon.

I started when the mantel clock began to chime. It was time to dress, so I rang for Gillian. Somehow, she had managed to install herself as my personal maid. Slow of wit she might be, but she was canny in her own way, and she was also a hard worker. Once she learned a task, she did it painstakingly and well. Add to these qualities loyalty and devotion, and you have an excellent lady's maid.

When I had washed myself, and Gillian had brushed and arranged my hair to our satisfaction, she lifted the gown over my head and settled it into place. The bodice fit snug and smooth over my breasts, leaving my throat and shoulders bare. A skillful arrangement of loosely pleated tulle encirled my upper arms and was caught between my bosom with one silk rose. The skirt, too, was garlanded with softly pleated tulle, caught here and there with pink silk roses, and when it was spread over the hoop, it hung in lovely graceful folds.

As for jewels, I had only a pair of pearl earrings. They were from John. "My Christmas present," he had said, adding that he was giving them to me early because he wished me to wear them to the ball. "I shall be sorely wounded if you do not," he had said solemnly.

In view of the fact that I owned no other adornments, I was tempted to laugh, but I did not. "They are beautiful," I assured my little brother. "I shall wear them with pride."

I was almost ready to join the others, when a rap on my door was followed by Elizabeth's entrance. Pale and distraught, she hurried toward me, her words coming all in a rush. "I must tell you, Victoria . . . it is *dreadful* . . . I scarce know what to do! Your father—Helaine! It was too, too awful . . . and Adam just stood there!"

Thunderstruck, I stared at her. Whatever was she babbling about? Elizabeth, who was always so calm and sensible! And then I noted that tears were forming in her eyes. I rushed forward, took her hands in mine.

But before I could speak, Elizabeth swallowed, took a deep breath, blinked back the tears. "I am not making much sense am I, little love?"

Suddenly we were in each other's arms, and she was sobbing against my shoulder. I patted her reassuringly on the back, but I could think of absolutely nothing to say.

All the while Gillian stood by, her eyes fairly popping out of her head. When my stepmother began to cry, Gillian, too, began to snuffle.

However, Elizabeth soon regained control and stepped back. But her eyes were wet and her nose all stuffy.

"Quickly, Gillian," I ordered, "fetch a clean handkerchief for the Lady Elizabeth."

Gillian jumped to do as she was bid, and Elizabeth accepted the linen gratefully.

While Elizabeth dried her eyes and blew her nose, I said,

"Now, dear Elizabeth, please tell me what has happened. Whatever has upset you so?"

Elizabeth drew another deep breath. "I am sorry, little love. I should not have . . . but I had to tell someone. It is Helaine. She came to me this afternoon and suggested that she should wear the Greystone emeralds tonight."

"Greystone emeralds?" But the memory came to me even as I spoke. They had been listed in the ledger I had found. I remembered them particularly because they had been so very expensive.

But Elizabeth was already explaining, "They were part of the collection of jewels that disappeared. But when I told Helaine we no longer had them, she insisted that Samuel would surely give them to me if I were to ask."

Elizabeth paused, and I interjected, "I don't understand. How does Helaine know about them . . . why does she think Papa has them?"

Elizabeth shook her head. "She gave no explanation, only demanded that she be allowed to wear them."

"I cannot believe that Helaine would be so bold!"

Elizabeth frowned. "Do not be deceived by that woman's beauty and charm."

As astonishing as her words were, they made only a small chink in the wall I had built around myself. But one comforting thought slipped through. *Perhaps, after all, I was not alone in my distrust of my sister-in-law!*

My stepmother had not finished her story, however, and she continued, "I told her all the jewels had disappeared years ago, but she refused to believe me. Imagine! She as much as declared that I was lying!"

Abruptly, Elizabeth seemed to wilt. "I had to tell Samuel, of course. He was furious. I have never seen him so angry. He went storming up to their quarters. I followed him . . . he spoke some very bitter words and demanded that Helaine apologize to me."

"And well she should!" I exclaimed.

"She refused to do so. In fact, she became so angry she threatened Samuel. She said that unless she was treated with the same consideration as the other members of the family, we would all rue the day we were born!"

"Why, she has been shown *every* consideration!" I broke in.

Elizabeth shook her head. "It was dreadful. . . ."

"Did not Adam have anything to say?"

Suddenly, Elizabeth's shoulders slumped. She turned away from me, her head bowed.

For a moment I thought I should choke on the anger that had been building inside me. Clearly, Adam should never have let things get so out of hand. Helaine was his responsibility. I knew it, and Elizabeth knew it. But Adam was her son, and I could only guess at the pain my stepmother must be feeling.

Nevertheless, I declared, "Obviously, it is all Helaine's doing. Adam would never behave in so unseemly a manner."

"That is not for you or me to say," my stepmother replied, but the sternness in her voice was belied by the sorrow in her tone.

My heart was touched. I put my arms about her and whispered, "Dear mother Elizabeth." I kissed her cheek, then drew back from her to ask, "What is it that I can do?"

Sighing heavily, Elizabeth replied, "Nothing, dear child. I just wanted you to be forewarned . . . prepared for whatever that woman may attempt."

"Do you really think she might do us harm?"

Elizabeth smiled weakly. "Well, she might prove a thorn in the flesh, but what real harm could she possibly do? No. You need not worry on that score . . . just be watchful."

We gave each other a smile then, rather sad little smiles. No matter what lay ahead of us, we had shared something very important: our mutual dislike and distrust of Helaine.

Chapter Fifteen

When we left my room a few minutes later, the sound of the musicians tuning their instruments in the hall below announced that the dancing was about to begin. Betsy and John were in the gallery before us. Betsy, attired in a gown of ivory mousseline de laine printed with tiny sprigs of holly and ivy, and trimmed with Irish lace, was as pretty as a picture.

Dark eyes shining, chestnut hair gleaming in the lamplight, her face aglow with happiness, she motioned for me to hurry. "Isn't it wonderful, Victoria!" she exclaimed. "I have to keep pinching myself to prove that I am not dreaming!"

Under my guidance and Miss Jones's tutelage, Betsy had blossomed—sweet Betsy, who had the spirit and the heart of a true gentlewoman. This was her first gala, and she was fairly bursting with excitement.

We all moved over to the rail and looked down. The walls of the great hall were festooned with evergreen and holly, and mistletoe hung above each door and from the rafters in each corner of the room. A multitude of brightly colored paper lanterns were strung overhead. Musicians, attired in red and green satin livery, powdered wigs upon their heads, were seated on a dais at the far end of the hall.

"Look," Betsy giggled, indicating a playful young couple who were exchanging a kiss or two under the mistletoe.

John, mischief dancing in his eyes, replied, "Mayhap we shall find our way into that very corner this evening, Miss Betsy."

Betsy's response was quick and full of fun. "Why, whatever do you mean, sirrah?" And she snapped open her ivory fan and gazed at him demurely over it's edge of downy ostrich plumes.

Just then the door of the room at the far end of the gallery opened, and Thomas stepped out. Impulsively, I kissed Elizabeth on the cheek once more, then turned and hurried off to meet him, both hands outstretched in greeting.

He met me midway, took both my hands in his. "Victoria," he murmured. "How very beautiful you look." But before he bent his head to kiss my cheek, I saw the concern in his eyes.

Nevertheless, I smiled at him. "Thank you, sir," I said lightly. "Such a compliment from so handsome a gentleman is praise, indeed."

He hugged me then, and said, "May I have the honor of escorting you this evening?"

"It is I who shall be honored," I assured him, and I thought how very lucky I was to have Thomas to lean upon. If only I could learn to love him. . . .

When we turned toward the group at the head of the stairs, I saw not only Papa, but Uncle Phillip and Aunt Drusilla as well, now stood watching Thomas and me. Each face was lit with a pleased expression, as if they all shared some wonderful secret. I looked from one to the other as we approached, questioning each one with my eyes, but no one spoke.

When we reached them, Papa stepped forward and smiled at me, a smile filled with pride and joy, yet tinged with sadness. "My dearest child," he said. "How proud I am to have such a beautiful daughter."

"Thank you, Papa," I replied, feeling a little embarrassed. Though I could not help but know I was the apple of his eye, Papa did not often speak so openly of his affection for me.

"There is something I wanted to do for your mother . . ." He hesitated and glanced at Elizabeth, who nodded and smiled, whereupon he returned his attention to me. Utterly mystified, I watched as he reached into his pocket and pulled out a rope of lustrous, shimmering pearls.

"They belonged to your grandmother," Papa explained as

he hung them about my neck. "I could not give them to your mother, but now they are yours. Merry Christmas, Victoria." Then he kissed me on the forehead and stood back, beaming with love and pride.

"Oh, Papa," I exclaimed. "Dearest Papa—" The clock on the landing struck the hour, the musicians began to play. The festivities had begun.

There was time for me to say no more, but I threw my arms about my father and kissed him. Everyone clapped. Then John, with Betsy on his arm, started down the stairs. Thomas offered me his arm and we followed after. Not until the four of us were in the great hall and turned to face the stairway did Papa and Elizabeth start down.

When they appeared on the landing, the crowd began to clap and cheer. They did not cease their ovation until Papa motioned them to silence. His welcoming speech was short, but obviously heartfelt:

"I am pleased and happy to see all of you here this evening. It gives me great pleasure to share the bounty of Greystone Manor with those of you who have been my friends for all these many years. Each one of you is important, both to me and to the land. I and my family thank you, and bid you welcome. Merry Christmas!"

At that the crowd broke into another cheer, and Papa and Elizabeth continued on to the dance floor. The musicians struck up a waltz, and we all took a turn about the floor before we went to sit on the dais to watch our guests. No mention was made of Adam and Helaine, although they were conspicuous in their absence.

As soon as we were seated, the musicians began to play the country tunes so loved by the people, and soon everyone was laughing and dancing. We joined in the merriment, clapping enthusiastically in time to the music. But Elizabeth's words, Helaine's threat, continued to hover in the back of my mind.

It was almost time for us to go upstairs to greet our other guests when a hush spread over the crowd. The dancing hesitated, the couples, one after another, stopped in their tracks, turned to stare up at the staircase. Even the music faltered, then ceased.

Dreading what I might see, yet unable to resist the urge to look, I turned my gaze upward. Upon the landing stood Adam and Helaine. My breath caught in my throat at the sight of her and, from his place beside me, I could not mistake Thomas's sharp intake of breath.

The dress my sister-in-law wore was of flaming red velvet over egg-shell satin. It was cut to leave her shoulders bare and revealed far too much of her creamy white bosom. Her hair had been dressed high on her head, and a fall of curls cascaded in a shining cloud of red-gold over one smooth shoulder. One graceful hand rested upon Adam's arm, the other lay upon her wide-spread skirt. Her smile was at once proud and enigmatic.

Back straight, head held high, she seemed to float down the stairs, and by the time they reached the floor, absolute silence reigned throughout the hall. As they advanced toward the center of the room, the crowd melted away before them.

Adam stared straight ahead, his face set and cold. It was Helaine who gave an imperious nod to the musicians. When they began to play once more, Adam took Helaine in his arms and they danced, alone, around the hall and then around again. Their performance might easily have been mistaken for a music hall spectacle, and my cheeks burned with shame that they should so dishonor Elizabeth and Papa.

At the end of the piece the music faded into silence. No one moved, no one spoke. Helaine turned to face the dais and curtsied, low to the ground, skirts billowing about her, arms flung wide. Rising to her feet once more, she stared boldly at Papa, and the expression on her smiling lips, in her glittering eyes, bespoke complete disdain. Then, with a toss of her head, she turned back to Adam and the two of them mounted the stairs once more.

Not until they disappeared around the bend of the landing did anyone move or speak. Then there was an uneasy shuffling of feet, a ripple of apprehensive voices. Thomas was the first to regain his composure. From the corner of my eye, I saw him signaling frantically to the musicians, who finally got his cue and began to play once more.

Several footmen then hurried to fling open doors on either side of the hall, revealing the tables laden with Christmas fare: crusty meat pies, cold sliced fowl, fat sausages, smoking hot and filling the air with the scent of sage. In addition, there were cheeses, bread and rolls, cookies and candy.

But for all around goodness and show, there was nothing to equal the mound of Christmas pudding, over which flaming brandy was being poured. A long, drawn-out *ahhhh* of approval from the crowd bespoke its praise.

Slowly the people began to move about, some to dance, some to eat and drink; but the gaiety was subdued. It was time for us to withdraw. Papa made another very short speech, we all wished our guests a merry Christmas and God speed, then went upstairs to greet our other company.

The mirrors that lined the walls of the upstairs ballroom were inclined at that precise angle which made it possible to view the entire room from any spot on the floor. And what a magical sight they revealed.

The light from the candles blazing in the chandeliers shimmered with an unearthly radiance as it was caught in the crystal prisms and shattered into a thousand tiny rainbows. In the ballroom below, the dancers in their multihued silks and satins, velvets and brocades, dipped and whirled, seeming to float over the floor on invisible wings.

Music, spilling down from the minstrels' gallery, filled the air, and even while I stood demurely in the receiving line, my toes itched to keep time with the joyous sound. In fact, it would have been one of the happiest nights of my life had not Helaine been at the center of it all. Each time I raised my eyes, no matter in which direction I looked, there she was, reflected in the mirrors. In her flaming red dress, surrounded by a bevy of admiring males, she dominated the room.

Still and all, I myself did not lack for admiring partners who told me how beautiful I was. I flirted with all of them quite shamelessly. I also drank glass after glass of champagne, and when Adam appeared at my side to claim a dance, I felt alive, happy, exhilarated as I had not felt in months.

The strength of his arms as he whirled me out onto the floor fed the fire burning in my blood. My heart beat faster; my indrawn breaths came quick and shallow; my body—lips, breasts, those secret places deep inside—tingled and grew warm. I gazed deep into Adam's eyes, and when he drew me closer, I did not resist. In fact, I smiled at him and whispered, "How handsome you look tonight."

He did not reply, did not, in fact, even smile.

"And will you not return the compliment, sir?" Never taking my eyes from his, I pouted, my lips trembling ever so slightly. I knew exactly what I was doing, knew also that my behavior was inexcusable, but the champagne had sharpened my daring even as it dulled my good sense. The nearness of him, the warmth of him, the desire I could see in his eyes, all fed the need throbbing within me.

The social veneer that had dictated my behavior toward Adam and his wife was weakened. All the pent-up longing, all the love and the anger were seething just below the surface. In that moment I was determined to make him want me, even as I hungered for him, and I didn't for one moment consider the consequences. And so I let my eyes say what my lips never could. . . .

Adam's grasp upon my waist tightened, and he said through stiff lips, "You are always beautiful."

I tossed my head. "La, sir, you only say that because you are my big brother."

His face darkened, and he answered sharply, "I am *not* your brother!"

"Why, how can that be, when you have called me 'dear little sister' all these months past?"

"Stop it!" The rising anger in his tone was unmistakable, and I could feel a tremor in his arm.

But I would not be warned. The champagne bubbled in my blood and Adam's anger spurred me on. I let my head droop, looked up at him through my lashes. "Now you are cross with me."

Abruptly I raised my head so that my lips were just inches below his. "Please don't be cross with me, Adam."

His jaw worked and he opened his mouth, but no words came, and I observed with satisfaction the frustration in his eyes, the tinge of white about his lips.

The music and the champagne sang in my brain, goading me on. "I remember when I thought —" I paused, gazed intently into his eyes, sighed. "But no, I was mistaken. You are, after all, only my big brother." Again my lips quivered — it was a trick I had learned as a child.

Through clenched teeth, Adam murmured, "We can't talk here . . ."

"Oh, but we are talking, are we not?" I should have been frightened by the expression on his face, but I felt only exultation.

"You know what I mean," Adam insisted doggedly. "I know you have not forgotten."

Suddenly I was tired of the game. I cut him short. "It was not difficult for you to forget. Why should it be any more difficult for me?"

The music ceased. I did not wait for him to reply. Turning my back on him, head held high, I preceded him from the dance floor.

There was a fanfare from the musicians, and supper was announced. Adam caught up with me just then, gripped my wrist and pulled me close enough to whisper, "After dinner, meet me in the library."

Before I could answer, Thomas appeared at my side, bowed to Adam, and offered me his arm. Adam's face went white. He glared at Thomas for a moment, but finally returned his bow. Then he spun upon his heel and left. My gaze followed him as he picked his way through the crowd toward the cluster of admirers about Helaine.

When I felt Thomas watching me, I tilted my head to smile up at him, hoping he would not notice my agitation. Whether he did, I could not tell. Or perhaps I did not really want to know. There was tenderness in his gaze, and I was comforted by his gentle smile.

As we walked into the dining room, Thomas chided me, saying, "Do you know how many giggling girls and motherly matrons I have danced with this evening, while you were playing belle of the ball?"

I laughed, and the tremor in my voice was scarcely noticeable when I replied, "Fie, sir. 'Tis I who have waited impatiently for you to rescue me from a host of callow youths and wily widowers."

Slowly I began to relax. I even enjoyed eating dinner. Talking and laughing with Thomas, I regained my composure and my good sense. True, I longed to throw all caution aside, to run to the library—to Adam—but I did not.

It was very late when the last guest said goodnight and the family prepared to retire. In fact everyone except Elizabeth and Papa, who were still in the great hall, had already gone to their rooms when Thomas and I reached the gallery.

"It has been wonderful to see you again," Thomas said.

"I'm so glad you were able to come. You have made it a very special evening for me," I replied.

At the door to my room, Thomas took both my hands in his and kissed me lightly on the forehead. "Until morning," he murmured.

The clock on the landing was just striking four as I entered my chamber. After Gillian had helped me with my buttons and lacings, hung up my dress, and added more coal to the fire, I dismissed her. I finished undressing and put on my nightgown. Then I pulled the pins from my coiffure and sat down upon the chaise to brush my hair.

And as I sat there, drawing the bristles through my hair, I began to wonder if Adam could still be waiting for me in the library. I had convinced myself, after carefully reviewing his past overtures, that his desire to see me alone had nothing to do with interest in the state of my mind. Still, it was obvious that his conscience was bothering him. Perhaps he sought only to gain my forgiveness.

But his whispered words, his expression, his intensity,

spoke more of an assignation than a plea for forgiveness. Oh, I was letting my imagination run away with me again! Why would a man with a wife as desirable as Helaine seek an assignation with another woman? With me? *Could* he be harboring some feeling for me after all?

He had been visibly shaken by my behavior, tonight. Indeed, his response had been more that of a frustrated lover than a brother. Was it possible that his marriage was not what he had expected? Quickly I thrust the idea from me. Such thoughts were—unworthy.

But the thoughts that came to take their place were hardly less so. My stepbrother and his wife, whirling about the floor like paid performers—it had been shameful. Helaine had gone too far tonight. Playing her mandolin and singing for a family dinner was one thing, but to display herself before the whole countryside in such a fashion was disgraceful! And Adam had not only let it happen—he had participated!

Poor Elizabeth. How shamed she must feel. Would Papa overlook the whole affair for his wife's sake? Or not?

Suddenly the door to my room burst open, and Adam stepped inside. I jumped to my feet and gaped at him as he strode toward me. His hair was disheveled and his face was pale. He did not stop until he stood close before me. He hesitated for a long moment, staring into my eyes.

Then, convulsively, he grasped me by my shoulders and drew me hard against his chest. His lips closed over mine, hungrily, while his hands, hot through the thin gown I wore, moved down my back, pressing my body tight against his own. I could feel the passion rising in him.

I had dreamed of his arms, his lips, so often, but not like this! However, I was too stunned at first to resist. It wasn't until he picked me up and began moving toward the bed that I started to struggle against him. "No, Adam, *no!* Put me down!"

He stopped, set me on my feet once more, but he did not relax his embrace. He buried his face in my hair, and whispered, "Isn't this what we both always wanted? I could see it in your eyes tonight . . ."

"No!"

Adam hesitated, raised his head, and his eyes searched my face. At length he asked, "Can you honestly say you do not love me?"

Love him? Of course I loved him. But this was shameful, I heard myself say, "Just go away."

His arms dropped to his sides. His face had gone dead white and a muscle twitched in his cheek. He took a deep breath and, the words slow and deliberate, said, "My apologies. I'll not bother you again." Having said that, he turned and left.

And when he had gone, I stumbled back to the chaise longue, sank down upon it, ashes in my heart. I tried to think about what had just happened, to make some sense of my feelings, but I could not. The fire that had blazed so merrily on the grate burned low and grew cold. Dawn was breaking when at last I rose and crawled into my bed.

The sound of sobbing wakened me. I thought at first it was another dream. But when I opened my eyes, I beheld Gillian, in the grey light of morning, her tear-stained face working against the emotions that wracked her.

"Please, m'Lady, please wake up. Me poor heart will break!"

Her words, her pitiful expression, the barely controlled sobs choking her voice, drove all sleep from me. I sat up and threw my arms about the poor girl, whereupon she lost all control and burst into heartrending sobs. I comforted her as best I could, waiting until she had gained some semblance of composure before I climbed from my bed and led her over to the chaise longue, where I insisted she sit down. I poured for her a cup of the tea she had brought for me, then gave her a clean linen to dry her face.

When at last she was able, she said, in a dull, flat voice, "It be Lueddy, m'Lady. Her be dead."

Chapter Sixteen

A long day, a long and colorless day; a day of which I remember little save the stillness and the emptiness. Somehow, breakfast was prepared and served to those guests who had remained the night. Unexpectedly, Adam shouldered the responsibility of saying the family farewells and seeing everyone off to meet the morning train.

When the guests had departed, the family gathered in the great hall. All trace of the previous day's festivities had been cleared away by servants who had labored until dawn. Now, Papa and Elizabeth sat side by side upon the settee, the one where my stepmother and I had sat the night Adam brought Helaine into our midst. John stood before the fireplace, head bowed, hands clasped behind his back. I could not sit still, but wandered aimlessly the length of the hall and back.

The fire burned low in the grate. A quiet, subdued servant entered, added a log, and it took hold with a lively crackle. The servant withdrew.

Elizabeth's eyes were red-rimmed, her face drawn. Papa looked pale and wooden. His eyes, too, were red, but his face, though marked by fatigue, was calm, composed.

Thus we waited in silence, in our grief drawing close, until Pastor Grewe came. Because Lueddy had no kin, and because she had held a very special place in the family, it was understood that she would lie next to the Lady Christina in the Garth family plot, adjacent to the village church. And when Pastor Grewe had come and gone, by mutual consent we each returned to our own rooms to nurse our grief in our own way.

With an aching heart I recalled how, when I was a baby, it was Lueddy's hand that rocked my cradle, Lueddy who held and comforted me; and after Elizabeth came, Lueddy had cared for both Adam and me. She had washed our faces and combed our hair; she had tended our scraped knees when we fell, and our wounded pride when Papa or Elizabeth saw fit to chastise us. It was Lueddy who had fed us and told us stories; but most of all, she had loved us — especially me, because I reminded her of her little bird.

I wished that Betsy would come to sit with me, but she did not. My suspicions and distrust of Betsy, occasioned by Helaine's cruel and tactless remarks, had long since been dispelled. And though I believed Betsy too young, too innocent to understand my sorrows and fears, her very youth and innocence were at times a balm to my weary heart. And so it was on that sad day: I wished that Betsy were there to sit with me, to talk with me, or just to share the silence.

Impulsively, I crossed to the connecting door, opened it, and looked in. She was not there. When Gillian brought my lunch, I asked her if she had seen Betsy, but she shook her head. Disconsolate, I picked up a book and tried to read, but the words flowed through my head in a meaningless stream. When I realized I was reading the same paragraph for the third time, I gave it up and allowed those thoughts that had been buried in my subconscious all the long day to rise to the surface.

Adam: the aftermath of the ball, the shame and pain of that tawdry encounter. Now, in the cold light of day, I acknowledged to myself how inexcusable my behavior at the ball had been. I had teased him, led him on. And yet, I thought, he should not have come to my room, should not have . . .

My cheeks burned at the memory. My head throbbed. I felt as if a huge stone lay upon my chest, making it difficult to breathe. When Gillian arrived with my tea tray, I was still huddled upon the chaise.

I must have sighed heavily, because Gillian turned from the table where she was arranging my food and looked at me. "Be ye all right, Lady Victoria?"

I tried to give her a reassuring smile. "I am fine, thank you, Gillian." While I had her attention I added, "Will you please ask Miss Betsy to join me? I would like her to take tea with me."

Gillian continued to stand gazing at me, eyes wide, a perplexed expression on her guileless countenance. "Please, m' Lady . . . I don't know where Miss Betsy be."

I made no comment, but waited with as much patience as I could muster for her to continue. I had learned long since that to question Gillian too closely only served to confuse her. She would, quite naturally, like a stream of water running down hill, unburden herself of all she knew, if one would simply wait and let her talk. Too many questions, on the other hand, posed for Gillian a riddle she must unravel, and by the time she had unraveled the riddle, the answer was long gone. I looked her in the eye, confident that the words would come, slowly but surely, until she had recited everything she could remember. And sure enough, her troubled eyes gazed into mine and the words began to trickle, then to flow.

"Her were that upset, m'Lady. Her said nary a word to me. Her just knelt there on floor, holdin' ol' Lueddy's hand 'til Pastor Grewe, he come. It were Betsy as found Lueddy, m'Lady. Every mornin' her comes an' her sits an' talks with Lueddy. Her takes her books an' her reads for ol' Lueddy—"

The retelling of the story became too much for Gillian, and she began to cry. "Oh, law, m'Lady, it were a terrible day," she managed to choke out between great, wracking sobs.

I told Gillian to dry her eyes and blow her nose, then poured her some tea, which she drank, hiccoughing noisily. At last, however, she calmed herself enough to continue. "When I went to the kitchen this mornin', Betsy were kneelin' there aside Lueddy's chair . . . Lueddy di'n't sleep much o' late, just sat and nodded in her chair . . . an' Betsy were holdin' her hand. Her face were all cold and hard, like, an' she said nary a word."

Gillian paused, sniffed mightily as she rubbed the back of her hand across her nose. "Oh, m'Lady, such a shock it were! I know'd right off somethin' were wrong with Lueddy. Her were sittin' . . . funny, somehow.

"I runned over t'ords her an' I seed Betsy there on the floor, holdin' Lueddy's hand. All big-eyed her were, an' . . . an' . . . an' still, like. I said, 'What's happent?' but Betsy said nary a word, an' I runned quick to fetch Bella. Then Bella runned to fetch the Lady Elizabeth, an' Paster Grewe, he were sent for, an' all the time, Betsy just stayed there on her knees, holdin' Lueddy's hand an' sayin' nary a word."

Gillian fell silent, and I could tell from the droop of her shoulders that she had repeated everything she could remember, so I asked, "Does Betsy have any family, any friends, anyone in the village to whom she might have gone?"

"There be no one, m'Lady. Betsy do be all alone in the world. Belike Lueddy were all the family Miss Betsy had."

This last remark startled me, for I had not known that Betsy had any special tie with Lueddy. True, I did have some vague memory of Betsy mentioning that Lueddy had known her grandmother; but, when I stopped to think about it, I clearly knew very little of Betsy's history. As I sat there, racking my brain, I seemed to recall hearing somewhere, probably from Elizabeth, that Betsy had been raised by her grandmother.

Betsy herself had never mentioned her past life. I had not asked questions, thinking she would speak of her childhood in her own good time, when she deemed it necessary—if, indeed, I had thought about it at all. Now I berated myself roundly for having neglected Betsy all through the day, and a sense of unease, of foreboding, mounted within me, until I was frightened beyond reason. All the vague and nameless fears that had hovered over me for weeks past suddenly crowded in upon me, and I felt completely inadequate and terribly alone.

However, there seemed nothing more to say to Gillian, so I dismissed her, instructing her to enquire amongst the other members of the staff to see if anyone knew Betsy's whereabouts. By myself once more, I paced the floor, trying to decide what to do. Where in the world could she be in this bitter cold weather—and it was now long past dark. Surely I should go to look for her, but where? I had not the faintest notion where to begin a search.

Then I considered asking for help; but who? Papa and Elizabeth had sorrow enough to deal with right now. Adam, I could not face, not even under these circumstances. Helaine would be of no use, even were I of a mind to seek her aid. John? Of course! Why had I not thought of him sooner?

I rushed to the wardrobe and pulled out my boots and a heavy pelisse, which I tossed upon the bed. I shoved my feet into the boots and fastened the buckles, then turned to the bed to get the cloak. Only then did I see, lying on my pillow, a folded paper with my name written upon it in Betsy's round, flowing script.

I snatched it up, tore it open, and read: "Dear Victoria, Please do not worry about me or seek to find me. I will be quite safe, and will see you early tomorrow morning." It was signed with an elaborate letter *B*.

It was too much. The excitement of the Christmas ball followed by that shocking scene with Adam, the pain and sorrow of Lueddy's passing, the worry over Betsy—I flung myself onto my bed and burst into sobs. I wept the tears of exhaustion, then fell asleep.

I wakened with a start to hear someone pounding on my door. I started up, rubbing the sleep from my swollen eyes. "Come in," I called groggily.

It was John. He strode furiously into the room shouting my name. Now completely awake, I got up and moved forward to meet him. At the sight of me he stopped, started to speak, then took a closer look. "Good heavens, Victoria! You look awful."

I opened my mouth to reply, but he waved his hands,

shook his head. "I am sorry. It has been a trying day. I know how much Lueddy meant to you."

Again I tried to speak; however, John had only paused for breath. "But Miss Betsy is missing, Victoria. What can have hap—"

I had to raise my voice to make myself heard. "I know, John!"

"You do?" He stared at me. "Where is she? Is she quite safe?"

"I don't know where she is, but I do not doubt she is safe," and I showed him the message Betsy had left for me.

John read it carefully, then raised his eyes to meet mine once more. "What does it mean?"

"We shall have to wait until she returns to discover that."

"But where could she have gone? She has no one but us, Victoria."

Now how did he know that? I wondered. But before I could pose the question, John continued.

"She was raised by her grandmother, never even knew her mother and father. When her grandmother died, Lueddy took her in because she had nowhere to go. So where can she be tonight?"

I was astounded! How had my little brother learned so much about *my* companion?

John, who had been pacing up and down my room like a caged bear, suddenly stopped, and turned to me once more. "Well?" he demanded.

It would have been funny, had the situation not been so grave. I seated myself on the chaise and motioned for my brother to join me before I replied. "She has gone of her own free will," I pointed out. "Her note says not to worry, she will return in the morning. I understand that you are fearful for her, but I also think your fear is unwarranted. Her message is quite clear: we are not to worry, she will return in the morning."

Looking slightly abashed, John stared again at the note Betsy had left me. "You are right, of course. It is just that I have been looking for her, and . . ."

Suddenly I reached out and ruffled his hair—a gesture that had made him furious when we were children. Now it brought a wry smile to his lips. "Do you know, Victoria, you were a real tyrant when you were ten years old?"

"And you were always underfoot!"

Our eyes met, and a host of memories flowed between us. Ghosts from yesterday, when an unwilling little boy had been sent to keep an eye on his sister and half-brother.

John's expression grew serious, and he said softly, "Victoria, there is something I should like to ask you."

I hesitated, mentally bracing myself, certain that he was going to ask why Adam had not married me. "I cannot promise that I will answer," I said at last, "but ask away."

But again my little brother surprised me. "Why," he asked, "do you suppose Adam married such an old woman?"

Chapter Seventeen

Dawn was just breaking when I awakened. It was much too early to be up and about, so I closed my eyes and tried to empty my mind of all thought, but sleep steadfastly eluded me. I tossed and turned, then finally gave up. And for a time, I entertained myself recalling the long conversation John and I had enjoyed the night before, once I had stopped laughing.

Only John could have asked such a question, I thought delightedly. And then I tried to imagine the look on my sister-in-law's face if she had heard herself referred to as "such an old woman."

Then, lying there in the early morning quiet, I began to wonder if I should have confided in John after all. But he was so forthright, so full of common sense. Perhaps he could find some meaning in my dreams—in the notes and the nightmares.

Slowly I became aware of the stillness within the house and I caught myself listening, for what, I knew not. The long day ahead, with the sorrows it entailed, burying Lueddy, filled my mind, and suddenly my only wish was to curl up into a tight little ball, pull the covers over my head, and nestle in the warmth and the dark forever. But I could not. I was like a spring that is wound too tight. Even Cyrano, snoring quietly on the foot of the bed, lent me no comfort.

Then it occurred to me that Betsy might have already returned, might even at that moment be in her bed. I threw back the covers and, unmindful of the cold, ran to the connecting door. Betsy was not there. Her bed had not been slept in.

When Gillian arrived with my morning tea, I was already up and dressed. I gulped down a cup of the steaming brew, gave my hair a perfunctory brushing, coiled it into a knot on the back of my head, and went downstairs. There was no one in the great hall or the breakfast room. The silence in the house bespoke sorrow, and I was loath to return to my room, so I went out into the park and walked aimlessly under the trees.

But the weather turned foul, the wind rose, and snow began to fall. Chilled, damp, not knowing what else to do, I returned to my room. And there, sitting calm and composed upon the chaise longue, her feet tucked under her skirts, stroking the head of Cyrano who sprawled sleeping across her knees, was Betsy.

"Betsy, Betsy, Betsy!" I cried, as I flew to the chaise and dropped down beside her. "Where have you been? Why did you run away?"

"I did not run away . . . truly, I did not." She hesitated, then asked, "Does anyone else know I was away last night?"

Her question took me by surprise, but I answered readily enough, "Yes, I'm certain all the servants know."

Betsy's lips tightened, and some of the color receded from her cheeks.

"And John. He was terribly upset . . ."

In the first joy of seeing Betsy, I had not noticed how tense and drawn she looked. Now I asked sharply, "Betsy, dear child, whatever is the matter?"

But before Betsy could answer, a brisk rap upon my door announced the presence of my stepmother. The sight of the two of us, there together upon the chaise, brought a relieved smile to her face. "I have searched high and low for you both. Betsy, my dear, if you have had your breakfast — you have, of course — go directly to my sitting room. Bella and

Miss Twitchle will make ready a suitable mourning costume for you to wear. When you are dressed and ready, you may return and accompany Victoria. The service is to be at three, so we must be in the carriage and ready to depart by half past two."

I knew that Betsy was loath to leave me, but she arose dutifully and departed, carrying Cyrano with her. When she had gone, Elizabeth took Betsy's place beside me on the chaise. Studying my face, her eyes filled with concern. "You look tired, little love. I wish I could spare you, but we must all be strong for Samuel's sake."

"How is Papa?"

"He is taking Lueddy's passing very hard. She was like a mother to him . . . he loved the dear old soul. I think none of us shall ever know how hard his life was when he was a child, or what a comfort Lueddy was to him then."

"What can I do?"

"There is little any of us can do. Be near when he needs us; let him know that we understand. . . ." She sighed, fell silent. And so we sat, quietly for a while, each of us lost in her own concern for Papa, her own memories of Lueddy.

At last Elizabeth rose and said, "Rest until lunch time, then. It will be another long day."

After lunch, followed by Gillian, I returned to my room and readied myself for the funeral. I was all but ready, just tying the ribbons of my bonnet, when Betsy entered. Somehow, amongst them, Elizabeth, Bella, and Miss Twitchle had managed to put together for Betsy a costume entirely of black, as befitted the occasion.

I dismissed Gillian, and Betsy and I descended to the great hall together. We were met there by Papa and Elizabeth. Adam and Helaine were also there, Helaine heavily veiled, Adam looking cold and withdrawn. John entered almost immediately and strode forward to meet us.

How like our father he is, I thought. How sturdy and strong he has grown. Then he was beside us, and he put his strong young arms about Papa. It wasn't until that moment that I realized Papa was crying.

The church service was short. I could hear a quaver in Pastor Grewe's once strong voice. He must, I thought, have known Lueddy for many years. I tried to imagine Lueddy as a young girl, her eyes bright, her cheeks rosy. Pastor Grewe would have been a tall young man then. Now his shoulders were stooped, his hair snowy white; and Lueddy, dear Lueddy was dead. . . . The hot salt tears blinded my eyes, rolled down my face, while in the steeple high overhead, the church bell tolled.

Thus we buried Lueddy. On her tombstone was written *Beloved friend of Christina and Samuel Garth*. And when the last prayer had been said and the coffin lowered into the ground, we returned to Greystone Manor.

Short though it was, I found the service at the church followed by the ritual at graveside, exhausting, and the sight of Papa's tears had completely unnerved me. All the way home I longed for the quiet of my room, longed to lie down, to shut my eyes, to lose myself in the oblivion of sleep. Yet the instant I closed my bedroom door behind me, I was overwhelmed by a crawling unease.

I had the distinct sensation that I was not alone. The muscles across my shoulder blades twitched. I hugged my arms tight across my bosom and glanced behind me, but the room appeared to be empty, save for me. With a compulsive jerk of my head, I glanced over my shoulder at the bottom of the tapestry beside my bed, half expecting to see again that ugly triangular head with its beady eyes and flickering tongue, weaving back and forth between the fronds of fern. There was nothing there.

I rang for Gillian, then took off my hat and gloves, dropped them on a table. Gillian arrived, helped me off with my dress, loosened my lacings, then bustled about putting things away. I donned a robe. Gillian offered to brush my hair, but I dismissed her, saying I could manage.

But all the while, the tension kept mounting inside me. I was fighting fear once more. Whence it came, I knew not. Like a foul miasma, something unseen, something unholy seemed to hang in the air, and suddenly I knew I could not stay alone. Driven by a sense of panic, I darted across the room to the connecting door and burst through, too obsessed by fear to knock first.

Betsy was not there, but the drapes across the French doors, which in winter were usually kept closed to shut out the cold, were drawn wide. The late afternoon sun had broken through the clouds and now washed the room in glaring white light. Without hesitating I rushed forward, and would have gone straight out onto the balcony had not a cold hand fastened itself about my wrist.

A high-pitched yelp of dismay burst from my lips before Betsy's hushed and ragged whisper could silence me. With the strength of desperation, she yanked me back out of the sun's light into the dark shadow cast by the draperies, shushing me under her breath.

As my eyes accustomed themselves to the dim light there in the shadow, I became aware of Betsy's terrified expression. Her eyes, wide open and glassy, were almost starting from their sockets, and her head wobbled upon its slender neck. While her fingers maintained their painful grip upon my arm, the back of her other hand was pressed tight against her mouth as if to stifle a scream.

We remained thus, standing as if frozen, while the seconds became minutes, and all the while her fear-filled eyes cautioned me to silence. Then, without warning, she began dragging me back toward the connecting door. She did not stop until we reached my chaise longue where she collapsed in a heap, dragging me down with her. Thereupon, she threw her arms about me, buried her face against my shoulder, and gave herself up to a fit of hysterical weeping.

In my concern for Betsy, I had quite forgotten my own fear. Gently I stroked her hair and whispered, "There, there," even as Elizabeth had whispered to me when, as a child, I had cried upon her shoulder. At last the shuddering of Betsy's body lessened, and the sobbing resolved itself into small, half-strangled hiccoughs, then ceased.

Only then did she sit back and look at me beseechingly.

Totally mystified and not a little upset by her behavior, I

said, "Whatever is the matter Betsy dear? What has frightened you so?"

Now she clasped her hands tightly together, and her tear-reddened eyes stared into my face. "If I tell you, promise you will believe me, Victoria," she implored, the words breathy and ragged.

Is it not wonderful how someone else's weakness, someone else's need, sometimes awakens in us a strength we did not know we possessed? So it was with me that day. Seeing Betsy's fear, I forgot my own; seeing Betsy's uncertainty, I was reassured.

"Of course, Betsy. I should never, ever doubt you."

I wish that I could relate, word for word, the things that Betsy then said to me, but I cannot. I will have to recount her story in my own words, setting events in order as best I can. Actually, much of the story I had heard from John the night before. But I did not interrupt Betsy's telling, though it was filled with jumps and skips, tears and back-tracking. As I understood it, this is what occurred.

She had spent much time with Lueddy, both while she was still working in the kitchen, and after she had moved upstairs and become my pupil and friend. Apparently there had been a blood relationship between Lueddy and Betsy's grandmother. For this reason, even as a small child Betsy had frequently been brought to visit in the kitchen of Greystone Manor. When Betsy's grandmother died, leaving Betsy completely alone, it was Lueddy who had interceded with Samuel on the child's behalf, and so she had come to the manor.

Things had gone smoothly at first. Lueddy, despite her advanced age, was well and alert, and she had clucked and fussed over the orphaned Betsy like a broody hen. However, soon after Adam returned to the family home with his bride, Lueddy had begun to fail. She kept more and more to the kitchen until, in fact, she rarely left the hearthside at all, but sat and nodded the whole night, as well as the day, in her chair.

Her mind as well as her body had begun to weaken. Her

manner became strained and secretive. Time and time again, she cautioned Betsy to silence. Though Betsy could not understand what she was supposed to know, or what secret she was expected to keep, she had tried to reassure Lueddy, to soothe her.

At that point in her narrative, I had stopped Betsy and asked, "Can you tell me exactly what Lueddy said about a secret?"

Betsy hesitated, then replied that as nearly as she could remember, Lueddy had said, "Don't ye never tell no one who ye be, child, an' stay away from the green-eyed demon."

Suddenly Betsy straightened up and looked at me defiantly. "I know it doesn't make sense, Victoria, but that is what she said."

I made no comment. The words made no sense to me, either, but I patted Betsy's hand reassuringly and asked her to continue. Taking a deep breath, she resumed her tale: Lueddy had told her only the week before she died that she, Betsy, was a lady born, and that her *uncle* lived in a fine house in London.

Once again Betsy interrupted herself to exclaim, "Truly, truly, Victoria, that is what she told me. I know it doesn't make any sense, and at the time I thought it only the maunderings of a very old woman . . . but that is what she told me. You *do* believe me? You must know I'm not making it all up."

"I do believe you, Betsy. I don't know what it means, or how it could be true, but I do believe that Lueddy believed it, and that that is what she told you."

Reassured, Betsy resumed. "Lueddy said to me, 'Ye can read now, child, an' ye must go to the churchyard where they buried yer grandmother an' see what ol' Lueddy tells ye be true. It say on another stone, near yer grandmother's CATHERINE, BELOVED SISTER OF CARTER."

Carter! The name hit me like an icy fist, draining my strength, leaving me weak and breathless. I sat there in a state of shock, staring at Betsy.

She was not looking at me as she talked. Rather, her head

was tilted back and her eyes were closed tight. The sunlight, streaming through a crack in the draperies, turned her chestnut hair into a halo of gleaming gold, framing her upturned face. Her fingers were knotted together in her lap, and her knuckles shone white. There was a greyish tinge about her mouth as though she were ill. Her lips were moving but her words came to my dazed mind in a jumble of far-off sound.

I tried to concentrate on what she was saying, but all the while the temptation to giggle grew and grew inside me. I was making a desperate effort to cling to the last shreds of my self-control when Betsy suddenly opened her eyes. The sight of my face, which she later told me had blanched to a greenish white, and my wild, staring eyes was almost too much for her.

She grabbed me roughly by the shoulders and started to shake me. "Don't look so, Victoria! I *swear* I am telling the truth!" And she began to weep once more.

Though a smart slap might have been better, the shaking had helped to snap me back to normality. I forced myself to draw several very deep breaths, and then I said, "It's all right, Betsy. I know you are telling the truth. Please, please tell me . . . everything you can remember."

She looked at me dubiously, blew her nose, then continued. "I loved Lueddy, Victoria. I loved her almost as much as I loved my grandmother, but I didn't really believe any of her stories until it was too late. I thought it was just her age . . . and she always told such tales."

I understood what Betsy meant. How well I remembered the long winter evenings when Lueddy, the consummate storyteller, had kept John and Adam and me wide-eyed with her wonderful tales.

I stood up, went to the wardrobe, and returned with a clean linen for Betsy. "Now, tell me what happened the night Lueddy died."

Betsy accepted the cloth, wiped the tears from her cheeks, blew her nose, and continued.

She recounted how she had gone straight down to the

kitchen after the ball to tell Lueddy about the dancing, and to show her her gown. She always went to say goodnight and to see if there was anything she could get for Lueddy before she, herself, went to bed.

She had found Lueddy in her usual place before the fire, in a state of extreme agitation. With much waving of her hands she had urged Betsy to come quickly to her side. Betsy hurried forward and dropped to her knees next to Lueddy's chair.

Lueddy had immediately grasped both Betsy's hands in her own and whispered, "Pray with me, child. Close yer eyes an' pray!"

Before Betsy could continue, I asked, "Pray for what?"

Betsy looked mystified. "Why, I do not know what Lueddy was praying for. I was so startled, she sounded so frightened, I just prayed that we might be kept safe from all harm."

"That was sensible," I agreed.

Betsy again picked up the thread of her story: Two cats that had been napping on the ledge in the inglenook had suddenly awakened, hissing and spitting, hair on end, and fled.

Betsy hesitated, then admitted, "I thought at first it must be because Mistress Helaine had entered the kitchen, though I could not think why she would be there, especially at that time of night."

"Why did you think they would react so because of Helaine?" I interrupted.

"Because the animals all fear her. Neither cat nor dog will stay in a room when she is there, and the horses are skittish when she is in the carriage. When the cats ran, I thought it was because of her." Betsy sighed and fell silent.

I did not urge her to proceed—my mind was busy worrying over this last strange bit of information. *Animals did not like Helaine?* Once more I felt that hysterical urge to giggle churning inside me. I was surprised to hear how calm my own voice sounded when I asked, "Then what happened?"

"Well, we sat thus, neither moving nor speaking, for ever

so long. I knew Lueddy was praying, though she made no sound. I heard the great clock on the landing strike the hour, and the kitchen began to grow cold. The fire was still blazing and crackling right beside us, but it was very cold. And then"—suddenly her voice broke, she swallowed convulsively, and her hands gripped themselves tightly together in her lap—"you must believe me, Victoria."

Her eyes bored into mine, and I nodded.

"I saw," and here her voice took on a hysterical quality, rising in pitch and becoming very breathy, "I saw, slithering along the floor just at the edge of the firelight, a serpent. I saw it! And it raised its head and looked at us, and its eyes were all bright and evil."

My flesh crawled. My heart raced. My mind whirled. I was dimly aware that Betsy's voice had broken upon those last words, and she had buried her face in her hands.

By the time she raised her head once more, I, too, had regained some semblance of control. Betsy continued: "I was so frightened I could not even scream, but I do not think Lueddy saw it—the serpent, I mean—for at that very moment, and I swear this is true, I was not asleep and dreaming . . . at that very moment, a lady I have never seen before came walking up beside us. Then she just leaned down and kissed Lueddy."

Betsy paused and looked at me. I did not speak, but she must have found reassurance in my face for she carried on. "I think she spoke to Lueddy, but I did not hear any sound at all. It was so cold, and I was so frightened. I closed my eyes and prayed. Perhaps I fainted, I don't know. The next thing I remember, it was morning and the cold was gone . . . the lady was gone . . . the serpent was gone. And I knew that Lueddy was dead."

With those last words, Betsy's voice had faded slowly into silence. Quiet tears spilled from the corners of her eyes and rolled down her face. After a deep breath she spoke once more, her voice flat, exhausted. "I didn't know what to do. Then Gillian came, and then Pastor Grewe."

I waited for her to continue, but she remained silent. Finally I asked, "Why did you leave the house?"

She started, as if her mind had been miles away. But after a moment she resumed. "I knew I had to find that tombstone, but I couldn't tell anyone . . . not even you, Victoria. I had to know for certain, you understand?" Again her eyes searched mine.

"Of course."

"I jumped up and ran out of the kitchen and up to my room. I changed as quickly as ever I could, wrote that note for you, then left by way of the back stairs. I ran all the way through the park and across the old bridge. I went straight to the churchyard and I searched and searched, and I found it: CATHERINE, BELOVED SISTER OF CARTER, BORN 1798, DIED 1814.

Again, at the mention of Carter, a chill raised gooseflesh on my arms.

Betsy did not notice my reaction. "It was late by the time I found the grave, and I had decided, in any event, to spend the night at my grandmother's cottage. Fortunately it is still unoccupied. I just went in, climbed up into the loft, where I had always slept, and went to sleep, wondering what it could all mean."

For a while, we were each of us lost in her own thoughts. The minutes ticked away, the clock sang out the passing quarter-hour in its tinkling chimes.

Suddenly Betsy asked, "What *does* it all mean, Victoria?"

I shook my head, "But," I said, "I, too, have seen the serpent, and I think I have seen the young woman."

Betsy nodded gravely and without surprise. It was obvious that she was spent, physically and emotionally, and though she sought no explanation, I added, "I have said nothing to anyone because I feared I was imagining these things . . . perhaps even losing my mind."

With a gasp of sympathy, Betsy reached out and took my hands comfortingly in her own. Once more the silence enveloped us. I jumped when Betsy spoke again: "Victoria, why do you suppose the cats so fear Miss Helaine? I fear her too, you know. 'Twas she who frightened me so just now in my room."

I was too startled by these words to reply, but Betsy continued, seeming not to notice my surprise. "I left the draperies drawn when we went to church this afternoon. When I got back, I went straight to the door to close them—the drapes I mean—and I heard another door along the terrace open. I don't know why, but I jumped back into the shadow, and then I saw Helaine. She was moving along very quickly, carrying a large wicker hamper. When she saw that my drapes stood open, she stopped, walked over, and looked into my room."

A shudder passed through Betsy, and she gulped for air before continuing. "She was standing close enough to have touched me had the doors been open. How she did not see me, I cannot understand. Neither do I know why I was so frightened. However she did not linger, but continued on to a little door in the tower. You do know there is a little hidden door there in the east tower, do you not, Victoria?"

Helaine knew about the secret door in the tower! I was dumbstruck by this revelation. I could only stare at Betsy while my mind seethed.

What could Helaine be doing in the tower? And how, in God's name, did she know about the little door? It was hidden so cleverly. Adam and I had discovered it quite by accident only days before he left for the Continent. But of course! Adam would have told her.

The thought filled me with rage. Was it not bad enough that he had married this woman? Did he have to share *our* secrets with her as well?

But wait. Betsy said she went in alone. Why had Adam not accompanied her?. Not that it really mattered. What mattered was the fact that Adam had revealed our secret to that dreadful woman! Indeed, I felt doubly betrayed, because it had always been an unspoken covenant, as binding as our love: the house and its secrets belonged to us, alone, even as we belonged to each other.

Another spasm of grief and anger shook me as I thought, by all that is right and holy, even now Adam and I should be exploring that tower together. In my agitation I had leaped to my feet, but when I went to take a step, I became aware that Betsy was pulling at my skirt.

"Victoria! What is the matter? What have I done? For the love of heaven, speak to me!"

I took a deep breath to steady myself, then sank back down beside her, patted her hand reassuringly. "You have done nothing, Betsy. It is what . . . someone else . . . has done." I hesitated, uncertain as to whether I should at last reveal to Betsy how Adam had betrayed me.

I did not ponder the question long. Betsy was my friend — indeed, she was like a sister to me. Slowly at first, then with complete abandon, I found myself telling her the whole story: how, just prior to Adam's departure for Paris, quite by accident we had discovered the secret door. There had been neither opportunity nor time before Adam's departure for us to more than step inside the tower.

I paused, then explained, "Once Adam was gone, I did not attempt to explore the tower alone, because I wished to share the adventure with him when he returned."

Again I paused, wondering if I should admit the truth. Then I thought, what is to be gained by dissembling? I took another deep breath and continued, "In truth, on the one occasion when I opened that little door and stepped inside, I was overcome by a sense of horror so great, it was like a physical presence."

I paused, studied Betsy's expression. There was only candor there. Reassured, I went on. "I was so terrified, I slammed the door shut and went straight back to my room. To this day, I find myself shunning that end of the balcony." And though I did not say it aloud to Betsy, I reflected that even so, with Adam to protect me, I should have faced that tower and whatever it might hold with perfect equanimity.

But Betsy was speaking. ". . . and she had just entered the tower when you came in."

Listening to Betsy's story, I had been wracked by many emotions, but at these last words my being filled with rage. "How *dare* she!" The words burst from me. "How dare she go snooping about in the tower!"

It was useless to remind myself that as Mrs. Adam Johnshaven Garth she had as much right as I to go wherever she chose in the house. My anger would not be calmed, and I continued my outburst. "Betsy, I hate that woman! I hate her with all my heart and all my soul, and I know that she is evil." I had spoken in a crescendo of fury, my final words sounding loud and clear in the quiet of my room.

Betsy drew back in fright, whispering, "Hush, Victoria, she will hear you!" We both turned and looked with apprehension toward my French doors.

Nothing happened. I do not know what we expected, but nothing at all happened. No sound penetrated the gentle eventide hush within my room. The winter sun had long since dropped below the horizon, and not even the wind broke the stillness. Then, through the gathering gloom, we heard the sound of a door closing somewhere nearby.

Betsy and I looked at each other, and I declared, "Betsy, I do not know what is happening here in Greystone Manor. Neither do I know what to do about it, but now I think I am not ready for Bedlam after all, and I would like some tea."

Chapter Eighteen

The knowledge that someone shared my delusions, if such they were, brought a quietude of soul I had not known for weeks, and I awoke the morning following Lueddy's funeral almost light of heart. I felt so good, in fact, that I did not even rebuke Gillian when I found my tea yet again too sweet to drink.

After a couple of sips, I got out of bed and hummed a gay little tune while I dressed. When Betsy peeked through the connecting door to say good morning, she admonished me with a stern shake of her head. "Sing before breakfast, cry before supper."

"Not today," I answered blithely. "There have been enough tears shed in this household of late."

The long hours of talking the previous afternoon had had a healing effect upon both of us. Somehow, as we shared our experiences, our fears and woes, they did not seem quite so monstrous, quite so threatening after all.

So what if I walked in my sleep? Lots of people walk in their sleep—it did not mean that they were mad. What if I suffered from nightmares? An unpleasant experience, but hardly proof of insanity. As for that strange note and the name Carter—well, the name, at least, could easily have been planted in my mind by one of Lueddy's stories. Nodding our agreement, Betsy and I again reminded each other of the many evenings when we had been enthralled by one of Lueddy's strange and wondrous tales.

Even Lueddy's warnings to Betsy could quite easily be explained away when we recalled how skillfully the old woman was wont to weave into her stories the names of people in and places about Greystone Manor. If, as she grew older, she actually began to confuse fact with fancy, jumbling the realities of her youth with the fantasies of her old age, that too was perfectly natural, completely understandable.

Of course, neither Betsy nor I could remember any such story, but it was not inconceivable. Finally, we declared that each circumstance that had seemed so ominous when considered alone was sheer coincidence or imagination, and promised one another we would think no more about any of it.

As for our feelings about Helaine, even these, once shared, seemed less urgent. If we disliked and distrusted her, if she inspired hostility in the servants and fear in the animals, it was because she was, as Betsy put it, "not a very likeable or trustworthy person." It was a remark that elicited a peal of giggles from me.

The one thing I had not revealed to Betsy the previous evening was my love for Adam. And it was unthinkable that I should ever relate to her that humiliating confrontation with him the night of the Christmas ball.

Even now, in the bright light of a lovely morning, as the memory of that disgraceful incident came flooding back, the happy little tune with which I had greeted the day died upon my lips, and I felt my face burn with shame. What a low opinion Adam must hold of me, that he could have made such dishonorable advances. Suddenly, I had no stomach for breakfast. I could not face the thought of sitting at table with the family—with Adam. Besides, my head had begun to ache.

I stood in my room, hand upon the doorknob, trying to decide what to do. I glanced at the mantel clock. It was still very early. If I hurry, I decided, I can get a book from the library, a cinnamon bun from the breakfast room, and be back here long before Adam begins his daily routine downstairs.

The plan was hardly complete in my mind before I was on my way. I hurried across the gallery, ran down the back stairs, along the corridor, and into the library. As the door swung to behind me, a draft of cold air caused me to gather my shawl more closely about my shoulders. But that was not all: some sixth sense was sending little warning signals dancing along my nerve endings, and apprehension slowed my steps until I came to a standstill, peering intently about.

The light, as it streamed through the leaded panes of the stained glass windows, was muted, transformed into shadows that slunk behind the chairs and under the tables, crouched in the corners of the room. There was no sound, but as my eyes sought to pierce the gloom, I thought I detected some movement near Adam's desk.

"Who's there?" I called.

The only answer was a faint, hollow echo. Fear ran its spidery fingers down my back. I caught my breath, strained my ears, seeking to hear any smallest rustle or creak. There was only silence. And all the while, I was goaded by the temptation to turn and flee.

Then, as I stood there, anger began to grow in me. Why should I be afraid in my own home? It was ridiculous! And clenching my fists, I forced myself to move forward.

When I reached the leather sofa in front of the fireplace, I hesitated. The room had grown perceptibly darker. A wave of nausea washed over me. I leaned against the back of the sofa to steady myself, but the feeling of nausea intensified, and my head throbbed. I reached up without thinking and pulled the combs from my hair. It tumbled down over my shoulders, fell across my cheeks in untidy wisps.

I raised my hand to brush the truant locks from my face, threw back my head. The fire in the huge grate had burned low during the night, and I could see quite clearly through the cavernous opening into the other half of the library.

And there, lounging against the sofa on that other side of the fireplace, was a man. Even standing at ease, he projected a magnetism, a sinewy grace that was at once fascinating and repulsive—and he was handsome. His face was as finely chiseled as a statue by Praxiteles, with wide-set eyes that glittered in the firelight. He was smiling an evil, sardonic smile that touched only his lips. His eyes, filled with malevolence, were cold and alert.

I remained as if frozen, gazing into those baleful eyes. I could not speak, could not think. It was as if time itself had stopped.

His hands, resting on the back of the sofa, were strong and graceful, and even in the murky light I could see, coiled about the middle finger of his left hand, a heavy gold ring fashioned in the likeness of a snake. The head, broad, flat, triangular in shape, rose up over the knuckle and was set with two black diamonds that caught the light from the fire and shattered it into a million sparkling bits. And as I stared at that singular ring, the man raised his hand with a languid movement, touched his fingers to his lips, and blew me a kiss.

There was something so hideous, so corrupt about that gesture, I feared that, being face to face with such evil, my mind, too, must shatter and fall into a million lost and empty pieces. Yet at the same time, an all-consuming hatred vied with the revulsion, and I think I even took a faltering step toward him.

He threw back his head and began to laugh, and though no sound reached my ears, I could hear him! I could hear his vile laughter inside my head, and the sound of it followed me down into the blackness of total oblivion.

When I opened my eyes I was lying on my bed, a silken robe thrown over me. The drapes had been drawn wide and the late morning sun shone bright on the balcony, glistened on the snow atop the balustrade. Betsy was sitting on the chaise, her legs tucked up comfortably under her long, full skirt. Cyrano, grown now into an exceedingly large and well-muscled cat, was sleeping peacefully, the whole long length of him sprawled across her knees. I thought to speak to Betsy, but I was so tired. My lids drooped, my eyes closed once more, but I did not go back to sleep.

Why, I wondered, was I lying in bed? Why was Betsy sitting there, so quiet, so still—and then memory came flooding back. The library—the man. I opened my eyes again and moved to throw back the coverlet, but before I could complete the movement Betsy jumped to her feet, dropping Cyrano unceremoniously to the floor, and was beside me in two long strides. She gave a tremendous yank upon the bell-pull, then took my hand in hers, calling urgently all the while, "Victoria! Victoria!"

Then I felt Elizabeth's hand upon my forehead, and the sound of Gillian's snuffling became audible. I opened my eyes once more and looked up into the dear faces all grouped about me. My stepmother leaned near and kissed my cheek, just as she had done when, as a child, I was confined to bed for one reason or another.

"There, there, little love," she soothed. "How do you feel?"

And without waiting for an answer, she raised her head and commanded, "Gillian, stop that snuffling at once, and fetch some warm milk for Lady Victoria."

Then to me, "Don't try to talk, little love. Its rest you need. Dr. Maerrie will be here soon."

The ormolu clock on the mantel chimed eleven o'clock. Where had the morning gone? I tried to remember what had happened, tried to speak, but the words seemed to get lost before I could utter them.

The lines of concern etching Elizabeth's pale, tired face deepened. "Oh, Victoria, baby," she asked, "do you hurt? Show me where it hurts."

Elizabeth had not talked to me so since I was a very little girl, and I realized how extremely worried she was. I tried to think why she should be so concerned, but I was too tired, and my head was muddled. However, I had not long to contemplate the situation, for Gillian returned almost immediately carrying a tray laden with a pitcher of steaming milk and a service of tea. She was followed by Dr. Maerrie.

Dr. Maerrie was a big man, solid and squarely built. His

countenance, buried in a thick tawny beard that curled in wild abandon down to the knot on his black cravat, appeared quite fierce. With his jutting brows and mass of wiry red-brown hair, he quite resembled a great growly lion. But when he spoke, his voice was low and soft and gentle, his hazel eyes were kind and sad.

He came directly to the bedside, handed his black case to Elizabeth, and took my hands in his own. Gillian and Betsy were asked to leave and then, assisted by Elizabeth, Dr. Maerrie proceeded with his examination. When he had finished, he said, "You must not worry, Victoria. There is nothing wrong with you that rest and cookies will not cure." But something in his eyes belied his comforting words.

Nonetheless, I gave him a smile—tremulous, I fear, but still a smile. When I was a child, no matter what my ailment, no matter what other dreadful-smelling, foul-tasting concoction he had felt it necessary to prescribe for my fevers and upsets of the stomach, he always finished with, "and cookies for Victoria."

When Dr. Maerrie and Elizabeth had gone, Betsy returned to my bedside. Cyrano, who had been sulking underneath ever since Betsy dropped him, emerged, and fixed Betsy with a most indignant stare. She reached down and gave his ears a scratch. Accepting her apology, he leaped up onto the bed and curled himself, with much purring and kneading of the counterpane, into a warm ball at my side.

I managed a watery smile, and Betsy started to speak, but was interrupted by the return of Elizabeth. She came straight to the bed and without preamble declared, "You, young woman, will remain in bed for the rest of this week, and you are to be very quiet thereafter for at least another two! Dr. Maerrie has left a tonic. He says you are just a little run down, and the shock of losing Lueddy was too much for you. You will soon be as sturdy as ever, but you must take care."

As she talked she fussed over me, straightening the blankets, fluffing the pillows. "Gillian is bringing your luncheon tray, and I shall stay to see that you eat every bite. Then, little love, you will take your medicine!"

Involuntarily, as she spoke the last words, a wry expression twisted my stepmother's face. Betsy laughed. I did not.

When Gillian arrived soon after, Elizabeth sent Betsy off to have her own lunch. As soon as both Gillian and Betsy had withdrawn, Elizabeth's face grew somber and she looked at me, searching my countenance with an expression I could not read. She shook her head, sighed, and finally murmured, "Eat, child, then we shall talk."

I had little appetite, but I picked at my food, and then Elizabeth brought forth the tonic, which, it seemed to me, she administered with far too much relish. However, the prescribed cookie followed directly after, somewhat mollifying my offended taste buds.

"Now," Elizabeth said, "let us talk."

I nodded, hoping my reluctance was not mirrored in my face. But I had no need to worry on that score. I soon realized that Elizabeth was too consumed by her own worries, too absorbed in what she had to say, to take much notice of my anxiety. She spoke slowly, choosing her words with great care. "Victoria, little love, I have no wish to speak harshly to you . . . to hurt you. You must know I could not love you more, were you my own child. Indeed, I have always thought of you as my own . . . my beautiful little girl."

Her strange words sent a chill of alarm through me; I could not understand why she should speak to me in such a way.

Sensing my dismay, Elizabeth reached out and took my hands in hers before continuing. "Your father and I know that the—events—of the past months were not easy for you to bear. For that matter, the situation has not been easy or pleasant for any of us."

She paused. Her eyes searched my face. I could only stare at her in confusion.

"Please understand, dear, this is very difficult for me to say, but it is for your own good, as well as for the sake of your father, who is greatly grieved by your unhappiness."

Suddenly I understood what she was driving at, but I could not think why she would suddenly choose to discuss it now. Neither could I think what she expected or wanted me to say.

When I remained silent, she sighed. "You simply must make an effort to stop moping about. . . ."

Moping about! The words were like a slap in the face.

"You must eat and regain your strength. You must begin to deal with reality."

Deal with reality! Was I not doing that to the best of my ability?

"Both Phillip and Drusilla commented upon your appearance, your loss of weight. Phillip even suggested taking you back to London with them, but of course with Lueddy's passing . . ."

Oh dear God, no! All the tranquillity, all the assurance that I had gained during the long hours talking to Betsy were destroyed. With her words, Elizabeth had sent my world crashing about me once more, and I didn't know what to do, which way to turn.

Elizabeth was shaking her head sadly, her brow furrowed with concern. "And now this latest collapse. Dr. Maerrie could find absolutely nothing physically wrong with you. Things cannot go on this way."

And still there seemed nothing for me to say. I knew, in my heart, that most of what she said was true, but . . .

"Did something unusual happen in the library?" she asked at last. "Did something frighten you?"

I hesitated, mouth working, and suddenly the words tumbled out. "There was a man in the library, Elizabeth, a dreadful man!"

"A man?" Elizabeth repeated dubiously.

"Yes, yes . . . a tall man." I fought to control the tears that threatened to choke me. "He frightened me."

Even as I uttered the words, I realized how childish they sounded. The memory of that long-ago time when I had tried to tell them about the man I had heard in the north wing came flooding back to further confound my mind. With a wretched, sinking feeling in the pit of my stomach, I realized it was useless to say more. Indeed, in that moment I was no longer certain of what I had seen, of what had happened in the library.

Elizabeth shook her head, drew a deep breath. Then, in an abrupt change of subject, she said, "We missed you at breakfast. Gillian said you were already gone when she returned to help you dress."

"I wasn't able to—" I started to say *sleep,* but I stopped myself in time. "I mean, I wanted to find a book," I concluded, but I couldn't meet Elizabeth's eyes.

"It was Adam who found you, lying on the floor in the library. You must have fainted . . . but why did you take the combs from your hair?"

I bit my lip, said nothing.

"Adam carried you here to your room. When you did not revive immediately, I sent for Dr. Maerrie." She was still watching me, expectantly. When I remained mute, she asked, "Do you not remember anything at all, little love?"

I shook my head. I could not bear to meet her gaze, and only stared in dumb misery at my fingers twisting themselves together in fruitless activity.

"All right, love. Rest now. I'll send Gillian to remove the tray and close the drapes. Then you must try to sleep."

The instant the door closed behind Elizabeth, a wave of fear and nausea engulfed me. I shrank down under the coverlet and huddled there in my bed, while the memory of the figure in the library burned in my mind's eye. So vividly had repugnance etched him there that when I closed my eyes I could see him again. And as I lay there remembering, it seemed to me that I had seen him before. But where? Not in the village, of that I was certain.

The ring—that ugly ring! Surely, if ever I had seen it before, I would remember. And he had blown me a kiss, I shuddered, and my skin crawled as revulsion engulfed me once more. Somehow I felt unclean, as if I had been touched by something evil, something loathsome. I wished fervently that Betsy would come back, but I knew she would not, because Elizabeth had said that I should sleep. And sleep I did, aided I have no doubt by the laudanum in Dr. Maerrie's tonic.

Chapter Nineteen

The New Year came and went, and even after Dr. Maerrie had pronounced me fully recovered, still I clung to the safety of my room. For the second time in my life I felt a certain resentment toward my stepmother, not because she had refused to believe my story, but because she had inadvertently confirmed my own fears: my mind was not to be trusted—I saw things that were not there.

John returned to Oxford, but for the rest of us, those remaining winter months were long and trying. The atmosphere throughout the household was strained. What Papa said or did concerning Adam and Helaine's deportment at the Christmas ball, I never knew. But it was obvious that a distance had grown up between Papa and his stepson.

As for me, I avoided Adam assiduously, though it had little to do with the spectacle he and Helaine had made of themselves. Actually, I avoided everyone as much as possible. Even Betsy. All the confidences we had shared seemed meaningless; all the ground that had been gained the evening following Lueddy's funeral seemed to have slipped from beneath my feet; I was mistrustful of everyone and everything.

Nevertheless, spring came as always. The snow melted. The midday sun shone warm upon the budding trees, the greening lawn. And on one such bright and beautiful day, John returned from school. Betsy could scarcely contain her excitement, though she did her best to maintain a ladylike air of decorum.

In celebration of Lord John's return, tea was to be served in the garden at four, and when the clock on the landing began to chime, I left the small sitting room where I had been embroidering and started across the great hall. I heard Papa and Elizabeth leave their bedroom, and a moment later Elizabeth's voice called, "Wait for me."

I stopped and glanced up. Papa came into view at the head of the stairs. He stopped, laid his hand upon the newel post, and made a half turn so that he faced up the gallery toward the room occupied by Stella.

I supposed Helaine would be in there—she often sat with Stella in the afternoon, though why they sat in the maid's room instead of in Helaine's lavish apartment, I could not guess.

On the other hand, it seemed likely that Helaine and Adam would join us for tea that day to welcome John home, in which case Stella would be, even now, putting the finishing touches to her mistress's hair, or face, or something. I smiled grimly to myself, thinking how my sister-in-law hated the bright light of day. It revealed rather too clearly the tiny lines about the eyes, the sagging muscles under the chin. Again I wondered just how old she might be, and almost laughed at the recollection of John's words: ". . . such an old woman."

While my mind toyed with these thoughts, my eyes watched Papa, saw him stiffen, step backward. I opened my mouth to cry out a warning even as he missed the top step, clutched wildly at the railing, then fell heavily over backward and came crashing and tumbling halfway down the great staircase.

For what seemed an eternity I stood paralyzed with shock. Then, somehow, I was kneeling beside Papa, who lay in a crumpled heap upon the landing. Elizabeth, pale as death, knelt beside me. I was but dimly aware of Adam and John shouting orders, of servants rushing about wringing their hands, of Gillian sobbing volubly in the background.

Miraculously, or so it seemed to my dazed mind, a stretcher was produced, and Papa was eased onto it and carried back upstairs. I wanted to help get him into bed, but Elizabeth said he should be left flat upon the floor until the doctor could examine him, ascertain his injuries.

Dr. Maerrie was at Papa's side within the hour, and Betsy, Gillian, and I were all kept hopping until far into the night. Everything that could be done for Papa was done, but the fall had broken both his clavicle and his left leg. The pain was so intense, only morphine could alleviate his suffering. Thus, it was decided that Dr. Maerrie should stay on at the manor for a few days.

It was very late when the household at last settled into exhausted slumber. Once the house was quiet I, too, fell at once into a deep sleep. I do not remember awakening. However, I opened my eyes to find the light in my room so bright that at first I thought it must be morning.

It was not. It was the moon, now at its fullest, that permeated my room with a blue-white radiance. I had fallen into the habit of leaving my French doors undraped, by night as well as day, because the tomb-like darkness that filled my chamber when the window was shrouded had become so oppressive to me.

Now I lay, propped high on my pillows, my arms resting upon the counterpane. Standing in the center of the room, regarding me with great, sad eyes, was the dark-haired woman. When her gaze met mine, an unbearable sorrow flowed through me. I could sense, more than see, the tears upon her cheeks. Her hands, clutched tightly together, were pressed against her bosom, and her breath came quick and shallow.

Her lips parted, began to move. Her eyes beseeched me. But I could hear no sound — even the vague ghostly sounds that inhabit all old houses had been blotted out for me. Each time the young woman appeared, I would find myself locked into this eerie, silent world.

But the senses of sight and smell, even of touch, seemed infinitely sharpened. I could *feel* the moonlight's cool caress where it fell across my bed, shimmering white upon the flesh of my arms. I could *taste* the sweetness of the wisteria—or perhaps it was the young woman's perfume. Yet all sound was lost to me.

At length she turned and walked over to the escritoire, sat down, rested her elbows upon the polished surface, and dropped her head into her hands. She remained thus for a long while; I lay unmoving upon my bed. When at last she arose and turned to look at me once more, her eyes implored me, commanded me, and I somehow understood that she had determined to communicate to me something of great importance.

At last, apparently satisfied that I understood, she turned back to the little desk and placed her hand upon one corner of the carved back. As I watched in fascination, a little drawer slid out from under the bottom of the writing surface. She did not allow it to remain open for even a second, but shut it again immediately.

Then she whirled about and retreated to the center of the room. How small and frail and defenseless she looked, standing there in the moonlight. Her lips parted in a gentle sigh and she raised her hands, clasped them together against her cheek, then loosed them again to flutter aimlessly to her throat, to twine themselves in the thick dark curls that swirled about her slim shoulders.

She stood as if dazed, swaying from side to side, until all of a sudden she started, fell back a pace, and stared fixedly at the French doors—or at something that moved just beyond them. Now I was aware of hatred flaming up within her, and there was fear in the set of her shoulders, in the tilt of her head, in her clenched hands.

When I followed the direction of her gaze, I, too, could see a figure pacing back and forth just outside. A man.

He hesitated, turned his face toward the glass. Horrified, I recoiled against my pillows. There could be no mistaking those finely chiseled features, the disdainful smile—it was the man I had seen in the library.

I'm dreaming! Surely, I am dreaming. But the sharp pain of my own fingernails cutting into the palms of my hands told me I was not.

Even as these thoughts raced through my shocked mind, the man stepped forward to face the doors, and grasping their handles, he shoved them wide. As the doors parted and swung inward, the young woman fell back another step, but she remained stiffly erect. Her gaze did not falter.

I watched them—him—in the brilliant light from the moon, and panic filled my breast. The still, quiet air was heavy with the cloying fragrance of the blossoms that covered the vine upon the balustrade, making breathing difficult, and I felt as if I were drowning.

But there are no blooms upon the vine! There have never in my lifetime been blooms upon the vine! As this realization welled up, confusion muddled my thoughts. *Was* I only caught up in a dream after all? Yet I could feel the labored beating of my heart, could see in minutest detail the drama unfolding at the foot of my bed.

Even while my mind wrestled with itself, my eyes continued to watch. So bright was the moonglow in my room that now, although his back was to the light, I could see the man's face, the same evil face I had beheld in the library. Sardonic, demanding, he was enjoying her despair, savoring it, touching it with his ugly warped mind. He moved slowly across the room until he was within a step of her. There he stopped, and as he lifted his hand, the moonlight shone upon the great ring he wore coiled about his finger.

The fury that I felt when I saw that raised hand knew no bounds. I flung aside the coverlet and literally threw myself from my bed, seeking to spring upon the beast, wind my fingers about his throat, scratch out his eyes. . . .

But in my haste I slipped, or tripped, lost my balance, and fell headlong into darkness.

Chapter Twenty

It was the burning, choking fumes of Elizabeth's sal volatile, administered by Dr. Maerrie that revived me. When my coughing and sputtering subsided, Dr. Maerrie picked me up and carried me to my bed. Then, as Gillian scurried off to fetch warm bricks from the kitchen to tuck about me, Betsy plumped my pillows. Elizabeth covered me with a soft down quilt, then dipped a cloth in the hot water Gillian had brought for my morning wash, and gently cleaned a crust of dried blood from my cheek.

I suffered her ministrations in dazed silence. My head ached, one eye was swollen shut, and I was shivering with shock and cold.

As soon as the women had me settled to their satisfaction, Dr. Maerrie took over. First he ran his fingers over my skull with a quick, light touch. Next he examined my blackened eye. Through the pounding in my head, I was dimly aware of Elizabeth and Betsy standing mute and anxious at the foot of my bed, and from somewhere behind them, of the sound of Gillian's loud blubbering. At last, satisfied that no bones were broken, no serious damage done, Dr. Maerrie gave me a potion to relieve the pain and make me sleep.

Thus, aided by draughts of laudanum, I drifted, half waking, half sleeping, through the week that followed. And for a while I neither remembered nor cared what had happened. Dr. Maerrie insisted that I stay in bed and be very quiet. Betsy, bless her, sat with me for hours on end, but I saw little of anyone else. Elizabeth, assured that my injuries were more painful than serious, devoted herself almost exclusively to Papa. Adam and John did stop by to see me every day, but neither of them lingered.

Toward the end of the second week, when the discoloration had all but faded from my eye, I was allowed to sit upon the chaise and read, even to walk a bit upon the balcony when the afternoon sun was warm. And while my body healed and memory returned, my mind was assailed once again by the fears, the doubts, the questions.

As my convalescence progressed, Betsy spent more and more time away upon business of her own. Helaine, on the other hand, seemed to take a renewed interest in my welfare. She came almost daily, and always when I was alone. On one occasion she said, "Dear Victoria, I am so sorry to see you ill . . . I cannot think what could cause you to so injure yourself. . . ."

I made no reply, only shrugged. The family assumed that I had gotten up in the dark, stumbled, and fallen, striking my head upon the bedpost.

Dr. Maerrie seemed unconvinced. I overheard him say to Elizabeth, "That tear in her face was caused by something sharp," but he did not persist.

I offered no explanation; I had none.

On another of her visits, Helaine made a point of telling me that people whose minds were unbalanced often saw visions and other strange things. "Like King George III, you know. They say he had all sorts of weird fancies . . . yet at times, he was as lucid as you or I."

She hesitated, but when I offered no comment, she continued, "It occurs to me that those American colonies would still be English if King George had had his wits about him." Much pleased by her own wit, she laughed merrily.

I had no desire to discuss the subject with her, and tried to distract her by showing her the book I was reading, some penny dreadful whose title I no longer recall.

But Helaine was like a dog worrying a bone. "They say that at first he suffered from quite dreadful nightmares." She simpered as if she were suddenly embarrassed, and said, "Oh, my dear . . . I do not mean to imply that because you have such dreadful nightmares, you are . . . no, no . . . you are just overly tired . . . That is it, of course. Now promise me you will think no more about my silly chatter."

After Helaine had gone, I lay in my bed feeling more tired and depressed than when she came. *And how did she know that I had nightmares?* Had I told her that, too, on the day when I confessed my unhappiness to her? I couldn't remember. I only knew that Helaine never missed an opportunity to remind me of my resemblance to my grandmother, the Lady Christina, and she never for a moment let me forget that my grandmother had been, as Helaine liked to put it, *different.*

"Not that you should worry, dear little sister. No, no . . . you are as bright as a button," she would assure me, but her eyes glittered, and the darkness that threatened to overwhelm me drew a little closer each time she came to call.

Once again I found myself wanting, desperately needing, someone to talk to. But whom? I would not soon forget that near disastrous attempt to confide in Elizabeth. That was a mistake I had no intention of repeating.

And the very idea of trying to explain to Papa filled me with dread. To Papa, even the innocent make-believe of childhood was anathema. I would never forget his stern countenance when Adam and I were but small children, if he caught us in some simple game of pretend. He would warn us in an uncompromising tone, "I'll have no foolish masquerades, no nonsensical pretenses in this house!"

Indeed, I remembered, all too well, how angry Papa had become when, as a child, I had ventured to speak of the dream girl as my friend. I quailed, recalling the unconcealed anger in Papa's eyes and voice on that occasion, when he had said, "I never want to hear such foolishness from you again."

Or yet again, when Elizabeth had told him of my—visitor. If he would not be convinced by the evidence of that note, but insisted upon believing it some childish ploy, a bid for attention, the invention of a too vivid imagination, there was nothing I could say that would convince Papa that—what? That dreams are real? That they write notes and burn paper? I laughed a bitter laugh. Not even I believed that.

There was Betsy, of course. Or John. Betsy would believe me—or would she? She had seemed, somehow, distant of late. As for John, he might be sympathetic, but, like Papa, he would never believe my dreams were real. But neither did I!

So I remained silent. And just as I could not bring myself to relate to anyone the occurrences of that night on which I was injured, neither could I bring myself to seek the drawer in the escritoire shown me by the dream woman. Is that not strange? I cannot reasonably explain why. I only know that I was afraid. I was afraid that I would not find the drawer, and, at the same time, afraid that I would. Either way, it would confirm that I was caught in some incredible aberration of the mind or the spirit. Either way . . .

Whereas in the beginning I had feared only for my sanity, I was now forced to the conclusion that I actually faced some physical danger. But did that danger arise from some hideous and unspeakable source, or was it possible that in my madness I was actually seeking to do myself harm?

But, I told myself, Betsy has seen the young woman, too. Hence, she must surely exist. Yet I knew she could not. And, my thoughts tormented me: perhaps even the conversation with Betsy had been all in my mind. All in my mind. Nothing was real. Perhaps even I was not real. . . .

So that was how I felt, some three weeks after my accident, as I lay upon my bed pretending to sleep. But my thoughts gave me no rest. I could no longer rid myself, waking or sleeping, of the dream woman's presence.

Oh, I do not mean she floated continually before my eyes like some dreadful apparition. Rather, I felt in some strange way that she was part of me. Or that some inexplicable bond existed between us. And the man, that villainous, satanic man — just the memory of him filled me with horror. I shuddered as with a violent chill.

Betsy was sitting beside my bed stroking Cyrano, who lay stretched upon her knees. Now she jumped up in alarm and laid her cool hand upon my brow. "What is it, Victoria? I thought you were sleeping. Are you chilled?"

I opened my eyes and looked at her. I wanted to tell her what I had been thinking, but I could not find the words.

"What is it, Victoria? Please tell me. I want to help you."

I mananged to say, "I don't know, Betsy."

"Are you cold? Do you feel a draft?"

"No, thank you. Perhaps someone walked on my grave . . ." I tried to laugh.

"That is not funny," Betsy admonished me. But she resumed her seat and picked up her embroidery, which had been abandoned when Cyrano jumped into her lap.

But despite what I said to Betsy, in my heart I knew, and at last faced, the truth: I must try to find that drawer in the escritoire, and the need was urgent. If I were not already mad, this wondering and fretting would surely make me so. However, even as I could not share my new fears with Betsy, so I could not share this quest. So I bided my time and once more pretended to sleep.

At last Betsy stood up and, after listening to my breathing, departed on some project of her own. After she had gone, I continued to lie very still until I felt quite certain that she did not intend to return immediately. Then I scrambled out of bed and hurried to the little desk. Heart beating wildly, I laid my hand upon the corner, just as the young woman had done. Nothing happened. I leaned down and scrutinized the elegantly wrought wood, but could see nothing unusual. Again I laid my hand upon the spot where her's had rested, and I explored the carved grapes and leaves with my fingertips.

Still nothing. So it was a dream, after all. All of it was only a dream, and I was mad—quite mad. Then, half in anger, half in despair, I grasped the corner once again and gave it a violent shake. Silently, the secret repository came sliding out.

I gasped, gazed at it, almost afraid to believe. Then I sank down into the chair and proceeded to give the drawer a careful examination. It was not deep, but was every bit as wide as the writing surface above. *And it was real!* I began to tremble with excitement. *There really was a secret drawer!*

I closed my eyes and drew several deep breaths, seeking to steady myself before continuing my examination of the drawer. It was lined with crimson velvet, and contained a slim, ornately carved ivory box, a packet of letters tied with a blue satin ribbon, and a diary bound in blue velvet on which was painted a white dove carrying a pale blue forget-me-not in its beak.

Trembling with excitement, I scooped everything up and quickly reclosed the drawer. Clutching the lot to my bosom, I climbed back into bed. Then I laid each item upon the coverlet and regarded them in awe. Now I had irrevocable proof that the dark-haired woman was not a mere figment of my imagination; and if she did exist, then I must assume that the man in the library existed—and, yes, even the snake must have some strange reality of its own.

But what did it all mean? These were ideas so strange, so new, that I really could not grasp them.

Slowly, I reached out my hand and untied the ribbon holding the letters together. Actually, there were only three. I picked up the one on top, spread it open on my knees, and began to read:

"Heart of my heart—All is now in readiness. I have only to carry you away, and that I shall do tonight. Dress yourself warmly and wait for me on the balcony. Keep yourself well hidden in the shadows over against the tower. I shall have you safe in my arms before the midnight hour. I love you, my darling, and shall be happy only when I have made you truly mine—you and our babe."

It was signed with the letter *C*.

My mind whirled. *C—for Carter!* Of course. At least, it seemed entirely possible. But to whom had the letter been written, and why the clandestine meeting? And the reference to a baby?

I picked up another letter and carefully unfolded it.

"My beloved—I can think of nothing but you. How sweet you are, how warm and pleasing in my arms. Would that I could come to you now, but we must do nothing to arouse suspicion until our plans are complete. I love you. C"

I raised my eyes and gazed at nothing, feeling more confused than ever. A forbidden romance? But who? I snatched up the final letter, opened it.

"My dearest one—How I long to hold you in my arms again, to taste your sweet lips. Never have I known such love as I feel for you—my treasure, my delight! I shall come to you again as soon as I am able. Until then, my life is without joy. I adore you. C"

When Betsy came bubbling into my room I was still sitting there, staring at the letters. Quickly, I slipped them and my other finds under my pillow, but my mind continued to race about in circles, and though I heard Betsy chattering away, I gave scarce attention to her words.

The diary, I thought; perhaps I shall find some answers there. . . .

"Oh, Victoria, I'm so glad you are awake. I have a surprise." Betsy continued to babble as she went to the bellpull and rang for Gillian. "Dr. Maerrie says you may go for a ride this afternoon. Indeed, he says it will be good for you to get out of the house. Hurry, now, get up!"

And that ivory box—what could be in that ivory box?

Gillian arrived and Betsy sent her scurrying off to fetch hot water. Then, with scarcely a pause for breath, she continued, ". . . and while you dress, I shall tell you where we are going."

I watched as she rushed about, choosing a gown, laying out handkerchief, gloves, bonnet, and slippers; but I did not really listen to her. My mind was too busy considering whether I should share with her my newest discovery. But before I could come to a decision, Gillian returned with the water. Still I sat.

"Victoria. Victoria! You are not listening to me!" Betsy's voice broke in upon my reverie.

I jerked my thoughts back and looked at her with, I am certain, a most sheepish expression.

She gave me a questioning look, then hastened to cover the awkward pause by repeating, "I said, come and wash. Pastor Grewe expects us at four o'clock, and at the rate you are moving, you will not be out of bed by then."

My complete bewilderment must have been written on my face, because Betsy gave her head a most impatient shake. "There! You have not heard one word I have said, have you? Victoria, dear, what is the matter?" And not waiting for an answer, she continued, "As I have already explained to you once, it occurred to me that it was possible Pastor Grewe might know about Catherine or Carter."

Of course! If anyone would know about Carter, it would be Pastor Grewe. Why had *I* not thought of that? Suddenly, I could scarcely contain the excitement that had welled up in me, set my pulses racing.

And all the while, Betsy continued talking: ". . . maybe

both. And so I made a point of getting us invited to tea at the parsonage. Was that not clever of me?"

She looked so smug and self-satisfied, I had to giggle. "Oh, Betsy, it's a wonderful idea."

I fairly leaped out of bed, feeling more excited, more impatient by the minute. Now my shaking hands became all thumbs. Obstinate buttons would not slip through eyelets, perverse hooks kept catching in lace.

Betsy, her eyes shining, did up my laces, then helped me brush my hair and arrange my bonnet. Ready at last, we crept down the staircase like two conspirators, as if by just seeing us, someone might guess our mission. But we met no one on the staircase or in the hall, and a groom was waiting for us at the entry with horse and surrey.

It had been almost a month since I had left the manor. Now I looked about me with surprise. I had forgotten how lovely it was to be out of doors, under the trees, close to the grass and flowers, to hear the birds singing overhead.

We arrived at the parsonage promptly at four o'clock, and were met at the door by Mrs. Grewe, a delicate and gentle woman who, I thought, must surely be in her seventies, though the smoothness of her cheeks and the quickness of her step belied the passage of time.

Pastor Grewe had addressed us from the pulpit in the village church for many years. His hair was snowy white and his shoulders bent, but his voice was still strong, and his eyes had never lost their youthful brightness, although his face was lined and often tired.

"Well, well. Lady Victoria . . . how very nice to see you. I have missed you at church the past few Sundays. And Miss Betsy. How pleasant to see you. I am so pleased the two of you could take tea with us today."

With such small talk, we were ushered into the parlor. The serving girl took our cloaks, then brought in the tea. We ate and chatted pleasantly, and when we were finished, Mrs. Grewe excused herself. Pastor Grewe sat silent until the door had closed behind his wife. Then he said, "Now, let us talk seriously for a while."

Betsy and I exchanged surprised glances. Throughout the past hour, I had been wondering how to turn the conversation to the mysterious Catherine and Carter. I was certain Betsy, too, had been wondering how we might introduce their names into the conversation. Now, it seemed that Pastor Grewe had his own reasons for inviting us to tea.

He did not wait for us to speak. "I have seen you on several occasions of late, Miss Betsy, strolling in the churchyard, stopping by the grave of Catherine. You must know, child, that I have carried certain information in my heart for many years, and I have often longed to share this knowledge with someone, but never has the time been right."

Pastor Grewe paused, took a deep breath, closed his eyes. For a moment I feared he had forgotten us. Not so. Abruptly he expelled the long-held breath, opened his eyes, and continued. "However, observing you, noting the air of anxiety with which you moved amongst the graves, it occurred to me that perhaps Lueddy, too, had some knowledge of what I know, and that perhaps she had communicated that information to you before she died. Have I guessed right?"

Mute, Betsy nodded her affirmation.

"Aye, I thought so," muttered Pastor Grewe, nodding his head in turn. Then, with a heavy sigh, he said, "What I am about to reveal to you young ladies, I would have preferred to tell Betsy when she is older, with a husband to guide and counsel her. Even now, I cannot help but wonder if 'twould not be better to tell the story first to Lord Garth."

Betsy drew herself up, face set, back stiff. "Lord Garth is my employer, not my father. He has been most kind to me, but if this information concerns my family, then I should be most grateful if you would impart that information to me."

Pastor Grewe blinked in surprise, then seemed to consider her words carefully. Abruptly he spoke. "You are quite right, Betsy. You are the one who should be told."

Again he paused. Betsy and I leaned forward expectantly.

"Catherine," Pastor Grewe said slowly, "was your true grandmother."

I heard a sharp intake of breath from Betsy, but otherwise she remained silent.

Pastor Grewe looked from Betsy to me and back again before continuing. "I do not know the family name, because Carter—he was her brother—felt that Catherine and her child, her illegitimate child, would be safer if no one knew who they were. He paid that fine woman who raised you to hide Catherine in her cottage and care for her. He planned to come for Catherine when it was safe and take her to a place of refuge. But something went wrong. Catherine died shortly after the baby was born. Then Carter disappeared. . . ."

Betsy and I sat like statues, staring at the old gentleman. He shook his head sadly. "I know these things because Carter first brought his sister here, to the parsonage, and sought my aid and advice. He told me that his sister had been presented at court the previous year. It was there that she met, and subsequently took the fancy of, a wealthy, powerful, and influential man.

"Catherine, being young and headstrong, ignored her father's wishes, her brother's advice, her mother's pleas. She chose rather to believe the lies of her seducer, for such he proved to be. Only when it was too late did she realize the man would never make her his wife, and only then did Catherine turn to her brother. She begged him to help her escape, before her baby was born and her disgrace made known.

"Hating the man who had so abused his beloved little sister, knowing the misery their father's wrath would call down upon Catherine's head, once her condition was known, Carter agreed. Though he was filled with sorrow and shame for the fate that had befallen his sister, he loved her. So he laid his plans for her escape with great care.

"Unfortunately, as so often happens, something went dreadfully wrong. By the time they reached our little village, Catherine, weakened by the rigors of her condition, was too weary to travel further.

"I was a young man then, and still unwed, or we should have been glad to keep Catherine here. However, Mistress Whittlesby was a fine, strong, young widow who I knew could be trusted. I took them there and explained the situation to her.

"Mistress Whittlesby did her best . . . but to no avail. Poor little Catherine was too small, too frail, too full of sorrow. The birth of the baby was too great an ordeal, and she died before her son was an hour old." Pastor Grewe's voice wavered, broke, fell silent.

Throughout this long recital, Betsy and I had sat mute, unmoving, scarcely breathing, in fact. Nor did we break the silence that now descended. Our eyes remained fixed upon his face, our hands clasped tight in our laps. And when Pastor Grewe again picked up the thread of his story, we continued to listen, spellbound.

"Carter paid Mistress Whittlesby well, and he came regularly, for a while, to visit the baby. Then . . . I don't know what happened. In any event, the last time I saw Carter, he gave me money in trust for the child. I continued to pay Mistress Whittlesby regularly until the money was gone. It lasted until the lad was almost grown."

Pastor Grewe drew a long breath, smiled at Betsy. "He was a handsome lad, your father. You favor him, you know. But he was a headstrong young man. Neither Mistress Whittlesby nor I ever told him his true heritage, Betsy. We feared that such knowledge would only bring him sorrow. After he married your mother and you were born, he settled down a bit. But even though he did not know who his mother really was, he was never a man of the soil. While you were still a toddler, he took your mother and left to seek his fortune. They planned to return for you, but they were never seen here again. Only the dear Lord knows where they may be today . . . dead, I fear. But Mistress Whittlesby looked on you as her own flesh. She loved you very much."

Pastor Grewe heaved a huge sigh and fell silent.

At last Betsy, who was pale and obviously shaken, said, "I know you would tell me nothing but the truth, sir, so what you say must be true. Now, what am I to do with this knowledge?"

The good pastor did not answer, but just sat gazing at her with sorrow-filled eyes, shaking his head from side to side.

An uneasy silence settled over the room. At length Betsy leaned forward to gaze into the old man's countenance. "Sir," she asked, her voice ever so soft, "sir, what is the *green-eyed demon?*"

The old gentleman started back. All the color drained from his face, and as he stared at Betsy, I could see fear in his eyes. At last he replied, answering her question with a question of his own: "And who spoke to you of the . . . of *him?*"

"Lueddy, sir. She told me to beware of the green-eyed demon." Betsy swallowed, took a deep breath. "It was the night she died. She said the green-eyed demon was back, and I was to tell no one who I am."

The pastor suddenly looked very old and very tired. He glanced from Betsy to me, then back to Betsy. When he spoke, the strain was clear in his voice. "I do not like to tell you two young women this, but with Lord Garth so ill and Lord John away, I see no alternative. Guard the information well, use it only if need be."

He hesitated, glanced around with a nervous twitch of his head. His voice dropped, almost to a whisper, as if he were afraid of being overheard. "The *green-eyed demon* is what the people in this parish called *him* . . . the one Lady Christina married."

Dumbfounded, shocked by his words, I felt as if my world were crumbling around me.

Outside, a dog barked. The laughter of a child rang soft and clear, somewhere beyond the open window. Amidst the branches of a nearby apple tree, a bird called cheerily to its mate. The sun shone bright in a cloudless sky.

But I could feel darkness pressing on my soul.

At last I forced myself to speak. "Surely you do not mean my grandfather?" It was an idle question, for had I not known for years that my grandfather was a scoundrel, a blackguard? But a green-eyed demon? It was too much to bear!

Pastor Grewe removed his spectacles and began to polish them, keeping his gaze averted. Even when he spoke, he did not look at me. "Yes . . . Lord Garth's father. He was an evil man . . . a wicked, cruel, and greedy man. So hated and feared was he, that after he disappeared people spoke of him only in whispers, and then not often."

"But how could that be, when Lady Christina loved him so?" Desperate for some shred of hope, I spoke without stopping to think.

Pastor Grewe remained silent as a puzzled expression clouded his eyes, spread across his countenance.

"Papa has told us his mother longed for her husband's return . . ." I paused, bewildered by the look on Pastor Grewe's face.

At last, shaking his head sorrowfully, he murmured, "I cannot explain the workings of a woman's heart. I only know that she was a beautiful bride, so happy . . . so young . . . so full of life and joy."

His eyes grew large with suppressed tears. "She was not so . . . later."

He cleared his throat noisily before continuing. "I'm not certain what happened. First her father fell down that staircase and broke his neck—he was dead before they could reach him. Then her mother . . . the poor woman just faded away. She died within months of her husband's accident."

Then, for a time, the good man seemed to forget that

Betsy and I were there. He sat shaking his head, whispering over and over, "Poor little Christina; poor child."

When I could stand the strain no longer, I asked, "But what happened to Christina . . . what did my grandfather do that was so dreadful?"

Pastor Grewe drew himself up straight, and his visage became stern. "I simply cannot repeat to you young ladies the excesses to which that evil man was given. You must believe me when I tell you this: within a year of her marriage, that man had broken Christina's heart and destroyed her mind. It was a blessing when he deserted her and disappeared. It is out of deference to the Garth family, out of love for the Lady Christina, her father, and her son, that today no one ever speaks of that perverted, unholy man!"

Betsy spoke not one word during this entire exchange. She sat, leaning forward in her chair, her eyes fixed upon the face of Pastor Grewe, her fingers first knotting, then smoothing the handkerchief she held in her lap. Not until we rose to take our leave did she speak again, and then only to say, "Thank you, sir. I enjoyed the tea very much."

Chapter Twenty-one

After Betsy and I had said our goodbyes, we went straight back to Greystone Manor. We spoke not one word during the entire ride, and mounted the staircase in silence. When at last we reached my chamber, we hesitated and looked into each other's eyes as if seeking reassurance. Then I opened the door and we entered, thinking there, in the sanctuary of my room, to discuss the day's events.

However, we had not yet had time to remove our hats and gloves before we were startled by a loud imperious knocking and Helaine swept in. She fixed me with an unblinking gaze and I felt a shiver start between my shoulder blades.

"So there you are, Victoria. Where in the world have you been off to? It is most thoughtless of you to be up and away without telling anyone. Don't you realize what a worry you are to all of us?"

So taken aback by her effrontery was I that I was left speechless. Not so Betsy. Eyes flashing, she faced Helaine squarely. "Dr. Maerrie perscribed an outing for *Lady* Victoria, and a very pleasant afternoon we have had, too."

Helaine stiffened. Her expression hardened and she glared at Betsy. Then suddenly she smiled, and her whole body relaxed. Turning to me she said, "Then you really are feeling better, little sister. I do hope you will join us for dinner tonight?"

"No." The word burst from me.

A gleam of amusement flickered deep in those glittering green eyes. "So perhaps the good doctor was wrong, and you are not strong enough to be out and about. . . ."

At last I found my tongue. "I am perfectly fine, Helaine. I shall take dinner here in my room because I prefer to do so." And, for once having taken a stand, I held my head high and returned her insolent stare.

Surprise, then amusement, flickered across her face. "Ah, yes. That is the way it goes," she murmured, shaking her head sadly. And with that obscure remark, she withdrew.

Spluttering with anger and consternation, I turned to Betsy. "How dare she! How dare she come into my room unbidden and talk to me that way!" I knew, of course, that these words would have been better said to Helaine, and I was furious with myself that I had not done so.

Tight-lipped, Betsy observed, "She is Mr. Adam's wife, and on the day Lord Samuel dies, who knows what power may fall to that woman."

"Don't be ridiculous!" In my frustration, I was even snapping at Betsy.

Ignoring my outburst, she continued, "I think she is already testing her power. Since you have been sick, and Lady Elizabeth so concerned with Lord Samuel, Helaine has taken over the running of the household. She does much as she pleases, for there is no one to say her nay."

Although Betsy and I had long since confessed our mutual distaste for Helaine, I was astounded by the vehemence of Betsy's words, and looking into her face, so pale and tense in the gathering dusk, my own confidence was shaken.

Nonetheless I said sharply, "But that's nonsense! The title, and with it the power, will go to John."

Betsy shook her head. "Think, Victoria. When Lord Samuel dies, though the title may be intended for Lord John, may actually go to him, the *real* power will remain in Elizabeth's hands."

"But Elizabeth wouldn't seek to take the title from

John. He is her son."

Betsy interrupted, "Adam is her first-born, and Lord Samuel did bestow the name Garth upon him. And consider this: Helaine and that maid of hers, they sit up there on the third floor, like two spiders in a web, spinning who knows what mischief!"

Was it possible? True, Papa *had* given Adam the family name—but no one had ever vouchsafed him the title of earl. And yet, by law—I didn't really know. Perhaps it was possible. . . . As for Helaine and Stella, I could believe almost anything of those two!

But Betsy was still speaking, and suddenly her words caught my attention once more.

". . . and poor Lord Samuel, lying there in his bed so pale and old. You have not noticed because you have been so ill, but—"

Betsy's voice fell. She shook her head, swallowed, then continued on a rising note, "He gets weaker each day. Thinner, and weaker, and older." She began to weep bitterly.

Struck dumb by these revelations, I could only watch while Betsy's face worked with the effort to control her emotion. Unable to stay her tears, she dropped her face into her hands.

Pulling my thoughts together at last, I managed to say, "But Betsy, surely Papa is much better. It has been over a month. . . ."

"No, Victoria, he is *not* better." The words came muffled through her fingers.

Unwilling to believe what she was saying, I insisted, "It does not take so long for bones to knit."

With a heavy sigh, Betsy raised her head once more. "Oh, the broken bones have healed, but something else has happened to Lord Samuel . . . something that Dr. Maerrie can neither explain nor treat. It is as if Lord Samuel has gone away from us. He will not leave his bed. He eats but little, and he seldom speaks."

"But why haven't *I* been told?" I burst out. "Maybe

there is something I could do...."

Betsy's shoulders drooped. "That is doubtful. Lady Elizabeth sits and tries to feed him. She talks to him, does her best to draw him out, but he only looks at her and sometimes shakes head, back and forth, back and forth, upon the pillow. Lord John and Mr. Adam have tried to talk to him as well, but they have fared no better than my lady."

I could not believe what I was hearing. I turned and started toward the door. "I must go to him, Betsy. I should have been told!"

Betsy grasped me by the arm and held me back. "No! Wait, Victoria. Of late he has refused to see anyone but Lady Elizabeth. He becomes so agitated when anyone else enters the room that Dr. Maerrie has forbidden even Lord John to try to see him."

"But surely there is *some*thing I can do!" I tried to jerk my arm from Betsy's restraining grasp.

She clung only more tightly. "No. Truly, Victoria. You would only upset him. Please, talk first with Dr. Maerrie ... please!"

But I would not listen. The thought of Papa sick and in pain was more than I could bear. Pulling free of Betsy's clinging hands, I rushed from the room, along the gallery, and into Papa's quarters without even bothering to knock.

As I burst into the room, Elizabeth rose to her feet and held up her hands, motioning me to stop. I ignored her and dashed straight to Papa's bedside.

He took one look at me and turned his face away!

I reached out and clasped his hand. "Papa! Look at me. I love you Papa. I need you...."

But he would not look at me, or speak to me. Elizabeth, her arm about my waist, finally prevailed upon me to leave him, to go back to my own room. "If there is any change in his condition, I'll call you immediately," she promised. I had to be content with that.

Heavy of heart, I returned to my room to find Betsy pacing the floor. She ran to me, threw her arms about me.

"I am so sorry, Victoria. I should not have told you . . . not yet. But I have been so afraid. I—" Abruptly, her words trailed away.

But there had been something in her voice, and though she said no more, I knew there was more she had not told me.

She must have felt me stiffen in her arms, for she stepped back a pace and looked searchingly into my face.

Her own countenance bore a stricken look.

"What else, Betsy? What have you not told me?"

All Betsy's resolve seemed to crumble. She swallowed, licked her lips, and then, in a flat, brittle voice, she replied, "I think Helaine is the green-eyed demon."

"Green-eyed demon?" My mind was still so full of Papa, for a moment I could not think what she meant.

". . . Though how she could be, when Pastor Grewe said it was Lord Samuel's father. . . ."

Betsy's words trailed off. Her eyes, searching my face, widened, and she grew even more pale. "But Lord Samuel's father is dead! He *is* dead, is he not, Victoria?"

I shook my head. I felt drained, numb, too exhausted to care. "I do not know . . . I think no one knows for certain."

Betsy's arms dropped to her sides. She turned and walked to the chaise, where she crumpled down like a rag doll. Her eyes, in her colorless face, were enormous.

What could I say? What could I do? My knees, too, suddenly felt weak, and a wave of fatigue engulfed me. I dropped down upon the chaise beside Betsy and took her cold hands in mine.

At that moment Cyrano appeared from somewhere, jumped up between us, and stretched himself luxuriously. Yawning and purring, flexing and curling his paws, he offered his chin for scratching.

His sudden appearance served to break the tension. He had grown into a beautiful animal, unusually large, with a powerful build. He was sleek of muscle, glossy of coat, and as lazy and spoiled a creature as ever was, is, or shall be. Betsy and I pampered and petted him, and he accepted our homage graciously.

As we stroked his smooth head, listened to his song, the color slowly returned to Betsy's face. As for me, I suddenly realized that I was hungry! I got up, walked over to the bellpull, and rang for supper.

Gillian brought our trays, and while we ate, Betsy and I talked. We went over each incident of the day, each revelation, and later, after Gillian had cleared away once more, Betsy and I continued to talk. We considered what Pastor Grewe had told us in every possible light. And when we had talked ourselves out, still we could draw no firm conclusions.

Nevertheless, we did feel reassured, in that now we knew Catherine and Carter were not figments of Lueddy's imagination, nor of mine.

And Betsy was gentle born! The wrong side of the blanket, perhaps; but nonetheless it was exciting news. If only we could discover Catherine's family name, or even the name of her seducer! The thought was tantalizing, but we could think of no way by which we might obtain the information.

We pondered Lueddy's warnings again. But with this new information, that the green-eyed demon was my grandfather, the whole business seemed even more unbelievable than ever.

Then we discussed the possibility of enlisting someone else's help in seeking out the truth. I thought of Uncle Phillip and Aunt Drusilla—or Thomas? I remembered that he had seemed to know all the court gossip. However, it was something that would have to wait for another day.

One final thing I did, before we said goodnight, was to show the secret drawer and its contents to Betsy. How I came to know about this hidden repository, I did not say.

Neither did Betsy ask. Rather, she pounced upon the letters and read each one carefully, not once but twice, for all the good it did. She could not think to whom the letters had been sent, any more than could I.

We considered my grandmother, of course. The letters had been kept in her desk. But from all accounts, she was a married woman who loved her husband despite his unsavory reputation; had mourned his disappearance and longed for his return.

As for the diary, though we were sorely tempted, we could not bring ourselves to break the golden clasp that bound it. "The key must be somewhere," I said, and Betsy agreed.

And so we left it, thinking to search for the key another day. At last, exhausted, we decided to put off any further attempts to solve the growing number of mysteries until morning.

There was only one other item in the drawer: the ivory box. Betsy snatched it up and handed it to me. Without a moment's hesitation, I flipped back the top. Inside was a large, ornate key.

Betsy's tired eyes opened wide in astonishment, and I daresay, mine did the same. "Now, whatever could that unlock?" It was a rhetorical question, of course.

Betsy answered, "Obviously not the diary!"

I could only shake my head in bemusement.

It was not until I had settled myself in bed, was, in fact, just drifting off to sleep, that I suddenly remembered that strange bedchamber in the north wing. My eyes flew open and I was instantly wide awake. Could it have been my grandfather's? I felt certain he had never shared this room with my grandmother—it simply was not done in those days. And no one had ever pointed out a room that had been his. If I were to search that chamber in the north wing thoroughly, might I learn something more about him—about a possible connection between him and Betsy?

Not tonight of course. Nothing would get me into that north wing at night. But tomorrow, while Betsy was busy with her lessons. Or better still, I would take Betsy with me. Two heads, they say, are better than one.

Having made that decision, I closed my eyes and drifted

immediately into a deep and dreamless sleep.

The next morning, while Betsy was busy with Miss Jones, I went over my room, and particularly the escritoire, with a fine-tooth comb, searching for the key to the diary. I found nothing. Still, I could not bring myself to break the lock on the delicate hasp. The little book was so beautiful, it would be a crime to deface it. Besides, to read something that contained the secrets of another's heart—it did not seem right to me.

It was not until after lunch that I was able to tell Betsy my plan about the bedchamber in the north wing. She was enthralled! I had not finished my explanation before she demanded, "When? Right now?"

And not waiting for my reply she was off through the connecting door, calling over her shoulder, "I must change into something more serviceable . . . I shall be right back."

Quickly I changed into the same grey worsted I had worn on my first venture into the north wing. Just as I buttoned the last button, Betsy came bustling back into my room.

"Well," I asked, "shall we be on our way?"

Betsy only nodded, but her eyes positively sparkled with anticipation.

Together, we made our way to the kitchen stairs, and thence to the door to the north wing. Since my previous visit, even more dust had settled, obliterating the marks left by my earlier passage, and everything, at first glance, seemed to be as it had been before. However, there was one difference: the door would not open. Try as I would, I could not move it. Even when Betsy leaned her shoulder against it and the two of us pushed with all our might, still it remained stuck fast.

At last we admitted defeat and stood back, panting. When she had regained her breath, Betsy said, "Surely there must be another entrance."

Ruefully, I admitted, "Yes, but I have no idea where."

"Perhaps on the third floor," Betsy suggested.

"No. The north wing has no third floor."

And for a few moments we fell silent, gazing at each other, deep in thought.

Finally I said, "I do have one idea . . . come along."

Quickly, we returned to the great hall. From there, I led Betsy around to the stables. The old buggy, where Adam and I had played as children, had long since been removed, and now a bright new surrey stood in its place.

It was not the old buggy that I had hoped to find, however. I moved on until we were face to face with the back wall. It had been white-washed, and hooks and shelves for tack had been attached to it.

My heart sank. In the corner where the little door had been there was now a set of wheels leaning against the wall. There was no sign of the little door.

But it *had* to be there! We moved forward until we were near enough to see the very texture of the wall, and sure enough, there it was. It had been painted over until the crack between door and wall was filled and all but invisible, but the door was still there. Down behind the wheels, I could see where the door handle had been removed and the opening covered over, a stout plank had been nailed across the bottom.

Looking at it, I laughed. It would have kept a child from entering, but it would not stay Betsy and me! When I glanced around, I found that while I had stood there congratulating myself, Betsy had been busy locating a lever with which to pry off the doorstop. In a thrice we had removed it and levered open the door.

Then we hesitated. The space beyond was shrouded in the inevitable cobwebs. Had it been so the day I followed the cat? I couldn't remember. However, there was a buggy whip at hand. It took only a moment to sweep aside the dusty webs, and Betsy and I entered the north wing.

It was gloomy and cold in the long, narrow corridor in which we now stood. "Now where?" Betsy whispered.

"I am not certain," I whispered back.

Then we both giggled nervously. Both question and answer had been irrelevant. From where we stood, there was only one way to go. However, we had not gone far before we came to a door that opened onto an outside stairway, which, in turn, led up to the western rampart.

I heaved a sigh of relief. "I know where we are." I assured Betsy. "It is not far now."

We all but ran along the walkway to the terrace, and around to the Venetian door. And there we stopped, out of breath and speechless with astonishment.

All the glass that remained in the sidelights had been cleaned! How could that be? Betsy and I stared at one another.

Then, still in a whisper, Betsy asked, "Did you do that?"

I shook my head. Slowly, I turned back to the door, put out my hand, took hold of the knob. It turned easily, and the door swung wide.

With the windows clean, the room beyond was filled with light, and everything looked different. Slowly, with Betsy close behind, I stepped across the threshold. Suddenly, it occurred to me that I had slipped, somehow, into another nightmare. Terrified, I turned to flee. . . .

Warm fingers gripped my arm; Betsy's whisper sounded in my ear. "Where are you going?"

I heard her! It was not a nightmare, then. Someone really had made up the bed, righted the chairs, placed the boots side-by-side. And the wicker hampers, the mousetraps, they were gone. Someone had taken them away. But why?

Slowly, I became aware of Betsy pulling at my sleeve, still whispering, "What is the matter? Speak to me! Victoria. . . ."

"It's all right. I was just surprised. Things are not as they were before." Suddenly, I realized I was whispering, too. "Why are we whispering?" I demanded.

Betsy jumped. "I do not know," she replied, then added, "Why were you about to run away?"

"Look about." I pointed at the various pieces of furniture. "This room was a shambles when I was here before. I was startled to see it so changed."

"But why would anyone try to clean and straighten this place?" Betsy's forehead puckered into a frown.

I only shrugged. "I don't know, but I guess we should get on with what we came to do. Shall we start with the wardrobe?"

We left the door and moved forward, holding hands like two babes in the wood. Abruptly, Betsy stopped, pointed. "Look," she said.

I followed the direction indicated by her finger. Now I noted that the table had been cleaned and polished, as, indeed, had the chairs. And on the table, there was a picture in a lovely silver frame.

"That picture was not there before. . . ." I was whispering again.

Now we hurried forward. I picked up the picture, the better to see it. It was an oil painting of a woman and a curly-haired baby.

Betsy studied it thoughtfully, then said, "The woman looks familiar."

I nodded. There *was* something familiar about the face, the set of the head; but I could not say for certain who it might be. I put the picture back on the table.

Without another word, we turned and proceeded to the wardrobe. The door had been closed since my first visit, but it opened easily enough. The garments that hung inside had recently been brushed and aired. In the drawers, the linens lay folded, smooth and clean, as if they had been laundered recently. But that could not be! Or could it?

"It was not like this when I was here before," I muttered, more to myself than to Betsy. "I am certain it was not like this. . . ."

It was Betsy who said, "I want to go . . . please, Victoria. Let us go quickly."

I did not argue. We turned and hurried from that room, back the way we had come. In the stable, we paused only long enough to close the little door and push the plank up against its bottom edge. We did not stop again until we were safe in my room.

We both longed for a good hot cup of tea, but our faces were streaked with dust, and our hair and clothing were draped with cobwebs. It would be best, we decided, to wash in cold water and change our frocks before ringing for Gillian.

At last, however, we were settled upon my chaise, with the tea tray Gillian had carried up sitting on a low table before us. Then, between bites of bread and jam and sips of tea, we discussed our visit to the north wing. Looking back, we realized that actually, nothing that appeared to be of any real importance had been discovered.

Because I had seen Helaine on the north terrace, we assumed that it was she who had been busy in the bedchamber, though to what end we could not imagine. Why clean those old clothes? Why make up a bed with damp, soiled linen? For so it must have been, considering the condition of the draperies.

And when all our talking and thinking and supposing was finished, we had to agree: not only had we found no answers, but we had added yet another mystery.

"I do not know about you," Betsy finally exclaimed, "but I cannot think about this a moment longer!"

"I quite agree," I assured her. "It is time we did something entirely different . . . something just for fun. How about a game of chess?"

And so we played at chess until dinnertime, and afterward we read aloud from Mr. Dickens's latest book, a gift from Thomas. It was late when Betsy finally yawned and stretched.

"Are you tired, Betsy? It has been a long day."

She nodded. "I think we should both go to bed. Perhaps after a good night's sleep we shall be able to think more clearly."

And so we said goodnight.

But just as she opened the connecting door to return to

her own bedchamber, Betsy hesitated, turned back. "Do you know, Victoria . . . I think the woman in that picture looked a bit like Stella." I shrugged, and said we would discuss it the next day.

Immediately Betsy had left my room, I prepared myself for bed, turned out my lamp, and tried to settle down. But Betsy's parting words had set my mind whirling once more. Now that I was alone, sleep would not come. I tossed and turned, seeking a comfortable position; I punched and pummeled my pillows; I counted sheep. Still my eyes refused to stay closed, and my mind insisted on racing in circles.

At last I sat up, thinking to light my lamp once more and read awhile. But as I held the match ready to strike, I heard a door open somewhere along the balcony. Only moments thereafter, a tall figure hurried past my French doors. Without taking time to consider, I slid out of bed, grabbed up a shawl, and followed.

I was certain it was Helaine. It was not the first time I had seen her walking the balcony at night, and according to Betsy, my sister-in-law also spent much time in the tower. It struck us both as strange that Adam never seemed to accompany her on these nightly promenades. Indeed, we wondered how it was that we hardly ever saw the two of them together, except on those rare evenings when they joined the family for dinner, or on some formal occasion.

Be that as it may, on that night all the worry, all the fear, all the anger that had plagued me ever since Helaine's arrival in our midst coalesced into a driving force that sent me racing after her. What I intended to do once I caught up with her, I did not know. At the time, I only knew that I had to follow her.

I reached my French doors just in time to see Helaine disappear into the tower. Not giving myself time to think, I ran across the balcony to the hidden door, opened it, and slipped through into the darkness that waited beyond.

Chapter Twenty-two

As the door swung shut, a wave of terror engulfed me. Only because I was too terrified to move did I remain there in the stygian dark.

Heart pounding, breath coming in gasps, I leaned against the wall just inside the door, and berated myself for my cowardice. I clung to the thought that there was nothing to fear—after all, Helaine was my sister-in-law. Rude and unpleasant she might be, but there was no reason to fear her.

Thus I cajoled myself, until the trembling in my knees had abated, my heart resumed its normal rhythm, my eyes accustomed themselves to the blackness. However, as my breathing slowed I became aware that the dusty, musty air of the tower was laden with another scent, a heady combination of jasmine and musk—unmistakably, Helaine's perfume.

Instantly, my own brave counsel forgotten, I turned and began fumbling at the door, seeking to escape back onto the balcony. Had I been able to get the door open, I should have fled in terror. But my eagerness defeated me. By the time my hand had found and clutched the handle, my self-control had exerted itself once more.

Mouth open, panting from my exertions, I forced myself to face the interior of the tower. Straining my eyes against the gloom, I could just make out another door. It was located further along the wall, at a spot that undoubtedly gave access to the western battlements, but it was secured by a stout wooden bar held in place by huge iron brackets. Helaine could not have gone that way.

Glancing upward, I perceived that a small glimmering of moonglow threaded its way in through the long narrow arrow slits cut through the upper portion of the wall. By that light, the stairs that rose round and round, following the curve of the tower, up into the highest reaches above, were clearly visible. Of Helaine there was no sign, only that lingering trace of her exotic scent. I knew I would have been able to see or hear her had she ascended the stairs.

Thus it was clear that, though I seemed to be standing on the lowest level, I could not be. Since Helaine was not above me, she had to be below—unless she *was* a demon . . .

The hair on the back of my neck began to rise and I quickly brushed that thought aside. I leaned forward and began to examine the floor, inch by inch. My eyes were thoroughly accustomed to the darkness by then, and I soon found what I sought: a large iron ring set into the floor.

Although I was literally weak with fear, my hatred of Helaine spurred me on. I grasped the ring and pulled. The trap door to which it was fastened was heavy, but the hinges swung freely and quietly, allowing me to open it with little difficulty.

The space beneath the trapdoor yawned black and menacing, and the sound of rushing water along with a dank smell floated up into the room where I stood. I realized, without stopping to think about it, that below me was water flowing through the moat. This door must open directly into the subterranean reaches of the manor.

I was still hesitating, observing that menacing black hole, considering what dangers I might be called upon to face below, when a furry white form emerged from the shadows behind me and stole downward.

Cyrano! I stooped and made a grab for him, but he was too quick. The die was cast! I dared not hesitate longer. I had to follow.

I remembered then that I had not stopped for robe or slippers. The stone steps beneath the trapdoor were damp and cold against the soles of my bare feet, and the very air was dank and chill. But at least I did not find myself lost in total darkness. Whoever had constructed that subterranean passage had arranged most ingeniously for light to enter from the outside. There was, in fact, more light there than in the area above the trapdoor.

The stairway was not long. It ended on a narrow ledge that was probably awash when the moat ran full during spring thaws, or whenever the river was in spate. The ledge ran straight ahead for perhaps a dozen paces, then seemed to disappear into a blank wall. Of Helaine and Cyrano, I could see no sign. There was nothing to do but move forward, and that I did, as quickly as I dared.

The water ran swift beside me, gurgling and swirling and sucking at the walls. I tried not to think of where one misstep would lead, but anger and fear had so heightened my senses, so piqued my imagination, I could almost feel the water closing over my head, tearing at me, hurling me headlong against the stone supports. . . .

When at last I reached the spot where the ledge seemed to disappear, I discovered, to my vast relief, a narrow opening in the wall, through which a long hallway led back at right angles under the manor, away from the rushing water. Straight ahead, not far from the spot where I now stood, I could see a low-arched opening in the foundations, through which the water poured to fall in a thundering cascade, down the cliff outside.

I turned and followed the hallway to its end. It was a tall, narrow, arched opening that gave into a cavernous vault carved from the living stone beneath the north wing of Greystone Manor. A flickering light poured through that opening.

Cyrano crouched just outside it, every muscle in his body taut, his tail lashing angrily back and forth. I knew his golden eyes would be fiery pools of liquid light. He took no notice of my approach, but stared through the archway into the chamber.

I hesitated, instinctively crouching against the wall, seeking to take advantage of what shadow there was in order to approach the doorway unseen. But I might as well have walked boldly in, for Helaine knew that I was there. Indeed, she was waiting for me.

Even before I reached the archway, she spoke. "Come in, sweet little sister," she crooned, her voice low and sibilant. "Come in, and I will tell you a story . . . such an interesting story."

She stood in the center of that great chamber, a tall commanding figure dressed entirely in black. She had lighted candles in several of the wall sconces, and in the flickering, flaring light, her shadow grew upon the wall behind her, monstrous, grotesque, writhing in a hideous, obscene dance.

"Enter, little sister, enter. It is too late to be afraid. Come in and see."

I stopped just over the threshold, gazing transfixed into her glittering green eyes.

"Come, little sister. It is only right that you should share my secret." Helaine's voice was soft in my ears, but as she continued to speak, the sibilance grew more pronounced. "After all, the secret of the tower door was yours, was it not?" She laughed low in her throat. "Adam, the fool, could not wait to share your secret with me." Her laughter grew malicious. *"You* would not have revealed that secret to anyone, would you, little sister?" Again she laughed, a harsh, ugly sound.

And for a time she fell silent, but her gaze never left my face. She began to back across the room, and I followed her, matching her movements step for step, as if mesmerized. She stopped on the far side of the room in front of what appeared to be a large cage suspended from the ceiling. I knew immediately what it was—a medieval instrument of torture.

Helaine's voice interrupted my thoughts. Her words came in a strange, sing-song cadence, as if she were repeating something by rote. "When I was a little girl, we lived in the West Indies, Maman and I. We lived alone . . . all alone. Maman told me about *mon père*—how handsome he was . . . so brave, so clever. Maman said he would bring us jewels . . . jewels fit for a queen."

Cyrano had crept forward and now I felt him crouch against my ankle, his body quivering.

Helaine droned on. "When *mon père* returned, I would be a princess . . . Maman promised it." The play of expression on her face as she spoke was disquieting, ranging from love, pride, to desire, but somehow distorted. I was fast beginning to rue my rashness in following her.

"But he never came! We waited and waited . . . but he never came." The light seemed to drain from Helaine's eyes, her shoulders slumped, and for a moment she looked old and tired. "When he did not come, when he sent no more money or presents . . . and even the letters stopped coming . . ." She sighed, shrugged her shoulders.

Then, abruptly, she laughed, drew herself tall once more, and her look became sly. "Maman was very beautiful in those days . . . *très charmante*. Rich men pay handsomely for the favors of beautiful and charming women."

Her hands moved seductively over her own body, cupping her full, rounded breasts, sliding down over the slender waist, smoothing and caressing the gentle curve of hip and thigh. "I made my . . . debut in Paris. I was an immediate sensation. So many admirers . . . so many beautiful presents . . . whatever I wanted."

She paused, gazed into space, as if contemplating something amusing. Suddenly she laughed. "Le Marquis de Chambray, fat old fool . . . he used to get down on his knees, weeping and begging for my favors."

With a small sigh she waved her hand in a languid gesture, as if brushing the memory away before continuing. "And then Adam came a-knocking on my door. It was as if the gods had heard our pleas at last. Adam Johnshaven Garth . . . another fool!"

She had gone too far! I opened my mouth to speak, to defend Adam, but Helaine silenced me with an imperious gesture. "Adam *is* a fool, you know. He could not distinguish between a courtesan and a lady of social standing! How easily I wound him around my finger. When his friends tried to tell him who I was, what I was, he wanted to fight a duel!"

I did not want to believe what Helaine was saying, but her words had the ring of truth.

"How Maman and I laughed! And yet we could not let that popinjay fight a duel. He would most certainly have been killed. No, no. Maman and I, we could not let that happen. It was necessary to our plan that we should keep the young lackwit safe until he should bring us to Greystone Manor." Now Helaine threw her head back, and her laughter echoed and reechoed through the vast chamber.

Then the laughter ceased, as abruptly as it had begun. She fixed me with a malevolent stare. "You see, Maman and I, we had only one desire . . . to find *mon père.*"

Abruptly her face twisted into a demonic mask. Hatred poured from her eyes. "Well, I have found him, and do you know where? Let me show you." She paused, then stepped quickly aside.

It took a moment for me to refocus my attention, and at first my mind would not credit what my eyes beheld.

The object that had hung behind Helaine was, as I had surmised, a great cage. Inside that cage, lying in a grisly heap, was what remained of a man. In the shock attendant upon this discovery I was overtaken by gagging nausea.

But try as I would, I could not drag my gaze from that heap of mouldering cloth that had been a suit of clothes.

It still retained the shape of the body that had worn it. Protruding from the collar a skull, patches of hair still clinging to it, lay pressed against the rusting iron bars that held the man prisoner. The arms, or what was left of them, were flung wide, the bones of the hands clearly outstretched as they lay on the floor of the cage.

But that was not the only shock in store for my battered senses. One thing perhaps more devastating than any other I had ever seen was now visible, there on one outstretched hand. Coiled round one slender bit of bone, its jeweled eyes gleaming in the torchlight, was the ring I had first seen in the library on the hand of a man who wasn't really there. . . .

At the sight, the blood roared in my ears and a darkness seemed to float before my eyes. Still, I could hear Helaine's voice.

"Yes, little sister, look well! That is all that remains of *mon père*. . . ." Her voice trailed away.

I wrenched my gaze from the grisly remains in the cage, looked back at Helaine. Her face mirrored an unbearable grief and she rocked her body from side to side, a soft moan issuing from her lips. But the moment passed and she drew herself tall, flung wide her arms, and the gibbous shadow undulated up the wall behind her.

"You see what she did to him, the *gentle* Lady Christina?"

She uttered the name with such loathing, such contempt, that I fell back a step and cowered before her baleful gaze.

"She locked him in that cage and left him to starve!"

Thrusting her hand into the folds of her cloak, Helaine drew out a crumpled piece of paper and held it out for me to see. "Before he died, he wrote it here . . . the name of his murderer. He wrote it with a pin dipped in his own blood, and he left it there"—she gestured toward the floor of the cage—"for me to find."

She paused, took a deep breath, then read from the slip

of paper. " 'The slut has betrayed me.' " Helaine raised her head and glared at me once more. "Your grandmother, the slut!" Slowly Helaine's eyes drooped shut. Pressing the scrap of paper to her breast, she appeared to have forgotten I was there.

I tried to move, to back toward the doorway, but my limbs would not obey me. My head was swimming, my skin was clammy, and my face burned. My legs threatened to give way under the weight of my body, and there was a roaring in my ears.

Helaine opened her eyes once more and fixed me with her glittering gaze. A sardonic smile curled her lips. "You see, Victoria, your family owes me much. How fitting that Christina's granddaughter should be the first to pay."

When she stopped speaking, the silence in the vault pressed against my ears. The cloying, musty smell of death and decay clogged my throat.

Helaine tilted her head to one side, looked me up and down, then gestured with her chin toward the cage. "Perhaps I shall leave you in there, with *mon père* . . ."

I retched. Darkness was growing inside my head and the blood was like ice-water in my veins. I would have run, but my legs would not move; I would have screamed but my lungs, my throat, would not . . .

Helaine's voice blended with the singing in my ears. "But first, let me show you my pet. You and the *kitchen maid* have your kittens and your pups." She spat out the words with derision. "But I have a pet worthy of respect. She laughed, and at the sound my head pulsed and throbbed.

Once more Helaine moved, and this time she placed herself beside a large wicker hamper. On top of the hamper was the mousetrap I had seen that day in the north wing, and there was a small grey mouse inside. Helaine picked up the trap, held it straight out in front of her. "I was about to feed my pet," she murmured. She smiled evily.

The mouse was her pet? Then why did she not keep it in her room? In a fancy cage? How strange that I should care, under the circumstances. I could hardly believe that my mind could be concerned with such trivialities.

While these thoughts were flashing through my mind, Helaine had walked around behind the hamper. It came to above her knees, and was rectangular in shape. It opened like a wardrobe. Helaine reached across the top, removed the large copper pin that secured the hasp. Silently, the doors swung outward.

God in heaven! It lay coiled there in the bottom of the hamper, its eyes glittering, its forked tongue flickering in and out; and as the doors swung open, it turned its wicked triangular head and stared at me. Then it began to move, slithering out over the lip of the box, across the stone floor, toward me.

Helaine's wild, derisive laughter together with the whimpering sounds of my own terror echoed in my ears. I could not move — I *could not move!*

Frozen in unholy awe, I watched as that great green, brown and mauve snake glided across the rough stone floor, its muscles rippling beneath the iridescent sheen of its skin. It stopped, not two short paces from me, slowly drew its body into a coil, raised its head to strike.

Like a flash of lightning, Cyrano pounced from behind me. He caught the creature in his strong white teeth directly behind its ugly head, and giving it an expert shake, he snapped its spine.

Helaine shrieked as if in pain, and terror overcame my inability to move. I turned and ran. My bare feet made little sound upon the stone floor, but I could hear the pat of Helaine's slippers close behind me. I could not have been more than one long stride in front of her when I reached the end of the corridor.

My bare feet clung to the damp and mossy stone as I sped around the corner onto the ledge, but the soles of Helaine's slippers must have been smooth as glass. I heard her scream once as her feet slipped from under her, then the sickening gurgle when she hit the rushing, foaming, sucking water. . . .

Chapter Twenty-three

I was a child once more, terrified, running through the cold dark rooms of the north wing, slipping, falling, scrambling to my feet again to run. Helaine's wild laughter blended with those other sounds, pursuing me, enveloping me. I fled over and over, as on a treadmill, in the cold, the dark, followed by the unholy laughter, the shrieks of hate and anguish, my own breath sobbing and aching in my throat. I was lost in some unholy world of mist and shadow, peopled by loathsome, slithering creatures with glittering eyes.

From time to time the darkness would lighten, and dimly, as through a thick and clammy fog, I would see a face. Betsy? John? Adam? Elizabeth? And I would cry out to them, begging for help. But the darkness would envelop me once more, so cold, so black, and I would hear the gurgling, sucking water. . . .

Then, one day, I opened my eyes and it was Thomas's face I saw floating in the grey mist. He held out his hands to me, and he led me back across the void. It did not happen all at once, of course, but after weeks of patient care, exercising all the skill he had acquired during his years of study in France and Germany, Thomas gave me back my sanity.

I awakened one morning to see the sunlight spilling in through the French doors. Betsy sat upon the chaise holding Cyrano, and Thomas sat beside my bed reading. How very strange, I thought, and I said, "Thomas?"

He put the book down and smiled at me. Betsy jumped to her feet and came to stand close by. My recovery from that day onward was rapid. And as I regained my physical and mental well-being, it was to Thomas that I was able at last to relate the details of Helaine's death.

Dear Thomas. He sat beside my bed and held my hands in his. "You must not feel guilty because Helaine is dead," he said.

"But I wished her dead," I countered. "I hated her."

"I know," Thomas acknowledged. "But no one can really help feeling either love or hate. It is the way in which we react to those feelings that is good or bad, right or wrong. Is that not so?"

"Oh, Thomas . . . it is not as easy as that. I not only hated her, I thought that if she were dead, I would be glad. But I am not." In my misery, I was scarcely aware of the salt drops that suddenly rolled down my cheeks.

Thomas took his handkerchief from his pocket and handed it to me with a reassuring smile. "Of course you are not, Victoria. Just as you could never willingly have hurt her, so you cannot feel joy at her death. You have done no wrong. But you are only human, after all."

I took his handkerchief and dried my eyes, thinking what a wise, what a good friend Thomas was.

He remained silent while I wiped the tears from my face and blew my nose. Then he asked, in a voice devoid of emotion, "Do you know that Stella, too, is dead?"

Stunned, I could only shake my head.

"You should know," he continued, "she lived only a few days after Helaine . . . disappeared."

"Stella has died too?" It was more than I could readily take in.

"Of course, I was not here at the time," Thomas hurried to add. "It was John who told me what happened."

"What did happen?"

"Is it not enough to know that she is gone? Must you know the details?"

"Please, Thomas. I shall not rest until I have heard the whole story."

"Yes," Thomas finally agreed, "I do believe you will be able to forget only when you have all the facts."

He then continued. "It was not until the following morning, when one of the maids reported that neither Helaine nor Stella had been in their rooms when morning tea was delivered, that anyone realized those two were missing.

"A search of the manor was mounted immediately, but no trace of them was to be found. It was then that Betsy told John about that room in the north wing."

"Surely they did not find her there?"

"Yes. She was there. And according to John, when they tried to bring her out, she became like a wild thing, biting, kicking, scratching. When they did finally get her back to her room, they were forced to tie the woman to her bed."

Before he could continue, I interrupted. "But why, Thomas? What was she doing there in the north wing? And why would she want to stay in that room? It was damp . . . the windows were broken."

Thomas shook his head. "Are you sure you would not rather rest? All this can wait for another day."

"No, Thomas," I insisted, "I must know now, or I shall never rest!"

Thomas gazed at me unhappily, but finally went on. "Well, it seems that that room in the north wing was used by your grandfather as his bedchamber. Apparently, he and Stella had . . . known each other, before he married the Lady Christina."

As Thomas talked, a strange idea was taking shape inside my head. That picture Betsy and I had found—the woman, though young and very handsome, had, indeed, resembled Stella. Abruptly, without giving myself time to consider, I spoke the question. "Was Stella Helaine's mother?"

Thomas looked thoughtful, then replied, "I suppose it is possible. But let me tell you what I know to be fact.

From the moment Stella was returned to her own room, she fell silent. They tried to question her concerning the whereabouts of Helaine, but it was useless. She neither spoke, nor ate, nor even moved, for over twenty-four hours."

"Why? Was she sick? Or was she just determined to tell them nothing?"

"I'm not certain. But Dr. Maerrie was here, to tend you, and apparently he could find nothing physically wrong with her. Nonetheless, the following day, Stella developed a high fever, and began to moan and wail and mumble in some strange patois resembling French. Both Adam and Dr. Maerrie, who speak French fluently, tried to make some sense of what she was saying, but her words were not wholly intelligible. What they could understand sounded like the product of hallucination. She died in the early morning hours of the fourth day."

Just as Thomas finished speaking, Cyrano sauntered in from the balcony, jumped upon the bed, and came to nestle at my side, purring mightily.

"Oh, yes," Thomas added. "The door to the tower is no longer a secret. Later in the day—the day when you were found lying on the balcony—old Cyrano, here, who had been trapped in the tower, set up a dreadful yowling."

How could I have left Cyrano behind! He had saved my life! I scooped him up and gave him such a hug, he emitted a startled *meow* of complaint. Still holding him tight, I apologized. "Sorry, old fellow. I promise, an extra large bowl of cream tonight." Then I gave him a gentle scratch behind his pink ears.

Thomas continued, "Adam said it wasn't until he heard those cries of indignation, seemingly emanating from the very walls, that he remembered the door the two of you had found just before he left for Paris.

"When he opened the door, out came Cyrano, dragging one of the largest vipers ever seen in these parts. It was assumed that Cyrano had followed the creature in through some small breach in the foundations, and had then been unable to find his way out again."

Suddenly apprehensive, I asked, "Has no one actually gone into the tower?"

Seeing my agitation, Thomas hastened to assure me that all was well. "No one else has entered the tower or gone down into that subterranean prison . . . at least, no one has mentioned it to me."

As he spoke, he leaned forward to pat my hand. But he looked at me strangely, and I realized that I had not told him about the cage or its grisly contents; neither could I bring myself to do so — at least, not then.

Suddenly conscience-stricken, I asked, "And how is Papa? Have you been able to help him, Thomas?"

Thomas brightened visibly. "That is another strange thing. It is one of those cases that proves the power of the mind to hurt or to heal. As soon as he was told about the snake that Cyrano brought out of the tower, Lord Samuel began to mend. He confessed to us later that on the night he was injured, while he was waiting for Lady Elizabeth at the top of the stairs, he had experienced a terrible shock."

"I remember," I interrupted. "I had just come out of the pink parlor when I heard her call to him. I looked up and saw him standing there . . ."

As I spoke, the whole scene replayed itself before my eyes. "I saw him look up and glance along the darkening gallery, in the direction of Stella's room." A shudder passed over me. Even in memory, the sight of Papa falling, tumbling, lying so still upon the landing, was painful in the extreme.

Thomas took up the story once more. "Lord Samuel says that when he turned to look, he beheld a serpent, gliding over the floor toward him. Startled, he jumped backward, missed his footing on the edge of the stair, and fell. When he regained consciousness and remembered seeing the snake, he feared he was losing his mind."

How well I understood Papa's feelings! There can be no

horror greater than the thought that one is losing one's sanity.

Thomas was still speaking. "He remembered all too well his childlike mother and her strange, obsessive fear of the creatures. He could not face the prospect of becoming like her."

"And he is all right now . . . really all right?"

"Except for a slight limp, he is fine," Thomas assured me.

"Thank God," I said, and my heart was filled with gratitude. "I want to see him, Thomas."

Thomas stood up. "Perhaps tomorrow. For now, I can see that you are tired. It is time for you to take a nice long nap."

How thoughtful he was. I gave him a grateful smile before saying, "You are right, dear Thomas, I am tired. But I cannot rest just yet. First, I must talk to Adam. There is something I must say to him."

Thomas nodded gravely, and I could read both hurt and understanding in his eyes. "Adam has been most anxious to see you. I'll send him right along." Thomas smiled his reassurance, and left.

Adam entered my room a few minutes later, and I was shocked by his appearance. His face was thin, pale, and drawn. There were dark circles under his eyes. "Are you really well again?" he asked.

"Yes . . . I am well."

Slowly, he crossed the room to stand at my bedside.

I had not thought it would be so hard to tell him, but I knew there would be no rest for me until I had done so. "There is something I must tell you. It is about Helaine."

His expression did not change, but he spoke through lips that were stiff. "You know where she is?"

I could find no gentle way to tell him. "She is dead. I'm sorry . . ."

"Dead?" He stared at me, as if he did not understand my words. "Dead?" he repeated.

"I'm sorry, Adam; truly, I am."

"But how?"

"She slipped and fell into the moat."

"But I don't understand—" Bewilderment was written clear on his face.

Seeing it, I could scarcely continue. "I followed her, Adam. Into the tower, down into a huge subterranean chamber." I swallowed against the lump that was threatening to choke me. "I followed Helaine, and Cyrano followed me."

Adam stood as if turned to stone—silent, staring.

I hesitated, wishing desperately that he would speak, but he did not. I continued, "Thomas told me Cyrano brought out the snake . . ."

My words were coming slower and slower—how could I tell him such horrors about the woman he had loved? Finally, I simply closed my eyes and blurted out, "It belonged to Helaine."

"That serpent belonged to Helaine?"

I opened my eyes. He was shaking his head in disbelief.

My throat was tight, but I managed to say, "She told me it was her pet."

"Oh, my God . . . my God in heaven!" The play of expression on Adam's face frightened me: first horror, then fear, then an agony of sorrow.

"Cyrano killed it . . . I was so frightened, I ran. Helaine was running after me . . . she fell into the moat." I could say no more.

"She is really dead. . . ." Adam spoke the words in a flat, expressionless voice, his staring eyes blank, fixed on nothing.

I remained mute, for I could think of nothing to say. In the lengthening silence I feared that my nerves, stretched almost to the breaking point, would snap. When I could bear it no longer, I opened my mouth to speak.

But Adam suddenly dropped down upon his knees beside the chaise and said, "Forgive me, Victoria! All that has happened—everything—it is all my fault!"

What was he saying? This did not sound like a grief-stricken husband. Had the shock been too much for him?

But he was holding out his hands to me. I took them in mine. "Hush, Adam, hush. It is all over now . . . we must try to forget."

"No—first I must know that you forgive me. Bringing that evil woman into this house—*two* evil women—betraying your love . . . can you ever forgive me?"

Two evil women. . . . "You knew?"

He nodded. "Not at first . . . but even when I found out what they were, I did nothing."

Adam's face was tortured. He could not meet my gaze as he continued. "Helaine told me the night I brought her here to Greystone Manor what a fool I was. She taunted me, told me she intended to see the family ruined."

It was too much. I could not take in what he was saying.

But now the words were pouring from his lips. "I was ashamed to admit how I had been duped. I convinced myself that there was nothing she could do to really hurt any of you . . . and I did nothing."

I could only stare at him in disbelief. "But you *loved* her. . . ."

Now he rose to his feet and began to pace about the room. "She was so beautiful, Victoria, so sweet and gentle, so kind when I met her in Paris. And I was vulnerable, lonely without you."

He gave me a beseeching look. "May I speak freely, Victoria? There are things I must tell someone, and you were always my dearest, most trusted friend."

With a sense of shock I found myself wondering if Helaine had, at least in part, spoken the truth about his foolishness. Aloud, I said, "Of course . . ."

"When we met," he began, "she was so understanding. She invited me to her *soirées,* then to quiet little evenings for just the two of us. She flattered me . . . what a fool I was!"

He paused, shook his head, ran the back of his hand

across his eyes. "At first we only talked. Then she began to—" His voice trailed into silence.

Suddenly he turned, so that I could no longer see his face. His voice was low and unsteady when he continued. "She did things . . . made me desire her . . . need her as some men need strong drink and drugs."

I stared at his back, and suddenly my heart was filled with pity, and with something else—something akin to contempt. Then I felt guilty. It had not been Adam's fault.

Again, he fell silent. I could tell by the set of his shoulders the strain he was feeling. When he at last continued his confession, his voice was so low I could barely hear the words. "Her knowledge of the pleasures of the flesh was unlimited . . . she—"

Again, his voice faded away. He buried his face in his hands, then mumbled between his fingers, "My God! I should not be saying these things to you."

"It's all right . . . Helaine told me herself that she was a courtesan. She seemed very proud . . ." The words were spoken before I realized my intent.

"She told you that?"

"She . . . she said you almost fought a duel with someone who tried to tell you . . ."

Adam groaned. "It's true. The . . . the pleasure she gave me blinded me to the lack of love, the purely lustful nature of our relationship." His voice fell lower, grew fainter, choked with the shame he was feeling.

Inexplicably, I, too, felt shamed.

He stopped pacing, turned to look at me at last. His eyes searched my face, begged for understanding. "Forgive me for speaking of such things to you, Victoria. Perhaps these are things best left unsaid . . . but I want you to understand, to know how weak and contemptible I have been. Only then can I believe any word of forgiveness you may someday offer me."

I wanted to comfort him, to assure him of my forgiveness, but shock had stolen my voice.

He began pacing once more. "She changed as soon as

we arrived here. She laughed at me. At first I was hurt and bewildered. Then I learned to hate her. But I didn't know what to do, to whom I could turn. She left me no pride . . . no honor. Knowing what a fool I had been, how I had hurt all of you who loved me . . . God! Was any man ever such a fool?"

Yes, he really was a fool, I thought, then quickly pushed the idea from me. "Oh, Adam," I whispered, "I'm so sorry. . . ."

He dropped on his knees again beside me. "No, Victoria, it is I who am sorry. It was I who brought all this horror and misery upon the family." He buried his face in his hands. "And the way I treated you, spoke to you the night of the ball. . . ."

"For that, I was partly to blame. I should never have—"

But he would not listen. "All the guilt is mine!" Then he raised his head and gazed into my eyes. "I can only pray that someday I may earn your forgiveness."

I touched his lips with my fingertips. "Hush, Adam. All that is behind us now. But there are other things that I have learned . . . dreadful things."

I then proceeded to tell him about the body in the cage, and everything that Helaine had told me.

When I had finished, Adam shook his head, his eyes full of puzzlement. "But I don't understand," he said. "Who was Helaine's father? Why did Lady Christina leave him in that cage?"

"I have not finished my story," I said. Then I told him all the things Pastor Grewe had related to Betsy and me.

Adam listened attentively, shaking his head sorrowfully from time to time, and when I was through he said, "Can it all be true? Is it possible that Helaine's father was married to Lord Samuel's mother?"

"It surely confirms all that Helaine said."

"But if that is so . . ." Slowly Adam's eyes widened, his mouth actually dropped open, and then he began to stammer, "But . . . but . . . that would mean that Helaine was as old as my mother!"

"It would appear so." I couldn't suppress a smile, despite the sorrow I felt.

Adam raked his fingers through his hair. "It still does not make much sense. It sounds like sheer madness."

I cringed, and the question formed itself unbidden upon my lips. "Do you think I am mad?"

Shock replaced the puzzlement reflected in Adam's expression. "Victoria! How can you suggest such a thing?"

But having put the question, I knew I had to tell Adam everything. I began with the first time I saw the lovely dark-haired girl, when I was ten years old and newly moved into the room with the beautiful little escritoire, and ended with the moment when she showed me the secret drawer.

"And I think," I told him in conclusion, "I know who she is . . . or was. I believe that dark-haired woman is more than just a dream friend. I believe she is my grandmother, the Lady Christina."

Chapter Twenty-four

Adam turned pale. "You cannot be serious, Victoria. Think what you are saying!"

"I do not mean my grandmother, literally . . . I mean her spirit. How that can be, I do not know, for I have never believed in ghosts. But what other explanation can there be?"

Adam listened to my words, his eyes troubled. "I don't know either, Victoria . . . but a *ghost?*"

"Perhaps because we are so much alike, my grandmother and I . . . oh, I don't know!" I hesitated, then added, "But I'm certain it was she. How else could I have found the secret drawer?"

Adam nodded, but he did not look convinced.

"Come," I said. "I will show you."

He helped me to my feet, then followed me to the little desk. For a moment my courage failed me. What if it had been a hallucination, after all? But there was no turning back. I took a deep breath, grasped the corner of the desk, gave it a shake, and out slid the velvet-lined drawer.

Adam and I looked at one another. I was trembling, but I was no longer afraid. I pointed to the packet of letters. "See? Just as I told you. I am certain now that Carter sent those letters to my grandmother."

Suddenly I was struck by a happy thought. "And if that is true it means that Carter, not the green-eyed demon, was my grandfather!"

I folded the letters once more, slipped the ribbon around them, laid them back in the drawer. Adam picked up the diary. "The clasp is locked," I told him. "I have not found the key."

Adam hesitated, looked at the clasp, then said, "Fetch me one of your hat pins."

Mystified, I did as he bid. In less time than it takes to tell, Adam had sprung the lock. We returned to the chaise and sat side by side as I opened the velvet-bound book. It was noted on the inside cover that the small volume had been given to Christina by her father on her fifteenth birthday. It was obvious from the inscription that Christina had been a much-cherished child. It was equally clear, from the entries that followed, written in a round and childish hand, that she had led a happy, carefree childhood.

We did not read in detail. Rather, we skimmed quickly over the first year's entries. It was shortly after her sixteenth birthday that she first mentioned *him*. She did not write his name, but it was clear that from her first sight of the man, she was fascinated. I was loath to read the words of love she had so freely written. Poor Christina, so innocent, so full of love. Once more we skipped and skimmed pages, hardly knowing what we hoped to find, yet knowing there must be something.

The day before her wedding, Christina had filled several pages. I almost cried as I read them. How happy she had been, how bright her hope, how full of joy her dreams.

We turned the page and continued to read. Suddenly, the hair on the back of my neck began to rise. Anger welled up within me, fierce and hot. The entries, from that page onward, were short and often incoherent; but we gathered that the marriage, from the very first night, had been a nightmare for Christina. The man she had thought so handsome, so gallant, so fascinating while he courted her, did not even wait for night to fall before he revealed his true nature: selfish, brutal, and depraved.

In addition to his perversions and unspeakable appetites, he had, on several occasions, struck the gentle Lady Christina with his fist, knocking her down and leaving great bruises upon her flesh. One entry in her diary read, ". . . and that ugly serpent ring cut a great gash in my cheek. When the blood ran down all over my dress, he laughed."

My quick intake of breath startled Adam and he looked at me questioningly, then in alarm. "Victoria, what's the matter? You've gone white as a sheet."

I pointed to the words. "It was my dream, the night my face was cut . . . at least, I saw him raise his fist with that great ugly ring. . . ."

Adam's gaze was uncomprehending. At last he said, "But it was only a dream."

I shrugged, and turned my attention back to the diary. To my surprise, I realized it really made little difference to me what my stepbrother did or did not believe.

A later entry noted that when *he* discovered that the very sight of a snake could reduce Christina to a state of near hysteria, he brought several home and kept them for pets! It was at about this time that he managed to squander all that remained of the family fortune, including all the valuable paintings and objets d'art.

But his wanton and degenerate appetites were insatiable. Insidious, ruthless, greedy, he was determined to have the one thing of great value that remained: the Greystone jewels.

But these jewels, at least, Christina had somehow managed to hide away, and on this one subject, she would not give in to him. "He will not kill me until he has the jewels," she had written. "I will endure!"

Sickened to the limits of my sensibility by these revelations, I put the diary down and said to Adam, "I do not understand why my grandmother, if it truly was her spirit that showed the secret drawer to me, wanted me to know these terrible things."

Adam shook his head, shrugged.

Perhaps, I thought, she just wanted someone to under-

stand how she had suffered. To understand why she was
. . . as she was, in her last days. It was a comforting idea. Aloud I said, "Or maybe there is something else in those last pages. We have read this much; we should finish it."

On the very next page, we found it. An entry made some six months after the death of her parents said, quite simply, "His name is Carter Hensley, Earl of Clyde."

At this, I felt a stirring of pleasure. Though I said nothing to Adam, I knew that I must tell Betsy at the first opportunity that her grandmother had been Lady Catherine Hensley, sister to the earl of Clyde—my grandfather. Why, that meant that Betsy and I were cousins!

Even as these thoughts passed through my mind, I continued to read: The Lady Christina had met Carter in the churchyard, where she had gone to lay flowers on her parents' graves.

Poor Lady Christina—terrified of her drunken, lecherous husband, anguished by the death of her beloved mother and father, with neither friend nor relative to defend her. Is it any wonder she was drawn to the gentle Lord Hensley? Soon a love blossomed between them that was stronger, more compelling, than anything else in their lives. Not long after, Christina realized she was pregnant.

My heart gave one great thump and began to race. I felt as if some terrible curse had been lifted from my head, and I murmured, "Oh, Adam, it is true! That evil man was not my grandfather, after all!" It was a selfish reaction, I know, but it was how I felt.

And once more, my feelings matched Christina's. The next few pages of her diary were filled with elation, joy, and hope as she and Carter made plans for their flight.

And as I read, even though I knew their plans had failed, I continued to hope for their success. It was their intention to flee to London and there sue for a divorce, so that the two of them could marry. However, the night Carter was to have taken her away, Christina wrote simply, "He did not come."

My own heart ached when I thought of the despair in

which Christina must have passed the ensuing days, weeks, and months waiting for some word from Carter, wondering what had happened, perhaps fearing in the end that he had not loved her at all—had only used her.

It was some two months later when she learned the truth. At dinner on that particular night, her husband drank even more than usual. But instead of leaving the table and going off to the village, as was his wont, he began to torment Christina. He told her he knew the baby she carried was not his.

"I told him I was proud to be carrying another man's child, that I would have killed myself before I would have brought flesh of his vile flesh into this world. His pride was stung by my words. He made to strike me again, and then I read it in his eyes. He had thought of another way to hurt me.

"In drunken glee, he told me he knew who the father was, and for a time he baited me. But when I would not rise to his jibes, his anger knew no bounds. And that is when he told me, bragging, how he had stabbed Carter and thrown his body into the moat."

As I read Christina's words, I could feel her agony. I was consumed by her loathing and hatred of the man who had destroyed not only her, but everyone, everything, she had ever loved. I was not even surprised when, on the last page of her diary, I read, "He wants the jewels . . . he shall have them."

Adam and I looked at one another, the same thought in both our minds. "You must go down there and see," I said.

Rising to his feet, Adam replied, "I will go immediately."

I paced the floor until he returned. When he entered my room once more he was pale and obviously shaken, but he maintained an icy calm.

"It is there," he said. "An oriental chest. The skeleton is lying over it, which is why we did not see it before."

Then we pieced the story together. It seemed obvious

that Christina took the jewel chest and placed it in the cage, then pretended to be so intimidated by her husband's threats and abuse that she agreed to show him where the jewels were secreted.

I can almost see her, leading him down along that narrow ledge, then into that huge, echoing chamber, pointing to the chest in the back of the cage.

And it is easy to picture him, blinded to any danger by his voracious greed, rushing into the cage and flinging himself down before the chest.

With what satisfaction Christina must have slammed and locked the door, then fled the room. I doubt she ever went back.

Unfortunately, or maybe fortunately—who is to say?—by the time Papa was born, Christina's mind was gone. She had lived through too much pain and horror. She became as a child again, remembering nothing of the dreadful man she had married or the terrible tragedy that had befallen her and the House of Greystone.

The man for whose return she had waited with so much love was, obviously, Carter.

The key in the ivory box opened the oriental chest. It contained everything that was listed in the ledger I had found in the desk in the library.

As for Stella and Helaine, it was not until we removed all Stella's belongings from her room that we discovered the final piece to the puzzle—a packet of letters, all dated between 1812 and 1815, all addressed to Stella. They were written in French and English; apparently Stella had understood far more than she ever let on.

Those letters confirmed what Helaine had said: The man Christina married was an adventurer who had never been interested in anything except the renowned Greystone jewels. To this end, he had arranged to meet and wed the innocent Christina, even though he already had a wife, Stella. In his last letter to her he had written, "Soon, I will convince the slut to give me the jewels. Then I shall return to you, my wife. I will be with you and our darling child before her next birthday."

When we had read those words, Adam exclaimed, "Good God! She *was* older than my own mother!"

And we laughed, though it wasn't really funny. Sadly, it was true. I reminded Adam of how Helaine had hated the sunlight, never appearing by day unless hatted and veiled. It was by candlelight that we always saw her—thus had it been in Paris, too, Adam recalled.

Adding the information in Stella's letters to what Helaine had told me in the subterranean chamber, it became clear that they, Stella and Helaine, had not known, until Helaine found the body in the cage, what had happened to Helaine's father. Only their jealousy and hatred of the Lady Christina had sustained them, driven them to the lengths that had finally been their undoing.

It also seemed likely that Helaine was so blinded by her emotions when she found her father's body that she, too, had failed to observe the jewel chest. Had she actually found the jewels, I dared not contemplate the fate that would undoubtedly have befallen the rest of us.

Among the personal effects in Helaine's room were several vials of strange substances, later identified by Dr. Maerrie. One of them, at least, was a deadly poison. Another was surely the cause of much of my distress: the nightmares, the sleepwalking.

Gillian admitted having allowed Helaine to put a "white powder" in my tea from time to time. She had convinced Gillian that it was something to make me sleep better.

Helaine's body was never recovered. Remembering her, I still find it hard to believe that that beautiful woman was more than twenty years older than Adam. I could scarcely imagine the vigilance necessary for her to insure that none of us ever saw her clearly in full daylight. Yet perhaps it had all been easy for her—by her own admission, her beauty and charm had been carefully cultivated, had been her livelihood.

We returned the jewels to Papa, with only enough of the story to satisfy his curiosity. Adam removed the body from the cage by night, and disposed of it in the proper manner, aided by Pastor Grewe and Thomas, whom we had taken into our confidence.

It was Thomas who offered the words that finally and forever put all my fears to rest. Some of his studies in Germany had dealt with the little-understood powers of the human mind. He took great pains to explain it all to me.

"Victoria," he said, his voice gentle, "your grandmother was a pure and gentle soul, and the guilt she felt as a result of having committed both adultery and murder would give her no peace. In her eyes, that her husband was both cruel and depraved was no excuse. This burden of guilt tied her spirit here, until someone should offer her absolution simply by knowing the truth."

"You mean there really *are* such things as ghosts?" I was still not wholly convinced.

"*Ghost* is not a very good term. Essence or energy might be a better description. It is a phenomenon that has as much to do with the sensitivity of the observer as the observability of the presence. Remember, you were still very young when you moved into your grandmother's room. It was easy for you to accept the manifestation as a dream. It is quite likely that that is what it would have remained — only a dream — had not Stella and Helaine come into the house.

"The energy produced by their fanatical hatred unleashed a power, precipitated a series of events that they were ultimately unable to control. Indeed, it is likely that those two were not even aware of the phenomenon."

"But what about the note . . . the burned paper?"

"It is likely that you did, indeed, write them yourself. Or rather, in some manner I do not understand, Christina *borrowed* your body to do the writing. For a few moments, you became the bridge between two realities.

"But don't worry about it any more, dear Victoria. I assure you, now that the truth is known, never again will you see either Christina or the shade of that foul man."

We did one final thing before we burned the diary and the letters: Adam and I told Betsy the truth, that her grandmother, Catherine, and my grandfather, Carter, were sister and brother, and thus, Betsy and I were cousins. Betsy herself, related this information to Thomas and to John.

And when at last everything had been explained, and all our sorrows had been put behind us, Adam came to me one day and said, "You know how much I love you, Victoria. Can I hope that one day soon you will consent to be my bride?"

How many months, and with what longing, I had waited to hear those words! But now that they were spoken, I felt nothing but sorrow—sorrow for all the days I had wasted, determined to cling to an infatuation born of the too-easily roused passions of youth; sorrow that it had taken me so long to recognize the true love only a woman's heart can know; sorrow, too, that I must now tell Adam.

But I looked him squarely in the eye and said, "You will always have that place in my heart reserved for a big brother, Adam, for that is what you are to me: my beloved brother."

Perhaps that was the answer he had expected, for he did not question my words. When he had left me, I ran out into the park, where I knew Thomas would be walking. When he saw me coming he smiled and held out his hands, but I threw myself into his arms and said, "Oh, Thomas, I love you." And I recalled for him that day when he had bidden me not to deceive myself.

"Why didn't you just *tell* me I was crying after a childish fancy? I think that you, dear Thomas, have always known what I was too blind to see . . . that you and I were meant for each other."

In reply, Thomas only held me closer, and kissed me, there in the park with the sun shining and the birds singing. He kissed me again and again, and the blood burned in my veins like warm wine. We were married a month later.

A year has passed since the day of our wedding. The jagged scar on my cheek still throbs when the wind blows cold from the North Sea, and my father's left leg will always be shorter than his right; but we are all very happy.

Immediately after Thomas and I were wed, Adam announced his decision to return to the Continent. We hear from him occasionally. He is making a name for himself in the art world.

John has completed his education and is home to stay. He and Betsy spend much time together. I can see them now through my window, hand in hand, crossing the garden. After careful consideration, we all decided it would be best not to pursue our connection with the Hensley family, so Betsy and I keep our blood relationship quiet and simply enjoy each other's friendship.

Thomas forwent a lucrative practice in London, and became our village doctor when Dr. Maerrie retired. We make our home in the manor, and will raise our children here. It is our hope that they may be many—our first born, a bouncing baby boy, even now sleeps in the old nursery.

And in the kitchen, in a soft warm nest in the inglenook, a fat mother cat is nursing a litter of snow-white kittens.

WHO DUNNIT? JUST TRY AND FIGURE IT OUT!

THE MYSTERIES OF MARY ROBERTS RINEHART

THE AFTER HOUSE	(2821-0, $3.50/$4.50)
THE ALBUM	(2334-0, $3.50/$4.50)
ALIBI FOR ISRAEL AND OTHER STORIES	(2764-8, $3.50/$4.50)
THE BAT	(2627-7, $3.50/$4.50)
THE CASE OF JENNIE BRICE	(2193-3, $2.95/$3.95)
THE CIRCULAR STAIRCASE	(3528-4, $3.95/$4.95)
THE CONFESSION AND SIGHT UNSEEN	(2707-9, $3.50/$4.50)
THE DOOR	(1895-5, $3.50/$4.50)
EPISODE OF THE WANDERING KNIFE	(2874-1, $3.50/$4.50)
THE FRIGHTENED WIFE	(3494-6, $3.95/$4.95)
THE GREAT MISTAKE	(2122-4, $3.50/$4.50)
THE HAUNTED LADY	(3680-9, $3.95/$4.95)
A LIGHT IN THE WINDOW	(1952-1, $3.50/$4.50)
LOST ECSTASY	(1791-X, $3.50/$4.50)
THE MAN IN LOWER TEN	(3104-1, $3.50/$4.50)
MISS PINKERTON	(1847-9, $3.50/$4.50)
THE RED LAMP	(2017-1, $3.50/$4.95)
THE STATE V. ELINOR NORTON	(2412-6, $3.50/$4.50)
THE SWIMMING POOL	(3679-5, $3.95/$4.95)
THE WALL	(2560-2, $3.50/$4.50)
THE YELLOW ROOM	(3493-8, $3.95/$4.95)

Available wherever paperbacks are sold, or order direct from the Publisher. Send cover price plus 50¢ per copy for mailing and handling to Zebra Books, Dept. 4040, 475 Park Avenue South, New York, N.Y. 10016. Residents of New York and Tennessee must include sales tax. DO NOT SEND CASH. For a free Zebra/Pinnacle catalog please write to the above address.